PRAISE FOR

CHRISTOPHER COE AND

SUCH TIMES

"Christopher Coe, a writer of ferocious talent and bravery, has crafted, in *Such Times*, perhaps the great novel of the AIDS epidemic: a story that could be told by no one but himself— and yet belongs to all of us."

—David Leavitt

"Coe outdoes himself in this lapidary new tale. . . . Deftly plotted and full of surprises, the novel showcases Coe's distinctive, occasionally superb writing, a brilliant verbal mirror of his narrator's obsession with flat-out, drop-dead elegance. The prose's elegiac beauty elevates what might have been merely an odyssey of gay sex and shopping into something deeply transcendent, reminiscent of both Oscar Wilde's and Marcel Proust's late writings. Angry, melancholy, and obsessed with the injustices of love, this may well be the gay novel of the decade."   —*Publishers Weekly*

"Christopher Coe is a delicious genius—he understands life, art, and the divinity of the well-timed remark. *Such Times* is an act of consummate bravery and sublime accomplishment—it is a heartbreaking, exhilarating romance, set amid an era of incomprehensible loss. The book never cheats; it simply and cogently argues for the triumph of love and Baccarat stemware. It is a work to be devoured and treasured, a fresh classic from the most elegant pen on the planet."

—Paul Rudnick, author of *Jeffrey*

"Mr. Coe is a daring writer, as unflinchingly honest about his characters' affectations and fatuous desires, their treacheries and small self-deceptions, as he is about the truth of their hearts. As Timothy, who narrates the story, shuttles back and forth through time, summoning up two decades of memories in a single night, he re-experiences the pain he has felt over his lover's needs. Yet to the author's credit, Timothy becomes neither pitiable nor mordant. Rather, in choosing to bear witness to the randomness of fate as well as the power of memory to redeem, Timothy is allowed to find reasons to live. In the process he gives voice to the dreams and terrors of an entire generation." —*The New York Times Book Review*

"*Such Times* is a Job-like story that resonates for anyone who has faced the demands of AIDS. But it is a tragic tale told in a grand, witty, and wonderful gay way. *Such Times* pulses with the confusions and heartbreaks of relationships—from the uninhibited and disposable to the hopeful and unrequited. Anyone who has been the third party in a triangular relationship will certainly empathize with the pleasures and pains Timothy finds in his love for Jasper. And anyone who has witnessed the changes in gay life over the last 20 years will find *Such Times* a must-read: Coe demonstrates how the AIDS epidemic has forced a whole generation of men into directions they might never have taken. Caught in its grip, Timothy refuses to see either himself or Jasper as victims. He remains unwilling to yield to the randomness of fate or to the misery of lost romance. He finds instead redemptive power in his memories, and as he unfolds his story, his voice elevates *Such Times* into a new classic."

—Jameson Currier, *Washington Blade*

"A wrenching novel about love, death, and AIDS whose author has no trouble at all supplying depth as well as truth. What sets *Such Times* apart is emotional sincerity, rich characterization, and a powerfully effective directness about AIDS. It's that kind of in-the-gut directness that separates *Such Times* from the rest of the pack: Its emotional honesty is as impossible to ignore as the reality of AIDS itself."

—*San Francisco Chronicle*

"Probably the most strikingly original novel to come along this year. It looks unapologetically and unsentimentally, yet with great compassion, at the sexual mores of a generation of men whose sexual activities have spanned the 'AIDS-barrier.' The characters are as real as you and your friends."

—*Phoenix Echo*

"In its tight control and formality, Coe's authorial voice recalls that of Kazuo Ishiguro's *The Remains of the Day*. He relates this very particular story in a precise prose that often dazzles with broad and universal insight. *Such Times* is more than simply a novel about characters dealing, in all manner of ways, with AIDS. At heart, it's a fascinating character study, an examination of the tenacity of human affection and will, matched against the ticking clock of mortality. . . . Coe takes what on the surface seems a rather idiosyncratic, even bizarre story and, by his artistry and talent, makes it pertinent, makes us care." —Michael Dorris, *Detroit News*

"One reason we read novels, as T. S. Eliot remarked, is to find out how other people live, and this is a novel about how people live when their lives have been taken from them."

—*New York Newsday*

CONTEMPORARY AMERICAN FICTION

SUCH TIMES

Christopher Coe grew up in San Francisco and lived in New York City. His first novel, *I Look Divine*, was published to wide acclaim in 1987. Mr. Coe died of AIDS-related complications on September 6, 1994; he was forty-one.

CHRISTOPHER COE

such times

PENGUIN BOOKS

PENGUIN BOOKS
Published by the Penguin Group
Penguin Books USA Inc., 375 Hudson Street,
New York, New York 10014, U.S.A.
Penguin Books Ltd, 27 Wrights Lane, London W8 5TZ, England
Penguin Books Australia Ltd, Ringwood, Victoria, Australia
Penguin Books Canada Ltd, 10 Alcorn Avenue,
Toronto, Ontario, Canada M4V 3B2
Penguin Books (N.Z.) Ltd, 182–190 Wairau Road,
Auckland 10, New Zealand

Penguin Books Ltd, Registered Offices:
Harmondsworth, Middlesex, England

First published in the United States of America
by Harcourt Brace & Company 1993
Published in Penguin Books 1994

10 9 8 7 6 5 4 3 2 1

The epigraph is from "The Last Cloak" from *Last Tales* by Isak Dinesen.
Copyright © 1955 by The Curtis Publishing Company. Reprinted by
permission of Random House, Inc.

The lines from "Stouthearted Men" (Sigmund Romberg, Oscar Hammerstein II) © 1927 Warner Bros. Inc. (renewed) & Oscar Hammerstein Pub.
Des. All rights reserved. Used by permission.

"Ode to Walt Whitman" (trans. by Donald A. Allen) from *Selected Poems*
by Federico García Lorca. Copyright 1955 by New Directions Publishing
Corp. Reprinted by permission of New Directions Publishing Corp.

THE LIBRARY OF CONGRESS HAS CATALOGUED THE HARDCOVER AS
FOLLOWS:
Coe, Christopher.
Such times/Christopher Coe.
p. cm.
ISBN 0-15-186426-8 (hc.)
ISBN 0 14 02.4143 4 (pbk.)
1. Title.
PS3553.034S8 1993
813'.54—dc20   92–35417

Printed in the United States of America
Set in Sabon

To Nancy Plese
To Sunny Rogers
To my sister, Kally,
and above all, to my doctor,
William Siroty

acknowledgments

For guiding me to a clearer understanding of the ways viruses and retroviruses work and specifically, the morphological complexities of HIV and its possible role in the pathogeneses of Acquired Immune Deficiency Syndrome, I am grateful to, in Paris, at Institut Pasteur,

> Catherine Transy
> Pierre Legrain
> Charles Dauguet
> Luc Montaigner

In New York, at the Irvington Institute for Medical Research,

> Anne Fleming

For encouragement freely given, when needed, I thank

> Joanna Laufer
> Abigail Thomas
> David Spear
> Liz Darhansoff
> Tereze Glück
> Amy Hempel
> Anderson Ferrell

I am grateful to PEN America for its support of this project.

The Duke of Alba, in Spain, who was a handsome and brilliant man, married a plain and simple-minded lady of the court and remained faithful to her, and when his friends, amazed at the fact, jestingly questioned him upon it, he answered them that the Duchess of Alba must needs, in her own right, and irrespective of personal qualities, be the most desirable woman in the world.

ISAK DINESEN
"The Cloak"
(Last Tales)

such times

one

THERE MAY have been a day this year when I thought of him as dead right off, the first time he came to mind. Most days I think of him as though he is alive. It can happen anywhere. Walking on a street, reading a magazine, I will see a listing for a concert, a review of a movie, a new place to go for dinner, and will think: Jasper and I should hear that, see that, go there. My mind then works out of habit to remember what date we made, when Jasper said we would see each other next. When this happens, it only takes a second, maybe not even as long as that; it is quick, not a time you can measure by a watch, but most of my life is contained in that time.

By most of my life I mean the years after I met Jasper. I had a mother, of course, a father, grew up in a house, was educated, but all that is behind me now. Sometimes I count Dominic. Tonight I am with Dominic, so tonight I will count him. But my life, all of it worth remembering, began really with Jasper.

Perhaps I shouldn't say worth remembering. It may only be remembered.

When I think of what is worth remembering, not much comes to mind.

There do happen to be a few things, though.

A little after ten o'clock on the Thursday evening just after Christmas eighteen years ago, Jasper and I, in towels, met at the Continental. The Continental was a bathhouse, popular in the early seventies. Before I met Jasper, I used to go there fairly often—once a month maybe, sometimes more. It was a way to have people around me without really being around them myself. That is how I would describe it, probably, to anyone who asked me why I went.

Mostly I went to watch. Sometimes, if a fellow in the steam room was what Dominic would call tasty, or had what Jasper called beautiful bones, I would let him touch me here or there, in a minor way, if he was so moved. I would not say that I went for that purpose exactly, and it didn't happen often, and when it did that was all there was to it, all I wanted, until I saw Jasper in a towel.

He was in the upstairs labyrinth. He was walking around.

Jasper in a towel was more than tasty.

I had better let it go at that.

The Continental has been gone for years, gone even before men in New York stopped going to bathhouses. But the address is still there, the same building, on Seventy-fourth Street just west of Broadway, and when I am in the neighborhood I will, more often than not, go a little out of my way to pass what used to be its door.

Sometimes I go far out of my way. I've been perhaps a dozen times this year. I used to go even when Jasper was alive. Just last week I went. The facade is unchanged. It is exactly as it was, though I have no idea what has been done to the inside or what goes on in there now. For a few years, in the late seventies, it became a place for men and women. They came to the Continental, renamed, to cavort in public, pretty much as the fags did, I imagine. I wouldn't know. I suspect it was pretty much the same thing. Last week a woman told me she had been there once or twice. She is not a woman I would have expected to have gone there. She is a married woman, a mother, runs a top photography gallery, is a social figure, always beautifully dressed, impeccably manicured, a woman with a polish. Really, she is the last woman I would have expected to go there, so I took her at her word that she had gone only to watch.

"It's hard to believe there used to be such times," she said.

Jasper was much more than tasty.

"Yes," I said. "It is hard to believe, isn't it?"

I didn't say this merely to agree with her. I really do find it hard to believe that there used to be such times.

———

DOMINIC HAS promised that the final question will turn everything around. He has told me what will happen tonight, and then for the rest of the week. It will be a disgrace, he has told me, I won't want to know him. For what will seem like forever, he will be left behind in answers and cash by a woman from Chicago, and by the second player, a young man Dominic calls the hot one, who was really pretty hot, he's told me, and was, as they learned after the taping, Dominic's neighbor here in West Hollywood, briefly, until the hot one moved back home. Dominic will stay in last place until the final question, on which he will risk everything.

He had no choice.

Having no choice turned out to be Dominic's good luck. With so little to lose, with nothing to hope for, Dominic turned his fate around. He came out on top.

This is not life, it's a show on television, a game show that was taped eleven months ago. We don't pretend it's life. Moving back home is what life is now.

Young men are moving back home. They are moving back home to Arizona, back home to Oregon, back home to Tennessee. Dominic says that West Hollywood is becoming a town of vacant apartments. I don't know if this is true, but Dominic tells me that in West Hollywood it is easier now than it has been in years to find a place to live. Last night at dinner we heard a man at the next table predict that if things keep going as they are pretty soon there will be no trouble finding places to park.

It is the summer of 1992. There are young men who have no homes, nothing to move back to, or those whose families will not take them in. Of course, not all the men are young. I knew a man who was sixty.

I know men who have been disowned.

Other men are doing the opposite. They are leaving home, coming from small towns to the big ones, hoping to find experts, treatments, to fit protocols and join drug study trials; they form support groups, coalitions, and they await the miracle.

Dominic has not been disowned. He could move back to San Francisco, where his mother still lives in the house on Pacific Heights that he grew up in. But Dominic says moving back home would be a defeat. San Francisco, he has said, was the death of him. He could as accurately have said New York was the death of him, Paris the death of him, Barcelona the death of him. I have been with him in those places and have had letters from many others, Palm Springs, Honolulu, letters scribbled in cafés or on beaches between bouts of sightseeing or of lust, and Dominic could have picked his death up in any of them, if it is true that it only takes one time. One exposure, as they say. I remember reading someplace, or maybe someone told me, that it takes one drop of blood, one ounce of semen, or several pints of saliva. I doubt these measures are exact. For example, I do not believe infection requires an *entire* drop of blood, and how often does one see an ounce of semen at one time? I believe far less is necessary, but who knows? If I believed everything I read or heard I would believe—everything.

I know a woman who claims to know exactly where

she got it, from whom; she can point to one man. I don't expect many can say this, but she is doubtless not alone. Her point, when she told me, was that one need not have been the all-time harlot of the world.

As for Dominic, any place he has been in the past five, ten, twelve years could have been the death of him. Some say twenty years. In any case, Dominic says San Francisco. In any case, Dominic says he will stay here in West Hollywood with his new eighteen-thousand-dollar brass and bamboo bed for what he calls the duration.

A few months ago he decided to give himself a pleasant bed. He bought it with some of the money that he won by risking everything and then by winning to the end of the week.

I want him to go home.

————————

DOMINIC HAS confessed that he was flustered by the hot one. It made him miss a question from what should have been his category: movie musicals. Ordinarily, this could not have happened, so I can imagine how flustered Dominic must have been by the hot one when the show was taped eleven months ago. The show will start any minute.

"Will you get in here with those cocktails?" he calls from the bedroom. I am in Dominic's kitchen, squeezing limes for our daiquiris, just about the only drink, he says, that still tastes right. When he told me that his doctor had encouraged him to have a couple of drinks each night, I wondered how that could be true. Liquor, like sunlight, like stress and almost everything else, it seems, is said to deplete the very cells Dominic is losing. Living depletes them. I wondered if Dominic was giving up, or if his doctor had. All I said at the time was that I would want a doctor like that even if nothing was wrong with me.

Jasper didn't have a doctor like that.

It was Dominic, almost twenty years ago, who taught me how to make the classic daiquiri. He told me I could travel the civilized world and find maybe one, maybe two bartenders who would know that a daiquiri cocktail must include a splash, just a few drops, of maraschino liqueur, without which, whatever you may think you are drinking, you are not drinking a daiquiri. Since then I have traveled the civilized world, much of it anyway, and have yet to find even one bartender who knew about maraschino in a daiquiri. I have wondered if the reason no bartender has known of it might not be that Dominic made it up. It would be like Dominic to do that, to invent for himself a world in which his preference is law. Dominic has always made up laws for life. He holds them as sacred and turns sullen when the world doesn't live up to them. He also likes grenadine in an old-fashioned. This, thank God, he has not made a law.

It will be twenty years next month.

Dominic kept maraschino in his room at school, in Berkeley, a school we both left when our romance gave us up. Almost twenty years later this will sound jejune, but when our romance gave us up we both had to leave that school. Everything became too poignant for us, for both of us. We became too poignant for each other.

Daiquiris were a part of our courtship. And we did court, we took a long time courting, we were coy maidens with each other for weeks. Dominic really was a maiden. I had been around a bit that summer, had been to art school in San Francisco, sketched a few models, even sold a few paintings, and had come down with hepatitis, gonorrhea, and crabs. I was with about forty men that summer, my first away from home. I was nearly seventeen.

Of course, there was no point in wondering who had given me the hepatitis, the gonorrhea, the crabs, because it could have been any one of them. Or any three of them. In a way, it was all forty of them. It was somewhat sobering to have all these things go wrong at once, and I decided to become more selective. That is why I was willing to play the coy maiden with Dominic, to let him court me as long as he wanted. It should have told us something that we were in no great hurry.

Dominic courted me forever with daiquiris and songs. He would sit on his bed in Japanese pajamas, in the lotus position, and sing me songs like "I'll Know When My Love Comes Along."

Dominic sang "When the Sun Comes Out." Dominic sang "Can't Help Lovin' Dat Man of Mine," "Stony End," "I'll Tell the Man in the Street," and, if I remember correctly, Dominic even sang "You've Got a Friend," a song I had heard all over San Francisco that summer; it played all the time, James Taylor's version, then Carole King's, at the Ritch Street Health Club.

Dominic sang other songs, which I would need to work a little harder to dredge up, there were so many of them. I'm afraid there was also a guitar involved in all of this and that at crucial phrases in the lyric Dominic would make his voice quaver more or less exactly like Buffy Saint Marie.

It was a Phoebe Snow number he sang to me the night we finally, finally tried. That was a night of busy fingers, busy lips, and a catastrophic lack of lust.

For one thing, we had courted too long. But there was more to it than that, of course. We tried again, put ourselves through many anguishing nights, many anguishing afternoons, but lust wasn't there. Dominic and I were possibly too much alike, or wanted the same thing perhaps, and we remained two helpless maidens. We put on a good face, acted as if we could not keep ourselves from each other, called each other every endearment we could think of, and lust would not come to us. It never came. It just never came. God must have known we were trying. One reason may have been, and this will sound worse than it was, I was disappointed when Dominic took off his clothes. That may be the primary reason for the lack of lust, which was mostly on my part, I'm afraid. I am sorry to say this, was sorry then, and of course I never told him this, but there it is.

Dominic knew, of course, must have known. He must have been through it before, with women. Dominic had been with women, two or three, the year before. One, Abigail Church, remained somewhat shameless in pursuing him, even after I had become a fixture in his life.

Miss Fingerstop, another woman Dominic had been with the year before, who also left that school and came to New York, lived with me about six months and then become a dominatrix, told me that the first time Dominic took his clothes off for her, she had been, as she put it, clinically disenchanted. This will be enough about that, except I will add that about five years ago, about the time it was becoming clear to him that any day the virus could kick in and make him stop feeling like his familiar self, Dominic summed up our failed romance. "Honey, let's face it," he wrote me in a letter—Dominic and I were always writing letters—"all the dykes at Berkeley could have handed us the shovels, and we still couldn't have gotten our ashes hauled."

I have been repeating these words to myself these last two days out here in West Hollywood with Dominic. Dominic liked this phrase the first time he heard it, as I had the first time I saw it. I saw it years ago, in print, attributed to Carole Lombard. It must have been in parlance in her time. Carole Lombard, who was known to be a candid woman, confided to someone—possibly the glamour photographer George Hurrell, though I won't swear to this—that on more than one occasion, when she and Clark Gable were finally able to be alone together, they'd be so worn out, so wearied by all the necessary subterfuge, by all their clandestine sneaking around—and so relieved to be out of the public eye—they would forget, as Lombard blithely put it, to get their ashes hauled.

When I gave this phrase to Dominic, he seized it at

once. Dominic has always had a flair for appropriating snippets of verbiage. He uses this phrase so often now, I'm sure he has forgotten that once upon a time he didn't have it in his repertoire.

Sometimes I'm a little sorry I gave it to him.

As summaries go, this one does its job. There you have it—no lust, classic daiquiris, seductive songs that stopped just short of abandon.

Twenty years of unhauled ashes.

————

IN HIS kitchen, Dominic's maraschino bottle is getting low. There is enough for a few more rounds, if that. This is not the bottle from Berkeley, but it has lasted Dominic more than ten years. I recognize it from other places he's lived: the house at the top of Telegraph Hill with the three-hundred-and-sixty-degree view of the city; the illegal sublet in New York, on Bank Street, which would have overlooked a garden if the window glass had not been blackened over with oil-based paint. Hardware had been screwed into the oak floor of that room by a previous tenant, and chains were heaped in a corner. Dominic has always said that he could live anywhere, and he has proved this more than once.

He has marked the maraschino bottle at every New Year. Next to these precise, hyphenated marks, usually less than an inch apart, he has written on masking tape, in perfect Palmer penmanship, "80–SF," "81–SF," "82–NYC," "83–SF," "84–SF." The rest of the years are marked "LA," except for this year, which, although we are eight months into it, remains unmarked.

It crosses my mind, briefly, that a new bottle would be a welcome gift. There are still times, even after Jasper, when I have to catch on all over again. Here in Dominic's kitchen, shaking the daiquiris while he calls out for me to come watch with him on the brass and bamboo bed, I catch on again that Dominic may need gifts that don't last.

I like knowing about maraschino in a daiquiri. I tend to stay close to people who can tell me things I like knowing. For years, Dominic has been one I could count on. Here is an item he told me today. It's not as worldly as the maraschino item, but, as fairly arcane information goes, it's a piece that suits me. And even if all the world has read it in the book where Dominic must have read it, it was not the world who told me, in the course of general conversation, that every skunk on earth is born in March.

"PERF," HE says, taking his first taste. "These daiquiris are perf."

Dominic is sitting up on the brass and bamboo bed, his ankles crossed under a mohair throw. He makes it a point that he is not "in bed," that he has not taken to bed again. He has been amusing himself with a massive coffee-table book on the Academy Awards. He has it open on his lap, and, though it is a costly book, he puts his drink down on the open page while he lights a cigarette. His doctor has urged him to give up smoking, but Dominic claims that the stress of trying to quit would be, at this point, worse for him than smoking the occasional cigarette. A lot of people say this. Of course, Dominic doesn't limit himself to the occasional cigarette; he smokes nonstop, like a crematorium.

The glass will leave a ring on the face of Eddie Fisher, who is seated at a table with a jubilant Elizabeth Taylor. She is beaming at her just-won statuette. Although her then recent, nearly lost battle with pneumonia had dominated the world press for days, she is photographed smoking a cigarette in a white, disposable holder. This photograph made the cover of *Life* and became a well-known image.

"How old were you in sixty?" Dominic asks me.

"You know how old I was in sixty," I answer.

Dominic picks up his drink and slaps the open page.

"This is an outrage," he says. "Read this paragraph with Elizabeth's acceptance speech."

I lean forward to read from Dominic's lap, to the line where Elizabeth Taylor thanks the Academy with all her heart. "She thanked them with all her heart," I say. "What's the outrage?"

"The outrage," Dominic says, "is that as a matter of fact she didn't say, 'Thank you with all my heart.' As a matter of fact, she said, 'Thank you from the bottom of my heart.' " He is adamant.

"Do you really think they'd get it wrong in a book that costs this much?" I ask.

Dominic groans, "Honey, they got it wrong."

"How can you be sure?" I ask him. "I mean, why would you necessarily remember Elizabeth Taylor's speech, thirty years ago, verbatim?"

Dominic looks at me astringently. "It's the short term that goes," he says.

I overlook this. "Not that it's a big deal," I say. "But actually, sweetheart, I think you may be right. I think I remember her saying, 'Thank you from the bottom.' "

"Of course she did," Dominic says, quite certain. He takes a drink, moans with pleasure at the taste. We are still in station-break commercials. "When is this thing ever going to start?" he asks. He has waited long enough to see his entrance, to see how he looked eleven months ago.

"Do you find anything a little odd about this conversation?" I ask him.

Dominic fills his glass from the cocktail shaker. "What's odd?" he asks me.

"Sweetheart, don't you find it a little odd that in 1960 we were six- and eight-year-old boys, and that on what was very likely a pleasant spring evening we were indoors, glued to the Academy Awards show? I mean, shouldn't we have been outside, climbing trees or something?"

Dominic flips ahead, to 1961. "Honey," he says, "we were boys, we weren't Debbie Reynolds."

"I think there is something here," I suggest. "I think there has got to be an insight, a revelation here." The theme music for the show starts up. Dominic has opined that it is by far the most hideous theme music of any game show on television.

"Save that revelation, honey," he says. "Here I come."

———————

A MALE voice announces Dominic as he comes onto the set.

This same voice will describe, at the end of the show, the prizes that the losers will take home. Even when a prize is something you may want, something you might buy for yourself, the voice makes it sound like a mediocrity you wouldn't have in your house. If you don't want the prize, there is no cashing it in.

"Our first contestant," the voice begins—as though we would not have noticed on our own that the other players have yet to appear—"originally from San Francisco, currently a fashion consultant in Los Angeles," and then the voice booms out Dominic's name. Dominic Tardiverri is Dominic's name.

The studio audience welcomes Dominic with applause while he takes a place behind a podium and is greeted by the hostess, who says, "Dominic, tell our studio audience a little about yourself."

Traditionally, a game show has a host. This show had a host for years. This is the first show to experiment with a hostess, she is part of a new format. I would not bet on her to last the season.

"Well," Dominic says, "I'm originally from San Francisco, and I'm currently a fashion consultant here in Los Angeles."

I roll away on the bed and cover my face with a pillow.

"What are you doing?" Dominic asks.

"Pretending I don't know you," I answer.

"Honey, just watch. That's what they all do on this show. Here comes the hot one, he'll do the same thing."

On the show, the show that was taped eleven months ago, Dominic, waiting on camera for the hot one to appear, runs his fingers through his hair. Dominic was always running his fingers through his hair, thick, dark, lustrous hair that he wore halfway down his back and called his coiffure. He parted it on the left side, and every morning and every night he would brush it for at least ten minutes with a pair of monogrammed sterling-silver hairbrushes that had belonged to his grandfather. In the morning, Dominic would brush his hair to, as he put it, compose himself; at night, before bed, he would brush it still wet from his bath—he bathed twice a day—in order, he told me, to give it gloss. Dominic told me that brushing his hair for ten, twenty minutes gave him, each night, a chance to review his day. He would savor any turns of phrase he might have used and think of retorts he hadn't been able to concoct on the spot. In all the time I have spent with him in the almost twenty years I've known him, Dominic has not missed a night, even when he was drunk, even when he would bring a fellow home, which he did with increasing frequency. Every night he would review his day with his grandfather's sterling-silver hairbrushes, always taking a bath, never a shower, first, even when it meant leaving the "hottest animal alive" alone in the bed.

Even in the eighties, when he cut his hair to work in retail, Dominic cared more about grooming than any man or any woman I have ever known. His hair had an unbelievable sheen, and Dominic was lavishly vain.

I would be just as vain if I had looked like Dominic did. Or, maybe, if I looked like Dominic, I wouldn't know it. I have no idea. I used to imagine that stunning-looking people were a different species. I thought they must have a different life, a life I would never know, and that they lived it anew every time they walked into a room.

I'm not certain I don't still think this.

Dominic had this kind of beauty. For a while I thought Jasper had it, too, but in fact Jasper didn't, not in the way Dominic did. Jasper was straightforwardly handsome, virile and blunt. There is something otherworldly in the kind of beauty Dominic possessed. Something in it goes beyond gender.

Tonight Dominic's head is bare. Four months ago, when he was treated for lymphoma, long black hanks of hair came out with each stroke of the sterling-silver hairbrushes.

He called me in New York.

"I have cancer hair," he said.

I said I hadn't known hair could become cancerous.

"Not hair cancer," Dominic said, too patiently. "I said 'cancer hair.' It's the chemo, honey. It's made my hair look like I have cancer."

"Oh," I said. "I see," I said. "I guess I see," I said.

For years Dominic and I have understood each other after small delays. "I'm holding a fistful of hair," he told me.

For a while I said nothing. I was not prepared. Jasper did not get lymphoma, at least none that was diagnosed. Of course, according to Jasper's doctor, until he developed pneumocystis Jasper only had the virus, nothing else, though Jasper lost, in pretty much this order, his youthfulness, his energy, all taste for wine, his appetite, his ability to swallow solid food, sixty-eight pounds, his ability to focus on a topic, his verbal flourishes, his sardonic stance, his ability to walk unassisted, steady breathing, and, I think, his will to live, but Jasper kept his hair.

Actually, that's wrong. His will to live was the first thing Jasper lost.

Jasper would have said that losing his hair was bad luck. After what may have been a reasonable amount of rumination, Jasper said that getting the virus was a bad piece of luck. He said it was nothing more than that.

I think otherwise.

Jasper had not called his hair his coiffure. Jasper had not prepared me for Dominic.

"What can you do?" I asked Dominic.

"I don't know," Dominic said, a reflex. "What a world," he said a moment later.

I suspect that it was on the telephone with me, after months of feeling tired, months of a steadily declining T-cell count, which was thought to mean everything then; after rectal surgery and seventeen weeks in the hospital; after his arms had turned blue from injections—it was only then, I think, telling me on the telephone about holding a fistful of hair, that Dominic was struck by the notion, the idea, and by a feeling, that his life would get no better.

Later that week, Dominic had his head shaved.

In fact, Dominic's life, or rather his health, the outwards signs, does seem to be getting better. Tonight, seeing him bald, you would not know that Dominic is ill. Eight months ago, in photographs—Polaroids he had his home-care givers mail to me twice a month—there was no mistaking it. He looked ill, horrifying really. I wondered why he was sending me these pictures and thought at first that he must have wanted me to be a witness to his decline. Then slowly, incrementally, photograph by photograph, he began to look a little better, a little stronger each time, until once again he looked almost, though not quite, as he had before.

Tonight, you might take the shaved head as a fashion

statement. Dominic remains, I would say, a preposterously beautiful creature. I do not say "beautiful man" or even "beautiful boy." To me, Dominic was always a beautiful creature. Yesterday, the first time I saw him bald, I thought the lack of hair was the big difference. Dominic has not lost weight, or rather he has regained most of what he'd lost and does not have the anxious, cachectic look that Jasper had, and that most men, most people, have in the stages that are called, and usually are, final.

It was not until we went to dinner last night and I saw the way Dominic entered the dining room, the way he ordered an old-fashioned, the way he asked for grenadine, the way he held the drink and the way he held his fork—especially the way he held his fork—his posture in the chair and the absence of animation on his face as he listened, that I noticed something missing from all of it, from Dominic's usual presentation of self—a lack of affect, a disengagement. It was not until then that I saw Dominic had lost his vanity. It had simply left him, withdrawn. Without his vanity, Dominic was without glamour.

It was glamour that had set Dominic apart.

He is still set apart, but it isn't glamour doing it now.

Tomorrow, before I return to New York, I will buy him a new bottle of maraschino.

———

THE HOT one is introduced as Todd, originally from Fort Lauderdale, currently a fitness trainer in Beverly Hills.

Todd tells the audience he's Todd, originally from Fort Lauderdale, now a fitness trainer in Beverly Hills. "At present," Todd adds. I don't find Todd all that hot. I knew I wouldn't. Dominic has always found men hot whom I find epicene. Except once, the time Dominic went after Jasper, which I didn't know about until long after, Dominic and I have not competed for men. Even then we didn't compete, because I didn't know it had happened.

"He wasn't a fitness trainer," Dominic says. "But they won't take you if they know you're an actor. Fitness was a job Todd could fake."

"He does look like he knows what a bench press is," I offer.

"That was almost a year ago," Dominic reminds me.

About five years ago, when he first learned that he might become ill, Dominic worked with a fitness trainer. Back then, it was believed that ten percent of the men testing positive for the antibody would become ill. Now, of course, the experts say closer to a hundred percent. The workouts were intended to relieve stress, but they were for vanity, too. If he was going to get sick, Dominic said, he wanted arms, he wanted a chest.

He joined a gym on La Cienega. He kept half of his appointments. The trainer offered to bring free weights to Dominic's apartment. Even then, Dominic kept about half of their appointments.

"Let's just chat tonight," Dominic would propose as the trainer started to set up.

Dominic did not get his chest.

"Now, of course, Todd could say he was a nurse," Dominic says. "We all know something about medicine now."

Dominic is right about this, it has come with the times. From Dominic, from Jasper, from here and there, I have learned about reverse transcriptase, T-cells, B-cells, macrophages, pneumocystis carinii, lymphadenopathy, cytomegalovirus, histoplasmosis, toxoplasmosis, mycobacterium avium intracellular, now called mycobacterium avium complex—because as many as eighteen bacteria can be involved.

Just lately, I have learned a little about mycoplasmas, which are being studied now in France. Some scientists believe they are a cofactor.

There could be many cofactors.

I have learned about azidothymidine, now called

zidovudine, known as AZT, marketed as Retrovir; about acyclovir, sulfadiazine, pyrimethamine, leucovorin, pentamidine, Bactrim, Dapsone, fluconazole, now called Diflucan; about rifabutin, clarithromycin, erythropoietin. If I were on this show and the virus were a category, I would not disgrace myself.

Next comes Dorothy from Chicago. She is originally from Chicago and is still there, a substitute teacher. She is also the reigning champion, having won four consecutive games. One cannot win more than five games, so, win or lose, tonight is it for Dorothy. It strikes me as being not entirely as it should be that the substitute teacher is put against the clandestine actor and the *soi-disant* fashion consultant, but I keep this to myself. On her own, without being asked, Dorothy adds that she has six beautiful children.

"She's too dowdy to have beautiful children," Dominic says.

Dorothy *is* on the dowdy side. I resist telling Dominic that he'd be dowdy, too, if he'd been through what Dorothy has, because in Dominic's mind he has been. He used to telephone me in New York, at five in the morning, after noteworthy encounters.

"Honey," he told me more than once, "it was so hot, I gave birth to fetal pigs."

Dorothy names each of her six children and waves to them into the camera. I notice, because how can I not, that she does not mention her husband. She says nothing at all about him. I comment on this to Dominic.

"What makes you think it's all one big happy daddy?" Dominic asks me. "Maybe Dorothy can't remember all the men it took to get those six little offspring. Maybe the men it took are countless. Honey, maybe Dorothy can't be bothered."

Dominic knows about countless men. So, for that matter, do I. That is, twenty years ago I did. Since then I've counted.

"Sweetheart," I tell him, "it's the exact repetition that sounds dumb. You didn't have to repeat 'originally from San Francisco.' " I let this sink in. "You could have said, for example, that you were a 'native San Franciscan.' "

Dominic ponders this until the questions and answers begin.

———————

IT TAKES Dominic five questions before he gives an answer, and when he does the answer he gives, Christian Dior, is wrong. The question was to name the French designer who said, "Fashion is beautiful and becomes ugly, style is ugly and becomes beautiful."

The correct answer is Coco Chanel. This is the kind of thing a man who passes himself off as a fashion consultant can be expected to know. Dominic says he did know but was under pressure, that it was the pressure, the monstrous pressure of the game, that made him say Christian Dior. Dominic says the pressure is obscene. The whole show, Dominic says, is about keeping your finger on the button.

He is penalized five hundred dollars for answering incorrectly. The worst part about being penalized five hundred dollars when he was too quick with his finger is that Dominic did not have five hundred dollars to lose.

Christian Dior put Dominic in the hole.

"Honey, I'll tell you what it took," Dominic says. "When the Chicago creature got Cyd Charisse, I slapped my face for *haute le monde* to see. I gave up on the hot one and started to play. I wanted that trip to Jamaica, honey."

Dominic, of course, meant *tout le monde*. For years, Dominic has spoken of *haute le monde* and *tout cuisine*. *Haute couture,* fortunately, is simply called *couture*. I have learned not to correct him. The one time I tried, he waited about twenty minutes and then said, about the gray cashmere blazer I was wearing, that untold polyesters had given up their lives for me to have it.

I watch. Dorothy *does* answer Cyd Charisse, Dominic *does* slap his face—not comically, but in anger—and then he *does* start to play. I am amazed by the answers Dominic can give. He knows what performer in what movie had the most costume changes, sixty-five, in motion picture history. He wins four hundred dollars for knowing this. He knows that the study of the evolution of the universe is called cosmology, that the study of bodies of fresh water is called limnology, that the age of a tree is discerned by rings in its trunk, and that a "V" indicates the growing of a branch. I might have guessed that one. Dominic knows that in the 1960s the equinox had progressed to Aquarius. So, I think, did Dorothy and Todd, but Dominic beat them to the button. When the question is to name the mountain on which the Greek gods lived, Dorothy rings in with "Mount Zeus."

Dominic rings in with Olympus.

"Mount Zeus," I say. "This woman teaches?"

"She teaches," Dominic says.

Dominic can name the three green avenues in the game of Monopoly and the actor who married two of the three Gabor sisters but cannot name the two U.S. presidents to be widowed and remarried in office, which Dorothy can. He cannot say that Louis Pasteur invented a vaccine for rabies or that the scientific instrument invented in the eighteenth century by the Dutchman Anton van Leeuwenhoek was the microscope, though I happen to know both of these, and Dominic does not remember the first four words spoken by God in the Bible.

I am sure he hates himself for this. He knew it, he says, but just couldn't think of it in time. In fairness to Dominic, who went to Jesuit school and was the favorite of the nuns, the game moves quickly and gives the players little time. On the spot, I might not have remembered, "Let there be light."

Before the final question, long before, I become tired
of the game. I don't know half of what Dominic knows,
none of the physics questions, few of the political ones,
and I have no idea whatever in the world could be the
capital of North Dakota. I start to think about dinner,
about *zuppa di pesce,* about *spaghetti alla carbonara* and
escarole d'olio. I think of a lunch Jasper and I had in
Imola, of the fried zucchini blossoms at Piperno in Rome,
of the sea urchin soufflés, served in their shells, at Le Pré
Catalan, and I try to remember, but cannot, the name of
the place where Jasper and I waited two hours under an
awning one rainy winter night eight years ago to have the
best steaks in Madrid. I'm so hungry I could kill.

The final question is supposed to be the hardest. The
players are told the category and must write their wagers
based on this, before they hear the question. The camera
pans over the players as they write, showing each one in
close-up. It is not always a simple matter of knowing the
answer; often all three players will know, and then it becomes a matter of how much each player puts at risk. The
disclosure of the category, then the time the players take
to consider their bets, and finally the thirty seconds in
which they write their answers are all meant to put the
viewer in a torment of suspense. Since Dominic has already told me he will win tonight and then for the rest of
the week, I am in no suspense. I have watched this entire
game tonight knowing the outcome before it comes out. I
have been denied the excitement of crisis and feel, as I
have before with Dominic, cheated.

Here is the final question, the one on which Dominic
risked everything.

Here is the question that enabled Dominic to buy the
eighteen-thousand-dollar brass and bamboo bed upon
which, unless he goes back home, he will quite likely, perhaps this year, perhaps in a matter of months, die.

For that matter, of course, he could have the bed
shipped. I will point this out to him tonight. Tonight at

dinner I am going to do whatever I can to persuade Dominic to go home. Here is the question. What Walt Disney animal grieves for its mother?

Eleven months ago, with a full head of hair, Dominic won this game because he knew the answer was Bambi. I didn't know. Neither did Todd or Dorothy, who guessed Dumbo and Old Yeller, respectively.

It could have been any question. But of all the questions it could have been, this is the question it turned out to be. What, I wonder, if the game tonight had been Dominic's life? What if his life itself had hung on one question?

I wonder if there may not be for all of us, or for some of us, one question we will be asked at a point near life's end, which some of us will be able to answer, while the rest of us look torpidly ahead.

Many times this year I've wondered what Jasper was thinking when he had his last thought. Actually, I think hardly at all about anything else. Now and then I wish all my wondering about this would stop, but it has its own life. Nothing can bring it to a close; it will not be satisfied, it will not even diminish.

Now and then, though, it takes a pause. Tonight it did. Just now, when the game was over, Dominic gathered strength from his little triumph and hissed to himself, "Why didn't I say 'native San Franciscan'?"

Hearing Dominic scold himself so bitterly brought all my thinking briefly to rest.

———

I USED to tell people that Jasper and I met at the Frick Collection. This after rejecting an all-Bartók concert by the Tokyo String Quartet and a handful of carefully chosen stores: Dunhill's, Crouch and Fitzgerald, the Argosy Book Store, where, I could have added, I was buying Montecruz 210s or a two-suiter for a three-day trip or was looking for a first edition of *Butterfield 8*. Wasn't I lucky, I would have said to anyone who had asked—if I had used one of these versions—to be buying cigars that day, or wasn't it the happiest coincidence that Jasper and I had both needed leather goods, or that I had gone to the Argosy on the day that Jasper happened to be looking for a first edition of *Absalom, Absalom*.

In fact, Jasper would never have bought a first edition for himself, though he did give me a few over the years. There is an indescribable feeling to holding, reading, and owning forever a first edition of Willa Cather's *My Mortal Enemy* or Truman Capote's *The Grass Harp* or Ben Hecht's *A Jew in Love*. You need to have the dust jacket for the full effect, and if the book is signed by the author that will increase the thrill. But the principal reason that a first edition of a good book imparts an unusual joy is that books were better made around the time that Willa Cather wrote them. Even in the Second World War, "wartime" books, for which every effort was made to conserve materials, were well-bound, sturdy volumes that still hold up, and fifty years later the pages remain white.

While it is true that Jasper and I used to smoke Montecruz 210s after dinner with snifters of Marc de Bourgogne, I smoked my first cigar of any kind with Jasper on my twenty-first birthday, at Lutèce, in 1975—when they still had banquettes in the glass-roofed room that is quaintly called the garden. So I could not have met Jasper in the Dunhill humidor in 1973, but until I came up with the Frick Collection that was the version I was partial to.

I had picked these places because each one seemed to me a situation in which one might conceivably enter into conversation with a stranger. I hardly ever enter into conversation with strangers, but there have been times I've wanted to, and if I had seen Jasper in any one of these places it is possible, in fact it is a certainty, that I would have made the effort.

Or Jasper might have spoken first, to me. In Dunhill's, Jasper might have been friendly, he might have been avuncular and asked how long I had been smoking cigars, since at the time we met I was nineteen. That is a question a man can ask a youth. I could have answered that I had been smoking cigars not as long as I expected he had been, since at the time we met Jasper was forty-one—though for the first several months he told me thirty-six. At the Argosy, he could have mentioned that he had read all of John O'Hara. Jasper now and then was friendly, so either of these scenes or a number of others like them could have happened. In time, however, I abandoned all these versions, because none of them seemed likely enough. Telling people that we met at the Continental has never seemed right, either. That we met by falling not into conversation but onto a mattress in a dark room filled with naked men is not something I have an easy time telling.

Once I settled on the Frick Collection, I stayed with it, like a name I had chosen for myself and was stuck with. I even picked the painting that Jasper would have found me looking at, a handsome little work that, as a matter of fact, I've looked at quite often, Hans Memling's *Portrait of a Man*. I like the face in this portrait. Once I knew a man in Paris who reminded me of the face in this portrait, a mistake I made in 1987. Dominic was the only person to whom I told the truth, until just last week when the woman who owns the photography gallery asked me where I had met Jasper and I found myself no longer in a mood to lie about the Frick Collection.

Jasper, in fact, had read all of John O'Hara. So, as it happened, had I. Except I was never able to get through *Pal Joey*, all that argot weighed me down. I had *Butterfield 8* with me at the Continental the night we met. When we left together, Jasper asked what I had in my bag. I always carry a shoulder bag with two or three books in it because I have for years been frightened that someday I will be stuck in some hellish place and find myself with nothing to think about. So I carry books with me.

The night I met Jasper I had two other books I don't remember now. I could probably remember them if I had to. Jasper said John O'Hara was an underrated writer, and we talked about this, about how unfair it was, when we left the Continental and went downtown for something to eat at about two in the morning. Jasper told me he had also read all of William Faulkner and that in his twenties he had made a map of Yoknapatawpha County.

It occurs to me tonight, waiting for Dominic to dress for dinner, that I never saw that map. It troubles me to have learned quite recently that Faulkner himself had mapped his county and that his map had appeared as early as 1948 in the *Portable Faulkner*. It troubles me that Jasper may have seen this map and simply copied it. The map Faulkner made is a simple one. Maybe Jasper's was more thorough, more involved. I like to think it was.

That night, I sat and watched Jasper across a table. He looked like a man who, in his twenties, might have mapped Yoknapatawpha—whatever such a man might look like—and I must have looked at him peculiarly, in a way he was unused to, because he asked me, "Why are you looking at me that way?"

I could not tell him that I was looking at him because he was the first man I'd been with who had read all of Faulkner, never mind made a map, but that is what I was thinking. I remember thinking it. I remember it as if it were, as they say, yesterday.

"How am I looking at you?" I asked him.

"That's what I'm asking you," Jasper said.

"I'm just thinking this is a first for me," I said.

"What is?"

"Leaving the baths with someone. I've never left the baths with anyone before."

I remembered then that in San Francisco I'd left the

Ritch Street Health Club one morning with a man who gave me a ride to my ten o'clock class. But that had been two years before, and it ended up as nothing more than a double espresso and a ride.

Not that it has much to do with anything at all, but I still remember that man, even his name: Carlton Gabrielson. Not as if he were yesterday, though; that man I remember as though he were quite a few years before yesterday.

That was a man.

I wonder if he's still alive.

"I don't do it very often, either," Jasper said, and added that when he talked with people after being with them at the baths he usually felt no need to talk to them for long. "Are you sorry you left with me?" he asked.

"Not at all," I said. "I'm glad I came after you when you walked away from me in the labyrinth. Why did you walk away?"

"It seemed silly," he said.

"What did?" I asked.

"What we were doing, groping each other with all those other people standing around. I knew someone was going to join us. I didn't want anyone to join us. Did you want someone to join us?"

"No," I answered. "If you had found me fetching, you wouldn't have walked away." I didn't want to sulk, but I couldn't help it, I was sulking.

"But I do find you fetching, as you put it," Jasper said, smiling a bit.

"Not enough," I sulked.

"What would be enough?" he asked.

"We were in the orgy room," I said. "You couldn't even see me."

"And you couldn't see me," Jasper said. "We'd already seen each other in the labyrinth."

"You were able to resist," I said. "You didn't find me irresistible."

"No one," Jasper said, "is irresistible."

"You are," I said. He looked at me as though I were very young and possibly a trifle slow. I was, of course: very young, possibly slow, and I wanted to be irresistible to this man.

It's laughable now, but in those years I wanted to be irresistible to every man who looked like anything. This was, of course, a fatuous desire, one that one must be young, and probably a little slow, to have. Most of my desires were fatuous then, no doubt many still are, but Jasper changed all that, or much of it, changed me somewhat for a time. Jasper gave me fewer desires, and more desire. He did not, unhappily, make me any less slow.

"I've never pursued anyone before," I said. This was more or less true, for the simple reason that I have always preferred to be the one pursued. I assume Jasper believed me, he didn't question me on it. "Are you one of those tedious men who come to the baths to be illicit and then go home to their wives, or are you really a fag?"

He laughed a little. "I'm a fag," he said. "I am a genuine fag."

"How old are you?" I asked.

"How old do you think I am?" he said.

"That's a silly game," I said.

"You're right," he said. "It is a silly game."

"I'm nineteen," I said.

"Nineteen," he said. "I was thinking you'd be more than that. I was hoping you'd be at least twenty-two."

What could I say to that?

"Even twenty-two is pretty young," Jasper said, giving it some thought.

"Will you call me after tonight?" I asked.

He paid the check. We got up to leave. He put on his jacket. He was wearing blue-gray corduroy trousers, a sports jacket, no tie, lace-up shoes that had cost some money.

Lord God, he was handsome.

"Would you like me to call you?" he asked, as though his life did not hinge on my answer.

"Of course," I said. "Don't you want to see me again?"

We walked across the street to where his car was parked. "You were going to ask me, weren't you?" I asked.

I saw him in the light that was coming from a book-shop that had quarter movies in the back.

"I live with someone," Jasper said. "I'm thirty-six."

I said nothing.

"We don't do anything," he said. "We haven't for years."

"Why are you telling me this?" I asked him.

Before he could answer—and I don't know what his answer would have been—I said, amazed that anyone could have a man like Jasper in the house and not want to be in bed with him every second, "You don't, you really don't?"

I thought it was decent of him to tell me, though I did not rule out the possibility that he could be making the fellow up to put me off, something I had done a few times, and just then, that early morning eighteen years ago, looking at Jasper's face in the light from the open door of the porno shop, I knew that I would be in bed with this man all my life if I could be, my whole life, all of it, just be in bed with him all the time and sleep my life away. This was a feeling I may have had once before—maybe once, sometime long before—but I think more likely it was new. It didn't feel familiar. It felt unfinished, not like something that had happened, or even that was happening—it felt like something about to begin.

To my credit, if it is credit, I have not felt this since. Not once.

Maybe it isn't to my credit. In any case, I will not feel it again.

"No," Jasper said to me that night. "We haven't for years."

"That's fine, then," I said. I remember standing with Jasper on the corner of Hudson Street, in 1973. A light snowfall was just beginning, and Jasper looked like wonder itself with snowflakes in his hair.

That night I didn't even care if he was lying.

DOMINIC TOOK two hours to dress for dinner. That is about as much time as Jasper ever took to *make* dinner. Jasper took no time at all to get dressed, but most of the times that I saw Jasper dress he was at my house, where he had only the clothes he had arrived in, or on a trip, where he had only the clothes he'd brought with him. Jasper traveled light. I like to have more on a trip than I need. Jasper could stay away a month with five shirts, three pairs of trousers, two jackets, a sweater or two, and six or seven books. The books were always from the public library, because Jasper didn't buy books. One time, when we went to Paris for eight weeks, just last year— the last trip we took together—Jasper brought two books, to read on the plane. He said he could read books we had in Paris. I thought it odd that he wasn't in the middle of anything. I had seen to it that we had quite a few books in Paris. I am, unhappily, no kind of homemaker, but I wanted our place in Paris to be like home for us, so I brought half a dozen books with me every time I came over. I also brought photographs. I was glad the books were there for Jasper, because Jasper would never have kept a library book overdue. He was especially prompt with books on reserve, always mindful that people were waiting for them. Also, Jasper would have hated paying a fine. Over the years I have paid hundreds—hundreds and hundreds—of dollars in library fines. Finally I just stopped using libraries, except to look things up; I like to read magazines from decades ago. Jasper did not understand my difficulty with library books and objected that I lived without discipline. This wasn't a point I would argue, because he was right to object. He did not ever complain, though, because Jasper knew that there are habits that *will not be* broken.

Jasper didn't keep a change of clothes at my house— no robe, no slippers. Even I don't have slippers. At my house Jasper kept an electric razor, a toothbrush, and he saw to it that I always had aspirin. He also kept a bicycle at my house, a racing bicycle. It is still there, I see it every day.

Other than the bicycle, the toothbrush, the razor, Jasper kept nothing at my house—no hat, no gloves, no scarf. He used my comb.

Jasper had overcoats, jackets, suits, shirts, sweaters, belts, shoes with shoe trees in them, scarfs, neckties, underclothes. Jasper had books, recordings, pictures on his walls—drawings, lithographs, silk screens, oils; Jasper had chairs, tables, he had rugs on his floors; he had dishes, glasses, crystal. He had a wine cellar well stocked with white Burgundies, red Bordeauxs—*grands crus, premiers crus,* a few Sauternes, some magisterial Italian reds; a linen closet stacked with bath towels, hand towels, blankets, quilts. He had magazine subscriptions and received catalogs and bills, which he paid by checks that bore his address, where everything he owned was kept, and where Jasper lived with the man whose name is Oliver Ingraham.

I have been to that house perhaps five hundred times. One time I met Oliver Ingraham there, by accident, in 1987.

Oliver Ingraham had even more clothes than Jasper had, and Jasper had a fair amount of clothing. Oliver Ingraham's shirts and trousers were left on chairs, all over the house. As far as I know, most of Jasper's clothing is still there, in that house—all of it hanging in closets or folded, by Jasper, in drawers.

Oliver Ingraham has all that to get rid of.

In my house, I have not even a necktie that was Jasper's.

IT HAS never taken me two hours to dress for dinner, but I used to spend much more than that on a dinner I would cook for Jasper. I was nowhere near as good at making a dinner as Jasper was. Jasper made glorious dinners for us: lacquered ducks with raspberries, baby pheasants stuffed with chestnuts and radicchio, which Jasper would steam briefly to take off the bitter edge, *gigot en croûte,* whole striped bass stuffed with oysters and figs, spaghettini with shaved white truffles. Even something as prosaic as a roast chicken Jasper could transform into something nearly lyrical.

One night he wrote out a four-course menu in French, a language he didn't know, though he did try to learn it one year. He wrote the French words carefully in his hand, accented them correctly—and this menu included the most glorious *homard à l'américaine* I expect ever to have in this world. I have tried more than once to make *homard à l'américaine* and have not ever had a triumph. This was years ago, of course—the night Jasper wrote out the menu.

When I told Dominic about Jasper's menu, Dominic asked what was so extraordinary about copying headings of recipes from a French cookbook. I suppose one could see it that way, as just copying from a book, but I was disappointed in Dominic for not seeing the wonder of it. To explain a wonder is to risk taking from it, making it prosaic, but I wished that Dominic had seen, as I did, that in the act of writing our menu in French, putting it down in dark red ink, in fountain pen, on fine gray paper that I had bought for him in Paris, at Papier Plus, Jasper was making a dinner, and the simple act of our eating it together, an occasion, an event, and that it is by gestures like this that daily life is made less daily. This by itself, making daily life less daily, strikes me as being an enterprise worth saluting.

———————

TAKING TWO hours to dress for dinner is nothing new for Dominic. For Dominic, two hours is almost record time. As he tried on and rejected just about everything in his closet, I began to pack for the next day's flight. Dominic dropped his grandfather's pair of silver hairbrushes into my suitcase.

"What are you doing?" I asked.

"I want you to have these," Dominic said.

"Sweetheart, I can't take these. They're part of your life," I said.

"That's why I want you to have them," Dominic said.

"Your hair may grow back," I said.

"In heaven, honey?" Dominic asked.

We went to an Italian place in downtown L.A. Dominic entered the dining room the same way he entered the place last night. I recognized this Italian place from two or three movies, and Dominic told me it had been featured recently in a film in which Faye Dunaway had played a madam. In a scene that Dominic said was pivotal, Faye Dunaway made a splashy entrance at the top of the staircase, whereas in fact, Dominic pointed out, the entrance is on the street; the street is what Dunaway would have come in from, not, Dominic insisted, the mezzanine.

This is the kind of detail that Dominic cannot let alone, and he said something about how the movie made it look as though poor Faye Dunaway was coming back to her table from the can. Dominic said it was a fraudulent use of locale, a piece of charlatanism. Dominic used to get twenty minutes out of this kind of thing. He used to be fun to spend time with, when I wanted to spend my time this way.

Tonight, the word "charlatanism" came out flat. I'm not sure he didn't want another word. There was no bliss in his inflection; Dominic doesn't seem to care anymore about inflections, whereas he used to be pretty much nothing but inflection.

I'll rephrase that. Dominic used to be a master of inflection.

Tonight, Dominic wants *risotto frutti di mare*. The *risotto* is for two. I am often disappointed by *risotto*. Actually, I somewhat dislike *risotto*. But tonight Dominic and I will be having *risotto*.

"How's Estelle?" I ask.

Estelle is Dominic's mother. We've not met. "She hates the new husband. It hasn't been two years, and she already hates him."

"I meant how is she taking it?" I say.

"It?" Dominic says. "I haven't told her."

"You haven't told her?" I ask. "Four months in the hospital, five months with nurses in your house round the clock, and you haven't *told* your mother?"

"They weren't nurses, honey," Dominic insists. He is impatient with me. "They were health-care workers, untrained, like hospital orderlies, except they weren't even as chic as *that*. Only one of them was a nurse, and she only came three times a week to give the IV, and then only twice a week, and she stopped coming altogether when I got off that odious amphotericin B. And the health-care creatures only came round the clock for about a month."

"Four months," I say.

"Whatever," Dominic says. He shakes his head. "God, they were awful."

"I know, sweetheart." I shake my head with him.

"No, you can't know," Dominic tells me. "All but one of them talked to themselves. They'd carry on endless monologues all day long. Endless, honey. You don't know how hideous it was, hearing them babble all the time, and when I'd ask them to bring me a lemon Coke they'd bring me a lemon *root beer*. Let me tell you, doll face, lemon root beer is *not* a lovely treat, and not one of them could figure out the asshole cappuccino machine. I mean, not *one* of them, honey, and two of them were thieves."

"Thieves?" I ask.

"One of them forged checks. One day she wrote herself a check for five hundred dollars, the next day she wrote one for a thousand, and the day after that was the last day I saw her."

"What did the other one take?" I ask.

"Julio liked Baccarat. I had eight lovely tumblers. He asked me, were they real crystal—as opposed to fake, I guess he meant. He didn't know, and, like a fool, I told him they were.

" 'Umm, what do you pay for things like this?' he asked me.

"I was beginning to catch on, so I told him I'd had them so long I didn't remember, and he said to me, this creature, 'They're beautiful.'

"Well, honey, the next time he brought me a drink in one of them, he said, 'Oh, Mr. Tardy-very'—that's how he pronounced my name—'one of these glasses broke, so now you only have seven.'

"I thought to myself, 'Oh, for shitting out loud, what's one glass?'

"The next day he said another one had broken, that now there were six left.

"So I said to him, 'Julio, please be more careful with the glass,' and he gave me this fiendish little smile and said, 'Oh, I will be, Mr. Tardy-very.'

"He waited a couple of days. Then he came and told me there were only five left.

"Well, honey, I hit the roof. I said to him, 'Julio, stop using these glasses. Just bring me my milkshakes in the *regular* glasses.'

"I was drinking milkshakes all the time to put some

weight back on, five or six of them a day, big, thick ones, with bananas and ice cream, wheat germ and raw eggs.

"And then one day I was feeling pretty down, so I said to him, 'Julio, please bring me a Punt e Mes in a Baccarat glass.' I knew there were only five left, but I was willing to lose one more, that's how badly I needed a lift.

"And the little beast looked at me, and he said, 'Oh, Mr. Tardy-very, they all broke.' "

Dominic had not told me this story before, but I had heard similar stories from men in New York who got out of bed one day and found themselves without copper pots, without Cuisinarts, without toasters.

One man got out of bed and found himself without aluminum foil.

They lived to tell.

I TELL Dominic that none of what he has told me would have happened if he had gone back home, and as soon as I've said this I regret it.

Dominic gives me a scornful look but goes on to tell me of an unpleasant day when Julio had looked Dominic straight in the eye and said to him, as Dominic quotes it, "You'd be *so* easy to kill."

I ask Dominic if it wouldn't have been easier to handle something like this if he'd had someone, a confidant, whom he could have picked up the telephone to call, to ask for help. I confide in him that if I had been bed bound and unable to walk, I would want someone to help me with problems like Julio.

Dominic shrugs. "Julio was supposed to help me. Do you know about the new husband?" Dominic asks.

"You've got to tell your mother, Dominic," I say.

"He used to be an alcoholic. He still is, except now he uses pills. He got disbarred years ago, so he's home all day, popping Valium."

"That must be darling for your mother," I say.

"It's very darling."

"Do you want me to tell her for you?" I ask Dominic.

Dominic looks at the couple across the room. "The whole day long," he says.

For a while I let Dominic go on about his mother's new husband.

"He has hairy nostrils and repulsive furniture. Picture, if you will, honey, the *eidos* of repulsive: plaid upholstered chairs, with ruffled skirts, all hideously brown and yellow.

"I went with him to his house to help him move his shit to Estelle's. He had little plastic fixtures over all the light switches, featuring cartoon drawings of happy little squirrels.

"Estelle said the first time she saw those she knew the marriage was unwise. But Estelle wanted a husband, and there aren't a lot of yummy men in San Francisco for sixty-year-old widows."

"Alas," I say.

"Estelle is nothing if not brave," Dominic says. "My mother likes a long cocktail hour, so Dan will get up and start playing his Hammond organ."

"He has an organ?" I ask.

"A Hammond," Dominic answers.

"Which he plays?" I ask.

"Which he plays," Dominic answers. "He *likes* to play, honey, and at dinner he's given to making remarks out of nowhere, remarks like 'Between Mr. Shakespeare and Mr. Shaw, I happen to prefer Mr. Shaw.' "

"That's worse than the happy squirrels but somehow not as dismaying as the Hammond organ," I say.

"He *likes* to make those remarks. When I heard that one, what could I say? So I said, 'Dan, I know what you mean. I know exactly what you mean. Take actresses, for example,' I said to him. 'Between Edith Evans and Susan Hayward, I *happen to* prefer Susan Hayward.' "

Dominic has not taken his eyes from the couple at the table across the room.

"Why doesn't Estelle get a charming divorce?" I ask.

"Estelle wants to get into heaven," Dominic answers. "But she *is* hoping he'll have an accident. Every twenty minutes she tells him he seems tense. 'Darling, you're so tense, why don't you take another Valium?' Then, when the man is stupefied, Estelle, who by this time has had several cocktails, tells him she's out of capers, would he mind driving to the stupid-market?"

Dominic chooses this moment to look at me. "He sings in a church choir."

"Oh," I say. Just as I am about to come up with something suitably scornful to say, the *risotto* is brought to the table, steaming.

Dominic contemplates it, lowers his head to inhale the fragrance. The *risotto* has a saffron color. It is strewn with the glossy dark-green shells and bright orange flesh of giant mussels from New Zealand and the grayish pinks of giant prawns from Santa Barbara. They are butterflied but otherwise left whole. This is a *risotto* you would never be served in Italy.

"Yum," Dominic says before he's had a taste. Then he does taste it and says, "This *risotto* will change your life."

I repeat my question: does he want me to tell his mother for him?

"No," he says. "I told two people when I first felt it coming on, and they got all goofy. Otherwise, you're the only one I've told. And of course my doctor knows. My doctor is the man in my life. He's on fire for me, honey. He is wild with desire. I'm going to write a memoir about our affair. First we're going to *have* the affair, then I'm going to tell the world."

"Sweetheart, I think your life would be easier if you had someone who knew," I say. "In fact, I know it would be."

Dominic does not pick up on this.

"Well, there *is* my pharmacist," Dominic adds. "He knows. Remember the ad, honey?—'Only her pharmacist knows for sure.'"

"What about the people you were with?" I ask.

"You want me to call out the fleet?" Dominic asks. "Who wants bad news? Anyway, I don't think I'm a carrier."

"Is that what the man in your life tells you?" I ask. "Sweetheart, forgive me, but of course you're a carrier."

We'd already been through this. We went through it four years ago in Rosarito.

Dominic looks at the man and woman across the room. The woman is overweight, overdressed in something midnight blue. It is shiny and much too small for her. She is younger than the man, though she isn't young. She looks like a woman who could have been a starlet twenty years ago, like quite a few women in Los Angeles, and it comes to me that she isn't all that much older than Dominic or me. The man looks prosperous, like quite a few men. Dominic says nothing to me while he studies them. Then he speaks in the slow, sullen tone he gives to every syllable when he wants you to be aware that he is taking great, unusual pains to make every word the unvarnished truth. He makes himself sound as if he's doing you a favor, that you should be grateful.

It isn't an inflection, exactly. It's a sound he has.

"I thought about it for a long time. I decided to tell you and Jasper, in case I was a carrier. I mean, just to be sure. Jasper is the only one I knew how to get hold of, but even if I could get to the others, why tell them? What could they do? Everyone is living as though he has it anyway, so what earthly difference would knowing make? I mean, to their lives? One way or the other? Anyway, Jasper doesn't have it, you don't have it, so I assume I'm not a carrier. Look at that couple. Isn't that sad?"

Actually, I don't believe that everyone is living as though he has the virus. I know this, in fact. Many people have it and don't know it; others know that they are carriers and are living as though they aren't. There are many who care enormously about their pleasure but not at all about the people who are giving it to them. And there are things people can do now to help themselves, new things, and newer things. They are not cures, but treatments. Dominic has been doing some of them, and this is not a time to make him feel responsible for anyone else, not that I ever could.

Jasper and Dominic did not keep in touch. At least I know this now.

I haven't told Dominic about Jasper.

I didn't tell Jasper about Dominic.

two

FOR THE first several days of 1974 I lived in torpor. I had nothing more urgent to do than to watch the telephone and to wait for the imbecile thing just to please Jesus ring.

Ordinarily, this is a woman's picture. Normally, there is a woman in it who has let this happen to her. In this picture, the woman is always waiting for a man to call. I began to suspect that I had turned, by a means unknown, into Greta Garbo in *Grand Hotel,* when she is alone in her room, quivering in Adrian plumes, hovering over her telephone, begging it to ring and to be John Barrymore, too. Barrymore has driven Garbo out of lassitude, has left her fulminating, twitching, all aflame. More than Garbo, even more, I had become Gloria Swanson in *Sunset Boulevard,* pacing the length of her swimming pool in her sweeping velvet robe, her nerves naked, asking poor, pitiful, down-and-out, good-looking William Holden again and again if "Paramount Studios" has called.

"Was that Paramount Studios?" Gloria Swanson would inquire every time the phone rang, her longing becoming each time more turbid, more suppurating—until, at the end, she is herself no more than a miasma of desiring.

I lay on the floor in the pale gauze of winter twilight, recalling all the Great Women of the Telephone. I thought of Luise Rainer in *The Great Ziegfeld,* of gnomic Norma Shearer in *Her Cardboard Lover,* of Barbara Stanwyck as a bed-bound invalid in *Sorry, Wrong Number,* who hears on the telephone that her husband, robust Burt Lancaster, is planning her murder for that night, and of the magnificent Ingrid Bergman in Jean Cocteau's *The Human Voice,* made for television in 1967. I thought of Joan Crawford in every picture she made after 1945, because, as Dominic had told me the year before, she'd had it written into her contracts. Crawford, Dominic explained, was a loner and preferred to act alone, without other actors getting in the way of her thespianism. She liked to dispense with the clutter of interplay, Dominic told me, when a scene called for anguish, as so many scenes in Crawford pictures do. So Joan Crawford would invariably have a telephone monologue, just as the incomparable Stanwyck, in most of her pictures as a star, would play at least one scene on a horse, and when she wasn't on a horse she was walking, striding that magnificent stride.

That first week in 1974, it seemed part of whatever wrapping the New Year had come in that I would join these women's company, beginning the year without any ability to do anything whatsoever, except to wait for Jasper to call.

The third of January came, the fourth of January came, the fifth, and so on.

"Ring," I shrieked to the vapid instrument.

When was Jasper going to call? Had he changed his mind? Had I done something, said something at the last minute that had made him think again? Had there been a sound in my voice he had heard, had I been dreary, verbose, had I lacked humor, seemed desperate, been a fool?

That was it. I'd been a fool. Would I be one all my life? What else could it have been that had made the man think twice? When I left him on the street, the Thursday after Christmas, had he looked after me, had he seen something in my walk? Had there been something wrong, something dreadful, in the way I had moved, had there always been? Was I too wide in the rear for his taste? How immensely undesirable had I looked to the man?

Had I looked to him just flat-out homely?

How bad was it?

Exactly how hideous had it been?

I lay on the floor, certain Jasper had decided I was homely. Maybe I was. Maybe I was, God help us all, just a homely, hideously ordinary-looking boy. Maybe he hadn't wanted to look at me for even one more second.

Had anyone ever told me otherwise?

A few, but who had they been? Who had they been to me?

I moved the telephone to the mirror that Miss Fingerstop and I kept in our foyer. The mirror was mine. So was the upright piano, that is, it would be when I finished paying for it.

I was practicing Chopin's nocturnes and had mastered no. 2. Such a lovely piece, it made me wish I played the saxophone. Every time I hear it, play it, I see the windows that line the quais of Paris, their windows black at three in the morning, and I hear the music moan the blues. Written for keyboard, for fingers, Nocturne no. 2 would sound, I was sure of it, just like a dream on a saxophone.

In our hallway, Miss Fingerstop and I kept an old metal barrel we had found on the street one night on a walk through the wholesale meat district. We shared a top floor on the edge of that district. Livestock cannot be slaughtered in Manhattan, but much of the meat that is sold in the city has been cut on or around Gansevoort Street. Miss Fingerstop had the idea to empty the barrel of the pigs' heads that were in it, to leave them on the street and roll the barrel home.

I called a glazier from a bar and ordered a three-quarter-inch piece of glass, cut on the round, with a beveled edge. This took a week. When it came, I put it inside the rim at the bottom of the barrel, which I had sanded clean with a rented sander and had spent most of the week lacquering in twenty-eight slow-drying coats of the high-gloss, almost-black color of Cherry Heering liqueur. I stood the much-lacquered barrel in the hallway, set it upside down. The open top rested on the floor, a good place to keep cash, I thought. Not even Miss Fingerstop would think to look under an old thing like this, with three-quarter-inch glass laid down on the bottom, now the top of it.

Flowers in water, in a glass vase on top of that, would make money hard to get to. With so much in its way, I thought extravagance—which is, I fear, my nature—would have that much more to overcome.

Of course, I spent every penny anyway.

I spent every last dollar as though it were my first. I had a trust. I could not break it until I was thirty. It paid me a monthly allowance, which was never enough. The trust took care of me and gave me some time. I had no urgent need for money, but nor had I the ability to walk into Steinway & Son and buy the first concert grand that struck my fancy.

I was buying the upright on time. Every month I had to send Steinway seventy-five dollars, and in those days seventy-five dollars was—seventy-five dollars.

I was always bouncing checks in those years.

I still am.

The first piece I bought was the mirror, my first antique. Its frame was Biedermeier. I hung it on the wall just over the lacquered barrel. I bought a round, heavy-rimmed clear glass vase, which looked good on the heavy round glass. I filled this vase with water for tall, fragrant speciosum lilies. These are flowers grown in Japan. Going out at night, I could see my face among their open petals and would look at myself just long enough to inhale their scent. I was fond of the Biedermeier frame, of its polished grain, of its black detailing, and I looked a little better in this mirror than I usually do in a mirror. I don't know why this was so, but it was, in fact, the case.

The glass and the mirror and the speciosum lilies all went together nicely, and I still do believe, even now, one should see something handsome upon coming home to a place.

———————

COMING IN, I'd leave my keys in a small silver bowl that I kept beside the vase. Miss Fingerstop picked up this habit, too. She was better at keeping it. She was much better at it, really. My problem is getting past the idea of a good habit. I always have the idea, but I'm poor at what Jasper called "follow-through." I'm just not good at it. It is unlikely I ever will be.

Jasper was remarkable at follow-through.

Without telling Miss Fingerstop about the money, I refilled the vase with fresh water daily, whether we had flowers that day or not.

Some weeks I forgot to buy flowers. Some weeks I couldn't afford them. But every day I changed the water.

When flowers were fresh I put aspirin in the water.

I did not let the silver bowl get dull.

The week I was waiting for Jasper to call, I carried the telephone to the mirror each day and saw in it the birds-of-paradise we had that week and homeliness. It was un-utterable, the homeliness.

Over those days of waiting, I would move, telephone in hand, from the mirror to the window, which I would open, which I would close. I could look down onto Wash-ington Street, where every night, just across from me, empty trucks were parked outside a warehouse, always left open, and at about two o'clock every morning they would begin filling up with men.

There was usually quite a number, sometimes as many

black as white, few Orientals, no transvestites at all. The transvestites had their own place to go, I'm sure. That is, I hope they did. They would not have fit the mood, exactly. I wore a dress to a Halloween party once. I put on false eyelashes, and Dominic did my makeup, to make me look, he said, like Katharine Hepburn in *Dragon Seed*. My triumph that night alarmed me, and I've done nothing like it since. That was as close as I will come in this life to cross-gender chic.

Those nights I slept with a cinnamon candle burning.

I WANTED to be the one who was called. Jasper had given me a number, and it had checked out with directory assistance. He'd given me his real number, his real name, which was more than I used to do. I could have called him myself, of course. That would have been easy enough—all I had to do was dial.

I did not dial. If I called him, how would I know that he would have called me anyway? I would not ever know the man had had me on his mind.

With Jasper, I needed to be the one to receive.

NO ONE wore white. In winter, men wore heavy down parkas. They were usually tan. I remember a lot of tan parkas, a lot of cowboy boots.

Wallets were lifted, fights were frequent, but almost every night there were men right there to give me what I came for.

Some men walked on their knees.

Living across the street as I did, and because I looked over it every night, some nights I went and looked it over.

Not every man would be good-looking, not all the time.

Most night I didn't do anything, but I liked knowing that I could have. I liked knowing those trucks were there.

Some nights I gave in. Things could get vicious when a fellow made a pest of himself, which did, of course, now and then happen. The best-looking men drew attention from those who were less coveted, and they, the less coveted, would sometimes get sloppy. Men who are not coveted can do this, they can get sloppy. You had to keep your pants up, or you would more than likely find a face in your rear while you were minding your own business. You would not know what places that face had been, or the tongue, either, but it seemed a fair assumption that if the tongue was in your ass, the face had seen the world.

Haute le monde, as Dominic would say.

Sometimes a fellow would be a little forward, would misbehave, but the mood was more often down to business, purposeful, and there was always something to see— some fellow getting slammed from the back while some other fellow—or two or three other fellows—took him off in front. This was a hard pose to imagine myself in, even when I saw it going on in front of me. Seeing this and things like it a few times helped me grasp a notion that had been slowly coming to me for a while. There are men who are not born for women. They are able to be with a woman, of course, they are capable enough, but they are not born for women, not made for them, really, and it is nothing more than this, it never has been, and there is a pleasure, or two, perhaps an ecstasy, that no woman will provide.

I don't mean anatomy.

That is, I don't mean anatomy *only*.

This is probably better not gone into.

Man, after all, is the provider.

———

O R S O I thought then.

Years ago, many years, I read a line in a Greek poem. It had been written long ago by Pindar, or more recently by Cavafy. I don't know by whom. Maybe it is in one of the monologues in the *Symposium,* though I don't believe I saw it there. When I met Jasper, I knew those monologues, every one of them; I knew what Aristophanes had said, what Agathon, the tragedian, had said, what Alcibiades had said. Until he met me, Jasper hadn't known the *Symposium,* which I found hard to believe.

I still do, given all that he had read.

I gave him a rather elegant edition, in a readable translation, with the Greek text on the left, illustrated by Giacometti, limited to seventy-five copies, printed in Verona, numbered, and signed by the artist. When I asked Jasper how he had found it, he replied he hadn't *found* it, I had given it to him. Jasper did this all the time. It amused him to do this to me. He did it whenever I asked him how he found anything.

"How do you find this?" I would ask him, about something I'd spent a day cooking.

"By looking on my plate," Jasper would answer. "It's right here," he'd say, and he'd look down at his plate.

So I asked him what he had *thought* about the *Symposium,* and he said he hadn't gotten around to it yet. At his house, I'd see the book on the table in front of his couch. It was always there, and every time I asked him about it he'd say he hadn't gotten around to it yet. Jasper had read all of Nathaniel Hawthorne, all of Herman Melville and Edgar Allan Poe; he had read all of Joseph Conrad, all of Edith Wharton, of course, John Dos Passos, Yukio Mishima, Alberto Moravia, Ford Madox Ford, Katherine Anne Porter, Truman Capote, every last word Willa Cather ever wrote, and, among the living, James Salter, Joan Didion, Gore Vidal, Philip Roth; biographies of just about everyone, also quite a few writers no one reads anymore, men like Ben Hecht and Nicholas Monsarrat. Jasper told me about a story by Monsarrat, "Leave Cancelled," that had moved him, he admitted, to tears. When I read it, I knew Jasper hadn't used this as a figure of speech; it made me weep, that story.

I don't believe Jasper ever got around to the *Symposium*.

Wherever the line appeared, it was given as an axiom, and it read: women for progeny, boys for pleasure, but a man for ecstasy.

I have many times thought about this line. I quote it only to make plain that the thought has been had before, by others, and does not originate with me.

The thought of man being the provider.

I like to pass it along.

It would be false to say I don't miss it now. I miss it all. There were times, even with Jasper, when I missed it. The pleasure, I mean; I had the ecstasy. It was fun. There is no virtue in denying now that it was fun.

Not too many lines were drawn. After one encounter, I did draw one: I let no one near me with chewing gum in his mouth.

A thing like that you don't let happen again. One night, though, I did. I forgot. So, in fact, it did happen twice. But not again after that, not ever.

One night a man showed up in a wheelchair. His legs were weak, paralyzed maybe, but he had them.

The three or four times I went to it with Tom, before it burned, there were usually a couple of men without legs at the Everard Baths. Their male nurses, strong men, would carry them up the stairs and settle each one onto a cot. That is, I assumed the other men were nurses. Maybe these men had been born without legs, maybe they had lost them. I couldn't tell, because I could not look at them for long. There were two of these men, and usually they took rooms next to each other. I guess they had made some arrangement with the management.

I was more than once surprised to see men going into

those rooms, paying visits to the legless men. One night a rather good-looking fellow went from floor to floor with his towel around his neck. I would have done the same, I'm sure, if I had looked as good as he did. This man was in every way presentable. I wasn't following him. In fact, I thought for a while he was following me. He looked in every room, everyone does that, and he paused now and then in a doorway, looked within, but he'd always move on.

This man was exceedingly presentable, a bit too perfect a specimen for me to approach, I felt. He was taller, though, than I like a man to be, by almost a foot, and, of course, I didn't approach men in the first place. But it pleased me to think he was following me, until he went into a room where one of the men without legs was sort of sitting on a bed.

That night I left the Everard believing that the world has something for everyone.

And gives it, too.

To just about everyone.

The man in the wheelchair found someone, too.

AT SOME point, almost every night, usually late, two or three police cars would pull up, and all the men would jump down from the trucks. They would scatter as I imagine Boy Scouts do, caught sharing cigarettes at camp.

Before I met Jasper, when I was sharing the floor-through with Miss Fingerstop, I had one or two good nights. One night I met a fellow who was a bit drunk but was just about perfect to look at. He fit my mood exactly, he was made for it.

He drove us through the tunnel, across the river to one of the towns in Essex County, where he lived in a shack near a football field. When we got inside he dropped his clothes on the floor. He didn't even empty his pockets, he just took everything off, fell onto his bed, and passed right out.

There he was—all handsome, all naked, all sleeping. I had nothing to do, so I picked his clothes off the floor, folded them, and laid them on a chair. It was the only chair he had. I had an idea that I could at least do this, could pile his clothes on the chair, that he might then be able to feel less shabby in the morning.

His trouser pockets were lumpy. I pulled out a handkerchief. It was unused and was wrapped around a wad of hundred-dollar bills, five or six thousand dollars in cash.

All these many years later, there is no point going into this, and I don't know why I am, except it was one of a handful of episodes that came to mind that week as I sat in the window and waited for Jasper to call.

It was still snowing, I remember, had been for days, and the man and his cash discharged in my mind. I watched the snow come down and remembered how easy it would have been, with the fellow so out of the picture, to slip away from the scene with all that cash. It would make a lot of payments to Steinway; I might even have been able to buy the piano. My mind filled itself with the thought of doing this; it was my only thought, and I wished that I were strong enough, had the stuff in me, just to take the money, call for a limo, and vanish from this oafish man's life.

I didn't. I did not have it. I didn't even count the bloody bills, and I put it in my idiotic mind, instead, that if I left the fellow's money where it belonged I might at some much later date, far in the future, be a little happy.

It turned out about the good-looking fellow from Essex County that he was a football coach who also did some counseling. I discovered this just by looking around. He had some notes. I read a file on a truant boy.

In the morning, when he saw his clothes had been folded, he went through his pockets. He was, I am sure, relieved to find the money there. The fellow stood by his bed, naked, superb, counting his money. He was a little on the beefy side, I saw, but far from gone to fat. He looked at me in some amazement, no doubt because the money was all there, and said he must have been out of his mind to go to the trucks with all that cash. I said I supposed he had been. Then he looked down, seemed pleased with himself, unembarrassed.

He looked at me.

I hadn't undressed. I believe, though, that he thought I had.

The fellow looked at me some more and then came toward me. He came right up to me. I saw he had a small scar, a deep, healed cut, under his chin, which I hadn't noticed until just that minute.

He was not exactly as handsome as he had been the night before—no man ever is—but he was still pretty superb, and he was ready. The man, all of him, was ready. He rubbed his face and asked if he should shave. I told him he should not. He pulled at my belt, pulled the whole thing off, reached in, and looked at me, met my eyes, and then he came so close I could not see him anymore. He asked me then, right into my ear, and rather charmingly, I thought, for a football coach, "Whose little boy are you?"

————

MEN WITH all kinds of voices would call up and ask for Mercy.

That's the name Miss Fingerstop had chosen upon launching her trade. None of the men came to the house, but Miss Fingerstop often had a female guest. Sometimes she had two. I would hear the women exchange words with Miss Fingerstop. There were arguments. In my room, I would hear Miss Fingerstop and the women call each other pieces of shit.

This all took place on the other side of the wall. A few, but very few, of the women stayed overnight.

Miss Fingerstop told me the one thing wrong with her life was that it lacked surprise. She said it would be exciting to her if I would penetrate her from behind. She didn't want to anticipate it, she said, she just wanted it to happen. She wanted me to come up to her from behind and bend her over the kitchen counter while she was frying an egg, for example, and plunder her, or what have you.

Frying an egg was the example she gave.

It was a new year. I asked myself, if I do this for Miss Fingerstop, will Jasper call me?

I wondered this stupidly. I was in torpor.

I was trying to think of a decent way—not to penetrate Miss Fingerstop, but to eject her from my life. I wanted to do this delicately, but quickly, in a way that would not make Miss Fingerstop feel discarded. Miss Fingerstop was a woman with a tendency to feel discarded. I liked Miss Fingerstop enough, she was—and still is—a good enough looking woman. She went to the School of Visual Arts. She wanted badly to be a sculptor herself and called herself a "sculptress," which, I suppose, she was. She was not a stupid woman, not at all, but she had about her, in many things she did, an air of mendicancy. A lot of people are mendicant, but they don't always have the air; they don't let it show, at least not all the time. With Miss Fingerstop, it lay about her. In her, it was raw.

Miss Fingerstop was a small woman with straight dark hair and almost porcelain skin. She knew how to make herself look like something in thrift-shop clothes, how to use makeup to make her eyes look big. If you saw her, you would say to yourself, "Boy, this woman sure knows how to use makeup."

She used it to make her eyes look not only bigger but more dramatic than they were—she had, in fact, rather narrow eyes—and she was not, I would say, a woman without charms, but there was always that air of mendicancy. It seemed to me that there could be no getting away from it, short of getting away.

I liked Miss Fingerstop. I want it to be clear that I liked her enough. We had some fun together. We did taxis. To do a taxi now and then was fun. When a cab was stopped at a red light, Miss Fingerstop would say to me, "Let's do this taxi," or I would suggest, "Shall we do a taxi, dearest?" Then, with enviably light-limbed stealth, we'd open the door and run in whatever direction the taxi couldn't turn. We also did the occasional dinner, skipped out on a restaurant check. No one noticed we were gone, until we were.

Miss Fingerstop would buy one tomato at Balducci's and walk out the door with a pound of Scotch salmon.

I really did like the woman enough.

I did not want her life.

I was waiting for my life to begin.

One night, after a three-hour darkroom class, I went to see Robert Mitchum in *The Night of the Hunter*. I went not so much to see Robert Mitchum, whose brilliance as an actor I was slow to recognize, or even to see the movie, though I had been happy to see dear Lillian Gish playing a saint who takes in orphans. Dominic had stated many times that Lillian Gish is the finest film actress America has ever produced—or probably ever will, he'd add. I went to the movie that night, and to movies generally, more or less to put off the inevitability of another night with what Miss Fingerstop had, by then, for me, become.

After the movie I had two grasshoppers at Julius. I was partial to grasshoppers. I still am, actually. At Julius, possibly the oldest fag bar in New York, not one man was good-looking enough even to talk to. I wasn't trying to meet anyone, but it would have been nice to be able to talk to someone. But there was no one. I'm not comfortable around unattractive men. This, of course, is my misfortune.

I got home around three. There, asleep, tucked in primly, in the front room, was Mercy in her dominance. I nearly awakened her. If she hadn't been tucked in I

might have had an urge. I could have taken her by surprise. I might even have made her happy for a minute or
so. I looked at her awhile and thought that a few minutes
of cunt would be a few minutes without Jasper in mind.

I let Miss Fingerstop sleep.

In my room, I found her note on my bed. She'd written, on paper torn from a dry cleaner's hanger, in pink
nail polish, "Jasper Eisendorfer."

She must have spent at least an hour writing out the
name in her stiff enamel.

She had spelled the name correctly, which made me
think that Jasper must have spelled it for her.

Even so, Miss Fingerstop had left a shiny pink question mark under Jasper's name.

"YOU SMELL of chlorine."

These were the first words Jasper said to me when I
came out of the West Side Y. It was still snowing, or rather
it was snowing again, and, according to the clock above
the door inside, it was four minutes before eight. It was a
Tuesday evening, the first full week of 1974, and I hadn't
waited for my hair to dry. I'd wanted to be on time, had
expected to wait, and there was Jasper, already there.

He was the first man I saw when I stepped onto the
street. I saw him first.

He was leaning against a low concrete wall, wearing
snow boots, wide-waled gray corduroy trousers that fit
him snugly, and a suede jacket the color of buttered cinnamon toast. He had on padded winter gloves, carried no
umbrella, and he was wearing a hat.

I asked him how long he had been waiting in the snow.

That was when he said, "You smell of chlorine."

"And good evening to you, too," I said.

"Don't you take a shower after you swim?" he asked
me.

"Where shall we go for a lovely cocktail?" I asked.

"Didn't you take a shower?" Jasper asked again.

We'd agreed to meet at eight, go someplace for dinner.

"I don't take showers here," I told him.

"You should, you know," Jasper said.

"I don't like to take showers with a lot of naked men dangling around," I said.

"You didn't mind it the other night," Jasper said amiably.

"The other night," I said, "I was with you."

At the Continental, Jasper and I had stood a long time under a shower head together. We had rubbed liquid soap, big green handfuls of it, over each other. We'd rubbed each other clean of each other, everywhere. The dark fur covering Jasper's trunk had turned white under the lathering foam. There had been a number of men looking at us. The two or three who looked at me also gave some attention to Jasper, but the men looking at Jasper did not notice me at all.

We walked south on Central Park West and east on Central Park South. I don't remember what we talked about, I suppose I did most of the talking. We were passing the New York Athletic Club when an alert-looking young man came out of it and looked at Jasper in a way Jasper had to notice. They both stopped on the street.

The young man said, "How are you?"

Anyone else would have kept on walking. I would have.

"How are *you?*" Jasper asked the young man.

"My God," the young man exclaimed.

The three of us stood there.

"It's been years," said the young man. He was about twenty-eight, I'd say, maybe not even that. He was wearing a heavy camel-colored overcoat that may have been cashmere and shoes that looked as though they had just been shined.

Jasper nodded at the young man. "It's been awhile," he agreed.

The young man shook his smiling, good-looking head. Even in the heavy overcoat, he looked like fitness itself. He was the kind of man who looks good when he smiles.

"God, it's been a long time," the young man exclaimed.

"Yes, it has," said Jasper.

I moved closer to Jasper and held my umbrella over him.

"How've you been?" the young man asked.

The fellow looked at me for half a second, possibly. He did not fully take his eyes from Jasper.

I didn't know what I should be wondering.

Jasper stood on the street, nodding at the man.

I examined the young man's face, broke it into pieces. I saw that it was not made up of arresting parts but was well composed of dull ones; he was decently assembled and generically good-looking. It wasn't a face I would study, except that Jasper, a man I'd gone after in a bathhouse eleven days ago, had stopped in the street to give the fellow the time of day.

Jasper stood, just nodding.

I wondered why Jasper didn't introduce me to the smiling young man. Possibly he'd forgotten the specimen's name?

"How's it going?" The young man tried again.

"We're on our way to dinner," Jasper said.

"It's so great to see you," insisted the young man, shaking his head all over again.

"It's been good to see you again," Jasper said to the young man.

The young man said, "You're looking swell."

"We're going to dinner now," Jasper told the young man and started toward Fifth Avenue. I followed. I did not know what, if anything, had been established, so I said nothing at all.

When we came to the corner of Fifth Avenue and Fifty-seventh Street, I mentioned, just to say something, that

Tiffany and Company was the first place in New York where I had established credit.

"What did you buy at Tiffany?" Jasper asked me.

This struck me as a dull-edged question, what I would ask if I were nervous. I *was* nervous, but I hadn't expected Jasper to be.

"Don't you want to know *how* I established credit?" I asked.

"I assumed your family arranged it for you," Jasper said.

"But that's not it at all," I said.

I TOLD Jasper how, when paying for a baby's spoon, I had found myself with inadequate cash.

"I told the woman I was terribly sorry, could she keep the spoon on hold for me, for just one day? I expected her to go off on a tirade, or at least snarl at me, but this woman was civility itself. She asked, without hesitation, would I like to open a charge? There I was, just off the street, you see. For all the woman knew, I could have been a ne'er-do-well, or an escapee straight from the asylum. Don't you think this was an immensely civilized thing for this woman to do?"

"We're turning here," Jasper said. "You don't look anything like a ne'er-do-well."

We turned east.

"Why were you buying a baby's spoon?" Jasper asked.

"I didn't have one," I answered.

"Why did you want one?" Jasper asked.

"Sometimes I like it for breakfast," I said.

"What? Baby food?" Jasper asked.

"Yes. It's good on a bran muffin, much better than jam, actually, or marmalade," I said.

"I don't believe you," Jasper said.

"It has less acid," I said. "Try it yourself. Beechnut peaches are really quite good."

"Do you have an ulcer, Tim?" Jasper asked me then.

I stopped on the street, just stopped.

"Timothy," I said.

"All right," Jasper said. "Do you have an ulcer, Timothy?"

"No," I said. "I hate being called by a monosyllable."

Jasper said he hadn't thought about that. He said he would not ever call me by a monosyllable again, and in fact he never did.

WE ENDED up in a Greek place in the East Fifties. Jasper ordered negronis for both of us. If anything, I liked his ordering for me, the way he took charge. Not many nineteen-year-olds know what to drink, they order gin and tonic in the pit of winter, and though it bothered me that Jasper was putting me into that category, I said nothing about it.

I'd never had a negroni, hadn't heard of them, except, of course, in Tennessee Williams's novel *The Roman Spring of Mrs. Stone,* and in the movie version, too, in which the dissipated Vivian Leigh replies, to the young and agonizingly succulent Warren Beatty, who, in her penthouse, has offered her a drink, "How clever of you to know I like a negroni." But I knew nothing else about them, and when I tasted one for the first time I liked Jasper's choice.

I thought this man could teach me everything.

The Greek place served, as it still does, surprisingly good lamb shanks with eggplant. Jasper said that the cooking was pretty good, for a Greek place. I agreed, though at the time I knew nothing about food.

Through that dinner I did my best to woo Jasper with words. In those years, and especially *that* year, I had a richer vocabulary than I have now. It was a time of life when I did not run out of words. I'm always running out of words now, and things have become harder to describe. I can't pin them down as I used to. There wasn't an adjective I wouldn't use, misuse, abuse. I also spoke with my hands. Years later, Jasper told me he had been startled that night by the way I spoke. He told me he hadn't before heard anyone speak quite as I did, and he told me that he had thought for a while that I might be the smartest person he'd met in his life. This made me wonder more than a bit about his life, but it was, of course, nice to hear.

He took it back, naturally, once he got to know me.

That night in 1974, he seemed amused by the way I spoke. I don't remember what it was I went on about. I do remember, though, everything Jasper told me that night about himself.

The early seventies have been called a candid age. Someone went so far once as to name them, in print, as the Age of Candor. Candor *was* afoot, and it became the fashion, more than it is now, I think, to reveal what could be known about one's character, openly, in detail, preferably all at once. Nothing was private, little was filtered. You were constantly bumping into people being open, disclosing every family nightmare, every marital contempt, every mother fixation, daddy fixation, all hatreds, all loves, everything oozed forth.

Jasper didn't ooze. He was not open in this way. That evening at the Greek place Jasper told me just a few things about himself. I remember them because they were few.

He told me he was of a German family, a Jewish family, a mercantile family, mostly in hats. In Germany, they had been prosperous, and in 1938 Jasper's father, who had been smart enough to have some gold, was able to buy his family's way out. The father, the mother, and Jasper sailed second-class and were, as were first-class passengers, waived through immigration. The Eisendorfer family was not detained at Ellis Island. Jasper was not yet six.

Jasper had been named after an Englishman who had saved his father's life in the first great war. Jasper said that it was not a name that German-Jewish families would ordinarily give their sons; it was not, for example, Jacob.

Jasper grew up in Indiana. He worked every day after school in the hat store that his father had bought with what money remained. In Germany, the father had owned a chain of stores; in Indiana, there was the one store. The mother kept the books, and the family had a maid, who cooked and lived with them in the house.

Jasper went into the naval air force, flunked his pilot's test, became an officer, and when it came time to reenlist didn't. He began graduate work, in business. He told me about what he called the nap rooms in the library at Indiana University. The nap rooms had little beds and could be locked from inside. Without going into detail, Jasper told me that as much went on in those nap rooms as reading did at reading tables. He went with young men into the nap rooms, but he got himself into a tangle with a young woman, too. Jasper was going to do the honorable thing, but three days before the wedding the woman miscarried. She wanted Jasper to marry her anyway, but, as he told me that night, Jasper felt he'd been handed a reprieve.

All this happened before I was born.

Business, it turned out, was misery to Jasper. One day he got in his car and drove straight down to Florida, to Miami, where he lived for a while, about two years, he told me, more or less off of women. He was young, handsome, and the rest of it and was able to make an older woman feel desirable again—possibly he gave her a late rebirth. Jasper said he saw nothing wrong in this.

Does anyone?

I'd thought of doing this myself. Miss Fingerstop and I had decided, back in Berkeley, that being in bed was the one thing we both did well and we made a pact to come to New York and become whores together. We thought we could rent out our parts. I looked forward to doing this for a while, actually.

Of course, I could not have rented myself out to women; after Miss Fingerstop, that would not be possible. Miss Fingerstop was as far as I would go in that field. Dominic had told me at Berkeley that Miss Fingerstop had given him an aversion to the female body, the way it's put together. I would not say this about a woman, even if I were convinced it was true, which I don't believe I ever could be. Miss Fingerstop did not give Dominic this aversion, nor did any woman, nor did any woman need to. Dominic was, I am sure, born with this aversion. Quite a few people are, including a number of women. People are born with this aversion, or with its opposite, or with something else; it is simply in the genome of one's being. It is one thing I know of that is blameless.

Sometimes it can go too far. In Africa, in some tribes, there is such abiding hatred of the female, of her fecundity, of her capacity for pleasure, that procedures are carried out, soon after birth, to remove or to maim her parts, to mutilate them, to render them useless, or to make the using of them excruciating for her. You can read about the horrors some African tribes perform on their female children, and of things the Chinese used to do, and the Indians, too, horrors so painful to contemplate that you must close your eyes at the thought of them.

It was Jasper who first told me about the prayer that is said nightly by men in a sect of Jewish Orthodoxy. Every night, these men go down on their knees, as their fathers had before them, to give their thanks to God. "Thank you, God," these men all say in prayer, "that I was not born a woman."

Jasper didn't tell me what a woman prays.

I can't say why I did not join Miss Fingerstop in the flesh business. Perhaps I was reluctant to join a life in which a man could look me over and go for a better deal across the street. I did not want to market myself in a world where I would, in time, be obliged to cut my rate. Imagine being an unsuccessful whore! I was, furthermore, not sufficiently convinced that it was illegal without reason. Although I was not a believer, we don't need to believe in order to know that it will not be the worst idea we could have, to live, when possible, as though we are in an eye of God.

Also, I was not keen on the prospect of putting myself out without desire. Doing this hadn't pleased Jasper for long, either. I expect Jasper got discouraged by a lack of spontaneity.

He didn't tell me this. This isn't a thing Jasper would have said. Like so many other things about the man, I come to this conclusion by way of speculation.

"AND TODAY?" I asked.

"Pardon?" Jasper asked.

"What do you do today?" I asked him.

"Do you mean sexually?" Jasper asked me, rather fliply.

"That I know. What I meant was what do you do for money?"

"Do you mean, Timothy, how do I earn my living?" Jasper asked.

"Yes, but what an ugly way to put it," I objected. "Do you like Henry Miller? He said, 'A man should never earn his living. If he earns his life he'll be lovely.' "

Jasper considered this. "I do like Henry Miller. Where does he say that?"

"He says it in one of the essays in *The Books in My Life*," I answered. "There's also an amusing little piece called 'Reading on the Toilet.' "

"What does he have to say about that?" Jasper asked.

"Read it," I said.

"Timothy, did you know that Henry Miller was without money for a long part of his life?"

"Of course, but not so long in retrospect, really. After all, he's still alive and not doing badly," I said. "When you read about his scrounging around, though, the way he describes it, he *does* seem to be at it just forever."

"Do you think he may have had contempt for money?" Jasper asked.

"Doesn't everyone?" I asked.

"Do you?" Jasper asked.

"Oh, please, what does a nineteen-year-old boy know about contempt?" I answered.

Jasper didn't go anywhere near this question. I think he knew it hadn't been asked with curiosity.

"Henry Miller probably adored money," I ventured, "but disliked the way it controls people, the disgraceful things so many people do to get it, the almost limitless vulgarity of it all, the way it can overtake a man's life, so that he becomes defined by what he does instead of by what he *is*."

"Timothy, do you work for a living?" Jasper asked.

"Not yet. I've sold some paintings, but I can't say I'm earning a living at it. I'd rather act than paint, but I'll have to work at something someday," I said.

This was not my favorite line of inquiry.

"How do you get along, then?"

"I have what I believe is called a little money. It's what I have instead of a family. You see, I'm a pitiful little orphan boy," I said.

Jasper ignored my tone. "You mean you're alone in the world?" he asked

"Not entirely," I said. "I do have Miss Fingerstop."

"Who's that?"

"A woman. We went to school together. I live with her," I said.

"How long have you been together?" Jasper asked.

"Oh, wait. I wouldn't say we're *together*, exactly. It's

not like that. We share a top floor in a house, a brown-
stone. She's got the front, I've got the back. It's not the
ideal setup, since I have to go through her space to get to
mine, and there are days when I don't want to see her.
But of course there are days I don't want to see anyone.
We had a tiny affair. It wasn't for me."

"What about it wasn't for you?" Jasper asked.

"I'd rather not get into it, if you don't mind," I said.
"The empty-handedness of it, I suppose. She wasn't what
I wanted to have and to hold, because she had nothing to
hold. You can understand that, can't you? I need something to grasp. You still haven't told me what you do," I
said.

Jasper collected himself. "I go to concerts, I go to the
theater, to dance, I travel quite a bit. Now and then I find
something I expect people would like if it were available
to them, and if it isn't too difficult I bring it to this country."

"Then you're a salesman?" I asked.

"No," Jasper said. "An importer is more of a liaison."

"Do you receive commissions?" I asked.

It was more complicated than that, Jasper told me.
But he conceded that it was a business based largely on
commission.

I asked if he imported anything illegal. He told me he
didn't, though he said he had been approached by people
who made him large offers to do so.

When I asked Jasper what had stopped him from ac-
cepting these large offers, the question startled him. That
is, it seemed to.

"I'm an impeccable citizen, Timothy," Jasper pro-
tested.

"Do you import anything that I may use?" Asking Jasper this, I felt uneasily like the clever, ghastly Dorothy
Kilgallen, in gloves, on the antiquated quiz show "What's
My Line?" You can still see episodes of this at the Museum of Radio and Television.

Jasper named a line of English marmalade and preserves, a variety of mustards, one of which you see in nearly every food shop, a line of French cooking oils, another of flavored vinegars and one of fruit syrups, and three spices I had never heard of. Some of these were items I'd seen advertised, but that year I didn't even own a mixing bowl.

I'd never used any of the items that Jasper imported.

"Do you do this just for the money?" I asked.

I hadn't meant this to sound as snotty as I'm sure it did.

"Not only for that," Jasper answered. "But if I couldn't make money doing this, I would have to do something else."

"Do you do this for a big company?" I asked.

"I am the company," said Jasper.

"A company of one?" I asked.

"I have a few people working with me, but it's my company," he answered.

"The people who work with you, do you mean they work *for* you?" I asked.

"They work for me, they work with me," Jasper answered. I liked that he'd said "with."

"What do you call your company?" I asked.

Jasper answered, "Eisendorfer and Son."

"Oh, so your father started it," I said.

"No," said Jasper.

"Are you the father or are you the son?" I asked.

"I'm the father," said Jasper, "and the son."

I was baffled. "So the 'and Son' is made up?" I asked.

"The *partnership* is," said Jasper.

"Did you choose the name because it sounds distinguished?"

"I don't know about that," Jasper answered. "It sounds trustworthy, I think."

"Even though it's all a bit of a lie?" I asked.

Jasper said he saw no dishonesty in it.

I thought a moment.

. "Do you use an ampersand?" I asked.

———————

ON THE street, in front of the Greek place, Jasper said, "This is where I parked."

It struck me as odd that he had parked where we were and had walked across town to meet me at the Y. I didn't ask him why. I imagined he liked walking in the snow.

He unlocked the car door for me. The car was mustard yellow, with a black convertible top. I knew nothing about cars then, know nothing more about them now, but I knew from an advertisement I'd seen years before that this model was unique. It was the only car designed, or so the ad claimed, so that the front and the back doors opened together in the middle. I knew that this model was no longer made in this fashion and hadn't been for some years. I have no idea why this feature was discontinued, or what advantages it had been fancied to offer in the first place, but, in any case, this model of the car was extinct.

"This is your car?" I asked.

"It's my partner's," Jasper said.

"Do you mean the fellow you live with?" I asked.

"Yes, my partner," Jasper said. "This is his car."

I wasn't happy, getting into Oliver Ingraham's car. I didn't even know Oliver Ingraham's name yet. Jasper hadn't told me, I hadn't asked. Nor had Jasper, until just then, described Oliver Ingraham as his "partner."

"Is he part of your company?" I asked.

"God, no," Jasper said, laughing at the thought.

I thought, they don't sleep together, they don't work together, what *do* they do together?

When we got to Washington Street, Jasper found a place on my block. I could tell from the light that Miss Fingerstop was upstairs. Miss Fingerstop had learned—

had no doubt been trained as a child—to turn lights off when leaving a house. She was not a woman afraid of coming home to a dark place. I had not been so trained: I leave lights burning, always. To me, a dark place is the Dark.

Miss Fingerstop had a peculiar manner of greeting people. Even if she had seen you that morning, she would greet you as though she hadn't seen you for decades and was overcome by the joy, the delight, of seeing you again. She made you feel that you were an expected felicity to her. This was one of many things about Miss Fingerstop that was really rather dear.

When I think of Miss Fingerstop now, this is often the first thought I have.

She greeted me in this thrilled-to-see-me fashion when I came into the house with Jasper.

I was not in the habit of bringing men home. In the seven months I'd lived with Miss Fingerstop, Jasper was the first man to come to the house. Except for Tom, a fellow I knew from acting class, and Robin, who had followed me out of a subway men's room, when the subways still had men's rooms, no men came to the house. Tom and Robin came separately, and not as men but as friends.

I like a rugged man.

I don't mean unshaven or ripe smelling or even particularly working-class. It's even more tiresome than that, I'm afraid. What I wanted then, and still do, was a solid man, one who would give me safety in the apocalypse.

And a man for whom I would do the same.

I was certain something like it would come, something like an apocalypse. I could almost feel it coming. Some nights I would lean against a back wall in a dark room at the Strap, the Mine Shaft, the Ramp, watching men in boxer shorts, in jockstraps, and there were shy ones, like me, who wouldn't even take off a shirt. I would look not so much at these men's bodies, though I did, of course,

look at them, but mostly I looked at their faces, the shapes
of their heads, their mouths, their foreheads. Some of these
men even had good-looking ears. Once or twice, in the
front rooms of these establishments, where there was more
light, a man would come over to talk to me a bit. I recall
a few conversations, and usually the men seemed fairly
smart, and this, if anything, confirmed a sorrow that I
felt. It was, in a way, too bad, I thought, that these men
would not be among those to repeople the earth. They
should be, I thought, through most of the seventies.

I am less convinced of this now.

I thought about carnal pleasure, and looked around
and felt certain that something cataclysmic was well on
its way. All of this is easy to say in retrospect, and I'm
not claiming prophecy. I'm not playing Cassandra. I did
feel, though, and I believe it is true, that disasters, all kinds
of catastrophe, are always coiled up and ready to spring,
and that the happening of them has been scheduled,
somehow, long in advance.

I didn't know when it would come or what form it
would take, nor did I know that no man can give another
safety in it.

There will always be one final everything—the last
word, of course, the last breath; there will be one last
check you write, one last nap, one last artichoke. There
will be a last time you chop scallions, a last movie you
will see, a last time you fly to Rome. It doesn't matter
how many coins you leave in the fountain. You will make
one last photograph, and be photographed one final time
by somebody else; there will be one last time you will
walk on a particular street, one last time you will go out
from your house or come back into it. You will have one
last dream, one last orgasm, one last cigarette. There will
be one final time you will see or will be seen by the man
or the woman you have loved, or the people you have
known, unless, of course, you outlive them all, which is
not likely.

You will lick one last stamp. You won't know it when you do.

Tom and I went to the Continental many times. He was with me the night I met Jasper. I would look around a little, but usually I'd end up reading in the bar. I brought earplugs, which worked against the throbbing music. Even so, it wasn't easy to read when all that flesh was on parade. It strains credulity, I know, but there were nights in those years when no man was bad-looking.

I read Zola's *L'Assommoir* on three different nights at the Continental with Tom.

I don't believe Tom ever went to any bathhouse unaccompanied. He always had me or some other fellow along with him. Tom introduced me to the Everard, which was on Twenty-eighth Street, a grittier establishment than the Continental, a darker place, more run-down, and Tom came to prefer it. The men tended to be more direct, and the goings-on more urgent, more animal-like, than at the Continental.

It was a manly place.

On the second floor, half the space was given over to a dormitory. It reminded me of the army barracks where the men in *From Here to Eternity* slept, or the men in *Stalag 17*. There were seventy or more beds in seven or eight rows in this wide room. A few of these beds were usually occupied by older men, who napped. Some men at the Everard were really pretty old. Sometimes even a young man would use one of these beds to have himself a little rest.

Then he'd get himself right back into the thick of things.

Tom was my age, and a fine-looking boy. Extraordinary-looking, really. In acting class, Tom was one of the two people able to get any further than the obligatory coffee cup or the obligatory sunshine. I was the other one. He also wrote, as I did for a while, thuddingly bad poetry.

Otherwise, we weren't alike.

In his couplings Tom was always the active, never the

passive, partner. I did not understand, then, why he always wanted someone to go with him to a bathhouse, because Tom did not, as Dominic would later do, assail me with the specifics of individual men with whom he had commingled. Tom gave me no lowdowns on any man's peccadilloes.

I have less knowledge of how things are going today, but in those years I found it invariably true that whenever two men had been physically conjoined it was the man who took the passive part, the submissive man, who could not wait to tell about it later. I have heard hundreds of postmortems of carnal doings, but not ever from a man who had been the one to do the real laboring.

Of course, many men take turns doing everything possible for men to do together, and for these men the different possibilities are, naturally, the point of it all. Still, I've heard tales only from men who received. The men who are only active men tend not to talk; it's almost as if they have nothing to say. They don't tell how slowly, how deliberately they proceeded, how the man beneath squirmed, or anything about what sounds were made. It is the passive man who gives these details, who testifies how deep it went, how long the doing took, how good it was overall. For this reason, I have been given many times to wonder if it might not be a simple truth that it is the man who gets slammed who is the man who has the story to tell.

Why do I go on about this, I wonder. I don't propose this as a universal truth. How could it be, with so many men who lie about what, or how much, they've done?

It is, at best, a postulate.

Perhaps I go on about this for the simple reason that, according to what I have read and been able to glean, it is, for by far the larger part, the men who have known the ecstasy of surrender who now are the men who are dying.

Not that the others will never get the virus.

In other words, men like Dominic.

I am not sure where Jasper fits in this.

I must have misunderstood one or two things.

Jasper among them.

I among them.

———————

ONE REASON I didn't bring men to the house was that I really did prefer the trucks, where I could, pretty much whenever I wanted one, get a blow job. I didn't always reciprocate. Once in a while some fellow might get me carried away. This was not usual.

After the summer in San Francisco, the summer I was always skipping drawing class, I could no longer trust myself in the horizontal pose. I would be fine as long as I had both feet on the ground, as in the movies of the Hays era. I believed that if there was no one above there could be no one below.

The few times I did lie down with a man after that summer, and before I met Jasper—and by a few, I mean three—it happened, without exception, in the other fellow's house.

I saw to this.

There are advantages in going to the other fellow's house. For one thing, you see different interiors and how men live. You are free to leave, you don't need to be the host, and you drink *their* liquor.

But the clearest-cut reason is that no man is apt to kill you in his house, where he would be obliged to get rid of the body. In your house, any man can kill you and be right out the door. He can be back on the street in ten seconds flat, and you can bet you won't see him again. You're dead. You can't call the police, you're dead. You will decompose in your own house, for days, for weeks, most likely in your living room—because you didn't get as far as the bed with the fellow. You're dead, he's gone, and you will keep right on decomposing, until your mother or your wife or your cleaning woman finds you, until your dog is hungry, until your door is broken down because someone has called the city about a smell.

They find you. They find out everything about you, and it has all come to this, all of it, from one mistake, when you were an unhappy judge of character. You know this now, of course. You, and everybody else. It does you no good, this clarity. You're dead, it's all your fault, and there's nothing you can do about it.

MISS FINGERSTOP was painting her toenails when we came in.

Jasper was somewhat stiff with her. I saw, as I hadn't before, that Jasper was, or at least around women tended to be, a guarded man.

As soon as Jasper and I were in my room, as soon as we lay down, Miss Fingerstop, who had until then shown no interest in the piano, began at that instant to attack it. She pounded on the low keys, on the high ones, and made loud, percussive, unmusical chords.

"Let's kill her," I said to Jasper.

"It's not her fault, she can't help it," Jasper said. We tried to ignore it. We made every effort. After a while Jasper said, "It's better on an empty stomach, anyway."

"I'm not kidding, I'm going to kill this woman," I said.

Jasper was putting on his shirt.

"I'm moving out of here tomorrow," I said.

"You'll have a hard time finding a place like this," Jasper cautioned.

"I don't need a place like this. I'd rather live in a maid's room than live one more night with this little twit."

"You're being too hard on her. You won't get out that quickly," Jasper said.

Jasper was right, I did have a hard time finding a place as good as the one I was leaving, and it *is* better on an empty stomach.

He was wrong, though, about getting out quickly. It took some doing, but I was out the next day. I took with me the piano, the Biedermeier mirror, the lacquered barrel, my baby spoon, and everything else in the world that was mine.

———————

THE PLACE I found was on Bank Street. It had no view of the trucks, but it did overlook a garden, which the fellow downstairs cared for lavishly. He grew rhododendron, hydrangea, strawberries, tomatoes, basil. I heard his piano, so I assume he heard mine. I continued to work on the Chopin nocturnes, kept on studying photography, did my developing and printing in the bathroom. But after I'd been seeing Jasper for a year or so I stopped going to acting class.

One Sunday in Soho, in 1975, I told Jasper about the one audition I'd been to, about the hundreds of hopeful creatures who showed up for it, how they all looked so driven, so eager, and so forlorn. I wasn't willing to go through the interminable preliminaries only to have a life of more auditions, more anxieties, and tiny parts I wouldn't get in shows that would close anyway.

Jasper listened to me that day with uncommon patience. He was not always a patient man.

We had seen that afternoon, among many other things in many galleries, an exhibit of fifteen-foot-square wooden boxes, about twenty of them. Each one had a different side, or part of a side, missing from it and could, through these, be entered. Some of them could be walked through. They were all for sale, and the lowest price was, if I recall, eleven thousand dollars. I'm not prone to sneer at works of art, but these huge boxes struck me as being an abominable waste of craftsmanship, like brilliantly well made movies that end up being about nothing at all.

Jasper, who spent a fair amount of time doing highly meticulous carpentry, said that these boxes were not, as huge boxes went, even terribly well made huge boxes.

What, I asked, would be the point of making an enormous, useless, three-sided box well?

Jasper answered that there is always a point in making a thing well.

"Look at this omelet," Jasper said. "This omelet is well made."

We were in a café that I believe no longer exists. It was called Yumburgers, and it served only omelets. There were about sixty different things you could have put in an omelet, and they were superior omelets. Jasper chose Roquefort and figs, I had watercress and dates. Jasper explained that the egg whites had been beaten separately and folded into the lightly whipped yolks, and that this was what made each omelet light, lofty, like a soufflé.

"You know, I don't think you will go far as an actor," Jasper said to me that day.

"But I'm good. I'm getting better. I think I could be quite a good actor," I argued.

"I don't doubt that, Timothy, I don't doubt that at all. That's not it," said Jasper.

"What is *it*, then?" I asked.

"I don't believe you have the drive," Jasper said. This answer surprised me. I had expected Jasper to say I wasn't handsome enough, something along those lines, that I had the wrong kind of body, lacked the presence, the force that an actor has got to have. I'd expected him to talk about things that can be changed, compensated for, counteracted in one way or, failing that, in another.

I didn't say anything for a while. Jasper didn't rush me.

"Don't you think," I was finally able to ask, "that drive can be cultivated?"

"Cultivated?" Jasper asked.

"*Developed*. Don't you think drive can be developed?"

Jasper replied, giving credit to Oscar Wilde, that only mediocrities develop.

"That's helpful," I said.

"I was trying to be light," Jasper said.

"Well, don't be," I said. I lack humor when it comes to being appraised. "That's just a dippy little epigram, whatever does it mean?"

Jasper said he'd read it so many years ago he didn't remember the context, but that it had, at the time, struck him as being true. He said he believed Oscar Wilde was saying that excellence is born or evolves and does not result from deliberation.

"You like doing things alone, don't you?" Jasper said. "An actor has to be part of a company. You don't even like people that much, Timothy. An actor has to wait for someone to offer him a job. He gets a job, he does it, and even when, even if, he does it brilliantly, the play closes, the movie wraps, the work is finished. It's over, and then the actor has to wait again. He spends his life waiting for the telephone to ring. He doesn't know what he's going to do the next day. It is not a life for you."

"Everyone spends his life waiting for the telephone to ring," I said.

Jasper looked at me then. His skin was dark. The man had thrilling skin. I told him once in bed that he did not look at all like any other Jews I knew, and he told me that all Sephardic Jews were dark skinned, that the Jews I knew must be Ashkenazi. In fact, they were.

Jasper told me that the Ashkenazi were of northern origin, mostly Russian, and were not really Jews. He told me that Sephardic Jews, who were from Spain or parts south, were, ethnically, the people of Israel.

I asked him, did he mean the Jews of the Bible, and Jasper answered that *was* what he'd meant.

For years I've been meaning to read about the Jews.

Jasper had the palest blue eyes I'd ever looked into. They were hydrangea blue, the blue of a summer mid-afternoon, or, rather, the blue that you find at the base of a flame. I never got tired of looking into them, of having Jasper to look at, or of having Jasper look at me. Jasper was, I thought, as handsome as a man can be, without his being Italian.

Sometimes in Rome, in fact every day in Rome, I have seen men more handsome than Jasper. You can see better-looking men than Jasper every day in the Piazza del Popolo or on the Via del Corso. In Rome, even the policemen are so handsome that Dominic, full of grappa one night, could not resist flirting with a group of them, at three in the morning, in the Piazza Barberini. They were amused, thank God.

But this is Rome, it is only in Rome.

It could be Florence, Siena, Bologna, Genoa, Venice, but it isn't. It just isn't true there. It is only in Rome that you will be overcome by the dark, opulent beauty of the men.

Dominic said that God knew what He was doing when He made Italians.

Of course, this is what all Italians say.

I was tempted, that afternoon in Soho, to think that a man as good-looking as Jasper has got to be wrong about a multitude of things. That should go with the territory. It hadn't, though, so far.

"And no one knows what he's going to do the next day," I said.

"Some people have an idea," said Jasper.

It struck me then that everything Jasper had cautioned me about as being the bane of actors, everything he had said about plays closing and movies wrapping, is true of every profession, that, in fact, Jasper *was* saying I wasn't handsome enough, that I didn't have the right body, but was telling me this in a gentle way.

His base-of-flame eyes convinced me I lacked drive. I had no drive particularly, toward anything. I needed to do something that did not require drive.

I like faces.

I like poses, not all poses, but I like the idea of people being posed. I like that people are able to pose. I like the way some faces can be made to look at different angles and under changes of light. I like the transformations that are possible in portrait photography, the control that is possible, and the surprises that can come, *with* control. Jasper had seen on my walls some photographs I had taken of acting students and had remarked at how beautiful one of the women was. I knew this woman was no beauty; her face had needed to be moved into position, she had required my hand, and careful lighting. She had turned out not at all badly, in black-and-white. In the darkroom I had been able to make her look as she should have, like the woman life had not given it to her to be.

Jasper and I went into a few more galleries, saw things even less worth looking at than the giant wooden boxes. In one gallery, though, we saw—and both liked—a photograph of a man about Jasper's age looking at an infant in a cradle. The man had one hand inside the cradle, and the other rested on the outline, seen through his rumpled boxer shorts, of his boldly tumescent member.

A proud, fatherly beatitude beamed from his face. You could see the man thinking, "This comes from me, from here."

The photograph was straightforward, not tricky in its execution. It made me get a little weepy. I told Jasper that if I'd had the money I would have bought the photograph.

Then I said, "I want to take pictures like this."

Jasper said, "Heaven forbid."

The way he said this sounded to me very like, "Why not?"

_____

I READ photography. I read nothing but photography for over a year and photographed nothing at all. Then I took another class, which required that I take some picture. Taking pictures became, as Edward Weston put it, "making photographs." But then it became just taking pictures again. I went through a disillusioned period. It lasted awhile. I took no pictures, made no photographs. I bought new cameras and didn't use them.

These were the years I started to cook. I read food. Everything I read was food. I read Brillat-Savarin. I read Jean-Jacques Rousseau's little work on gastronomy, M. F. K. Fisher, Waverly Root. In those years there was a wonderfully readable restaurant critic named Jay Jacobs who used words in a lively, flavorsome way. I read cookbooks front to back. I got Jasper to read many of them. We talked to each other incessantly about food, and I was always finding new things to do. I seemed never to run out of notions, or patience to try them, to fail and try again. There was so much to learn, such an abundant, absolute endlessness to all of it. Parsnips alone are just staggering things, and, my God, what you can do to a cabbage—and then, of course, there is the miracle of the lemon.

I started pickling everything I could think of, started adding cardamom and turmeric to mangoes and pineapples and pears. I could not improve upon the raspberry. In Milan, in 1981, I tasted ice cream made from sage. It was a revelation to me. Jasper didn't like it, but it was a revelation to me.

One afternoon I cut into a large globe-shaped cherimoya and was struck by the giant, glossy blackness of its seeds, by the sheen that clung to them. They were like cavair in close-up, in a web. Years later, I would think of their sheen as being rather like the membranes enclosing viruses I had read about.

That day, I set the camera on the tripod to take a long exposure. I used six rolls of film.

Food brought me back to the human face.

I began to use models, began showing work. Then I started getting assignments. It was a good way to see a lot of the world, without joining the army. I could not believe that so many people had the patience not only to stand still but to trust me with their faces, and to give me money for it, too.

Until recently, when people wanted color portraits, I would tell them I did not work in color. This made it sound to them as though color were beneath me. Actually, I didn't know color. I still don't. Since Jasper's death, once I could work again, I have started telling people the truth, that I don't know color. They had been willing to accept that color was beneath me, but now, when I tell them I don't know it, people look at me in smiling disbelief, thinking to themselves, I'm sure, what a modest man I am.

Heaven forbid, Jasper would say.

three

TONIGHT THE *risotto* has
sea scallops. I used to like them. I made them many times
for Jasper, with nothing but butter and cream. Sometimes
I added a few gratings of nutmeg. Sliced, sea scallops could
be made delicious in five minutes flat. They tasted like
more than they were.

Tonight, with Dominic in Los Angeles, I ask our waiter
to bring another plate, and when he does I pick out every
one of them. Even removed, their pungent flavor over-
whelms the dish. Dominic does the same to the squid.
He objects to the way it's been cut. His disdain is vig-
orous.

"Sweetheart, maybe your mother can help you, and
you can leave her with a feeling she'd done something for
you."

This is my suggestion to Dominic.

A minute loses itself.

"Who's talking about leaving? Who said anything about
leaving, did I say anything about leaving?"

"A slip of the tongue," I say.

"Excuse you," says Dominic.

He looks at his glass, then looks into it. "This is the
first time white wine has tasted at all the way it used to."

Dominic and I are drinking a perfectly chilled Gavi dei

Gavi La Scolca, a wine Jasper and I drank many times on picnics.

"This is nice wine," Dominic says.

I look at the familiar lettering on the familiar black label and remember drinking this wine with Jasper, especially the first time we drank it, in Rome, on a picnic deep in the Villa Borghese. That trip was long ago, before Jasper and I stopped playing.

"Actually, sweetheart, this is a lovely wine," I say to Dominic.

The light in this downtown L.A. dining room glares on Dominic's head, not unbecomingly. He keeps his head smooth with frequent shaving. A man comes to his house twice a week and does it for him.

"Yes," Dominic says, "it is."

He says this with partial conviction. I doubt he is tasting deeply. I see, even more clearly tonight than before, that it has become impossible for me to take a sip of this or any other good wine—of a Brunello de Montalcino, a Corton Charlemagne, or a Batard Montrachet—as it is impossible for me now to bite into a piece of anything that has been cooked with the smallest flourish of excellence—even this somewhat pallid *risotto*—or to taste on a salad green a sprinkling of pear vinegar, or to smell avocado honey, without having at once a thought of Jasper.

I cannot lie in bed alone without his coming into view. Some nights it feels that he is almost in the room. Not that he's with me, but that he is in the room. If I could hold the thought, hold it long enough so that everything was in it, Jasper would appear in a corner, even perhaps at the foot of the bed.

He would look at me, I'd see his face. Then, physically, he would occupy a chair, stretch his legs out, make himself comfy, and we would talk again.

There are times I hear him.

When I do, his voice is as it was. It speaks as he did

and talks about places we've been. He invents nothing new; everything he talks about happened.

He names the places he wants to go again. He wants to bicycle again to the Bois de Vincennes, to promenade again in the Jardins des Plantes. He wants to watch the shirtless boys splashing one another under the tall sprays of the Trocadéro fountain. He wants frog's legs again at L'Ami Louis, to be in Rome when *porcini* are in season, to bite into them again the way they are grilled at Sabatini, in Trastevere. He tells me calmly that he would like another bellini at the Hotel Excelsior on the Venice Lido.

He wants to return to the island of Torcello, where we saw twenty-year-old men playing soccer in front of an old church with boys who looked twelve or eleven, their younger brothers, probably. Their game looked improvised. Jasper and I watched them for a while, and they summoned us, in a friendly way, to join them. I think we would have if we hadn't had a boat waiting to take us back to Venice.

Jasper asks me, will I take him with me when I go?

"Of course I will take you, papa," I tell him.

We talk aloud.

Sometimes I think, though, that he wants only to be in the places again. He hasn't made it clear that he wants me along.

Among the dead, nothing goes without saying.

———

NOW AND then Jasper and I called it "toss and catch."

There was a reason for stopping, at least a reason to give it a rest. The reason had nothing to do with immunity, or with fear of losing it, which was small to us back then. Jasper and I stopped playing in 1982, before the pandemic was well along, before the virus had been isolated. A few people, a dozen or so, had made the back

pages of big-city newspapers by coming down with illnesses that, though they'd been seen before, had been seen
infrequently, and not in young men, and not in combinations. Kaposi's sarcoma, for example, which may or may
not be a skin cancer and can affect organs other than the
skin—in which cases it is definitely a cancer—had been
seen before, in elderly Jewish men in the south of Italy,
and no one had called it Old Southern Jewish Italian Men's
Syndrome. One reason for this may have been that
OSJIMS does not make a tidy acronym.

The cause of these infections may or may not have
been, it was speculated, multiple partners or the use of
nitrate inhalants. There was talk of urban men in their
twenties, in their thirties, who had already, in such a brief
time, coupled with thousands of others.

"So many men, so little time" was a popular T-shirt
slogan in the very early eighties. No one wears them today. At first, and then for years to come, this was the
prevailing image.

It was, in fact, the only image. Perhaps for the simple
reason that not many people who are not urban men in
their twenties or thirties—and few who are—manage
anything like these numbers, there was little sympathy given
to those who first became ill.

Some of us hoped that farm boys would get it.

Many were ill too early.

An eminent retrovirologist proclaimed recently, in a
women's magazine, that "heterosexual AIDS is a myth."
Many believed they could escape by leaving New York or
San Francisco and moving to Seattle or Salt Lake City.

The truth is that the afflicted, the tainted, however they
end up being described, must live in New York City, or
San Francisco, or in Los Angeles, or on these cities' pe-
ripheries, because these are the cities at the vanguard for
treatment. It isn't where you live that gives it to you, and
multiple partners aren't necessary, though they will help,
no doubt.

Dominic knows this. Jasper didn't.

The entire epidemic was thought to arise from what was called a "life-style"—a word with condescension built into it, a xenophobe's word. No one knew any better, though they should have. In Kenya, in Uganda, in Zaire, there is a slightly different virus, but the epidemic is similar—except that in Africa it is more rampant among women than among men; it is in the cities as well as the bush, neither of which has much in it that can be considered akin to the urban American "life-style." There isn't a lot of faggotry in Zaire, and people don't use nitrates there, or so I've been told by a young man who spent two years there in the Peace Corps. He told me that in bars female prostitutes are so thin it is assumed by everyone that they have the virus. Men will only dance with these women. There are few, if any, male prostitutes. In one bar, one time, Wayne told me, he saw two young men in lipstick and asked an older man, in Lingala, if these young men were "little fuck boys." The older man shrugged and said they must be.

Wayne has read a lot, knows a lot, is only twenty-six, and is always good to talk to. He grew up in a Baptist family, in Florida, where until quite recently the houses of infected people were still being burned. Possibly they still are but no longer make the news. When he came to New York, Wayne hadn't decided which direction he wanted to go with his youthful and no doubt considerable energies. He likes boys but also likes women, and it was an agony for him to make up his mind. For a while he was thinking that he could live in both worlds. I told him about Miss Fingerstop, how she had felt every time I was with her, that what I really wanted was to be with a man. I told Wayne she'd been right and added that when a man cannot decide which sex he prefers, usually at least three people will be made unhappy. In the end, or what seems to be the end for the time being, Wayne decided it was easier to be with boys. His reason was, and probably still is, that faggots are less expensive than women. Faggots, Wayne believes, do not expect to be taken to dinner and to the theater, or to receive presents, as, he feels, any woman worth bothering with will. Men just don't expect this from one another, Wayne believes, and faggots are more likely to pick up the occasional tab. It is also true, though Wayne didn't mention this, that fagots are quicker to fall on their knees or even roll over and play dead for a good-looking man than a woman will be. I would hate to know that a man was with me because he considered me a cheaper date, but there is, I expect, an unending supply of men who are not offended by this in the least.

In the early eighties, I had wondered about the until quite recently unheard-of business men had started doing to each other by making a fist. I don't imagine this was newly invented, but it was new as a conversation piece. I had seen one man doing this to another in a film that was shown at the Museum of Modern Art in the seventies, and it had looked to me both horrifying and thrilling beyond description.

Tom told me he had done this to a few fellows who had pleaded with him for it. He said that with one of them he had gotten his arm as deep as the elbow, and the fellow, Tom told me, had wanted more.

"There isn't any more," Tom had said to the fellow.

The fellow, Tom told me, had contorted in a way Tom had never seen before, even in the dance.

I was still stuck at the thought of a man pleading for this. What did he do, did he just come right out and ask?

It was unlike Tom to go into detail, and he asked me how did I think a fellow could be satisfied by just a weenie after being filled by a forearm? I answered that I didn't imagine that anyone could be.

This seemed a good enough reason not to do it.

"I wouldn't want anyone to go as far into me as that," I said, meaning this rather lightly.

"Not even Jasper?" Tom asked.

I had to think about that; I hadn't before. I then told Tom that Jasper got as far into me as I wanted any man to go.

"I can believe that," Tom said.

"What do you mean?" I asked.

This question made Tom smirk. "I've seen him, Timothy."

"Where?" I asked.

"All over," Tom said.

"You mean at the baths?" I asked.

"There, and other places," Tom said.

"What other places?" I asked.

"The Hole," Tom said.

"That I don't believe," I said. "Jasper wouldn't go to the Hole."

I hadn't been to the Hole. Tom had tried to get me to go with him a few times. A fellow could fit quite a lot through the holes, Tom had told me, but not, of course, everything, not all at once. I've always enjoyed looking at people—I've liked it enormously—but I like, when looking, to see an entire picture. For example, a face in its own peculiarity of rapture.

"I wouldn't have told you if I'd known you'd get so touchy," Tom said.

I doubted Tom would have told me any of this if he hadn't been confident that I would, as he put it, "get touchy."

WHENEVER WE went to a place where a tie was called for, Jasper would remind me how immensely he preferred to wear a silk scarf around his neck. This was more than a desire to break from tradition, it was more than vanity, though some of these did, of course, come into it.

Jasper disliked neckties and despised a buttoned collar. More than anything, Jasper demanded comfort in haberdashery. Usually, there is something behind a dress code, some reasoning. Unlike Jasper, I don't argue with places that demand that men wear neckties. One complies with codes, with conventions, for the comfort of others. It isn't so agonizing, really.

There used to be a place in San Francisco, on Market Street, near Dolores, that enforced a code of undress. It may still be there. Footwear was allowed in this place. Otherwise, everything was checked behind the bar, with a man who kept his clothes on. He would give you one half of a cut-in-half tarot card. You would carry this in your sock and give it back to the man, reclaiming your clothes on your way out.

Most fellows wore heavy white athletic socks. In this place, with its undress code, you could rest your eyes on the best-looking gonads on this earth, and all you could do was touch them. You could not lick them, and you could not get yours licked. You were allowed the play of your hands—only the play of your hands. One night I was startled when a fellow licked my ear.

This was in 1982, the beginning of the crisis, and new places opened in New York, in San Francisco, in Los Angeles, places with rules, and in some of these places the rules were actually enforced. There was, for some, an excitement in the strictness of rules, to so much being forbidden. I was aware, though, as was everyone, why so much had to be forbidden, and these thoughts gave me more than pause.

It was impressive, though, the way everyone did all he could to make the best of things.

One reason nakedness was required, apart from any lubricity that might inhere to it, was, I now believe, that unless he had them only on his feet, which has been known to happen, no man could hide any markings, Kaposi's lesions, that he may have had on his skin. Of course, not everyone gets Kaposi's, and it isn't every man who will enjoy himself strutting among others in nothing but his shoes. Dominick didn't give this place his business. He went once and called it "Jackie O."

I only went twice, because it was true, what I'd told Jasper, about not liking to take showers with a lot of naked men around. It wasn't the showering I didn't like, it was the shower room. A shower room full of naked men is far too much to study, especially when so much is being made of the soap.

But the two times I went, I liked the place on Market Street, with its undress code. It had no shower room, though there was a sink with soap and a roll of paper towels, and there is something that will always be endearing, almost heartbreaking to me, about naked men standing around together in nothing but their shoes.

———

AT HIS house, Jasper kept free weights with which he did routines twice daily. He also did sit-ups, but not in front of me. Jasper, I was sure, was a favorite of nature, genetically blessed. This was a topic we talked about, how Jasper had been blessed, how I had been gypped. I talked about this more than Jasper did.

I've always suspected I was somewhat shortchanged, genetically. And I don't mean shortchanged; I mean gypped.

Some things, you just know them. You can't brood about them long, because you could brood about them all your life. Soon enough, without brooding, you will see pretty well that having been gypped a little by genetics is not the worst thing you could have been, not by far. You could have been less. You could have been nothing at all.

Recently I heard about a woman who had been given an abortion in her seventh month because the fetus, if it had been born, would not have had a brain.

The human male produces about two hundred thousand sperm each day. This is the average man on the average day. I suppose most people know this, but I hadn't until quite recently. Some men produce a greater number and can release in one burst as many as half a million. When a man releases all this into a woman, only one will fertilize an egg. Triplets and such come about from an egg that has split.

Once it is penetrated by the single sperm, the egg becomes impervious. To me, nothing could be clearer from this than that everyone alive could have been one of the sperm that ended up as nothing. Looking at it this way is to see, to know, that to be alive at all, to be anyone at all, is to have already triumphed over unthinkable odds. Looking this way at myself, I am less inclined to brood over whatever blessings may have been withheld.

I knew well enough that no man gets from nature a set of stomach muscles as toned as Jasper's, as rippled. But I only came to know of Jasper's regimen by noticing the weights one day and asking, were they his, did he, in fact, use the things?

I was hoping he would tell me the free weights belonged to Oliver Ingraham.

Discovering that Jasper used the weights faithfully, and all the rest, made him seem more ordinary than I had thought he was. In this way—only in this way—Jasper took on normal scale. Many times I wished I hadn't noticed the free weights.

THE NIGHT I turned twenty-one, in 1975, when we'd been together two years, Jasper gave me an avalanche of presents. The best was a platinum print, which are hardly ever made today, eleven by fourteen, of the photograph we'd seen the year before in Soho, the black-and-white image of the man looking at his infant son in a cradle, with a father's pride on his face. Jasper had returned to the gallery and bought it the next day. Then he waited more than a year to give it to me. Some of the presents were better than others, but none was better than this one.

I opened all the presents on the bed, and among the wrappings Jasper and I did the things we knew. They were the things we always did, and that night we took a darling nap and did them all again.

That's enough about that. Jasper and I always called this playing. We only sometimes called it "toss and catch," which was, perhaps, a little too illustrative for Jasper.

The night of my birthday, our naps were engulfing. Mine was over before Jasper's, and when I woke I watched him as he slept. Jasper asleep was a marvel to see. He looked like a man who took sleep seriously, and, in fact, he was. Jasper was exactly such a man and looked earnest as he slept.

I have not ever been able to think of anyone Jasper looked like. He resembled no one.

That night, another of my presents was a bow tie. It was blue and silver and had wide stripes. While we were dressing for dinner, Jasper spent a long time trying to teach me how to tie it. When different steps must be mastered in the learning of a thing—when, as in the case of tying a bow tie, there are two steps, or more, that must be mastered in order to learn one thing—I do not learn them all at once, and when the learning is difficult, when it is impossible, I worry that I may be just a trifle backward.

This, of course, would be genetic.

That night, Jasper's patience wore out before I got the knack. He ended up tying the bow tie for me. After that, Jasper always tied my bow ties.

I can't tie one, even now.

I watched Jasper tuck a scarf into his open collar, and it came to me that the reason he despised a buttoned collar must have been a consequence of all that dutiful weight lifting; it had probably made his neck too big around for his collars. When I suggested this, only as a possibility, Jasper said it wasn't so. He was short with me, in fact.

He had been lifting free weights every day since before I was born, he said, long before it became fashionable, that is to say obligatory, for every man in the street under seventy to carry around with him at all times the physique of a butch cartoon, to be a Tom of Finland hero incarnate.

Soon after, Jasper began having his shirts made to measure and admitted to me that the new collars were, when buttoned, gentler than he had ever imagined.

A FUSS was made at the door about Jasper's scarf. The house provided a tie. This displeased Jasper, but he went along with it.

"It's a good thing you don't turn twenty-one every year," he told me.

Under a glass roof we sat side by side, à deux, on a banquette. They no longer have a banquette at Lutèce, but they did have one in 1975. I would have preferred looking at Jasper across the table, without needing always to turn my head the few degrees that were necessary in order to see him as he spoke. Though it was nice on the banquette to be able to look down at Jasper's legs, and into his lap, to have those parts of him so near.

"There aren't any prices on this menu," I said.

Jasper explained that at Lutèce, and a few places in New York of its ilk, only the host was given a menu that included, in addition to the bill of fare, the cost of the bill of fare.

"How can they tell I'm not the host?" I asked.

"They just can," Jasper said. "It doesn't matter where we go, people will always notice how much younger you are, and then there is the matter, dear Timothy, of how you dress."

"What do you mean?"

"You have frightful taste in clothes," Jasper told me.

"Look at the men here, how are they dressed? Then look at what you have on tonight."

I looked at the other men. Most were dressed somberly—a different lack of taste. The thought gripped me then that amidst these men I was as hideously put together as the woebegone newlywed in her nightmare dress played by Jeanne Crain in Joseph L. Mankiewicz's *A Letter to Three Wives*.

The difference was that Jeanne Crain had had enough on the ball to recognize her dress for the horror that it was, whereas I had believed, until Jasper indicated otherwise, that I was glamour itself in my five-inch platform shoes, my yellow silk trousers, and my blue and gray blazer bedizened with gold threads. I'd felt snappy in the bow tie Jasper had tied on me. Most of the clothes I was wearing I'd bought to wear that night, and Jasper liked none of them. If he hadn't shown a bit of amusement, I would have almost thought he was ashamed to be seen with me. Then I worried that he was, and was hiding it behind the show.

I asked, "Am I so disgraceful?"

"You shouldn't be let loose in a store," Jasper said. Saying this, he smiled with chagrin. "You don't know how to buy."

This was his conclusion.

"Will you come with me next time, papa?" I asked him.

"You don't need me with you," Jasper said. "Just ask yourself, 'Do I really like this, will I want to wear this next month, will I wear it next year?' Every time you see something, Timothy, and think you like it, ask yourself, 'Do I want to own this for the rest of my life?' "

"Is that what you do?" I asked.

"I don't have to," Jasper said.

"Oh, I see," I said. "Not to be a trifle smug, or anything. It's a tad severe, wouldn't you say?" I asked.

Jasper considered. Then he smiled in a way that had

thought in it, a smile well worth waiting for. "Maybe it is," he said.

We agreed together that it was optimistic to expect me to learn from my mistakes, that this could end up being a costly self-instruction, that I might waste a heap of money. It was agreed then that Jasper would be with me the next time I bought anything to wear, even just a belt. Thus began a long period wherein Jasper approved, or did not, of everything I bought, or didn't, to cover my skin. I learned from Jasper how to look at merchandise, how to appraise by touch the care of its construction, to judge how well it fit my body, and finally, if it passed these tests, how it looked. Jasper told me the thing to care about was how an item looked on me, not how I looked in it.

One will follow the other, Jasper said.

This looking at clothes together lasted until 1986, when I got a little willful one morning in Rome, on the via del Babuino. That is where Missoni sells its wickedly costly sweaters, and those eye-catching scarves.

Even as we came to this agreement at Lutèce, it did cross my mind that I wasn't the one who had been stopped at the door.

We nibbled, then, meager *amuses-gueules*.

AN IMPECCABLY coifed woman, a blonde of consequence seated next to him on the banquette, gasped upon the steaming arrival of Jasper's first course. It was a mosaic of boned frog's legs, morels, and I don't know what else. It was handsome to behold, exceptionally fragrant, but this woman would have gasped, I expect, at anything that had been set in front of Jasper.

"Mmmm," the blond woman moaned. "That smells *délicieux*."

She was dining with a stolid-looking man, who appeared deeply unconcerned by what the woman was doing. She wore sapphire earrings, and her ring was a diamond of irrefutable substance. You wouldn't have wanted, really, to call it vulgar.

She looked wide-eyed at Jasper and smiled ear to ear.

I was accustomed to waiters flirting with Jasper, but beglamoured Frenchwomen suppurating over him in dining rooms alleged to be tony were new to me.

Jasper asked the creature if she would like a taste.

"Mais oui," she moaned again. This time, though, her moan was more of a squeal.

That was what she sounded like to me, like a woman squealing.

Jasper swirled a piece of frog's leg and whatever else in his saffron-colored sauce and passed his fork to the Frenchwoman.

He held his napkin under it for her.

She closed her eyes, no doubt to taste with deepened rapture.

"C'est formidable," she groaned.

"You must taste just the sauce," Jasper suggested, and presented his spoon.

"Bien sûr," the Frenchwoman moaned again.

She wore too much perfume. I have to admit, though, she did come close to beauty.

"You would like to taste mine?" she asked.

"I would," said Jasper.

"May I present you with the breast?" she asked. "Or would you prefer a piece of leg?"

"I'll leave that to you," Jasper said.

Jasper could have had at her right there on the banquette. She would have gone under the table for him in a second, I was sure of it, if Jasper had lifted one finger to point the way for her.

I could tell. Anyone could.

One fact was on my side, and it could not have escaped the Frenchwoman: Jasper was with me.

The older man looked at me. If he felt left out, he didn't show it.

The Frenchwoman sliced a piece of quail breast. Then she stabbed a little pastry with her fork.

Jasper took her fork and, not tasting from it, as she had done from his, lowered the Frenchwoman's food onto his plate. He slid the morsel from her fork with the blade of his knife. Only then did he taste it, and told her it was very nice indeed.

"But I fear that it is far less sublime to that of you," the Frenchwoman said.

She was petulant.

"I agree with you," said Jasper.

This was more or less the end of it, though this would not be the last time a thing like this would happen.

It happened again, eight years later in Paris, with a Ganymede who had the greenest eyes.

I may come to that in its time.

I RECOLLECT an anemic soufflé Rothschild, which thrilled me that night, it being my first dessert soufflé. Jasper produced from his breast pocket a cigar case made of lizard skin. It held three Montecruz 210 cigars. From his trouser pocket he then produced a cigar cutter, which he taught me how to use, showing me that it worked like a guillotine. It was a one-step process. I had no trouble learning it.

Jasper flamed one end of a cigar in cognac. I had not seen this done before. Where had he learned this? I asked. I don't know what I was expecting him to answer—that he'd picked it up from a colleague in his Miami days— but he told me that as a boy he had seen his father do it. He said this casually, as though it were a flourish every boy who's ever lived has learned from his father.

Jasper gave me the dipped cigar and dipped another

for himself. He taught me how one lights a cigar, holding its tip just above the flame, so that the cigar will not scorch. I liked learning this from him. I tend to like things I'm able to learn.

I liked Jasper's teaching.

That is, much of it.

————

THAT NIGHT, Jasper was driving Oliver Ingraham's new black Jaguar. It was my birthday, we'd had a splendid dinner, and I wasn't going to fret about riding in Oliver Ingraham's car. I wasn't going to think about Oliver Ingraham for one minute. I despise automobiles, the way they've ruined cities, their toxic belching into the air, but the blue leather seats in this new Jaguar smelled faintly expensive and were nearly the color of Jasper's eyes. It was a comfy place to finish the first cigar of my life.

Oliver Ingraham was away, and Jasper and I'd had three bottles of wine, including a Château d'Yquem. Jasper had wanted an Yquem from 1954, the year of my birth, but the sommelier told us that no Yquem had been sold that year. I liked that the château did have its standards. When I commented on this, Jasper said that when a château sells an inferior wine it is throwing away not only its reputation but, in a larger sense, its history. According to lovers of the wine, Yquem reaches its perfection when it is thirty years old. Lutèce did not have a half-bottle of Yquem, so Jasper and I had a full bottle. It was glory itself. We didn't finish it, so I took it with me when we left.

I asked Jasper, did he really want to drive all the way home with all that lovely wine in him? This was as close as I could come to asking Jasper to stay the night, that is, during the week. He stayed with me every weekend, but not ever during the week.

He declined to stay and dropped me at my door. I

stood at the top of my stoop and watched Oliver Ingra-ham's car turn the corner.

I went upstairs with the last of the Yquem, too drunk to do anything but finish it. There wasn't enough to save for Jasper and me to have another glass, and, of course, once a wine is opened it will not be as good again.

It was after midnight, and the fellow downstairs was playing what sounded like Scriabin. That month I was up to Chopin's Nocturne no. 10, but I was in no mood to work on it. It's hard for me to learn a piece. To learn Chopin, I had been listening for more than three years to the piano of Tamàs Vàsàry. I picked up the notes from listening; I don't read music. That night, with Jasper gone, I felt older than I ever had before. I realized then—I was.

This was the first time the thought had come to me with anything like the sharpness it had for me that night, after Jasper left me on the street: every new day I lived, I would be older than I'd been the day before.

This minute, I knew then, was the oldest minute of my life, as would be the minute after it, and then the min-ute after that. It occurred to me that everyone in the world was at that instant the oldest he had ever been, that, briefly, every minute is the oldest minute of everyone's life, while at the same time it is the youngest minute of all future history.

I finished the Yquem, looked at the yellow Holland tulips in the clear fresh water in the clear glass vase. What is lovelier than tall green stems, cut on the diagonal near their base, standing in clear water, in a clear glass vase?

Nothing, I thought.

I poured a bit of Benedictine in a pony.

The bedroom floor was littered with wrapping papers. They made me restless—claustrophobic—I needed to get out, to walk. A pony is hard to hold, to grasp, while walking. It didn't feel right, and the pony glasses had been in my family three generations. They reminded me that I was the end of the line; I would be the disposer of the name, the last of the Springers. Sometimes this seems almost to rebuke me, to be a heavy price to pay for a simple preference of male anatomy.

Other times I think, "Too bloody bad, tough Titania," and that possibly there is more to it than anatomy.

Not that anatomy isn't reason enough.

I poured the pony's contents into a brandy snifter. I could hold the bowl between my fingers, easily. I'd bought this snifter myself, it was mine, it had no history. It was just Swedish glass.

It was easy to carry it down the stairs and through the street door. I started walking with it toward the river.

I was still wearing the bow tie Jasper had tied.

There used to be an open pier a few blocks south of Bank Street. Late at night, the end of it was a good place to sing. In the Village, in those times, there were many piers along the waterfront. They were what was left of New York's great harbor days, relics of another age, and had been abandoned long ago. Many of them were covered, buildings with roofs. Inside, there had been vast space for cargo and, up dark, enclosed flights of stairs, large rooms. Years before, these must have been splendid offices. There were gigantic windows that looked out over the already closed upper ramp of the West Side Highway, and if you turned around you could see the Hudson and all the way across it.

There was no glass in any of the windows.

One of the piers, the biggest one, I think, had in the mid-seventies taken the place of the Washington Street trucks. Just as at the trucks, there were men in this pier every night, even in cold weather, and in the early mornings, too. There was more space, so there were more men.

There seemed no end to men answering the flesh, the demands of it.

Even in daylight, men carried on in this pier, upstairs and down. For more than a few summers, this old pier was something to see on a Sunday afternoon.

For years, no one was killed in it.

At night, the rooms downstairs were so flooded by street light from the highway that, Tom told me, you could see what all the men were doing. If you looked awhile, when your eyes adjusted, you could get a fair idea, he said, of what every man in the place looked like.

Time, weather, and long neglect had taken the piers beyond dilapidation. At some point in the early eighties they were barricaded. Their demolition took months, and finally all the detritus was hauled away, and I noticed, one day, that the piers were no more.

The last time I went down there, the uncovered pier was still hanging over the slate-gray water. I have never seen that river blue. But it has been years since I walked as far west as the river. Recently a young man, the one who grew up in Florida as a Baptist and now goes out with boys instead of women because boys are less expensive, told me that many of the bars that used to be there still are. Until then, I had assumed that all the activity of the waterfront, or what used to be the waterfront, had been pretty thoroughly wiped out, a casualty of the plague. But they are still there, Wayne reported, still packing them in.

That surprised me. It did. But the covered piers are gone, now a part of a many-parted past.

The waterfront thrived for a time and will thrive again, I've no doubt, though next time it will probably thrive in some other place.

It was thriving the night of my birthday.

I went to the pier that night for nothing more than the quiet of the river and a breath or two of air. I had thought I might walk to the end of it and try out a song Tom had introduced me to two weeks before. I didn't go for a blow job, but this wasn't something I asked Jasper to believe when I saw him walking toward the covered pier.

He was shirtless.

I don't know what it was about him I recognized first. Jasper had said he would be able to spot me in a crowd, to pick me out at once. That night I recognized at once something about him. Whatever it was, I recognized *it* before I recognized him.

He wasn't wearing the clothes he'd worn to dinner. He was in button Levi's—but barely in them; the top button was open, so that they hung low on his waist. I knew these trousers, knew how easily they could be pulled over his hips. I'd done this myself; Jasper had no hips. Since dropping me at my door, Jasper had changed everything—everything, that is, except his shoes.

His shoes were the ones he'd worn to Lutèce.

Since that night, I have wondered many times if Jasper changed his clothes inside Oliver Ingraham's car, or if he'd made it easy for himself and made a quick change in the street.

When I saw him, these were not my first thoughts. I had other thoughts. I didn't want to see Jasper there, where he wasn't mine.

"Papa?" I called out.

It was the first thing I did, a reflex.

It wasn't until he turned that I saw his face. He was smoking the third Montecruz, the one left over. He didn't look pleased to see me. He walked toward me and sat himself on a low block of wood. I took the place next to him and did not wait for him to speak.

I set the snifter of Benedictine between us and began to eructate words.

Jasper took a taste from the snifter. He made the face he always makes at something much too sweet.

Nothing would have been a smart thing to say. What conversation could we possibly have had there, then? We'd been together twice that night, our bodies linked, and everything I said to him on the pier was ignited by this fact.

"Can't I be enough for one night?" I asked.

I'm sure Jasper took this as a reproach. How else could he take it? It *was* a reproach, I'd meant it as one.

I reproached myself: I hated that I wasn't enough for him.

Jasper looked down at the space between his knees and said, "It isn't going to work."

"Is that all you're going to say?" I asked.

I didn't know how to proceed. I don't think either of us did.

I took a taste of Benedictine. It was sweeter than it really had to be. I hurled the glass to the ground, an object despised. I heard it smash against the pier, a good smash, but the satisfaction, the relief I'd hoped for, I didn't get. I should have broken the pony.

Jasper did not react.

If anything, I was less satisfied. Sitting with Jasper, the longer we sat, the longer it went on, the worse it was.

"Say something," I said.

"Doesn't it make sense," Jasper asked me gently, "that when I want sex, I'm going to want the most sex I can have?"

I wasn't sure I had heard this. I asked him to repeat it. He did.

He used the same words. I thought he could at least have tried new words.

I was sorry I'd asked.

"It would make sense to want the *best* you could have," I said.

Jasper thought about this, but not for long. "Sometimes the most *is* the best," he said.

"Do you think so?" I looked at his chest and remembered how its covering of hair had felt just hours ago against my skin, and all the many times before. I was weak in his presence. That's just the way I was with him. Sometimes, when I wasn't with him, I'd think about his body. I knew it as though it were my flesh, and even better than that. I knew all the things about it that are unique.

I still do.

I know how Jasper felt to me, but I didn't know what he felt *with* me. I wondered how he felt enclosed by me.

I still do.

There was no getting away from it: I liked Jasper's face. It owned me, that face. It was a face I had known in boyhood, in a dream I had once. I only had it once, and in this dream I was rescued, carried away by a man from trouble, from danger. Who knew what the danger was? I had this dream at night, but there was daylight in it. It was in this daylight, this bright, hot daylight, that an able, handsome man appeared, a man well made, and he lay down with me on a white sheet, in a room with many windows. Every one of them was open, and the white sheet, when I looked at it again, had changed to white sand. The room became a beach, a wide stretch, and the tide was turning on it, going out. I lay with the man, admired his face, trusted him on sight, knew he was wise without his saying a word, knew he had abilities, every possible ability, without his doing anything. I touched his flesh, found much, and waited for something to happen, for the man to make a move. He made none. He lay without moving on the sand, looking out quietly from behind blue heroic eyes, up into a towering sky.

I did not look away from him, nothing happened, and I did not have this dream again.

The man in the dream had a face no man had. For a long time I was frightened I'd invented him, that I would not see his face again, until I saw Jasper and recognized, though not at once, the face that had been in my life for years, waiting to be found.

On the pier that night, I looked away from him. "Do you think you could button your trousers?" I asked.

I looked away because I hadn't wanted to see Jasper feign surprise.

So I don't know if he did. I think he probably didn't.

"Look around this place," I said to him.

"I know what it looks like, Timothy," Jasper said.

"Look at it. See that fellow, over there? He's getting blown through a window by someone who won't even get out of his car. See those fellows huddled there? Is this what you want?"

Jasper looked not at the figure reaching to grasp the head of the man inside the car, not at the dark figures out on the pier, but at me, directly. "I do this three times a year, if that," he said. "I'm not making it my life."

"Give it up, then," I said.

"What for?" Jasper asked.

It's telling, what you love at first—the best face, the best handful of flesh. These can be what you end up with, too. I knew then that sitting beside me on a pier used for lust was a face that had waited until this minute to embody for me all the disequilibrium of living.

I said to him, "Except for the infrequent *frisson,* you're the only person I do anything with. That's because you're the one I want. I don't want to be with other people, I mean *be* with them. Now and then I see a fellow looking at me, we talk a bit, but I don't go through with anything, I disappear." I said all this to Jasper almost in one breath.

"Why?" Jasper asked.

"I want to be yours."

"Except for the infrequent *frisson,*" said Jasper.

"Oh, you know that's nothing at all—Boy Scout stuff," I said.

Jasper made a gesture that took in the pier. "Why do you think this is more than that for me?"

"Can you tell me it isn't?" I asked.

He looked down. "No, I can't," he said.

And then these were his words—"Monogamy is antithetical to the homosexual life."

Those were his words, exactly. How could I make them up? How could anyone? How had he?

What did he mean, *the* homosexual life? I wondered, at the minute Jasper said this, if I was the only faggot in the world who hates men.

It struck me that there had to be something just a little infantile about *the* homosexual life, or, rather, about ours.

We stayed on the pier awhile. I said what I said, Jasper said what he said, and neither of us came round to the other.

I left.

Jasper stayed.

Until now, I haven't talked about this night. I didn't speak of it again with Jasper. I don't know that Jasper thought about it much. I am now the only one who knows it happened, and that is as it should be. It isn't something I will talk about with Dominic, but tonight, with Dominic in Los Angeles, as I watch him devouring *risotto frutti di mare,* the pier, sitting on it with Jasper, seeing Jasper with his shirt off—everything about it comes to me again, like a doubt I'll have forever.

———

ONE NIGHT, a year or so before Tom said he would not have told me about seeing Jasper at the Hole if he'd known I'd get touchy, we were going, Tom and I, to dinner at the old Trattoria da Alfredo, on Hudson Street, when I saw Jasper with a nicely put-together-looking youth. They were leaning against a parked car, waiting for a table together. I didn't get a close look at the fellow. He was about my age, I'd say, maybe a little older. When I saw that he was better-looking, I turned around quickly and told Tom we had to think of another place for dinner.

I would have turned around if the fellow hadn't been better-looking but probably not as quickly.

Tom took a long look at Jasper before he caught up with me down the block. He said it was too bad we couldn't go to Trattoria da Alfredo, that he had been looking forward to the *spaghetti puttanesca.*

They used to do a nice *puttanesca* at Trattoria da Alfredo, which has been gone now many years. Jasper and I must have had at least a dozen dinners there, but we would not go there again. I did not tell Jasper I had seen him with the nicely put-together fellow.

Tom and I went to Le Jules Verne, another place that has been gone for years. It's been three different places since. Tom, who missed nothing and was not without a vicious streak, had a good idea of what I was feeling, I'm pretty sure.

Neither am I without a vicious streak.

Jasper was the least vicious man I've known. I would have preferred, though, if he had thought to take his boys to dinner in a different neighborhood. Why did he need to have dinner with that confectionery-looking creature just three blocks from my door?

"I've seen him at the Hole twice," Tom said.

That was how much Tom wouldn't have told me.

I knew that Jasper was not an exemplar of monogamy, but I was certain Tom was lying. I could not think of Jasper being satisfied by a cutout in a wall, though it occurred to me that I might be.

Jasper, alas, could not have given a good blow job to save his skin. He didn't seem to love it, didn't seem all that happy doing it, and he would use his hand to rush it along. *No one* should do that. Over the years, I'd had blow jobs without Jasper. Some I still remember. And that is all I did with other men. I'm sure this sounds like Doris Day, but there it is.

That is, until 1987, when I met Claude. Claude is the man I knew in Paris who reminded me of *Portrait of a Man,* the Hans Memling painting that hangs in the Frick Collection.

Claude, as I have said, was a mistake I made.

Claude was my lunacy.

This isn't the place to talk about Claude.

Actually, it is the portrait, the face in it, that reminds me of Claude.

I didn't consider getting a blow job as an infidelity to Jasper, because Jasper couldn't give them. It might have been different if he could have. The man couldn't give them, that's all. It wasn't the end of the world to me.

"Tell me the truth, have you ever done anything with Jasper?" I asked Tom then.

"Of course not," Tom said. "I don't like a man with chest hair."

"As opposed to a woman with chest hair," I said.

Tom laughed at this.

I hadn't meant it to be funny.

four

ONE AFTERNOON in 1980, after I'd known Jasper almost seven years, it struck me, just by looking around a room, that many good things in my house had been made by him. Not the art on the wall, but the wall itself; not the books on the shelves, but the bookcases; not the plates or the glasses, not the candlesticks, but the table I would set them on for a dinner we were having that night.

Jasper had built for me six walls of bookcasing, not simply mounted shelves but pieces, each one self-standing, with a bottom, two sides to it, a top and a back. Like the dinner table and like the table by my bed, the bookcases, which were tall, narrow, and handsome to look at, had been joined by finely sanded prongs. The prongs had rounded edges that fit into finely finished grooves. I didn't believe I would ever own enough books to fill these cases, but now I have far too many, and so few of them, alas, read. The dinner table, at which he himself would dine, was not, as one would expect it to have been, any more finely crafted than the bookcases.

Jasper built things to last. "They can go with you when you move," he told me, the day he brought them in a rented truck and hung them on my walls or placed them on the floor.

Nothing was nailed.

It was unlikely I would move. When the man down-stairs moved out I bought his floor. I put a darkroom in down there, and I had the garden in the back.

The bookcases built to hang could also be self-stand-ing; they hadn't been designed any differently. When I asked Jasper if he could hang them upside down, he an-swered that it would be more difficult but, of course, he could.

"Why do you want them upside down?" Jasper wanted to know.

I hadn't put it into words for myself.

I thought for a bit. "Papa, these bases are massive hunks of wood, they're heavy-looking. How high will they be from the floor?"

"That depends on whether you want them to adjoin the ceiling."

"What do you mean, 'adjoin'?" I asked.

"Touch, Timothy," Jasper said. "If they touch the ceiling, they will be twenty-eight inches from the floor."

"How do you know that?" I asked.

"I measured," Jasper answered.

"When?" I asked.

"When you were in California," Jasper answered.

"The last time?" I asked.

"The time before," said Jasper.

"Papa, that was more than a year ago," I said.

"It was sixteen months ago, and the ceilings are still the same height. Do you worry they've shrunk? Tell me, why do you want me to hang these units upside down?"

"Units!" I nearly shrieked. *Units?* I hated hearing Jas-per say that word. It gave me the same feeling I get when-ever an ice box is called the "fridge," or when a dinner is called a "meal." Jasper, thank God, never said *that*. Words like these, terminologies of that order, or nomenclature, or whatever it is, hearing it, take me close to the edge of revulsion. A pint of blood is a unit. A mobile home, or anything packaged in cellophane, a pack of jockey shorts, for example, or a carton of cigarettes, these are units. A blow job is a unit.

Jasper was waiting for my answer.

I hadn't put it into words for myself. It took me awhile to get over the "unit" business.

Actually, I didn't get over it. I blacked it out. "If you don't hang these handsomely made cases upside down," I said very slowly, "the goddamn heavy bases will pull down the ceiling. They'll squash the room and make it look like fifty cents."

I heard what my voice was doing. I knew I was being the pansy bitch of the world. I couldn't help it. Just could not. I hated that Jasper had said "units."

Jasper wasn't bothered by my tone, but he looked painfully surprised.

"Jesus, I didn't think of that," he said, and he sounded almost dejected.

I wished I hadn't said anything. What difference did it make what a room looks like? Who cares? "Let these units wait," I said. "They can do that, can't they? They can wait. Let's toss the ball."

———

JASPER LIKED tools—saws, clamps, sanding machines. He liked the different grades of sandpaper; he liked useful things. I think he may have loved them only because they *were* useful, though I'm not, of course, sure of this. Jasper taught himself to use tools, without ever taking a carpentry class. He hadn't even taken shop in high school. It was the last class of the day, and his father needed Jasper's help in the hat store. Jasper built things more or less by figuring them out. He didn't spend a fortune on carpentry books, as I have done on photography books, but he knew how to find the right book in a library, and he devoured catalogs. Many of them were free.

Jasper wasn't able to build a chair. The man could not suck a cock, and he could not build a chair. We ended up buying chairs. That is, I did. Jasper helped me find them, a set of six eighteenth-century Venetian chairs.

Last year I gave two of them—the two that have arms—to my friend from Berkeley, Abigail Church, who had come to New York a few years after I did. Abigail had graduated with distinction from Berkeley, which Dominic, Miss Fingerstop, and I had left. Dominic left between semesters; I at least finished out the year, and it was Abigail who got me through it. We would go to drive-in movies with canned margaritas, brandy Alexanders, anything that we could get cold in a can. I don't remember ever taking a bottle. We saw Elizabeth Taylor's great romping in *X, Y and Z,* also called *Zee and Company,* a broad piece of fluff about adultery in London, in which a brazen Elizabeth Taylor triumphs over Michael Caine, Susannah York, and the splendid Margaret Leighton, stealing the movie with such dazzling aplomb that you pretty much forget that other players are in it at all. After the drive-in movies we'd go to a twenty-four-hour place, drink from glasses, and talk interminably about Dominic. Abigail and Dominic had been close enough to tell each other everything about each other, which is, of course, unwise—especially with a creature like Dominic. With Dominic, the game of self-disclosure is an exchange without balance: Dominic judged others too quickly and himself not at all.

Abigail got me through the year because I could talk with her about Dominic. She needed to talk about him as much as I did, and this was the basis of our early friendship.

Of course, Abigail also knew Miss Fingerstop.

Abigail was the only witness to an event on Telegraph Avenue, an event that gave me a sickening delight. We had seen an instantly forgettable movie and were in the twenty-four-hour espresso place. The espresso place was also a pizza place. In those days, I didn't know that the olives had come from a can, that the mushrooms had also. I didn't stop to wonder how many chemicals and different artificial flavors were in the pepperoni that some scullion had dumped on top of it all. I was busily devouring the sizzling, overspiced grease when a tall woman with a long red braid stopped at our table. She was with a long-haired man. She put her hands on our table and said to me— and I remember her words exactly—"I've been looking at you, and I couldn't leave without telling you that you are just really incredibly beautiful."

I looked at the woman. She was tall and rather pretty. I clutched my neck defensively. My instinct was to assume that she was playing a vicious joke. I wished the long-haired man would agree with her or, failing that, take her away.

"What a nice thing to say," I said. "Sweet God, no one's ever said *that* to me. Thank your lovely heart," I babbled, moronically.

"I just had to tell you," the red-braided woman said.

The long-haired man smiled but said nothing.

"Thank you, thank you awfully," I said to the woman.

"Good night," she said. Then she was gone.

Abigail looked at me as though I were something new that she had not seen before. "I've never been with anyone who had this happen," Abigail said.

"Perhaps not in a pizza dump," I said.

"Aren't you thrilled?" Abigail asked.

"Why would I be thrilled?" I asked.

"Timothy, does this kind of thing happen to you all the time?" Abigail asked me.

"It's never happened, except once or twice from Dominic, when he was trying very hard to be pleasant, usually because he wanted something. And there was a man in San Francisco on the cable car who found me somewhat acceptable one afternoon, but otherwise this is the first time, and it will probably be the last."

"What makes you say that? You've just been paid the highest possible compliment, and you're not enjoying it," Abigail said.

"It's not as though she said I was brilliant, or uniquely talented, or anything, really, at all. All she said was that I was nice-looking, and that, my sweet, is hardly the highest compliment going around."

Abigail said, "She didn't say 'nice-looking,' Timothy. She said 'beautiful.' "

"Actually, she said 'just really incredibly beautiful.' But what does she know?"

"She knows what she sees," said Abigail.

"I don't think so, sweetheart. She was on something," I said.

"How can you say that?" Abigail said.

"She was tripping on something. Acid or what have you, monkey dust, angel crap, who knows. I was one of her hallucinations."

Abigail said I was a fool. Then she said I was incorrigible, and I said *that* was a compliment.

Abigail came to New York in 1975, largely at my urging. She said she was going out of her mind in California. Back then, I thought of New York as being the answer to any conundrum. In some ways, but not as many, I still do.

Abigail became a medical writer. She knows Latin and Attic Greek, and that helped. She found herself a man and married him. I gave her the armchairs when she married Gary again. They weren't divorced—they just wanted to get married again.

Jasper liked an armchair at a dinner table. I don't, and it didn't matter anymore what Jasper liked. I suspect Abigail thought I was too preoccupied to go out and buy her something, which I admit I was, last year, but I doubt that Abigail has any idea what she could get if she cashed those chairs in.

They don't look like they're worth much, but they cost

money when I bought them, and they're worth something now. Jasper told me I was throwing money away. He said this about many things I did with money, and he was often right. It has never been necessary for me to lay hands on money; I don't need to touch it. All I have to do is look at money and it will evanesce.

In the case of the Venetian chairs, however, I consulted a reputable man, who told me they were *underpriced*. I had heard of this man through a woman I knew in California who had, in her bathroom, a lapis-lazuli ashtray. There was also a lapis-lazuli vase, and these were the only things in the room that weren't white.

About his inability to build a chair, Jasper observed that people tend to get tired of chairs. A good table, Jasper said, accrues character.

Someone wrote, I think long ago, that a chair by itself in a room will look quite alone. To prove this, a photographer took a black-and-white picture of a chair in an empty room. It was all by itself. In this photograph, which appears in many anthologies, the chair looks bleak in its complete aloneness. If it weren't a chair, you might almost think it was lonely. I remember reading a comment that an unoccupied chair, unlike a table, on which one can write a letter or arrange flowers or pile books or leave one's mail—and which can always, if nothing else, be set— a chair needs someone sitting in it and has no other utility.

Even an empty bed can be made to look inviting; you can plump up pillows; you can turn a bed down. There isn't much you can do with a chair.

A chair just haunts a room.

———————

THE NIGHT Jasper told me he had not ever heard anyone go on in quite the way that I did on our first date, at the Greek place, was an August night. It was years later,

1980 or '81, I think. We were in Provincetown, our third or fourth time there. It was late, after dinner and after an after-dinner drink. We were walking out on a long jetty built of boulders, huge uneven stones, a massive effort made by hardy, enterprising people many years before. It extends out over the bay.

Jasper and I had walked out on this stone jetty half a dozen times, always at night, without ever getting to the point where it stops. In daylight, on bicycles, we could see how long it was—it goes a long way out over the water. At night, walking on it, we had no idea how far we had come.

It took an effort to get out even as far as we did, more than just walking; you had to jump the rocks, or climb up between them, and you had to watch your footing.

Jasper, who was far more agile than I will ever be, was faster over the rocks. He'd always get ahead of me, and he'd stop, every fifty feet or so, and wait for me to catch up to him. Then he'd be off again. In one or two places, Jasper had to pull me up between the rocks. This pier was not a promenade for me.

Sometimes, when Jasper was far ahead of me, I wished I could be more agile for him. I wished I had for him an athlete's grace, that I could just glide over the rocks, swiftly, with ease, as though they were a path to lead me to him. I wished that I could be, for him, his able, agile, good-looking young boy.

That night, we got out far enough to leave the world behind, away from the bars, the discos, the boisterousness of too many people having all the fun they could manage. We got ourselves away from all that.

Farther than we'd been before, we found a rock smooth enough to lie on, so we lay down on it. We looked up, into the night, through a canopy of stars. They seemed themselves bewildered at being where they were, to have been burning so long, alive all their millions of years.

We were quiet awhile with each other in the immensity. We lay close together, and Jasper produced from a pocket a thin silver flask. It had a small cap to use as a cup. We sipped green Chartreuse from this and tasted it on each other's lips, from each other's mouths.

"Yours is better than mine," Jasper said.

"You think?" I asked, and tasted his.

"I know," Jasper said.

"I like yours more," I said. "Give me some of yours."

"This is a nice way to drink Chartreuse," Jasper said.

"Give me more of yours," I said.

The sky, which had been clear, became even clearer. Jasper told me he had never seen such a multitude of stars. Nor had I, I told him, and it was true: I hadn't. Jasper began to name a few of them, some constellations that he knew—the Big Dipper, the Pleiades, Aldebaron.

"Hush," I said. "Give me more of yours."

He did.

We had many fine evenings. There were winter evenings in New York with Montecruz 210s and Irish coffee with real cream. There were summer sunsets with champagne framboise on the Quai d'Orléans. Now the fine evenings seem fewer—though I know that they were many. They may also now seem finer than they were. If I exaggerate, I do so only a little. There were nights with Jasper, many nights, and days, that gave me almost all that I had ever dared to want. The evening with the stars and with the green Chartreuse is only one of them.

———————

THIS IS the place to state that it was my nature to be faithful to Jasper.

This should have been true. It almost was.

Before I knew Jasper, I had a notion that love has got to be something. It hadn't been with Dominic, but I didn't admit that at the time. I believed that love must live up to itself. I still do. Eighteen years with Jasper did not convince me otherwise. People make a mistake, I think, love wrongly, when they love without demands. Jasper always told me that he loved me in his fashion, that he was true to me, in his fashion. It may be to his credit that he made no promise on which he didn't deliver. There may be a kind of honor in that. I'm not sure there is, but possibly there is. I didn't need Jasper to love me absolutely, I didn't want anything impossible, but I did want him to love me *almost* absolutely. Very early on, though, I decided I would have Jasper on his terms rather than not at all.

In the last decade more than a million men and women have died, many from loving without demands. Possibly, many of them loved without expectations. There are other reasons, other causes: I'm not suggesting that every death is due to a lack of demands. It's not a moral statement I'm making, though no doubt it sounds like one. I'm not saying that the uncrested waves of death are in any way a retribution, though sometimes it is hard to think of them as being anything else.

I do not speak of the thousands of children who are *born* infected.

Abigail's husband, Gary, is a pediatric social worker. He works in a hospital with children who have the virus. He works with their families, too. One night Gary told me about a thirteen-year-old girl. I was impressed to hear about her, that she had survived with the virus as long as she had. Infants and the elderly have less native immunity than young adults. Gary told me then that this child hadn't been born with the virus, the virus had been passed to her after birth. Gary said there are many of these children. They are not in the public press or made anything of by Republican senators. In fact, one has to go out of one's way to know about them, unless, of course, one is a pediatric social worker. Gary told me there are thousands of these children in this country alone, little boys as well as girls, who have been infected by their drug-using fathers, or by men on drugs who were not their fathers. They may have been infected by the lovers of their mothers, the boyfriends, the johns. In families where drugs are used, Gary told me, incest is more or less a given.

Abigail said that the latency period makes testing not at all useful and that it will do little, if anything, to eliminate the crisis, to reduce, or even slow, the spread. Gary told Abigail she's right. He says he knows of five cases, just in his hospital, in which the virus was passed to children by fathers who had *known* their antibody status.

The last time I was in Paris, in 1991, I saw large posters on the rue Saint-Antoine and in the Metro stating that, in Paris, a child is born with *SIDA* every fifteen minutes. It cannot be said of these children that they loved without demands.

I know a man who was a boy in Texas. He's in his early forties now. One morning when he was nineteen he was in his family's garage making some repairs to his car, and the car exploded. Eighty-five percent of his skin was burned. He no longer tries to describe the pain. He spent three years in and out of hospitals and received more than three hundred blood transfusions. He finished college and went to business school in a wheelchair. He doesn't need the wheelchair now, though he still has difficulty, sometimes, when climbing stairs. On a good day he can walk fifteen blocks at a regular pace. He could easily have given up, but Bob chose to survive. I don't know him awfully well, but I have not once seen him in bad humor. About eight months ago he learned he has the virus. He wasn't cheerful about it, of course, but he didn't blubber, either. He told me he wished he'd had more sex, and he said this pensively. I asked him if he had kept in touch with any of the people he'd been with. He was in touch with all three of them, he said. I asked if they were positive. Two of them were negative, he said, and the third will not take the test. I asked Bob if he could look on things a bit differently: I offered him the notion that by having been with few people he at least had the comfort of knowing he hadn't infected as many people as most others have. He didn't take much comfort from this and pointed out that if he had infected only one person, which he wasn't sure he had, he has put everyone that person has been with since at risk, and everyone those people will be with subsequently, and so on, exponentially.

I knew this. I pointed out to him, however, that no one can put another adult at risk, at least not all on his own. Bob told me he is trying to find a way, while taking nucleoside analogues to halt its replication, to think of the virus as his friend.

Maybe Bob did love without demands—I don't know, I wasn't taking notes under the bed—but that is not how he got the virus.

I can only speak of my case. It is only of my case I can say that everything that has come to me has come because I loved without demands.

———

IT WAS nothing in my nature that kept me faithful to Jasper. I have all the ordinary appetites. Possibly, I have more of them. Show me a man with enough of everything, with more than enough, and I will be undone every time, without fail. Sometimes I will remember a man, as a specimen, even if I only watched him cross a street eleven years ago. I wish I *were* exaggerating. Just a man's face can get to me, and there is also the sound of a voice. The pitch of it, the timbre, words a man says, will sometimes stay with me, even if I only overheard him saying them to somebody else.

This doesn't happen all the time, but it has happened. I remember a man I saw years ago. He was passing in front of my table at a café near Centre Georges Pompidou. It was early evening. Some musicians were playing on the street, and the man stopped to listen. He leaned, all of him, against a railing and stood with one foot propped on a middle rung, his leg bent, akimbo. He pulled what looked like a peach from what must have been a gym bag and bit through the skin. Juice burst from the fruit and splashed onto his shirt, which was white and clung to his state-of-the-art chest, to all the major discipline of his torso, until it disappeared into his trousers, which were snug at his narrow, perfect waist.

My thought was that if the world hadn't wanted me to look at him it should not have brought him around. There was, in the way he stood, in the way he ate the peach, in the way he moved his mouth, the way he chewed, and in how his body weight shifted in the lowering evening light, a lewd perfection. It made me want to follow him wherever he would go, and though I'm not sure of this, I think he saw me, think he knew I was devouring him. For an instant, he seemed to look at me, too. I could have made a fool of myself so easily—a spectacular fool, because this man was out of my league—and I would have, if I hadn't decided years before that Jasper was my preference.

Even so, I thought about this man off and on for most of the week. More than just being with him, I imagined what it could be like to *be* him, to be him being with himself, being able to touch himself whenever he wanted, to have himself there, all of him, every minute of his life.

In other words, there were times I had to remind myself, to demand that Jasper be my choice.

What I had to do, each time, was remember.

This will explain why I stopped going to the baths with Tom, and to the piers and to the backroom bars. I didn't need to throw myself into their quagmires of temptation. That's what they all were; they were quagmires.

When Tom and I saw each other, he usually brought along a bit of hashish, and we listened to Prokofiev, who is staggering enough without hashish. We hadn't known each other long enough to have many memories in common, but now and then we would talk as though we did. We'd talk like old men about what we'd call old times, about plays we'd read, parts we'd memorized and no longer remembered, about bars that had closed, people who had moved away.

Instead of going to the quagmires, Tom and I began to have what we called "performance nights," until Tom ended up calling them "recitals." We would read to one another aloud, and we would sing. I taped one of these nights in the late seventies. It wasn't yet the age of video, so I have only our voices, the sounds that we made together. I listened to the tape just a few days ago. On it, Tom reads Sylvia Plath so that the language sparkles in the doldrums. He takes away from it the I'm-sticking-my-head-in-the-oven-and-here-comes-the-gas squeamishness that I often get from her. I read Lorca's great chant and invective, his *Ode to Walt Whitman*. Even in translation, it is a staggering poem. The poem exalts Walt Whitman's natural love of men and has only scorn for the sleek simpering of what Lorca calls "pansies of the cities," by which he means, I am sure, New York, because that is where he wrote the poem.

> *. . . I do not raise my voice, aged Walt Whitman,*
> *against the little boy who writes*
> *a girl's name on his pillow,*
> *nor the boy who dresses himself in the bride's trousseau*
> *in the darkness of the wardrobe,*
> *nor the solitary men in clubs*
> *who drink the waters of prostitution with nausea,*
> *nor the men with a great stare*
> *who love man and burst their lips in silence.*
> *But against you, yes, pansies of the cities,*
> *of tumescent flesh and unclean mind,*
> *mud of the drains, harpies, unsleeping enemies*
> *of love which distributes crowns of joy.*

Against you always, you who give boys
drops of soiled death with bitter poison,
Against you always,
Fairies *of North America,*
Pajoros *of Havana,*
Jotos *of Mexico,*
Sarasas *of Cadiz,*
Cancos *of Madrid,*
Floras *of Alicante,*
Adelaidas *of Portugal.*

Pansies of the world, murderers of doves!
Women's slaves, bitches of their boudoirs,
opened with the fever of fans in public squares
or ambushed in frigid landscapes of hemlock.

Tom said the poem was judgmental. That's what Jasper would have said, too. I've never understood how so many people can be frightened of making judgments, of saying, simply, "This is better, that is not as good." How can a choice be made without making a judgment? Without making a judgment, what will stop anyone from reading Rod McKuen all his life?

On the tape, to compensate, I sing for Tom, "Rockabye Your Baby with a Dixie Melody." No judgment there.

Tom sings old English odes and folk songs with titles like "Where Have You Been, Lord Randall, My Son" and "Sometimes I Feel Like a Motherless Child." In Tom's versions these songs are nearly all refrain, which doubtless they are, no matter who sings them. Until I played the tape again, I had forgotten how fine Tom's voice was; even singing these inert odes, his was a deep and handsome voice, and it had musicality.

We sang together that night a song Tom had introduced me to the week before. "Starlet, Starlet on the Screen, Who Will Follow Norma Jean" was written by Dory

Previn, who also sings her wondrously bitter lyrics with a snap that still stays with me.

The way that Dory Previn sings the song is also the way I heard it from Tom, and the way I learned to sing it myself. The words are broken, even the monosyllables, so that the lyrics go as follows:

> who do you have to fuck
> to get into this pi-ick-sure
> who do you have to la-hay
> to make your way
> hooray for Hollywood . . .

When Tom and I sang this lyric we both tried to do it justice. I tried to sing it in somewhat the way Marlon Brando sings "Luck Be a Lady Tonight," toward the end of Joseph L. Mankiewicz's *Guys and Dolls,* but the Dory Previn is not that kind of song, and I failed miserably. I think anyone would fail, because no one but Brando could do what he does with his face while he sings. He could have been a riveting song-and-dance man.

Fortunately, I hadn't told Tom I'd had Marlon Brando in mind.

To Tom, English ballads were the way. Tom wasn't an Englishman, but these were the songs he could sing with something resembling verve. So that's how he tried to sing the Dory Previn when we sang the song together.

We didn't even get to the first "hooray for Hollywood." We laughed on the word "la-hay." Tom laughed first, and we went on from there. It's a bitter song, you can feel the quiet rage in it, but Tom and I had adopted it as our hymn to the world.

There are two or three seconds on the tape where Tom is laughing and I am asking him to stay with me and with the fractured lyric. It sounds, on the tape, almost as if I'd had a drive to finish the song. Without the tape I wouldn't remember this. In fact, even hearing the tape I don't remember it. There it is, though, determination in every broken syllable, with Tom and me, on tape, intact.

———

ONE AFTERNOON Tom showed up at my house with a chilled bottle. "Let's drink this," he said.

I was making bay scallop ravioli for Jasper, who was coming at six. I didn't feel like drinking, but the bottle Tom had brought with him was a bottle of Cristal.

"Where did you get this?" I asked.

As I do, Tom always carried a shoulder bag and, in cafés, would drop into it envelopes of sugar, ashtrays, the occasional wineglass. He'd take his bag into men's rooms and return with rolls of toilet paper. I agreed with Tom that it's thudding to buy an item like toilet paper, to spend money on it. Toilet paper does cost too much for what it is, but I would find it mortifying to be caught stealing it from a men's room. Bottles of Cristal, of course, are harder to come by.

"I stole it from my dad," Tom told me.

"Do you know how *good* this is?" I asked him. I wondered if Tom knew that this champagne had been created for the Romanovs, that when the Romanovs went out of power Louis Roderer made no Cristal for almost fifty years. Probably everybody knows this. I hadn't, until just weeks before. I asked Tom if he knew this about the Romanovs. He didn't, he said. I told him he should take the bottle back, that his father would miss it. Telling him this, I pulled two champagne glasses out of the freezer.

"I don't give a shit," Tom said.

The bottle of Cristal opened with the usual soft pop. "Let's drink to that, then," I said.

We drank to Tom's not giving a shit.

Tom plopped himself askew in one of the Venetian chairs. He threw a leg over an arm. He settled in. I sat across the table from him, just for a minute.

"He's not going to pay my rent anymore," Tom said.

"No?" I asked. Tom's rent was approximately nothing.

"He doesn't want me to be a queer."

"Where does he want you to live?" I asked.

"With him," Tom told me.

"Come talk to me while I cook. I thought your father was living with a woman," I said.

"With her, too," Tom said.

"He wants the *three* of you to live together?" I asked.

"He wants more than that," answered Tom. He sounded rather sour.

I waited for Tom to go on. He didn't go on. He sat on my kitchen counter, drained his glass in two swallows, and poured himself another.

"What exactly do you mean, *more?*" I asked.

I distributed tiny bay scallops, tossed with coriander and transparent slices of ginger, along one side of a sheet of pasta, which I'd just rolled out when Tom showed up.

"How do you know that about the czars?" asked Tom.

"Jasper knows things like that," I told Tom. "I think he read it in Truman Capote. What is it that your father wants?"

"This morning, after breakfast, he made me do a three-way with them."

I looked up, said nothing.

"He wanted to see if I could function as a straight."

"That's straight? And could you?" I asked.

Tom shrugged.

I hadn't met Tom's father, so I couldn't picture Tom in this trio. As I tried to envision this group, Jasper's old observation about lust being better on an empty stomach came to me at once.

"You didn't go through with it, did you?" I asked.

"He made me," Tom said.

I had made these ravioli before and had thought they needed something. I spotted every other raviolo with just a few dots of oscetra. I passed Tom a spoon, with a taste on it.

"How exactly did he *make* you?" I asked.

"He gave me an ultimatum. He said if I didn't do it, he wouldn't even think about my rent," Tom said. "He said if I did, then he *might* pay it."

"That was crafty," I said. What I thought it was, I kept to myself.

"This caviar, it's different," Tom said.

I thought it was diabolical. "Probably you've only had beluga," I said. "So if you did it for him, he'll pay, won't he?"

"No," Tom said. "Once the thing was done, he took it back, so I got screwed. I've never had beluga, Timothy."

"Wait, he didn't *screw* you, did he?"

Tom shuddered, a mock shudder. "Of course not," he said.

"Still," I said, "he almost gave you his word, but not quite, not enough to break it. Was the girlfriend there when he told you he might pay it?"

"Yes," Tom said.

"He negotiated this whole thing in front of her?" I asked.

"Of course," said Tom.

"And she sat there and listened," I said.

I folded the bare side of the pasta over the mounds of scallop filling. This took two hands. An ash fell from the cigarette I had going in my mouth. This only happens when someone's watching. I scooped up the ash with a teaspoon. "That makes her a witness," I said. "Will she take your side?"

"Not likely," Tom said. "She's been going to him for six years," Tom told me.

"She's his *patient?*" I asked.

"Sure," Tom answered.

The pasta was rolled a little too thin. I could see the gray spots of caviar showing through it faintly. I worried that these ravioli might break apart in rolling water.

"This is just so horrifying," I said. "So what was the worst part of it, being with her?"

"I didn't mind being with her—except that it was *her*," Tom said. "I guess the thing I hated most was having my dad there watching, and when I was inside her he put his hand on me and pushed me into her from behind."

"Oh," I said.

I pressed the top layer between the mounds. I had to cut quickly, before the dough stiffened. When it was cut into ravioli, I decided, I would brush each one very lightly with egg white. This would reinforce the seal. I tried to focus on these logistics and not to picture an older man pushing his much younger son into the body of a woman. The effort was superfluous: I could not have moved this picture even as far ahead as the point at which the father touches the son.

It all stopped there for me.

The woman I didn't see at all.

At Berkeley, Dominic, Miss Fingerstop, and I had tried something once. We crowded together on a single bed. I was between the two of them, and I saw them lean together over my body, over my face. In every threesome one person is *always* the third. That's one thing I don't like about a threesome.

When I saw Dominic and Miss Fingerstop kiss this way, I got up and left the room.

I ran from it, actually.

"That's obscene," I said to Tom.

Again, Tom shrugged. I realized we were talking about his father, and possibly Tom didn't see it as I did. "It's the first time I'd seen him with a full hard-on," Tom said.

Possibly I was being a bit of a prude. Prissy. I'd hate

that. If this was the first time Tom had seen his father with a "full" hard-on, did that mean Tom had seen him before with an empty hard-on? Possibly things like this might have happened so many times before that they were, to Tom, not obscene but typical. If Tom's father could make his son share a woman with him, wouldn't it be in order for Tom to take his father to the Hole and shove his bare ass against an opening in a wall, and watch as an unseen man on the other side of the wall plowed deep into his father?

The only difference between these events is that Tom isn't a bully.

It occurred to me that Jasper would consider these ravioli a waste of caviar. I worried then that they were.

Even with Tom still in the room, still telling me his story, I began thinking about how I would tell it to Jasper.

JASPER SAID the ravioli with oscetra was the best thing I'd made in a while. Even so, he put one of them aside, without comment.

It was unlike Jasper not to object to cigarette ash in ravioli. Years before, he'd offered me a thousand dollars to stop smoking for a month, that's how much he wanted me to quit. Because I like things in pairs, I told him I would quit for *two* months, for *two* thousand dollars. He agreed; I lasted two weeks.

I don't know why the cigarette ash didn't bother him. I didn't know what about that night was different. I never saw Jasper in anything I would call a mood.

When I told Jasper that Tom's father had made him perform in a threesome, Jasper dismissed it as a bad doctor story. "Typical," Jasper called it.

My opinion of physicians is not as low as Jasper's, and Tom's episode had seemed more than this to me, though not so very much more, really.

This was the night Jasper told me about a man named David Moss. They had met in Kansas City. They didn't live together, or anything close to that, but when Jasper moved to New Orleans David Moss had followed him there. Jasper stayed in New Orleans about seven years, until he came to New York in the sixties. By that time David Moss had married, had fathered two daughters, but every year since Jasper left New Orleans David Moss had sent a card and telephoned Jasper on his birthday.

When Jasper told me this story, it was 1982, and the birthday cards and telephone calls had been coming, without fail, for sixteen years. Nineteen eighty-two was the year Jasper had hepatitis.

I liked hearing about David Moss, liked knowing about this man who had uprooted his life to follow Jasper, just to be around him. I liked knowing Jasper had changed this man in some way, to a point—but only to a point: David Moss had kept his life. I liked thinking about him and his two daughters, about the birthday cards and telephone calls. The whole story pleased me; I liked everything about it.

Five months or so after I'd made the oscetra ravioli, I had a call from Tom's sister, whom I had not met. She said she had something to tell me that she didn't want to say on the telephone. I assumed Tom's father had committed him somewhere. This seemed the kind of thing a man who had pushed his son by the backside into a woman would be likely to do. Tom hadn't talked much about his sister. In fact, until she introduced herself on the telephone I'd not heard her name: Gloria.

When she came to my house, the first thing she noticed was a photograph I'd made of Tom, in a black turtleneck sweater, holding his black cat. The turtleneck was formfitting, except for the collar, which was loose and floppy. It was my sweater; I'd asked Tom to wear it to give the image a strong circular line. I adjusted the neck so that it covered an edge of Tom's chin and then fell away from his neck, showing his jawline, which, by the way, was superb. It was about Tom that Jasper had said "beautiful bones."

It had taken time to set the collar right, and the cat didn't help matters. I would rather have skipped the cat, but Tom insisted on holding it. He must have wanted some softness, a homey touch, and, of course, the cat *did* give the image all the homeyness anyone could want. Otherwise, I can't say it added much to the picture.

All you see of the cat is its cat face in Tom's hands. Tom is not the subject of the photograph; the subject of the photograph is Tom's beautiful bones, and not a great deal else. Tom had been a good model, because he liked to pose. Jasper was the opposite: Jasper would not hold a pose for me, and all I have of him are some shots I took in the woods or on trips—Jasper leaning against a big tree or in front of a Roman or Mayan ruin, some landmark.

It takes time to make a man look in a photograph as he does in life, and to get the world into his face. It's work to get a man *that* way, and it needs something from him as well, not so much posing as yielding. Jasper would not yield, and he did not ever give my camera his quintessential image.

I had dry-mounted the portrait of Tom and hung it on the wall. I worried it was hackneyed, an embarrassment. Tom's bones looked far too beautiful in it. Tom would like that about it, I thought.

When she saw the photograph, Gloria said it looked more like Tom than Tom did. This is something I hear often; it's the standard compliment people pay a photographic portrait. This isn't to say I don't like hearing it. Sometimes people really mean it.

I opened a bottle of Lachryma Christi, and Gloria, sitting in the chair Tom always sat in, told me that three days before she had found her brother's body. She had found it lifeless. Tom had emptied three bottles of sleeping pills, each one a different kind—he'd emptied them into himself, Gloria said. Each prescription, Gloria told me, had been filled at a different pharmacy. Tom had used his father's prescription forms and forged his signature, too. He had also self-prescribed Compazine, so that he wouldn't throw up the sleeping pills. Tom had never done anything like this, Gloria told me; she believed Tom must have put in long hours to forge their father's signature. This would mean he had planned it, Gloria said, that it had not been an impulse.

Tom had left no note.

Where do things like this come from? Tom had been a smart fellow, extraordinary-looking, and he would have been a good actor if he'd stuck to it. All along, I'd been sure of that and had told him so, for whatever it was worth. Tom had been one of not many people I knew who was all but guaranteed a good life, if that can be said of anyone. Possibly there had been one or two unhappy romances, some parts in plays he'd wanted and didn't get, and, of course, there was that father, but none of these were reasons, I thought, to toss everything off and check oneself out after twenty-six years. It takes more time than that to know that twenty-six years is just a driblet of time, and now Tom never would.

Gloria drank the wine like a thirsty woman and talked about what her brother had been to her. She told me they had liked going to discos together, where they would pretend to be boyfriend and girlfriend and, by making themselves unattainable, torment as many people as possible. They had both been so good-looking, Gloria confided, everyone had wanted a crack at them.

Cautiously, I began appraising Gloria. I started with her face. It was an older version of her brother's face, a much older female version. She looked about ten years older than her brother and had a hardness to her that Tom hadn't. Her coloring was the same—white skin, dark eyes, dark, reddish hair. She had her brother's bones, some

of them, and ten years before she might even have had
something remotely akin to Tom's boyish appeal, but these
were not handsome on her.

She went on about how they had moved together on
a dance floor, how provocative they'd been. Hot was one
of her words. Sexy was another.

Racy stuff, I thought.

I know hot. I may even know sexy. I know them when
I see them, and I know it when I don't. What Gloria was
showing me, what she was proving incontestably, was how
unbecoming vanity will be when it is unwarranted.

Something more than this bothered me about Tom's
sister. It picked at me. I didn't know what it was, exactly.

We finished the Lachryma Christi. Ordinarily, I would
have opened another bottle. I didn't for Gloria. I wanted
Gloria to leave before she gave me another image of Tom,
one that would replace the image I had.

She told me there would be a gathering, a sort of me-
morial. It wouldn't be anything like a service, she assured
me, but more of a party, something casual, where people
who had known Tom would talk about him, share anecdotes. I'm not keen on this kind of thing, but I told Gloria
I'd come. I asked when it would be. She said she'd let me
know.

As she was leaving, she asked if she could buy the
print of the photograph I had made of her brother. For a
moment, I nearly gave her the one on the wall. Then I
wondered if maybe she'd been right: maybe it did look
more like Tom than Tom had.

"No, this one is not for sale," I told Gloria. "I'll make
another one for you, and of course you won't have to pay
for it. I'll bring it with me to the . . . gathering."

"I'd rather have it now, Timothy," Gloria said. I think
she really wanted it.

"No, that's not possible," I answered. "This is not a
first-rate print. I don't let second-rate work go out of this
house, and that, dearest Gloria, is that."

Gloria gave me the look of a woman who was unfamiliar with exactitude. I could not wait for her to leave.

Later that night, watching Tom's face come to life in developing fluid, then as I watched it fix, I knew what had bothered me about Gloria. It bothered me that she had been the one to survive.

———————

"THINK OF all the education," Jasper said. "All the books read, all the dinners eaten, and think of all the fucking enjoyed."

"Not enough, it would seem," I said. "I think of all the money poured into the assumption of long life."

"You make Tom sound like an investment," said Jasper.

"That's what every child is," I said.

"And now all for nothing," said Jasper.

"Maybe not for nothing," I said. "We're talking about him. In a way, that keeps him alive."

It had taken Gloria seven months to pull the tribute together. Jasper parked Oliver Ingraham's new Porsche on West Broadway. The tribute was being held in a loft around the corner.

"How long do you think that will last?" Jasper asked me on the street.

Then we were in an elevator, ascending to the tribute. I had brought Tom's photograph with me. It was mounted and overmatted, and I'd slipped it into an envelope for Gloria. I'd spent time on it.

"I've thought about him every day since he died," I said. "And it's been almost a year."

"Do you really think about him every day?" Jasper asked me.

I said I did.

"Would you if he hadn't died?" asked Jasper. The elevator opened onto an enormous space.

"Here we are," I said.

MORE THAN a hundred people were in a vast room. No one came to greet us.

Entering this space, the first thing anyone would notice was the limousine. It was a long, dark-gray British town car from the thirties, I'd say, a stretch limo before they were called stretch limos. It was a handsome specimen, and doubtless would have been much more than that to those who like this kind of thing—Oliver Ingraham, for example, would probably have been gripped by a lust to acquire. The car must have been dismantled and brought up in the elevator in pieces, then put together again. Several people were standing around the front of it, and I saw that the hood had been removed and where the engine would have been was a hollowed-out space, which had been made into a bar. A giant glass bowl was filled with ice, which did not seem to melt, and settled in this were bottles of different vodkas and of aquavit. There were two bartenders seeing to all of this, and everyone in the room was drinking one colorless liquid or another from expensive-looking drinking glasses.

The limousine's doors were open, and six people were sprawled inside, on deep seats covered in peach-colored leather. These immobile passengers faced each other across a low table that was built into the floor. It was made of polished veneer and topped with dark-tinted glass. Two people appeared to be entangled with each other, interwoven. Up in front, under an open roof, a mannequin, a blackamoor in chauffeur's livery, sat erect behind the wheel. The blackamoor's posture was the best in the room; the mannequin looked straight ahead, with the pride of a professional.

Other than the dark, waxed limousine, the space was devoid of furniture. There were round glass vases, like great globes, perched atop black lacquer pedestals, with thousands of dollars in cut flowers bursting from small openings in their tops.

There was nothing to sit on. There was also nothing to eat.

Jasper and I went to the limousine, and Jasper asked the better-looking bartender for two glasses of red wine. The better-looking bartender gave Jasper the disdaining expression long ago patented by catered help and replied that only clear liquor was being served.

We both took an aquavit and stood by a window, one of many in the room, and I looked around for Gloria.

Hanging on the far wall was a large painting of a pale man in a plaid flannel shirt. The painting looked as though its colors had bled away. The man's hair was pale, his eyes were pale. His face was pale, and his expression, no expression. The painting was almost photographic, and the man in it appeared never to have been troubled by a thought. The painting was bigger than life, that is, its dimensions were, and I saw that other paintings like it were hung from other walls. I began to look at them, then felt something cold. When I turned around to see what it was, what I saw was Miss Fingerstop, holding a glass to my neck.

I hadn't seen her for about nine years, since the night she invited me to dinner, when Dominic was there. Miss Fingerstop also looked pale.

"Miss Thing," she trilled.

I said, "Aren't you a surprise."

Miss Fingerstop was one of very few women in the room not wearing black. A few wore gray, a few white, but most were in sleek black dresses. Many were strapless. They weren't in mourning, they were in style. Miss Fingerstop wore a loose, flowing dress the pale yellow-green color of a key-lime pie. She was with a young man who didn't look like much. Miss Fingerstop introduced us; the young man's name was Justin Graft.

"You remember Jasper, don't you?" I asked Miss Fingerstop.

She looked at Jasper. "How could I forget?" she said. None of us shook hands.

"Justin did all these brilliant paintings," Miss Fingerstop enthused.

"Good for him," I said.

"I've been looking at them," Jasper said.

"He's doing me now," Miss Fingerstop told us.

"Is he?" I asked.

"It's a real challenge," Justin Graft began. "I'm painting her from a photograph. I've captured her straddling a guy with her high heels jabbing his abdomen. She's got this expression on her face, real nasty.

"For a while I tried to show her doing it, but I couldn't get the flow," Justin Graft told us.

I looked at Jasper. He was absorbing all of it unflappably. "It's more important to get her facial expression, or possibly that of the recipient, isn't it?" I asked.

"It makes me proud in my bones to know every night that I'm bedding down with the most expensive dominatrix in New York City."

To this, I had no handy reply. "Is that a fact?" I nearly said, or "Are you sure?" or "I had no idea," which would have been true, because, in fact, I hadn't. I wondered how Justin Graft could be sure of this and began to suspect that he had invented this credential to impress me. And it had. There has got to be a distinction to being the most expensive *anything,* no matter what, if only for a time.

Looking at Miss Fingerstop in this enormous space with its eviscerated limousine, I thought that if one is going to be a dominatrix in New York, one had better be the most expensive, because when a man pays a visit to a dominatrix he will want, I imagine, to know that he is getting the best discipline obtainable in New York City.

"I'm glad to hear that," I was able to reply.

I spotted Gloria across the room. She was more or less crawling out of the limousine.

She saw me with Jasper, with Miss Fingerstop and Justin Graft. She waved at us but also looked around the room, I assumed to see who else was there. I held up the giant envelope, which induced her to cross the room. She took the envelope, thanked me for it. She said hello to Miss Fingerstop and Justin Graft, both of whom she seemed to know, and, tiring of holding the envelope, she leaned it against a window ledge. I introduced her to Jasper and asked if we had come too late for the tribute. Gloria gave me a baffled look; she showed no sign of having any idea what I was talking about. I assumed the gathering had gotten out of hand, that she was flummoxed by it, so I didn't push the matter.

"This is a *loft*," Jasper said.

"Yes, whose is it?" I asked Gloria.

Gloria looked around, giving it a thought, as though it hadn't occurred to her, until asked, to notice where she was. "Someone I've been seeing," she answered. "I've got to get out of here, I'm late for something else."

"You're leaving so soon?" Miss Fingerstop asked.

"*Soon?* I've been here for *hours,* Eleanor," said Gloria.

Miss Fingerstop grimaced. Eleanor is the name she was given at birth. It had been the first thing to go. Everyone is entitled to a change of name, but I wonder if it may not be wise to wait until one is fairly sure of who it is one wishes to be. I did not believe Miss Fingerstop would want to be "Mercy" on her dying day.

"If you're leaving now, Timothy and I will go with you," Jasper said to Gloria.

"Yes, we could give you a ride," I said. I was as eager to get out of that place as Jasper was. It had given me a pleasure to see Miss Fingerstop again, but I didn't need more of it.

"I could use a ride," Gloria said. She and Jasper began moving through the crowd, toward the elevator.

Gloria had left Tom's photograph on the window ledge. Because I had spent some time making a better print for her than the one she had seen, I was put out, more than a little, in fact, by Gloria's indifference.

I gave the photograph to her again, in the elevator.

Gloria asked if we were going anywhere near Eighty-second and York. We weren't, but Jasper said we'd drive her there. We had a dinner reservation on Twenty-sixth Street; if we went there directly, we'd be just on time. I was raging with hunger and didn't know why Jasper had taken it upon himself to be gallant to Gloria.

Gloria sat on my lap. She seemed unimpressed that Jasper was putting himself out for her. "I'm seeing this guy I met last night, and I can't be late. Actually, I already am. I should've been there an hour ago. Maybe he didn't wait, maybe he's gone out, given up on me already. God, he's so fabulous. You know what he did? He peeled off one of my nylon stockings and tied it around his cock and balls. What can I tell you?" Gloria squirmed on my lap; it wasn't enough for her simply to turn her head to look at me. "He gave me head through my other stocking. He says there's something about the way nylon feels on his tongue that just gets him going. To tell you the truth, he doesn't have much of a cock," Gloria said, and she scowled a little. "But what he has is perfect asshole size."

It was difficult to take this sitting down. I looked at Jasper. His face showed nothing. He said nothing at all, and kept driving.

"And he's not even all that great-looking," Gloria admitted. "But a man who goes down, and likes it, that's hard to find. But tonight he'll probably just fuck me."

We dropped Gloria off at a doorman building.

Jasper and I started downtown. We were somewhere in the Sixties when Jasper said, "I've never heard *men* use language like that."

"She wanted to be one of the boys," I said.

I thought that covered it. I also thought it was terribly sweet of Jasper to believe that a woman should be less obscene than a man. There was something very dear to me about Jasper's thinking that.

Under my feet, on the floor of Oliver Ingraham's Porsche, was Gloria's brother's photograph.

five

The blood is composed of exceeding small particles named globules, which in most animals are of a red color, swimming in a liquor, called, by physicians, the serum; and by means of these globules the motion of the blood becomes visible, which otherwise would not be discoverable to the sight. These particles, or globules, are so minute, that one hundred of them, placed side by side, would not equal the diameter of a common grain of sand; consequently a grain of sand is above a million times the size of one such globule.

ANTON VAN LEEUWENHOEK
(1632 – 1723)

DOMINIC IS telling his neurologist story. He almost spits when he says the man's name: Greenwood.

"Every day, he came to call. He's a tower of a man, and he's got this *hairdo*. It's short, it's dark, it's sculpted. This is hair with edges, honey. This is high-tech, hardcore hair."

For this story, Dominic retrieves some of his old inflections. He even tries out some new ones, as though he's in rehearsal.

"It's maintenance, and he wears a suit. It's gray, it's navy, you can't tell. That's how dark it is. He's got three of them, four of them, and they're fitted *to the tits*. Honey, we're not talking off the rack, we're talking costly, we're talking money. Suits like those, you get them made."

"I know about those suits, Dominic. I've owned a few. They're cut kind of amply in the crotch, and they make everything look mysterious," I offer.

"Yes, if that's the first place you look," Dominic replies loftily. "This Greenwood is urbane, he's debonair, he's *soigné*. And the man has diction, he's summa cum laude from the Orson Welles School of Enunciation."

"It's a pity more people can't afford those suits," I say. "They're vastly more appealing than tight trousers

· 153 ·

that push everything forward and let you calculate more or less precisely what's there, to the pubic millimeter."

Dominic looks around the room. "Where's our red snapper?" he implores. "Will that red snapper ever come?"

This is not a time to tell Dominic that when he was in the men's room I asked our waiter to give us an interval between courses. There wouldn't be any point in telling Dominic this. I like a cigarette between courses. It's one of my favorite times to smoke. If smoking between courses was good enough for Julia Child, and still is good enough for Marcella Hazan, both masters of the palate, what do I care when people I dine with, in restaurants, call me a barbarian?

Instead of telling him, I give Dominic the floor.

"Greenwood buffs his fingernails, and he doesn't smile. The man cannot smile. He's not a doctor, he's a layout."

Dominic pauses to open his cigarette case. He is the only man I know who carries one. He pulls it from his trouser pocket. Dominic has had this same silver cigarette case for almost twenty years. He doesn't lose things. When you give Dominic a gift, if he keeps it at all he keeps it for life. More often, he will give it back, telling whoever gave him a gift, whether it be a drawing, a sweater, or a pair of candlesticks, that he would prefer to receive—"especially from you, darling," he will add—something closer to his style, more to his taste. Dominic knows that this is, at best, a breach of etiquette. I think he even knows how rude other people find it, but there is such gentleness in the way he says "especially from you, darling" that I forgive it every time. I've heard it a lot of times—and every time it strikes me as a genuine candor between us. Dominic would not, I am sure, have declined a gift from his grandmother in this way, or from a casual friend. I believe it is Dominic's assumption that I will accept this from him as being, in its unusually gnarled way, a sign of love for me, or at least a showing of regard.

I do not rank other things Dominic has done. I don't

know what to make of his pursuit of Jasper. There was no sign of love in that, nor did it show regard; it was free of those, void of them. He started to talk to me about it once, and I slid my hand slowly through the air in front of my face, dismissing the topic.

I did not want to hear about it from Dominic.

I would have disliked hearing it from Jasper.

So I did not tell Jasper I knew about it.

This isn't generous or delicate, really. It just takes so much time away from us when we are unforgiving.

Dominic's silver cigarette case is a very old present from me.

———————

A GOOD-LOOKING waiter produces a light. Dominic adores having a man light his cigarettes. Come to think of it, so do I. Doesn't everyone?

"Every morning at ten-thirty sharp, Greenwood comes into the room and asks me what day of the week it is. What month is it? Is it or is it not morning? Who does he think he's talking to, Olivia de Havilland in *Snake Pit*? Frances fucking Farmer? Will there *ever* be a morning, honey?

"He tells me to recite the alphabet backward. 'It's not a race,' he reminds me. How could I forget, when he says this every time? So I go through it, slowly. I do the whole thing, going forward in my head. You have to go forward in order to go back, because after *z, y, x,* who knows? You get the picture?"

I tell him I do. "Another thing I find rather wearisome at present is the ubiquity of the new hairless-chested male, all these nearly identical specimens who shave themselves the better to exhibit their identically developed pectorals and their tight-fisted abs. Why do they all insist on neutering themselves in this way?"

"You're raving like a madwoman," Dominic answers.

He dismisses the question, wanting to get back to his neurological anecdotes.

"Then Greenwood says, 'Give me four words that rhyme with strive.' So I start from *a*. Alive, connive, deprive. I stop at survive.

"He touches his ear, his nose, whatever, and he asks, 'What am I touching?'

"Every time, it's the same routine, honey. Every goddamn day he points to some part of his fucking person and asks me to tell him what he's touching, and one day I finally get so sick of it that when he points to his chin and asks what it is, I answer, 'Is it black cock?' "

"Was he amused?" I ask.

"What do you think?" Dominic answers. "When you're lying there wondering if you've got the dementia, and when you ring for the Xanax that will keep you sane—that is, if they ever bring it to you, which they do, three hours later—you cannot say to your neurologist, 'Oh, Dr. Greenwood, sweetie, I don't think I need you today.' "

"I guess you can't," I agree.

"I had to *ask* him to give me the lumbar procedure." Dominic flicks an ash. "That's the gun, the vacuum, it draws out some spinal fluid, and if the virus is there, its next stop is your brain."

"I know what the lumbar is," I say.

Dominic looks at me. He goes on. "Greenwood gives me the lumbar. Then, of course, he goes on vacation for three weeks. He's gone, and no one is authorized to tell me the result.

"I'm wondering, does everyone *know* I'm demented, and are they simply not going to tell me?"

I wonder if Dominic asked. Dominic was probably smart enough to know that if he had asked a nurse if he was demented, the only answer he'd get would be: you'll have to ask your doctor.

"Honey, one night you're lying there with the IV plugged into you, pumping you full of God knows what.

You've called out for Chinese, because the hospital food is so truly vile, and you're full of Peking duck and pork fried rice, and all at once you've got to shit like a bag lady, but you can't make it to the toy-toy because the IV tubing isn't long enough. All you can do is stand there between the bed and the toilet and wobble on your feet, and try to figure out what the hell you can do in the next five seconds.

"You fiddle with the needle, but before you can get it out you lose control. You lose all control, honey, and it just starts to happen. You're taking the all-time dump of your life, and you're taking it right there on the hospital floor."

"Oh, sweetheart," I say.

"So you get back in bed, delighted you didn't beshit yourself *there*.

"A few days later, Greenwood returns. He comes in the door and says, 'I understand you have experienced some incontinence.' Notice the use of the partitive—not simple incontinence, not major, not minor, but *'some.'*

"The man never stays more than a minute, but every time he steps into the room, every time he inquires who the last five presidents were, he gets a hundred dollars."

"Did you remember the last five presidents? I couldn't do that," I say.

The red snapper arrives. So does some fried polenta. There are grilled boletus mushrooms. One good-looking waiter fillets the fish. An even better-looking one pours out more Gavi.

"I forgot Carter," Dominic says.

"What did it all come to?" I ask.

"Greenwood? Twelve thousand dollars," Dominic answers. "That's for one hundred and twenty minisessions, less than three hours of his time."

"Your insurance covered it, didn't it?" I ask.

"Not without raising my premiums," Dominic snaps.

"It sounds like extortion," I venture.

"Honey," Dominic snaps, "it's what Ezra Pound called *usura*."

Dominic fastidiously slides a small bone from his mouth and deposits it on the rim of his plate. We start talking about a hospital chain in Tennessee, recently in the news. These were private hospitals. At one of them Tylenol had been marked up to something like twenty dollars a capsule. When this was in the news, the report stressed that the hospital in question did not operate on a not-for-profit basis. Dominic says a lot of people are making fortunes off health care, especially off of this epidemic, not just people like his Dr. Greenwood, but people who run private nursing services, drug companies that hold patents, companies that manufacture condoms, people smart enough to have bought stock in those companies, and possibly, Dominic says, even the orderlies who clean up the vomit, just because there is more of it to clean.

If all the world's private wealth were seized and gathered, then released miles above the earth, would it all fall back, funnel down, Dominic wonders, into the same hands?

I've been asked this question before. It's one of those questions I can never answer wittily. I take them seriously, that's my mistake. A few months ago I was at a dinner party where every guest at the table was asked who he would choose to be stranded with on a desert island. Your choice could be living or dead. The only person I could think of was Jasper, but I couldn't let that be my answer—that would not have brightened the party. I chose Diotima, the woman in Plato's dialogues who is wiser than Socrates. But few at the table had heard of her. No one found her an enchanting choice, so I gave the matter shallower reflection and answered, "Then I'll take Porfirio Rubirosa."

Everyone had heard of Rubirosa.

Tonight, my answer to Dominic's question is that if money were smart, it would take itself someplace else entirely.

SOMETIMES I wonder how things might have gone if Jasper, not I, had picked up the phone.

The Saturday night Dominic called—in Paris it was Sunday morning—Jasper was asleep, but I could not sleep at all that night.

What if we'd had a telephone in the bedroom? I've often wondered.

"Timothy," Dominic said.

"Sweetheart, are you in Paris?"

"No," he said.

"Then you're in Los Angeles?" I asked.

"Yes," he said.

"You sound as though you're right here."

"Are you sitting down?"

"Oh, God, don't ask that, it's always bad news," I said.

"I have the virus," Dominic said, wasting no time.

I hadn't been sitting down.

"What virus?" I asked.

"The virus, honey," Dominic said.

"Wait, do you mean *the* virus?"

"That's the one," Dominic said.

"How do you know you have it?" I asked.

"I had the test," Dominic said.

"What test?" I asked.

"The ELISA," Dominic said.

"Well, that's a fallible test, isn't it?"

"Yes, it is," Dominic answered.

"Well, then," I said.

"Then I had the other test."

"What other test?" I asked.

I heard Dominic light a cigarette in Los Angeles. I carried the telephone into our little foyer and closed the sliding door.

Dominic said, "The western blot."

"Which is new, isn't it, and also fallible?"

"The western blot is considered fairly accurate," Dominic said.

I began to feel responsible.

"The lab must have made a mistake," I offered. "We're not the kind of people who get this thing, sweetheart."

"We are exactly the kind of people who get it," Dominic said. He said this too emphatically.

"Why in the world did you have those tests?" I asked.

"My doctor wanted me to have them," Dominic answered. "I had ulcerative colitis."

Dominic has always had medical problems. It occurred to me that Dominic might have remained a nice Jesuit boy if I hadn't turned him into the shrieking faggot he'd become. I know this sounds a tad narcissistic, but it was the first thought I had upon hearing Dominic's news.

One afternoon in 1972, on horseback in Sonoma Valley, Dominic shrieked, "Bring out the K-Y, my anus is a hotbed of intrigue." It was to me he shrieked this. I was the only person there on a horse that day.

I didn't bring out the K-Y. When we finally did it, two years later, I'd known Jasper almost eight months and had been with no one else. Dominic was stopping in New York after a long stay on Mykonos, which he had documented in several letters to Miss Fingerstop. Every letter had the same P.S.: "My warmest regard to Miss Timothy Springer."

When he came to New York he stayed with Miss Fingerstop, who was having a great success as "Mercy." She asked me to dinner, omitting that Dominic would be there. It doesn't matter how, but Dominic and I ended up together—I did it to him; it was over in about twelve seconds.

Until that summer afternoon, Dominic had, in his words, kept his sphincter intact. I remember Miss Fingerstop shrieking to him in San Francisco, in an enchilada place, over blue-corn tortillas, "Oh, Dominic, no one gives a shit about your sphincter."

When it was over, Dominic asked, "Is that it?"

They hadn't been twelve especially stunning seconds, I'm afraid. I felt I'd misused us—both of us. Worse, somehow, though it didn't involve him, I felt that I'd done something shabby to Jasper.

It only took twelve seconds because twelve seconds was all I could take. Or, rather, all I could do.

The night Dominic called me in Paris, Jasper was asleep in our bed, and it was thirteen years after the summer afternoon on Bank Street. Since then, Dominic had been with hundreds of men. On a trip we took together in 1983 there had been more than a dozen in Paris alone, not that I counted, and we were only in Paris five days. Dominic had gotten himself slammed behind a bush, standing up, in the Tuileries. The shrubberies have since been clipped, but there was a time when men could do anything behind them.

In Barcelona, Dominic spent three afternoons at the baths. Dominic said that for him the most important part of foreign travel was meeting the people. At Sitges, a beach resort about forty minutes out of Barcelona, Dominic went looking to meet people in a notorious section. He had to walk through thorns to find people, but he did find them, three of them to be exact. He came back three hours later, the skin of his arms and legs ripped by thorns and bleeding.

It was cocktail hour. I was on a terrace with a glass of sangria, which I decided could not possibly be good, given what it is, but it was refreshing. I was watching the sun go down and reading David Hume. As Dominic approached I came across these words in *An Enquiry Concerning the Principles of Morals:* "It is sufficient for our present purpose, if it be allowed, what surely, without the greatest absurdity cannot be disputed, that there is some benevolence, however small, infused into our bosom; some spark of friendship for humankind; some particle of the dove kneaded into our frame, along with the elements of the wolf and the serpent."

I watched Dominic checking out men on the beach.

"Have fun?" I asked.

"Fabulous," said Dominic.

I don't have Dominic's flair for travel.

Dominic had met one person in the hotel lobby, in Paris. He brought the fellow, who was Egyptian and looked about fifteen, up to our room at three in the morning and asked me, didn't I have a rock to go climb? I spent that morning trying to get another room—anywhere. But there was not a vacancy in Paris, not in any arrondissement. Everyone on earth was in Paris that week for the fall couture, and for some colossal tennis event.

I did not want to be with Dominic in any hotel room anywhere on earth. I did not want to be awakened again by the smell of, as Dominic enjoyed calling it, smegma. It can smell, smegma. It can be exceedingly pungent after a dinner with three wines and an *eau de vie de prune,* and drinks, after all that, in a *gai* bar.

Dominic could dress quickly when a change of clothes was called for. To get oneself slammed after dinner in Paris, appropriate attire is *de rigueur,* but the change requires little time, and no imagination, because one has done it a thousand times before.

One evening, changing for a postprandial fling, Dominic stripped entirely; he turned his back to me, spread his legs apart, bent over, and reached behind to separate his buttocks. "Come take a taste of this," he beckoned, and between his knees I could see his face, laughing upside down.

I took no taste. Traveling together, Dominic and I would sometimes kiss good night, but when we went to bed we went to separate beds.

That was over between us.

In Paris, in 1983, Dominic told me one thing I remember. I remember because I had believed the opposite.

"I love it when they're almost there," Dominic confided, "and they pull back and wait for it, and then you feel them shoot it up your ass. That's when you know it's really been hot."

Heat was something I would want to have had at least an inkling of *before* that point. I didn't say this to Dominic. Jasper hadn't done this with me, but I remembered fellows doing it the summer in San Francisco, my hepatitis summer.

It only happened twice; both fellows had. been pretty toothsome, up to that point. When it happened, both times, it struck me as being not in the nature of ardor, this finesse that Dominic had told me he loved a man to make. It must be in the instinct of ardor to bear down, to be embedded.

Actually, I know it is.

I expect everyone does, except Dominic.

Jasper proved as much. The one time I asked him to do this, he didn't. He just couldn't, he told me later.

It had not occurred to me that either of the fellows who did this had meant this flourish to thrill me. I'd thought at the time, or actually a little later, that what they'd wanted was for me to know that it was happening, as if I'd needed proof.

Was it possible, I wondered, that either of these men had pulled back for *my sake*? If so, I must be even slower than I have thought; maybe I'm not quick enough to know when a fellow is trying to be sweet, trying to do me a favor, when he's making a gesture, an effort, a sacrifice—which it would no doubt be, at such a juncture.

I decided to make this my last holiday with Dominic.

Except for a weekend in Rosarito a few years later, it was.

In Paris, I finally found, in the Fourth Arrondissement, a hotel with a vacancy. It was on the rue des Mauvais Garçons. There was a sink in the room, a toilet down the hall, and I spent more than a hundred francs on it.

That night, drinking *eau de vie de prune*, I presented Dominic with the key. I told him he could receive his new friends there. I didn't think he'd actually use the room. I'd only meant to make a little statement. But, as it happened, later that night I left Dominic upstairs in the bar on the rue Jacob, the bar with the drab blue door that looks like an entrance to nothing at all.

It is the only facade on the street without a vitrine, without displays of books, fabrics, antiques. That's Le Trap, a place with a spiral staircase inside, on which men sit, pose, and ascend to a dimly lit balcony with many subdivisions. Within these, dozen of sweet- and rough-looking young men can be seen, in a faint rose-colored light, doing nothing more salacious than kissing one another.

The next morning Dominic, in a snit, told me in detail about his evening in "the black rectum of Calcutta."

———

"WHO ELSE knows?" I asked.

"My doctor," Dominic answered.

"Anyone else?"

"Honey, I'm not exactly hanging out a sign," Dominic said.

I carried the telephone into the kitchen, poured a little pear brandy, and sat down with it at the table. I lit a cigarette and said to Dominic, "No one really knows what this virus means, do they? How are you feeling?"

"What are you drinking?" Dominic asked.

"Williamine," I answered.

"That sounds perfect. Hold on, honey."

I heard the receiver smack against Dominic's glass table in West Hollywood. I could picture Dominic walking to the trolley cart he uses as a bar, could see him bending over to pour something into a glass. Dominic has always had handsome cocktail glasses, standing ashtrays on pedestals, and huge, lumpy chairs that somehow always come with every place he rents. He has no end of pricey things to wear and never anything comfortable to sit in. Dominic has always lived in places that feel temporary, no matter how long he lives in them. As I waited for him to come back to the telephone, I was aware of the quiet on Ile Saint-Louis at that hour, how comfortable I was at my kitchen table, and of how soothing ripening papayas are, heaped in a blue ceramic bowl.

Dominic told me, "I'm not feeling marvelous."

"Have you ever, sweetheart?" I asked him.

"Not for a while," Dominic said.

"Maybe you shouldn't fret. Aren't they saying that only a small percentage of people who have it end up getting sick?" I asked.

"There aren't any long-term figures," Dominic told me. Although I already knew this, it was a chill, hearing it from Dominic. He added, "Not everyone who has it checks out, but that may be because they haven't had time."

"You have to get pretty sick before you check out, though, don't you?"

"Not necessarily," Dominic said.

"What do you mean, 'not necessarily'? You don't just drop dead the day you're diagnosed," I said.

"There was someone here who got his diagnosis and was dead two days later," Dominic said.

"Someone you knew?" I asked.

"I knew *of* him. I knew people who knew him. He was supposed to have the Dick of Death."

"So you've only heard about this, really. You don't know how long he could have had it. I mean, he could have had it for ages."

Six thousand miles away, Dominic was quiet. I did not expect he was thinking what I was: I was hoping Dominic would not be one of the men I'd heard about who, knowing themselves infected, continued to go to quarter movies, exposing others at random in dark little cubicles. Of course, Dominic could argue that anyone who would make himself available in a cubicle would in all likelihood have already been exposed—that anyone who would get

Dominic's virus would get somebody else's sooner or later.

That is true, of course. Not many people think about the risk of *re*exposure.

"Have you and Jasper had the test?" Dominic asked.

"We've talked about it a couple times. Jasper won't take it."

"Tell him about me," Dominic said.

There was a tightness in his voice. It pulled everything together.

"Jasper was with you?" I asked.

"He didn't tell you, I take it," Dominic said.

"When?" I asked.

"Years ago," Dominic said.

"I don't believe it."

"Just tell him to get himself checked."

"How many times was he with you?" I asked.

"One night. Three times. Enough," Dominic answered.

"Jasper's never done it three times in the same night," I said, then realized that I had, of course, no way of knowing this.

"He wasn't the only one doing it," Dominic said.

I could not picture it. I wondered, were they in the room on Bethune Street with the blacked-over windows? Were they standing up?

Did Jasper lie on his back?

Were Jasper's legs in the air?

I did not see Jasper in that pose. I never had.

––––––––––

WHEN I finished with Dominic, though it would have been the natural thing to do, I did not awaken Jasper. I thought about boiling a pot of water and waking him with that. I thought about sputtering oil, about sizzling butter. Ordinarily, these are things one can be trusted not to do, but there are times when trust is a grotesque presumption, beyond arrogance. These thoughts of water, of oil, of butter, did not ripple through my mind. They were not mere tingles: I stood in the kitchen looking at the copper pots and held these thoughts a long time. Then I held them longer.

I had enough sense to get out of the house.

At the tip of Ile Saint-Louis is a small triangular park where the island ends at a point. Trees with hanging foliage enclose this little park, give it privacy and shade. People across the river cannot see through the shrubbery, which stands in dense clusters, taller than a man. Since the park is not much frequented, the trees, the shrubbery make it a retreat from the city, a calming place to hide oneself away. Jasper and I went almost nightly to this park with whatever we were reading and glasses of whatever we were drinking and would have a quiet cocktail hour together. Some evenings we had the park almost to ourselves, as though it were our garden.

This was where I went that early morning in June 1987. It was about 5:00 A.M., no one was out, except in the park. In the park, the world was out.

I'd heard that years before men used to gather at night in the gardens behind Notre Dame. No one had told me that when the city locked those gardens all the men who used to congregate there had simply crossed the footbridge and brought themselves here.

In the three years that Jasper and I had owned our place on this island, I had not known about what this park becomes at night.

I wondered if Jasper knew of it, if this was where he came when he took his late-night strolls. It had seemed to me he must have become unduly enamored of Place des Vosges. That's where he told me he'd been, whenever I asked. Wondering this, I knew it would be harsh of me to blame him. We hadn't played for five years, or longer, and when we stopped Jasper had said to me he *had* to do something. Of course he had to do something, how could

I argue with that, unless perhaps to point out that he had *always* needed to do something—with someone else—even when we *were* playing together all the time.

I hadn't the alertness to point this out to him then, and I was in a park that, at five o'clock in the morning, was unexpectedly seething with testosterone, working myself into a rage over a suspicion that Jasper had amused himself with some *tapette* he'd coaxed into a bush.

It was idiotic to be in the state I was. I knew that. It was unworldly, I told myself; it was shallow, possessive—everything ugly, everything petty. It was infantile even. I told myself this to make myself believe it.

This failed. I did not believe it.

In the park, I asked myself a question aloud: what did it matter what Jasper does in a bush? I didn't care if every man in the park heard me. I answered aloud: these days everything matters.

I walked to the far end of the park, sat on the balustrade above the Seine, and looked at men going in and coming out of the bushes. I tried to picture Jasper with Dominic, but the thought of the two of them together, linked, took my mind away.

There is something that happens at five in the morning to men who are waiting in a city park for one thing to happen. No one wants to take himself home unsatisfied, and men who ordinarily would not look at each other begin to look good to each other. On this early morning, the park was full of men with eager-looking eyes, letting their standards down.

It happens.

A man had followed me to the end of the park with his weenie hanging out. As flaccid weenies at five in the morning go, it wasn't bad. I realized at that instant that I could have been with just about any man I wanted in the park that morning and would not have been happy, even for a minute, even with the best of them.

There wasn't a best of them, really.

The man approached. I squeezed him, gave him a shake, admired his appendage politely. I met his eyes and told him with mine that the time wasn't right, wasn't it a shame? I turned away and went toward the gate. The man called after me, as a crazy man would. Why was I leaving him? Would I be back?

Walking home, it occurred to me that any man in the park could be carrying the virus, any one of them could give it to me. Earlier that year, I'd had a cyst on my neck. Soon I had three. The dermatologist could tell just by looking, he said, that they weren't Kaposi's, but I asked him to do a biopsy, to be sure. He said to me, "You get it by being passive," that if I had it—"it" being the virus—it would be as a result of something I had done twelve years before. This was the first time anyone in medicine had spoken to me about the virus, and it seemed to me that the doctor had told me this to put my mind at rest. It didn't.

Thirteen years before, I'd met Jasper, and, except for the twelve seconds with Dominic, I'd been with no one since. That is, in the sense of being conjoined; I could count on one hand the blow jobs I'd been given. Of course, I would have needed to use the one hand more than once—six, seven, eight: you can count to infinity on one hand.

It was possible that a fellow had had bleeding gums, that blood might have passed through a microscopic tear, which I gather most men have, or that virus could have entered through my urethra, but all that seemed unlikely. According to what I understood about the ways of transmission, Jasper was the only man I had been with in a way that could have passed the virus to me.

When Jasper had hepatitis, he told me I was the only person who could have given it to him. He was gentle about it. I was gentle, too, when I reminded him that I'd already had hepatitis, in 1971, that I couldn't have it again. What Jasper had tried to do was sneaky, possibly even low, but I wasn't angry.

I suggested he must have gotten it from an unclean fork.

It was six months before we could drink wine together again.

That night, I left the park, came home, made coffee, put some cognac in my cup. It was Sunday morning, and the church bell rang, as it always does, at eight o'clock. Jasper and I were flying to New York on the one-thirty flight. Soon he'd get up, he'd begin to pack. It would take him five minutes, no more. I put an almond croissant in a low oven for him.

I took coffee to him in bed and watched him sleep. Jasper claimed he didn't dream. He'd often made this claim, and I had told him that everybody dreams. Not he, he claimed, he didn't. That morning, watching him in our bed, I could almost believe him; his face looked as it always did, just as handsome, slightly troubled.

There is something just to proximity, to having known a man's body by touch, to loving the forces behind it, the voice that comes out of him, the words he selects, and then, too, something to having been away awhile—a week, a day, an hour, time in which you were removed, briefly free of him, even—and to coming back into a room and finding him still there, unchanged, the same as he was when you left him. There is something to this, to finding that you cannot possibly fill in what the man was in your absence, cannot imagine him as having been anything at all, even just alive, lying motionless without you, and something about this is bound to overcome you.

This happened to me when I brought Jasper his coffee. It swayed me. It had been easy enough to go away, to sit in a park and hate him for an hour, but being again in his proximity, seeing the way he hugged a pillow as he slept—a thing as minor as that—made hating him, even for a second, feel like a crime. Watching Jasper sleep, I decided not to tell him about Dominic's call. I decided not to go to New York with him that afternoon, to stay another week in Paris. I'd cancel six or seven photo sessions.

These things decided, I wakened my love with a fingernail scratch.

———————

SOME TIME later, a year or so, when I began to regret what I had done with Claude and was ready to tell someone about him, it was Abigail I told. Abigail was the one person I could expect to stay calm. I thought she would make some sense of it. This proved to be too much to expect. When I told her what I'd done with Claude, Abigail nearly recoiled. She said that in my life I'd done some idiotic things, unconscionable things, but this was beyond beyond. All she could think, she told me, was that I must have had a death wish.

Abigail didn't get it. I'd had nothing like a death wish. I hadn't *wanted* to get the virus—that would have been insane. If I had, I wouldn't have stopped at Claude; I would have been rapacious, I would have traipsed all over Paris, slutting around, impaling myself on every pole I could grab.

Abigail couldn't see that what I'd wanted was *one* other possible exposure. I'd stayed in Paris the one week to do one thing: to be one time with one other man, so that if in five years, or ten, I found myself infected, I would not be able to point to Jasper.

I wanted another man whom I could point to, hold accountable.

I have said, haven't I, that Claude was my lunacy?

I found him upstairs in a bar I chose just north of the Louvre. I chose the bar from a guidebook, which indicated that it had what the guide called a "joy room." This meant, I assumed, that men coupled on the premises. This assumption proved correct. The guide stressed that this bar was not recommended—"stay away" was what it cautioned.

Fetching young boys danced to a pulsing beat—I felt the floor throbbing with it—while older men stood and watched them from the bar. I was thirty-three that year and belonged to neither group.

On a giant video screen the great panther known as Eartha Kitt slithered against the bare torsos of muscle men and growled a song about mink coats and Cadillacs. It was a hissing number that was a hit for her that year.

In my real life, I don't frequent places like this. That's why I was there. My real life wouldn't do.

"Avez-vous l'heure?" I asked and asked, man after man. Finally, at three o'clock, I went upstairs with my fifth drink. The upstairs room was long and narrow. In the front, on another video screen, three well-built specimens cavorted on the tailgate of a pickup truck. It was parked in a desert. The men looked American. So did the desert. So did the pickup.

The screen gave off the only light.

I circled around a group of men who were watching the screen and began investigating the length of the room. Figures leaned against walls. Some were bent over, some were on their knees. In the middle of the room seven or eight men stood together, forming a boundary. One man was short enough for me to crane my neck over his shoulder. All these men were looking at three others, who were linked together in a chain fuck. The three men were the same height, roughly, and seemed to fit together well enough to keep the act going awhile. I wondered if that had been the principal attraction each had offered the other—the fit. Even in movies, where separate shots can be pieced together, men linked this way don't stick together long.

As expected, there was a smell.

There was more than one.

There were the usual smells.

I pushed through the barrier and went closer to the three men, the ones who were linked. The man in the middle, who was slamming and being slammed, reached out to me.

I chose Claude because he was the man in the middle.

"Aren't you being naughty enough?" I chided him in English.

I took a careful look at his face, so I'd recognize him when he came downstairs. I did not take stock of his body.

I DIDN'T have to approach him, he approached me. He asked, in English, if I was an American. I asked how he could tell. He said it was the way I looked at things. I did not see what was American about the way I looked at things and did not confide to him that I was looking at things as I was because I was without my glasses. Without them, I can't read a sign across a street. I'd had a lot to drink, to get my nerve, so I don't remember what we said. I must have made some allusion to having seen him upstairs, and he let out the highest, most out-of-control laugh I had ever heard. It was so high it startled people; men turned around to see from where it had come. It was the laugh of someone who probably didn't care much, or at all, about what people in a place like this thought of him. Or it was the laugh of someone who doesn't know how to laugh. It had merriment in it but was also ugly-sounding, piercing.

"Do you want to get out of here?" he asked me.

"You mean, take a walk?" I asked.

"Yes, we could take a walk," he said.

We left the place. We took our bottles of beer. We walked a few blocks and came upon a street I'd not seen before. I asked Claude the name of it, and I liked what he said: rue Tiquetonne.

It was a quiet street, a block or two long.

I pushed this man against a huge black door and pressed myself against him. I rubbed up and down. He had a bit of a stomach, it was in the way, so I unzipped his trousers, reached in, and grabbed.

"Jesus, you walk around with these?" I asked.

He laughed again. I covered his mouth with my free hand.

"Not a sound," I said.

He stopped.

I pressed hard against his mouth.

"Let's have a look," I said. I yanked his trousers down around his shoes. I let out a breath. I wasn't impressed, I was staggered. He was clearly pleased.

"*T'aime la grosse?*" he asked.

I just gaped.

He did to my trousers what I'd done to his.

I wasn't as ready as he was. I never am, not right away, and I felt incidental, beside him. If I went around all my life with what he went around with, I wouldn't bother with anyone who goes around with what I do. In fact, I don't. Who would? Jasper was ample and was, of course, far more handsome—but, I have to say this, Claude was more than ample.

We stood together in the quaint street with our pants around our ankles. I wanted to strip his off altogether, to see him bare. He had good thick legs, unlike Jasper, whose legs were thin, and Claude's had thick, heavy hair on them.

Of course, we couldn't take our clothes off on rue Tiquetonne, and it didn't seem likely we would do much of anything there, until Claude put his bottle on the sidewalk, crouched in front of me, and swallowed me into his face.

"Clean," he declared.

Something perfect was happening. A man with a bit of a pot, a giant's dong, who smelled of French cigarettes and what he'd done half an hour ago upstairs in a sleaze bar, not only had me in his mouth but had an excellent idea of what he was doing. Both his hands were devoted to me; he did not touch himself. I looked down at his crouching legs. He looked stranded down there between them, heavy and lonely, so I bent forward, leaned down, and gave him a grip.

He filled my hand.

There is just something different about being blown by a man who is bigger, who is much bigger, and if, on top of that, he does it adroitly and seems to like it, then that is really *something*. One of his hands was playing with my rear, a little too demurely. I told him what to do with it. I couldn't believe I was talking this way on a street. I'd never talked this way to Jasper, never talked this way in a bathhouse, and I was on a street in Paris giving specific, lurid instructions to a man I didn't know, as though I did this every night.

Maybe I should have. Maybe I should have done this all my life.

I spat in my hand and gave Claude long, slipping strokes. I could hear the slickness of it when I slid my hand down to his root.

If anything, he grew.

I moved myself around on his finger.

This was close to what I'd chosen him for.

I turned around, and he put his mouth on my backside as though it were all he'd ever wanted. I gripped his head and pressed it closer, harder against me.

I moved up and down on my feet.

"Can you do more?" I asked.

"Here?" he asked.

"Right here," I said.

He looked around, let out a breath.

I pulled him toward a car that was parked on the street, bent myself over the hood. It wasn't perfect, but it would do. He began tentatively, and I raised myself off the car and pressed up against him. It didn't hurt much, which surprised me, so I squirmed myself up, coaxed him in deeper.

Then it did not hurt at all.

He began.

"That's the way, fella," I said.

Except for us, the street was quiet.

Had I really called him "fella"?

All the windows on the street were dark.

I'd never called a man "fella."

Every tenth or twelfth time, every twentieth, he pulled himself all the way out. I felt him leave completely. He made me want more. All I wanted was more. I felt his hand under my shirt. He touched me in front. Then he jabbed into me again. He'd do a little more, then pull out again, then he'd force his way back in. Doing this, he moved himself from side to side. I'd never had it this way. Jasper hadn't done it this way.

A thought came to me then from far back, what Dominic had told me four years before, over an *eau de vie de prune,* about what a man can do so that Dominic could tell it had been hot.

I asked Claude to do it. I told him to.

This must have pretty much done it for him. I felt his excitement build.

He lifted me from the car, angling my body for a deeper lunge. He pounded down in me a few dozen times, quickly. Then I felt him pull back, almost withdrawing, and he held himself there. Then I felt him giving me exactly what I'd wanted.

He'd done it.

He bore down again, pressed himself against my back. He licked my neck.

It was everything I'd wanted.

And Dominic was right. It had been hot.

I felt him contract in me. I pulled away and picked his bottle off the sidewalk. I shook it and rinsed him off with foamy, tepid beer. This must have surprised him; he didn't laugh.

We straightened ourselves up. I watched Claude stuff himself into his trousers. He watched as I did the same, though with me it is a simpler operation. We started toward the corner. I walked behind him, to see whatever it was he did to get himself around. It was not something I could see.

Just then a taxi came into the street. A man and woman in evening dress alighted from it. They went into a building, through the door against which Claude and I had begun our deed.

Claude laughed at this. It was fine for him to laugh. He could laugh at everything now.

I let him laugh.

———————

THE BEDROOM window was curtainless, but it was not sunlight that awakened me. Claude snored, but it wasn't his snoring that awakened me. It was the smell. It made me look in the direction it was coming from, and because the smell was of urine I noticed, as I hadn't before, Claude's foreskin, a major flap of skin, which, hours before, I'd overlooked.

Looking at Claude, I remembered how, in the school in Canada that I was sent away to, the Carlisle twins from Buenos Aires had been the first uncircumcised boys I'd seen. The Carlisles were fraternal twins. One was a tall, handsome, oversized athletic fellow, who at thirteen already looked like a full-grown man. His name was Ian. The other, his brother, was smarter though not as well liked; he was a puny-looking thing, not handsome at all, and because I knew he was the second born I thought of him as the thing that had come later, that is, as Ian's afterbirth. It was the smaller one whom all the other boys called "the faucet." No one called Ian this, though Ian was just as uncircumcised as his twin. In fact, being the bigger of the two, he might have been said to be *more* uncircumcised. Of course, little boys don't often tease bigger, stronger, more strapping ones.

Seeing Claude put me in mind of an article I'd read a few years back about a surgeon in Texas who offered restoration to men who had all their lives felt incomplete because they'd been unsheathed. The procedure was a complicated one and was not, of course, bona fide restoration. What the surgeon did was take loose skin from a man's elbow, from between his toes—who knew from where?—and graft it onto the long ago denuded instrument. When the article appeared, in the early eighties, this Texan was said to be the only man in the country to perform this procedure, and he was well paid each time he did it.

Most of the men who had this surgery were from New York City, and because the procedure was done in stages, over several months, these men spent much time and more than a little money flying back and forth from Texas, all for their spanking new twenty-or-so-thousand-dollar foreskins. Claude's foreskin had cost him nothing, and I wished he didn't have it. I didn't like the look of it. I don't even like the idea. To see that flaccid collar of flesh undoes it all for me, and, of course, it entraps all kinds of smegma, and worse.

What I was smelling was more than a whiff. Claude smelled like a long-established, one-man history of micturation. Looking around Claude's room, I regretted being in it, regretted what drinking the night before had made me do with him in the rue Tiquetonne—until I remembered that I'd resolved to do it before I'd even *had* a drink. Drinking had made it sloppier, that was all.

I investigated Claude's—abode. It needed cleaning, it needed paint, it needed what it wasn't getting. It was beyond remedy, I thought. In addition to the bedroom, with the mattress on the floor, there was, through a doorless passage, a living room, with clothing for all seasons strewn about.

There was an upright piano and a piano bench. In one corner was a cello; in another a saxophone. Since all I'd needed from Claude, from anyone, was the one event on the rue Tiquetonne, I didn't know why I had come with him here.

I wondered if Claude would be able to play the Chopin nocturne on the saxophone.

In the bathroom, I washed myself. I used an unclean towel. Then I went into the kitchen and found a bowl to use as a basin. I filled it with hot water and looked around for a sponge. The only sponge appeared to have been used to scrub floors, though the floors didn't look scrubbed. I rinsed the sponge as well as I could, lathered it, squeezed much black water out of it. I took it in the bowl of hot water, with the soap, into the room where Claude was sleeping.

I knelt on the mattress and began washing him. The sheets were dry; all the smell was of Claude himself. I was pulling back his foreskin, looking at everything under it, geishalike, when he awakened.

Although I could not imagine it being any clearer, he asked me, "What are you doing?"

"I'm cleaning you," I told him.

"Why?" he asked.

"Because, frankly, lambie-nuts, you're fragrant," I answered.

He gave that laugh again. He didn't seem at all insulted. I saw that a back molar was missing—something else I hadn't noticed in the dark.

Then he said, not laughing, "You must love me a lot to care so much about me."

What response could I give? I didn't see how an effort to eliminate an odor could be so quickly taken as a sign of love. It occurred to me that possibly no one had done this for him before.

Possibly he hadn't done it for himself.

I was uneasy just touching him, at seeing where leftover fluids had crusted: dried white paste flaked around the wedge. Of course, the night before I'd more than touched him, but this wasn't then; it wasn't dark anymore, I wasn't drunk anymore; this was a fresh morning, a day that hadn't been.

Claude lay back and let me work on him. He put a hand on my head and messed with my hair. I realized that some of what I was cleaning could have come from me.

"Do you play the saxophone?" I asked.

"I'm a composer, I play a lot of instruments," Claude said.

"Are you a serious composer? Do you write serious music?" I asked him.

"What other kind is there?" Claude asked.

"Oh, there're all kinds of other kinds," I said. "There is background music, Broadway musical music, motion picture music, there's airport music."

Claude took my hand with the sponge in it, pressed it against himself, selecting places for me to clean.

"There are two kinds of music," he said. "There is music that is heard, and there is music that must be listened to. My music must be listened to."

"Is it that simple?" I asked. I was soaping his gonads. He had such handsome ones. They were superb and more than made up for all his excess stomach. "Are you a good composer?"

The answer Claude gave this foolish question was so assured, so without aggression, he made me believe it might be so.

"One of the best" is what Claude said.

———

CLAUDE WAS French Canadian. He was in Paris because the province of Quebec had given him a pretty—as opposed to a handsome—sum to live there for a year. The grant was given with the idea that he might write some music, but Claude explained that no music was demanded.

He was working as hard at music as if it had been demanded.

If my ear were sharper, I would have heard differences between Parisian French and what Claude spoke, but my ear is not good for this, and I heard no difference. In any case, we spoke mostly English, which was too bad, because it has for centuries been accepted, I believe, that the best place to learn a language is the bed.

Claude took me to a concert where one of his pieces was performed. It was a six-minute piece for oboe and piano, and Claude was the pianist. The piece was highly energetic, and its piano section reminded me of pieces Jasper and I had heard a few years ago by Xenakis, whose music, though exciting, can be hard to listen to. I liked Claude's music, and seeing him perform gave me a chance to look at him more critically. His stomach *was* a bit much, he *was* rather chunky in the rear, and then there was the matter of his face. Everywhere I looked there was too much or too little of it, and almost every part of it was wrong: the chin was too square, the lips too thin, the nose bulbous, but, as is the case with just about everyone, compliments could be paid to the eyes.

Claude's were alert, smart-looking eyes, and so dark that on stage they appeared black. His was the last piece performed that night, and after the performance it turned out that he had some friends in the audience. He introduced me to them as his lover, put his hands all over me. I was embarrassed by just about all of this. Two of his friends were women, both singers, and it struck me that what Claude was doing was not only indiscreet, which I didn't care about, but unworldly. Thank God, no one asked him how we'd met. He would have told them.

Five of us had dinner on Boulevard Montparnasse, which killed off forever the notion that there is no bad food to be had in France. Some of the vilest food on earth is dished up in Paris nightly. It was at this dinner that I was exposed to Claude's passion for steak tartare.

I watched him crack a raw egg over a mound of the rawest-looking ground beef I'd ever seen, and he mashed it all together with capers, salted it heavily, and asked for, and was brought, Worcestershire sauce. When he did all this it was the only time he gave me less than his total attention, and when he began to eat it there was no mistaking his delight. Claude said that he did not consider it a good day unless he had eaten at least one portion of excellent steak tartare.

"You eat this every day?" I asked.

Once again I heard that laugh. He laughed, I expect, at the horror he'd heard in my voice.

"Twice, if I'm lucky," he answered.

We went to dinner a few more times, always at places that served steak tartare. The night before I left for New York, I was in need of a good dinner and took Claude to a place I'd always liked, owned by a chef named Rostang. Claude looked nice in a tie. When he saw that Rostang had no steak tartare on his menu, he sulked. Rostang had ravioli with langoustines, cold lobster consommé with chives, he did wondrous things with oysters, with pigeon, with quail, but none of these were steak tartare. Claude seemed crestfallen, and that was hard for me. I pointed out to him that steak tartare is not a test of a kitchen. Claude said he didn't care about testing a kitchen, he cared about eating steak tartare.

I asked the captain if someone in the kitchen could improvise steak tartare, and of course someone could. It was done. That made Claude happy.

Claude said many times that he was amazed to be loved by anyone so beautiful. God, that was nice to hear. It was a little sad, maybe, but it was an awfully pretty thing to say—what faggot *doesn't* adore flattery?—and, in a selfish way, it thrilled me. It went to my head. I hadn't heard anything like that from Jasper.

I began to have a thought, one I shouldn't have had. I wondered about men who are not handsome, who are not everyone's ideal. Could it be that they make, because they are more grateful, better love?

Many things shamed me when I thought about Claude. It shamed me to be evaluating the prowess of a man whom I would not ordinarily desire. It was such a shabby thing to ponder, especially to ponder it while he was at it. There were other regrets: that I'd chosen Claude for the reason I had. That was shabby—hideous, really—and it shamed me that I'd begun to find a way to look at him, as though at a slant, that made him not at all bad-looking. I became fond of his face. I liked being with him more than I'd expected.

I began to be afraid that I might be enough of a fool to slip into love with Claude.

I even hoped, for his sake, that he didn't have the virus. For mine, too, I suppose.

Claude always touched me when we walked on a street. In cafés, he'd squeeze me under tables. In bed, he would pass me a lighted postcoital cigarette. With Jasper, there were no postcoital cigarettes. It was bliss to smoke with Claude in bed. What most surprised me, though, was the absence of pain: Claude had given me none.

I'd been prepared for pain.

THE REASON Jasper and I had stopped playing five years before was that in 1982 I had an abscess. Because I was taking some classes at Columbia, I was examined by a doctor affiliated with the health service. This doctor did not advise me of anything I could do to relieve the pain. Instead, he said three times that he suspected I was homosexual and had used my body in a way it had not been designed for.

He told me that was why I had the abscess. What did I expect? he asked.

This doctor had clearly not read his Sade, who argues,

in his *Philosophy in the Bedroom,* that if God had not meant for men to join together, if this were anathema to Him, He would not have supplied men with an orifice so well suited to the purpose. I did not waste Sade on this doctor. If he'd been a good doctor, what was he doing at the college health service? Of course, I haven't found many people who buy Sade's argument. I don't know that *I* buy it. But it is an argument.

The abscess grew. I could feel it through my trousers, sitting was painful. One morning I was taking it uptown to a real doctor, a specialist, and the whole thing burst under me in the backseat of a taxi. My trousers were soaked. It was hard to believe that something the size of an acorn had released such copious liquid and such a stench. There is simply no reason for anything to smell so foul. That this putrescence had issued from *me,* that it was *I* smelling I, was—to say the least—disquieting.

The cabdriver was a man about seventy. He had probably seen the nadir of the world in his taxi, but he was either devoid of olfaction or was an immensely civilized man. He did not comment on my mishap. I counted myself lucky to be in his cab and not with one of those snarling curmudgeons who hate you the instant you set foot in their cab.

Since I knew that one in every fifteen hundred people do not come out of it, when I had surgery I refused general anesthesia. This annoyed the surgeon, who began to cut before the local or the sedative had taken effect. I felt his knife but was also somewhat loopy and asked him if he could, since he was cutting me down there anyway, toss in a buttocks lift while he was at it.

This was a way to handle the pain, but the surgeon told me not to talk. He scolded me for not making sense. I'd heard what I'd said; it had made sense to me. I disliked this surgeon; his cutting was sloppy, as was his poststitching.

Three years after the surgery, the unhealed scar still

hurt on occasion. Even now, ten years after the procedure, five years after Claude, it is sensitive when touched.
It is, in fact, exquisite.

I don't know why the abscess had to stop everything
with Jasper. What Jasper wanted was the one thing I had
to stop. It was, by the way, the only thing I had to stop.
I would have been happy with a lifetime of frottage. But
this was not enough for Jasper, who thought of frottage
as being the aperitif and of a blow job as the hors d'oeuvre.
Either would have been ample for me. Some of us are not
German.

Also, in 1982, I was aware, though dimly, of what
was at that time called GRID. Gay-related immune disorder. It's odd how partial the world is to acronyms, as
though by naming something, by assigning a word to it,
we risk making it real. "Why can't they give it a real
word?" I would object to anyone who would listen.

Recently, though, I read that in the latest supplement
to the *Oxford English Dictionary,* AIDS has been admitted into the lexicon. Today it is a proper word, a noun,
just like "eggshell" or "pomegranate." This rise in its status doesn't make me any happier to use it.

Even when it was called GRID, I knew probably as
well as the next fellow how it was being transmitted, and
it may have been something more than remembering the
pain of surgery that kept me from Jasper. I may have
worried that being with Jasper, being passive with anybody, would put me at risk. I don't like this, and I tend
to deny it, but possibly some trust was lost. If any love
trundled off with it, I must not have noticed.

MY SECOND week back in New York, Jasper made
for us what he called a simple repast. We had spaghettini
with slivers of white truffle, a leg of lamb marinated for a
week in Barolo and a sprig of rosemary, a salad of Swiss

chard glossed in walnut oil. We had three cheeses, and tangerine ice. All this was a lifetime away from steak tartare.

Claude had sent a turbid letter. I wrote back two pages that topped, I am sure, anything Lana Turner ever wrote to Johnny Stompanato. Why I did this, I can't say, but when Claude wrote again so did I. Putting things on paper to him, gushing, I didn't feel convinced. I'm not sure I wanted to.

I didn't tell Jasper everything about Claude. I told him that I'd met a composer in Paris whose work had reminded me of Xenakis, that we'd had a few dinners. I didn't tell Jasper I had found Claude in the middle of a chain fuck, that I had looked for him there. I didn't tell Jasper about the rue Tiquetonne or the five times after it. I can't say why those other times happened. Telling Jasper these partial truths was of course, more dishonest than it would have been to tell him nothing.

After dinner we went downstairs with a large snifter of a superb cognac, a *fine champagne* we had found on the rue du Mont-Thabor. Jasper put on some Xenakis. Then he surprised me with news.

"I had a blood test," he began.

"You did?" I asked.

"It came back negative, so I'm still a clean machine," Jasper said.

"That's good to know," I said. "That's awfully good. Were you worried?" I asked.

"Timothy, I don't worry about things like that," Jasper said.

"What do you mean, *like that?*" I asked.

"Things I can't control," said Jasper.

"You mean things you *couldn't* control, don't you, because you *can* control them now?" I asked.

Jasper looked at me, and the Xenakis slid into an odd, tinkling passage.

"What do you mean?" he asked me.

I looked back at him. I looked at him closely. "I hope you're not playing without rubbers, papa."

Jasper's entire expression changed. I will not forget his troubled look. I still see it all the time and hear him saying, "I don't think I could fuck with a rubber."

He was so earnest about it.

"You don't *think?*" I asked. "You mean you haven't tried?"

"I don't think I could do it," said Jasper.

"Then you'd better not fuck at all," I said.

"Sex is very important to me," Jasper said.

"I know it is," I said.

"It used to be important to you," Jasper said.

"If you weren't worried, why did you have the test? What would you have done if it had come back positive?"

"You know I don't speculate," Jasper said. "I was hoping it would be negative, and it was. I imagine yours would be, too."

"Are you telling me to have it?" I asked.

"No, I'm just saying that since I'm negative, if you *did* take it you would very likely be negative, too," said Jasper.

"Were you prepared for a positive result?" I asked.

"How can anyone prepare for that?" Jasper asked.

"That's just it," I said. "No one can. I'm not prepared. I won't have the test."

"You haven't been with that many people, have you, Timothy?" Jasper asked.

This was the first time he had asked me this. He hadn't seemed to care before. If he had asked me a month ago, I could have told him there had been no one. I remembered Dominic, of course, that I'd been with him once, for twelve seconds, thirteen years ago, but because it had been I who had done it to Dominic, because Dominic had done nothing to me, because he'd claimed that his sphincter was "intact"—and because it had been thirteen years ago—I expect that if Jasper had asked me a month earlier, I would have told him there had been no one at all.

I could no longer tell him this.

I said to him, "It only takes one."

"Maybe you've been lucky," said Jasper.

BEFORE I took the test, I began looking in the streets for signs of illness. I noticed men who looked thin. I took notice of the way everybody walked. An amazing mass of people walked steadily and appeared untroubled. I studied people's eyes, alert for that anxious cast, which I had not seen before, until I saw it in the eyes of the infected, the ill, in photographs, in magazines. For many people, I believe, possibly for most, the prevailing image, and what people still expect to see, is a ravaged face, like Rock Hudson's at the end. That is what I looked for on the streets of my neighborhood. It is what I expected to see all over New York, thousands of men looking like Rock Hudson, with those same frightened eyes. Not everyone looks that way.

I didn't know yet about cytomegalovirus, which can among other things cause retinitis, and in turn alter the pigmentation and the outward appearance of the eye. It can also make the eye sightless, legally blind. It wasn't this I was looking for, though. I looked into faces, to see if they were wasting, and at people's skin, around their necks, on their legs in summer, if they wore shorts, to see who had and didn't have Kaposi's.

I don't believe I ever saw a Kaposi's lesion on the street. This for a long time was a problem of the epidemic, and still is, that the streets are full of, teeming with, thousands of men and women who have the look of health. You see people at the rallies who don't, and at ACT UP meetings, though infrequently; you see people emaciated or in wheelchairs, and some have facial lesions, but you do not see them every day in line at the bank, on subways, or in restaurants. Taking a weeknight stroll in the Village or on

the Upper West Side, you would not know, from what
you will see, that fifty percent of the men in this city—
that is, men who have been drawn to each other—are at
this minute, even as we speak, said to have the virus
working in their bodies, eating their immunities.

These men are one part of it. Many people are afraid
of this illness—they had friends who have died, they have
seen photographs, and they are afraid, without knowing
exactly of what. It is something other than, more than, a
fear of death. A woman I know, a friend, an executive,
has been this year with three married men. None of these
men used protection; the woman feels safe and dismisses
me when I speak of risk, and in restaurants this friend
will not taste food from my plate.

I waited to take the test. I was afraid. Even today,
when much can be done, there are men afraid to take the
test. Men who will not be tested, and women, too, who
will be undiagnosed, will not be treated, or will be treated
too late, and these man and these women will, in time,
find themselves in a final condition.

Sometime in the eighties, the then surgeon general
commented, when asked, that he did not believe there will
ever be a cure for acquired immune deficiency syndrome.
When I read this prediction, which was quoted in *Time*
or *Newsweek,* not in any arcane journal, I thought of all
the men and women in laboratories around the world
working on the virus, and of all the millions of people—
men, women, children—who are infected, and ill, and
holding on. What does a remark like this, by the surgeon
general, do for any of them? Will it make research fund-
ing pour forth increasingly? Reading this, I thought it would
have been better left unsaid. I also thought that the surgeon general was very likely a fine, perhaps even a superb,
physician, but that he was not God.

In 1987, when I was reluctant to take the test, there
was reason to be. There was not at that time any FDA-
approved antiviral medication, and, worse, only a sketchy

understanding of the virus. And, of course, not every scientist believed that the virus was the cause of the illness. This is still true. There is a retrovirologist in California who insists that HIV is an old virus, quite harmless. He has said he wouldn't mind being injected with it. He has not yet put his life on the line to prove this, however. There are people in advanced stages of the illness in whom the virus cannot be found. In 1986, in 1987, many physicians, including mine, were opposed to the test. So little could be done for a patient that to test positive for the antibody was, at that time, more or less tantamount to a death sentence. It was thought by many, perhaps rightly, that the anxiety of testing positive, the stress, would further weaken a person's already weakened immunity. A handful of men who were ill as early as 1980 live today. They are no less real for being exceptional. In fact, it must be said of these men that they are, if anything, more real, because they have put up a fight, have had a hand, have had a say, still do, and insist upon life. No doubt there are many who have tried as hard who did not succeed. Then, there are those who do nothing at all for themselves. I've known a few. There are people enrolled in drug-study trials who miss appointments—they're feeling good that day, they want to forget—and many stop taking medications. Many give up and die. I don't know if there is courage in dying. There may be. I don't know enough to say. I am sure, however, there is not any courage in being dead.

I waited six months. That was the time it would take, if Claude had given me the virus, for antibodies to show in my blood.

Jasper still spent every weekend with me, but we did nothing physical together. If I tested negative, I would speak with Jasper about monogamy. Maybe he would be ready for it now. If he would give me his word, we could do everything together again.

Until I had the test, I could not go near him. I still had

a great affection for his body, and it was lovely to think we might play again.

The day I was to take the test, I found a postcard under the door. It was not stamped, hadn't come through the mail. Curiously, it was a pen-and-ink drawing of Frédéric Chopin, and the first thing it made me think of, before I flipped it over to read the message, was the early morning that Claude had taken me down to the Seine, below Ile Saint-Louis, and played for me, after practicing a few days, the Chopin Nocturne no. 2, under the bridge, inside the arch of it, which gave a rich echo to Claude's bass saxophone. Claude played the Chopin cleanly, gravely, reaching low notes that were something to hear. The melody was free of clutter, without filigree, stripped to its barest line. It made me happy, and when Claude finished the piece I thought for an instant of inviting him up—my windows were just above us, and I had chilled champagne. I didn't, though; I wanted it to stay just Jasper's place, and mine.

Even for a postcard, the message was terse. It said, "Claude was killed last week in Paris. They told me you should know." That was all. The writer closed by identifying himself, not by name but as a musician from Vienna. He said he was in town for a few days, on tour. He took longer at this than he did with the news.

One thought came to me, and it was that I had not before heard anyone introduce himself as a "musician." Doesn't a cellist introduce himself as such, a pianist as a pianist, a trumpeter, a trumpeter?

I thought about the word—killed. What did the writer mean by it? The word told me nothing; it didn't say whether Claude had been shot by someone, stabbed by someone, hit by a car. I read the message again and found no more in it than I had. It was void. Why hadn't this musician from Vienna put himself out enough to call me on the telephone? What kind of person is it who slips news of death under a door?

I found the telephone number for the *commissariat de police*. It really is true, you can find anything you need in that little book of maps that cabdrivers use, *Paris par arrondissement*. I gave my name, and Claude's, and spoke to a few men, who were not helpful. Then I spoke to a woman, who was. I asked her if it was true. She said it was. I asked her where Claude had been found, and by whom. She could not tell me by whom, but Claude had been found in his apartment. Was he dead when he was found? I asked. The woman said he was. How had he been killed? I asked. My French was such that I had to rephrase the question. When she realized I was asking how it had been done, the woman told me a knife had been used. They had not found the killer, she told me, when I asked.

I did not have my test that day.

————————

MONTHS LATER, the day I took the test, I ended up not taking it. My doctor drew blood, and because he knew I like to walk, and because he thought I was of sound mind, he gave it to me in a tube to take downtown, to an address on First Avenue at Twenty-first Street. I left my doctor's office with a white paper bag, almost as if I were going to school with my lunch. The lab was about fifty blocks from my doctor's office, and on every block, at each street I crossed, I thought only of the blood in the tube, and of my life and whatever was left of it.

A building next to the lab was being demolished. There was a Dumpster on the street. It was filled with things that had been cut down, hauled out, walls, windows, floors, and such. It was right there, that Dumpster; you couldn't miss it. So I peeled the label from the tube and threw my blood away.

six

six

"IGNORE THE note," Jasper instructed my answering machine. "The note is not accurate."

I went through the mail that had accumulated in the two weeks I'd been in California and found nothing in it from Jasper. Jasper was seldom warm on the telephone, but when I played the tape back I was sure I heard something in his voice I hadn't before.

My first thought was that Jasper had written to tell me that after seventeen years he was tired of me.

When Jasper and I were together—when we were bicycling in Paris, for example, or the twelve or so miles from Provincetown to Truro, where there is such a magnificent beach; when the same picture in a gallery would catch us; when Jasper told me stories from history, as when, one night at dinner, Jasper told me a long, complicated narrative that took me more than my best to follow, and in the story there was an emperor or a duke, I think, and a stolen hat and finally Jasper said, "And that was the beginning of the First World War," when he was talking this way to me; and when we could enter a dining room together and entertain each other through a spectacular dinner—there was never anyone better to have dinner with than Jasper—at those times I would know without question that it was having been with Jasper so long that gave my life whatever shape it had. I knew that keeping Jasper amused, making him happy, and keeping myself deserving of him, was my one achievement.

Hearing Jasper's voice on the tape, hearing him instruct me to ignore his note, I thought that there must be an absolute moral balance of right and wrong. Something in Jasper's voice was telling me that three years before I had made a mistake in being with Claude and that I was losing Jasper now because of it. I believed it would be that simple, that tit-for-tat, that nickel-and-dime.

Then it came to me that I was to ignore the note because he had changed his mind. This wasn't something I believed in a thoughtful way, it was more of a seizure. It came from nowhere and gripped me. As it turned out, it was true. In a way I had lost Jasper.

"Do *not* read the note," Jasper said on the tape.

After seven or eight tries I finally got him on the telephone.

"What note?" I asked.

"The note I sent you," Jasper said.

"There's no note from you here," I told him.

Jasper was silent.

"When did you mail it?" I asked.

"The sixth of April," said Jasper.

It was odd, I thought, that he could answer so precisely.

"Maybe you forgot the zip code," I suggested.

"Timothy, I don't forget zip codes," said Jasper.

In fact, Jasper frequently forgot zip codes.

"What did you say in the note?" I asked him.

"I'll tell you when I see you," Jasper answered.

"Papa, if something's happened I wish you'd tell me."

"It can wait, Timothy," Jasper said.

"*What* can wait? Tell me, please," I said.

"We'll talk about it when we see each other," Jasper said.

Jasper had a way of bringing conversations to a close. Everything stopped, was final, and when he did this he yielded nothing. When Jasper closed a subject that subject was closed.

"I hate it when you do this," I told him.

"I can't help you," Jasper told me then.

Always, when Jasper came to my house, when I heard his key turn in the lock, I'd put myself in front of the door. Jasper did not have to look around for me, or to call out; he did not ever find me in the darkroom, on the telephone, or in the shower: I always waited for him by the door. I was always the first thing he saw. Usually, I stepped up barefoot onto his shoes. No doubt, with Jasper, I was much like a friendly dog.

That night I had negronis ready for us. It had been a while since we'd had them together. I made big ones. Most nights we sat together on the couch. That night Jasper sat in the enormous leather chair, which put him at an angle to me.

"The note never came," I told him.

Jasper leaned back in the deep chair. "As you know, I've not felt right since Mexico. I've been to half a dozen internists, and none of them could understand why the problem hadn't cleared up."

We'd been to Cabo San Lucas over Christmas, then went to Puerto Vallarte for New Year's. The problem that hadn't cleared up for Jasper was one that afflicts many North Americans in Mexico. They usually suffer for a day or two, they run to their room, praying that the hotel maid is not that minute cleaning it. Usually, people take paregoric or eat some cheese, and that's it, it's gone, they're good as new. Nothing had made Jasper good as new. We'd been to Mexico before and hadn't suffered. That's why Jasper's affliction was a puzzlement. All we could think was that it had been the oysters, which we has watched a man shuck for us and had eaten on the half shell, just down the beach from where we were staying. That night

Jasper took to bed. He said he was feeling more wretched than he'd ever felt before.

We'd been back from Mexico four months. Jasper was still not quite right. I doubted an oyster could remain pernicious for so long a time.

"I know that. It's why you haven't been coming into the city, and why we haven't seen each other as much. That's not what you put in the letter, is it?"

"Too much negroni juice," Jasper said. He hadn't called it that for a while; I realized then that I'd missed hearing him call it that. "I found out I had the virus," he said, "and I tried to kill myself."

It is odd how hearing something you hadn't heard before, something you would not have known without being told, makes it all at once a fact.

Instantly, the fact became irrevocable. When Jasper told me this, I heard, at first, nothing but the fact. I did not hear his bitterness, his hatred of having this to tell. Jasper showed none of this, kept it from me, but it was there for each of us to know.

It was my turn to say something. All I had was my first thought: I was glad he had failed. I didn't say that, though. What I said was, "That is not a thing to do."

We looked at one another.

"How did you try?" I asked.

"I took some pills and tried to asphyxiate myself."

I couldn't picture Jasper doing either of these things. I could not imagine him contemplating them. None of what Jasper was telling me connected to anyone I knew, to the man I had *known*. Instead of Jasper, I thought of Tom and his three prescriptions, of Sylvia Plath sticking her head into the oven. These thoughts came automatically. They were reflexes. In the years since Tom checked himself out, I had not been able to think of it as anything but giving up. Tom had made the wrong choice, I thought. He could have made another; Tom had not been without choices.

This isn't a generous way to think. I know it isn't large. My sympathy is finite, and what I have of it is for those who choose to live.

"How did you try to asphyxiate yourself?" I asked.

Jasper said, "I left the car running and lay under it."

"Why didn't it work? Did Oliver find you?" I asked him.

"Do we have to talk about this?" he asked.

I held back. I didn't ask him if he was going to try again. I told him I was glad he had failed, and I asked him, wasn't he, too?

"I didn't want to fail," Jasper said.

I heard that slowly, word by word. I couldn't think about it, couldn't take it in. I wasn't ready to. The thought I did have was this man, whom I loved more than anyone alive, had not thought of me when he tried to take his life. He knew I had the virus and was willing to leave me with it. He was what I lived for, and he had been eager to take himself away and leave me without him.

I did not tell any of this. What I did say to him was, "You know, papa, if I hadn't known you I might never have had a negroni."

"But you have known me," said Jasper.

THE MAN I mentioned before, the one who got out of bed one day and found himself without aluminum foil, was me. I'd become sick a few months after Jasper tried to kill himself. Like Dominic, I had health-care workers in my house round the clock for many months, and *that* after seven months in the hospital. Unlike Dominic, I'd never gotten around to insurance—I just hadn't thought of it—and because illness requires medical attention, which is expensive in these United States—every other country in the civilized world protects its citizens—a year and a half of treatment took just about all the money I had.

There was nothing to do but start over.

I went into the hospital with two infections, pneumocystis and chicken pox. This was in 1990, and I had opportunistic infections, OIs as they are called. They are what I had instead of immunity. In the hospital, I got new infections. These are so common they have a medical name: nosocomial infection. Many patients get these illnesses in hospitals, even those with normal immunity; without immunity, one is just that much likelier to get them.

The human immunodeficiency virus is not airborne; it is not easily spread. Nosocomial infections, however, are very easily spread; they are parasites, and every hospital is full of them: microorganisms, bacteria are simply at large in the air. They flock to and thrive within people with lowered immunity. Staff members will have unwashed hands, or unchanged gloves; nurses may have uncontrolled coughs, or be carriers of streptococcus, or there will be mycoplasmas in the water pipes. If a *doctor* has unwashed hands, or in any way infects a patient, if he prescribes the wrong medicine, it has a different name: iatrogenic disease. In some hospitals, patients with the virus—that is, AIDS patients—are isolated. Sometimes this is for the patient's safety, but more often it is done for what is considered the safety of others. Actually, it does make sense to isolate patients with the virus: it may give *them* a little safety from everybody else.

Of course, some patients will want visitors.

Of infections treated in hospitals, about one-third are nosocomial. Hospital stays are extended to treat them, often by more than a week, and the annual cost of treating nosocomial infections in the United States is estimated at three billion dollars per annum, and like everything else it's going up. All this, and not one good glass to drink from, or a proper ice cube anywhere.

One night I moaned to Jasper about the shaved ice and about how sick to death I was of paper cups. Two days later, when he came to see me again, he came through the door carrying an ice chest filled with big cubes of handsome ice. Nestled in it was a thermos filled with pre-mixed negronis. Jasper had made them as I like them, with Bombay gin, and had thought to bring along with him, from his house across the river, two superb tumblers for us to drink from.

I watched him as he poured the red ambrosia into the lovely clear glass.

I had never tasted such perfection in a cocktail. Jasper pulled a chair closer to my bed. He saw me as I was, with herpes zoster lesions covering my face and an IV dripping acyclovir into my arm. These grotesque herpes, which began as chicken pox and became herpes in the hospital, were only on my face, they were nowhere else, but they were *all over* my face. When a doctor, not my doctor, brought interns into my room to look at them, *in vivo* as it were, I referred to them as my "carbuncles."

The interns looked at me with grave faces. The shingles were red and purple; some were the size of shirt buttons, some the size of chestnuts. For three months I hadn't been allowed to shave for fear of spreading them. They spread anyway. I could not keep my hands off them. They were fascinating to the touch. Jasper had always disliked facial hair, abhorred it, really, but he had brought me superb negronis, and poured them over wonderful ice into a handsome glass for me, and he was able to look at what was possibly the ugliest beard on the earth that night.

He was having a cocktail hour with me. He was handsome, he was charming—he was there—and though I felt, and must have looked to him, like the end of the world, Jasper gave me a perfect hour.

That night I was loved.

———

IN 1988, when I heard my test result, it was about six months after the postcard from the Viennese musician. I'd had blood drawn, not by my doctor, and I had dropped it off myself at a place near Sheridan Square. I was told to use any name I wanted and that the result would take about two weeks. Since Jasper had tested negative, I thought I had a chance. There was no knowing about Claude. Two weeks passed, then three, then four. Jasper and I went to Paris in June.

Most places that test for HIV will not disclose results over the telephone. The place I went to did. That was why I'd chosen it.

I didn't make the call, though. In Paris, I could think of little else, then of nothing else, and on a late afternoon I called New York. Jasper was out on his bicycle.

Until I heard it, I hadn't known how immense a terror one word can contain: positive.

It was hard to tell Jasper, but I told him at once. His first piece of advice was that I tell no one. He said it wasn't a challenge I should put to a friend. This seemed good advice to me at the time, and I took it.

For two years I remained asymptomatic. That's not my word, it is what you are called when you still look like everybody else. You can also feel like everybody else, except that knowing you are positive can make you live in dread. Only Jasper knew my secret, and that is what it was, a secret. It became shameful, hideous. Tonight, in Los Angeles with Dominic, after a year and a half of illness and half a year in a highly medicated remission, I believe that Jasper's advice was not as wise as we had thought. When you live with a secret you will live *like* someone with a secret; and it may show, it may put you on edge, and you may end up looking like your secret.

You cease to be yourself, you become your secret. People may be unusually observant and tell you that you are letting yourself go. If they are kind, if they care about you, they may want to know why you are letting yourself go. One friend, an awfully good one as as smart as they come, said, "You don't have AIDS, so what is your excuse?" She wanted to know.

The loneliness of keeping the secret can bury you. It helped bury Jasper. It hasn't buried Dominic yet, and I am hoping, of course, that it won't.

THE FIRST image I saw of the virus, as opposed to images of people who carry it, was in the *National Geographic,* in the summer of 1986.

I've read quite a bit about it since. Back then, and still, most images in the press or on television showed people in such advanced states of wasting that they appeared less lively than dead people I've seen in paintings and photographs. I've not ever seen a dead person live, in the flesh. There was a room in the funeral home where both my father and then my mother were, as they say, "laid out." I'd seen enough of them alive, I felt no need to look at them in death.

The image of the virus was impressive and was rather beautiful, I thought, against its black background. The curve, which was of a lymphocyte, looked like soft, voluptuous flesh, and the clusters of deep blue, almost purple, dots in the image had a kind of majesty about them. It was elegant-looking and difficult to connect with the cachectic people, invariably men, who had posed for cameras on their last days.

In captions, they were frequently called victims and were photographed, usually, on hospital beds. Some effort had been made to groom them for the camera. They did not look, these men, as though they had made this effort themselves. They appeared to lack even what strength is needed to hold a glint of rage in their eyes.

I wanted to know what it was that had come into my body, and into Jasper's, that could make me look, in time, worse than dead, and to feel whatever that would feel like, too.

I was more afraid of how I would look than of how I would feel. The appearance of the people with the virus, how they look physically, is more widely documented than what they feel under their skin, inside themselves.

I did not believe, of course, that any of it would happen to Jasper.

It was mine for life, this virus, barring a miracle. If it was going to be part of me, I was obliged to know it well.

What was it, exactly, that, left to itself, could take light away? Cytomegalovirus had blinded many.

What was it that could stop my breath, my heart, and be the last part of me to die?

The image in *National Geographic* had been magnified to thirty-five thousand times its size. No mention was made in the article or in the captions of artificial colors being used. Most readers of *National Geographic* will doubtless know, without being told, that they are looking at the work of a coloring artist. But I didn't, not right away. In fact, it hadn't occurred to me that anyone would disguise or in any way fictionalize the virus. Why would anyone want to see a false image when there is a real image to be seen? Why would anyone want to glamorize a nightmare? It took me awhile. I had thought, when seeing this image, that the reason I had been feeling askew was that my blood was overwhelmed by thousands of blue dots the size of pinpoints.

Three years later, I was able to see the virus without artificial colors. I saw it magnified to three hundred and fifty thousand times its diameter. This opportunity did not fall into my lap. I had to ask around and write letters and put myself out to make it happen. It took weeks to get an appointment with the scientist in charge of the electron microscope at the Pasteur Institute, in Paris.

It took persistence.

I'd wanted to see the virus move. My idea was that if

I could see the thing in motion, I would then know what it was that I had to try to stop. This was, of course, naive, grossly uninformed, but I didn't know that, so it didn't stop me.

The scientist who showed me the virus, who knew as much about viral morphologies as any man in the world, explained that the electron microscope is unable to examine living virus. It can only look at cultured virus.

He showed me how he does it. He puts a drop of virally infected blood into a green medium, which is like a paste; he puts it under high heat, and by this process the intricacies of a virion are highlighted.

In the microscope, the virus is monochromatic, and it is in stasis.

Before a virus particle is prepared for the electron microscope it must be made static. It must be dead. No one, not even the greatest retrovirologist in the world, has seen the virus in motion in the microscope.

I LEARNED as much as I could about the virus so that I could tell Jasper something about it. Jasper had gotten into a habit of saying that he would not live to see this or that.

WHEN JASPER died, I stopped reading about the virus for a while. There is not a great deal of readable prose in the field. Scientists care about their peers. That is who they write for. Also, I wanted to learn something else, Italian maybe, or how to make color photographs, that is, how to light and print them, which is something I should have known years before. I also had some curiosity about the use of nanometric light. When Jasper was alive, I thought that if I could tell him what the virus is, what it was he had, he would know it well enough then to give it a contest.

I wanted him to oppose it with me.

Sometimes it is just a bit too onerous to oppose a thing alone, and now that I am doing it I feel I'm staying alive for no one's pleasure but mine.

ONE AFTERNOON, the last time we were in Paris together, the day before I left so that Oliver Ingraham could come for the Bastille Day—Jasper and I walked all the way home to Ile Saint-Louis from an exhibit at the Musée du Petit Palais at which we had seen jewels designed by four generations of the Cartier family.

Designs were shown from the 1860s up to the 1950s. The galleries at the Musée du Petit Palais were crowded with men and women who had alike been made to gasp at works of incomparable beauty, the splendor of which we are unlikely to see again.

Many of the jewels were laid in unimaginably intricate settings. You could look at them, you could study them— but without seeing them you would not have been able, not in the richest life, to *imagine* them. Looking at them directly, even when they were right in front of you, you still could not imagine them.

The most spectacular, the most opulent designs had been executed in the thirties, during the world's Great Depression. I was struck especially by a summer parasol. It had been made in 1928, of apricot-colored silk covered with Chantilly lace. Its shank was of carved coral and ivory interlaid with strips of black laquer. The rounded handle was made of coral, delicately crafted to fit in a small woman's hand. Little diamonds were embedded in it.

This was displayed in the large central gallery, superbly lit, and surrounded by diamond bracelets that had belonged to Gloria Swanson. There was an emerald neck-

lace created for Merle Oberon. Bow-tie pins of enamel
and sapphires sparkled behind glass set into black walls.
Platinum cigarette holders were ringed with rubies, vanity
cases and *nécessaires* were encrusted with diamonds, and
a pink-flamingo brooch with ruby, diamond, emerald, and
sapphire plumage had been commissioned by the Duchess
of Windsor. Spectacular jaguar pins had been made for
Nina Dyer, the Princess Aga Khan.

Many of these treasures had been repurchased by Cartier, but some remain today in private collections.

A cigarette case arrested Jasper. It made him stop. It
had been fashioned to look like an envelope. In its upper
right corner, where it belonged, a postage stamp had been
etched in the yellow gold. A facsimile postmark—London, June 20, 1932—had also been etched, and inscribed
on the front of the case was the name and address,
in Kent, of Randolph Churchill, Esq. This inscription
had been made to look tossed off, like handwriting. This
piece of utterly preposterous handsomeness had been
given by Winston Churchill to his son on his twenty-first
birthday.

I thought it was a pretty nice bibelot for a man to give
his son and that there must have been love in the giving,
but Jasper told me the father and the son had not gotten
along awfully well and that what was in the gesture, other
than ostentation, had to be somewhat more complex than
love. Probably there was an apology in it, Jasper offered.
I did not see much contradiction; I thought that love should
always include apology.

We left the exhibit happier than we had been in a while,
each one of us gladdened by things we'd liked.

We walked along the Champs-Elysées, through Les
Jardins de Marcel Proust, and stopped in the Tuileries.
We sat in the chairs that are set out in summer around a
fountain. There are goldfish the size of trout in that fountain. That day, a pair of them writhed iridescently in inky
water.

This was the time to tell Jasper some of what I had learned about the virus.

I wasn't going to tell him all.

"I've read a fair amount about the virus," I began.

"And what has your reading taught you?" Jasper asked.

"You know it's a coil of nucleotides, don't you?" I asked.

"Timothy, I don't know what a nucleotide is," Jasper said.

I had thought that Jasper, who was encyclopedic about so many things, would know what a nucleotide is.

I wasn't sure myself, not altogether. "They're components of RNA and DNA," I began. "There are five of them all told, four of them are in DNA, and the virus ends up being composed of these four elements, repeated in different sequences."

"I don't remember much about RNA," Jasper said.

"No one knew how it was composed until 1953, so you probably didn't study it in school," I said. Then I added that I hadn't studied it, either.

"There are such appalling gaps in your education," said Jasper.

"Bodies are made up of two nucleic acids. DNA is one of them, and it is in just about everything."

Jasper was waiting.

"It's in these goldfish, this algae, these trees. You are made of it. It contains your chromosomes and makes you what you are. It gives you your blue eyes. It's what makes you smarter than most people, and it's what makes a few people smarter than you, possibly. It gives you your arched feet, and me my flat ones. It gives you every one of those marvelous chest hairs." I gave him my smile. "In a way, it predetermines everything, and it is in everything that I love in you," I said.

"And now it gives me AIDS," said Jasper.

"No," I said. "That's not the way to think, papa."

Jasper gave me a quizzical look.

I wasn't going to tell him yet that the virus begins as RNA. I didn't want to confound him. He did not need to know that it is the conversion of RNA to DNA that characterizes a retrovirus, that the conversion, also called polymerase, is achieved by an enzyme, reverse transcriptase; Jasper did not need to know that it is the presence of this one enzyme that tells a scientist that he is looking at a retrovirus. The enzyme is the hallmark, the giveaway.

This is hard for anyone who is not a scientist to grasp.

I got through a lot of costly education without ever studying biology. "Let x equal the number" is about as far as I can go in any of the abstruse disciplines.

I told Jasper only what I thought it essential for him to know. "The nucleotides have names, they are cytosine, adenine, guanine, and thymidine. In RNA there is one called uracil, instead of thymidine. You don't need to know all this, though, really."

"Then why are you telling me?" Jasper asked.

"It can't hurt you to know, can it? You can look them up. What's important is that the virus consists of these four components, and they repeat themselves in a chain, a spiral, and that the chain is nine thousand nucleotides long. Actually, it's a little more than nine thousand. It's nine thousand seven hundred and then some. There is always the same number, but in every man who has it, every woman, and in all the children who have it, the sequence is different," I said.

"The sequence of what?" Jasper asked.

He didn't like this, didn't want it, I could tell.

"Of the nucleotides," I said, a little sharply. "And therefore of the virus. That's why it's too simple to think of it as *the* virus, as the newspapers are so fond of calling it, and the sloppy television journalists. You can't think about it that way, because, you see, there isn't just *one* virus."

I stopped until our eyes locked together. "What you have," I said, "is *your* virus."

I waited for this to sink in.

"Timothy, even if that's true," Jasper asked, "what difference does it make?"

He was annoyed.

"Don't you see it?" I asked.

I was imploring him to see it.

I drew a circle with my finger on the concrete rim of the fountain. I wished the surface were flatter, that it had more area.

"This is the virus," I said.

Actually, the virus isn't a circle, it is more of a sphere. It is unimaginably small.

I was drawing only to give Jasper an image.

I did not burden him, though he seemed to feel burdened. I gave him no account of the difficulty I had put myself to in order to learn what little I had. I didn't tell Jasper, for example, that our internist at the American Hospital had not had even the courtesy to respond to a letter, which had taken me hours to write, in which I asked if I could see the virus in the hospital's electron microscope. This physician, when I asked him three weeks later why he hadn't answered, even by telephone, shrugged and said that no one had cooperated. I doubt he asked anyone.

This wasn't something Jasper had to know.

I did not speak about another American doctor who had shown me slides of the virus. This doctor had no projector, no screen, but had a table lamp to which I could hold up the slides. I did not tell Jasper how many times this doctor had insisted that I not touch the transparencies. "Don't even think about it," he told me three times, as if I knew no better than to smudge an image with my fingerprint.

I did not tell Jasper that one of these slides had the name Gallo written on the top and bottom of its white cardboard frame, and of how this doctor, when I asked him if he had any slides from Montagnier's lab, had hesitated a full fraction of a second before answering that the slide with Gallo's name on it had turned out to be, in fact, from Montagnier's lab.

I did not tell Jasper how reluctant half a dozen scientists had been to talk to me. One woman was candid enough to tell me that scientists tend to be uncomfortable talking to lay people, nonscientists, who, they fear, are apt to misunderstand what they say; this woman said, quite properly I thought, that there is a problem of language, that scientists speak in code. This woman, who is also the mother of three young children, guided me around the virology building at the Pasteur Institute and introduced me to other scientists, few of whom extended much welcome, which puzzled me. Possibly it is my fault, something I extrude.

Possibly they are correct in thinking what they do. I've done a few things, accomplished this or that in my life, but I did not cure polio, did not invent penicillin, and I have isolated no virus. I have not banished illness, have not wiped out pain, or added at all to human prosperity.

Good God, imagine changing the world in one's time.

I didn't want Jasper to know the difficulty, or how humbling it had been for me to talk to these inaccessible, almost lordly researchers, didn't want him to see that his virus, and mine, had taken over every other interest in my life; how they had, in short, become my life.

———

I DREW an oval inside the circle.

"This is the nucleus," I told Jasper.

Jasper nodded.

I jabbed once with a fingertip. "Think of this as a nucleotide." I jabbed again. "And this is a different nucleotide, and so is this, and so is this."

I jabbed my finger again against the concrete, describing spirals.

"All these are nucleotides," I said.

"I don't see it," Jasper said.

I looked at him. I thought for a moment.

"Think of this nucleotide as an emerald," I said, and jabbed again. "And of this as a diamond." I jabbed the concrete again. "And here is a sapphire, and here a ruby. That's it, that is the virus."

I knew that there were also membranes and crystals and proteins and enzymes, but I was trying to keep this as simple as it could be kept. "Now, picture these as separate gemstones, each one is distinct, but much, much too small to see. Close your eyes and try to picture them. Make them gleam in the dark. Let each one glisten infinitesimally, each one separately."

Jasper did not close his eyes, he would not indulge me. I made tapping sounds on the concrete with my fingernail, retracing the spirals. "My virus may begin with an emerald, and then go: diamond, diamond, sapphire, ruby, emerald, emerald, ruby.

"Your virus may begin with a sapphire, and if read from end to end, which they can do now in a laboratory, it might go something like this: sapphire, diamond, diamond, sapphire, ruby, emerald, diamond, ruby, ruby."

Jasper looked at me as he would look at anyone who was going insane in front of his eyes.

I went on. I retraced the oval and said, "This is the membrane of the nucleus. Here and there it has tiny holes, like punctures, and through these the virus can pass."

Jasper looked bemused.

I pointed outside the oval, but within the circle. "This is called the cytoplasm."

"What is it?" Jasper asked.

"It's part of the whole virus. It's almost like an empty space, except it contains an enzyme and a number of proteins, and the virus replicates within it. Researchers are still isolating proteins, and no one knows what all of them do." I pointed at an arbitrary spot in the cytoplasm and took a risk. "This enzyme is called reverse transcriptase. It copies the original virus, which begins as RNA, a single-stranded virus, and then it makes a double-stranded DNA copy of itself. Once this is done, the DNA can replicate within the cell ad infinitum."

"What does it do then?" Jasper asked.

As he asked me this, a woman approached the fountain with a preposterously groomed, fluffed-up dog. It was one of those little rats on leashes that lead women around Paris, yapping. You see them in parks. Some parks don't allow dogs, but the Tuileries is not one of them. Jasper and I had seen these animals on white tablecloths in quite a few restaurants. We would watch the women cut their *plats du jour* into fastidious bites, which would be quickly devoured by the unconscionably pampered little beasts. That afternoon, when Jasper saw the woman walking the rat in the Tuileries, he was more eager to look at them than he was to hear from me.

I should have known better than to talk to Jasper about reverse transcriptase. It is complicated. I didn't understand it well enough then to say much about it. I still don't. Even if I'd wanted to, which I didn't, I could not give Jasper a biology lesson. I certainly could not give him a retrovirology lesson. All I hoped to give him were one or two facts.

I wanted those to give him hope.

"Look at me," I said. I would not be interrupted by a woman who was walking a rodent.

"Some of the proteins are needed for the virus to function, others of them may not be."

I paused. Actually, I believed that soon enough every single protein would be proved necessary. It was unlikely that this highly efficient virus would carry any superfluous baggage.

Jasper looked at me, and I saw that he did not think of his virus as something to talk about.

I started to tell him how, in the double-stranded DNA,

the two strands spiral in opposition to each other, that one forces up while the other forces down. I was going to tell him that an adenine nucleotide in one strand can pair only with a thymidine on the other—just as a cytosine will pair only with guanine. This is true of all DNA, not only of the virus. I could have made this clear by telling Jasper that an emerald will pair only with a diamond, a sapphire with nothing but a ruby.

I thought better of it, though: the fact that the nucleotide pairings are invariable, that one strand of DNA rigidly dictates the other, takes more away than I wanted taken from Jasper of the notion I was determined to instill: that every virus is different.

Of course, that is true. I wasn't telling lies.

I wasn't fibbing. Every man's virus *is* his own.

"If every virus is different," Jasper asked, "how can it be studied?"

"Every sequence breaks into sections. It's a kind of natural scissor. There are ten nucleotides per turn of the spiral, and four nucleotides, I believe, in each scissored section. I've also heard it said that there are only three nucleotides, that these are in a way rather like a sentence, which contains instructions, and the fourth is simply a kind of punctuation. That is *one* way it can be studied," I answered.

"Then how important can the differences be?" Jasper asked; his voice had more doubt than question in it. It was clear that Jasper did not believe that any difference would matter much.

"Why do you think people get different infections?" I asked. "Why do some people get Kaposi's but not toxoplasmosis? Why have some people lived with their virus ten years, and why are some of them still living, while others die within a few months of diagnosis? The reason it matters, papa, why it should matter to you, is that another man's virus may have killed *him*, but your virus, yours, hasn't killed anybody yet."

"It might have, Timothy," Jasper said.

I could hear a sadness in his voice. It sounded like regret. He must have been thinking of boys and young men he had been with. I wanted to enclose that regret, to crumple it up, throw it away, get rid of it. These were not thoughts Jasper should be having.

"What good can you do anyone by thinking about that? None, papa, none. What's important is that it hasn't killed you yet. It's yours to challenge, to stop if you can, and certainly it is yours to slow down. Your virus and mine are individual, as different as our lives."

Jasper, the cynic, shook his head. His face became sarcasm itself. "Timothy, dear heart, this is all a bit too Ayn Rand for me."

I laughed, but not at what he'd said. I laughed at how easily the man could make me feel like a fool.

———

OLIVER INGRAHAM stayed in Paris six days. A week before I was to return to Paris, Jasper called to tell me he had started to feel unwell. He had reserved on a flight leaving Sunday. I asked him what exactly he meant by unwell. The question seemed to irritate him; he said that by unwell he'd meant unwell.

I asked if I should come over to help him get to the airport. I knew this would anger him, but he'd been losing strength in the weeks we were in Paris. Even though I'd seen him just two weeks before, I pictured Jasper alone, too tired, too depleted, to walk to a taxi stand. Jasper didn't know enough French to call for a taxi, and they almost never come anyway, I have found, at least not promptly.

This picture of Jasper came to me because years ago it had been a picture of me. A waiter had told me in a café that he was out of beer, all beers, though he was serving beer to everyone else. The French do have a way of withholding welcome. Nothing like this had happened to me before, except once, years ago, in New York, when a bartender at the Four Seasons was not altogether satisfied that I was wearing a jacket. I had on that day an item that was cut unusually; it may have looked a bit outdoorsy at the Four Seasons, but it was made of superb suede, had cost a fortune, and I thought it more than qualified to pass as a jacket.

I told the bartender it was a jacket, most definitely. He gave in.

This happened before Jasper began helping me choose my clothes. It happened before I knew Jasper. It was years ago, when the Four Seasons was, unofficially, a cruise bar for faggots who fancied themselves to be debonair. I think there is less of that now. It was before faggots had an identity. Now they have political correctitude.

In Paris, a taxi driver had shouted me out of his cab. I'd given him an address on Boulevard Saint-German when I'd meant to give him one on Saint-Michel. I had forgotten where I was going, actually, which in retrospect is not hard to understand. I was going to Boulevard Saint-Michel to pay my telephone bill, which was long overdue. It would require a long wait, and paying a telephone bill is not something worth waiting for. Standing in line, even for a good movie or a great exhibit, is a big enough bore; to do it for a phone bill is hateful.

I must have looked like *merde en croute* that day. The driver left me on neither street. Then his cab got stuck in traffic, for which I thanked the Lord.

It started to rain, and all I could do with my mind was brood and mull endlessly over everything I should have shrieked to that cabdriver in brazen, vulgar, illiterate French.

I dragged myself home brimming with rage.

The next day it took every effort, and was a thousand times harder than usual, just to get myself to the airport.

I upgraded to first class and ranted when a negroni

could not be provided. I bitched about the champagne, hissed at the stewardess that I despised Dom Perignon. I was grandly unpleasant about everything. This can be one of the many characteristics of toxoplasmosis.

I hated to think of Jasper being as I had been. That was why I asked him if he wanted me to come. He said he didn't. I asked him if he was eating. Of course he was, he said sharply.

Actually, I don't believe he was.

Dominic has told me how things came back to him pretty much in the order he had lost them. In this case, the first thing to go was his appetite. Dominic had never been all that vehement an epicure, but his appetite was, he has said, also the first thing restored.

He'd had no need to get his libido back, he told me. At first I thought he meant that he had no use for it, but, as it turned out, what he'd meant was that it was the one thing that had not left him.

————————

JASPER CALLED the day he got back. He was tired, he told me, needed a nap. He'd call the next day, he said.

He didn't.

I tried to get him all week. On the sixth day, the first of August, I was frightened. In Paris, when I had mentioned a friend in San Francisco who had joined the Hemlock Society, Jasper had shown a morbid interest.

Abigail had told me that people who fail at suicide will try again, usually within the year. This is especially true of single men with life-threatening diseases, she told me.

"Thank you for saying 'life-threatening,' " I said.

Abigail was cutting into a cherry pie. She looked up from it, perplexed.

"I mean, as opposed to 'terminal,' " I said.

"Oh," Abigail said. She put an immense piece of the

cherry pie on a plate for me. The crust was lovely, and the plate was a pretty one. The cherries were from the tree in Abigail's garden, picked that morning, pitted that morning, too. That's what Abigail does to calm herself: she bakes a pie, she makes a soufflé. She can cook for hours and feel almost complacent, she says. I'd like to have that gift. When I cook, even when I plan everything step by step, which I never do, one thing goes wrong, then another, and I feel that I'm racing from panic to panic. Abigail knows how to start and finish things. It isn't always easy for her to ghost a doctor's article on anemia or heart disease, but she can get it done, she can meet a deadline. She can fabricate a readable article from a doctor's haphazard notes; she loves to play with her little boy, and he likes it when she does. I even believe she still loves Gary. She'd have to, I suppose, to marry him again. They've been together almost as long as Jasper and I have. The difference is that Gary and Abigail have been together day after day, which is, I suspect, somewhat different than week by week.

Abigail knows what every organ of the body is for, the ways each one can malfunction, and she can name all the amino acids. She does not toss off a phrase like "terminal disease" casually. She does not think of me or anyone who is still with the virus as being a cripple, or a victim; she doesn't rush in to smother a fact with a word like "disability," and she makes a dazzling cherry pie.

Of course, she also has more counter space than I do.

When I was bed bound, Abigail came for lunch one day and gave me the choice of a Quarter-Pounder or a Big Mac. She would have the one I didn't. She also brought french fries. They were still good then, still tasty, fried in beef fat, I believe. Now they are fried in something like canola oil, which may be more wholesome but is less flavorsome in the bargain. The potatoes are not the same at all. They taste much more like nothing now.

Abigail sat with me awhile and said that she would not accept my death.

She gave me the idea that I need not accept it, either. She was the only one to put it to me that way.

I chose the Quarter-Pounder.

That day, it tasted as good as the best food I'd ever had. It yummed me back to life, I'd say.

That was more than a year ago. I still remember the taste.

"I don't think of Jasper as a statistic," I told her.

"Of course not," Abigail said. "And you shouldn't."

"God, this pie is bliss," I said.

"Is it a little too sweet?" Abigail asked.

"No, no. No, no. It's perfect."

"I think maybe I used too much sugar," Abigail said.

"This pie, these cherries, should give you a place in God's heaven," I told her, meaning it. "Have you got any heavy cream?"

"Ice cream, will that do?" Abigail asked.

"No," I said. "You know, I can't imagine hating life so much that I wouldn't want it anymore."

"I know you can't," Abigail answered.

"How could he do it?" I asked her then. "Does he own himself so completely, every ounce, every breath? Is every heartbeat his, every brain wave, every synapse? Does he hold the patent on himself, so that every part of him is his, and only his? Can be really just abscond, take himself away from me? How can he even think of it? How dare he! Isn't there a part of him that was mine, an inch of skin, some particle that he had no right to take, and didn't he think of that at all? Didn't he think for a minute, for one instant, that he is part of me, and that by killing himself, or trying to, or even just by wanting to, he is taking part of my life with him?"

Abigail cut herself a thin piece of the pie. "I doubt he did think about that, Timothy. He was probably out of his mind, temporarily," she said.

"That's what I said to him. But it made him angry to hear me say that, and he told me he'd known exactly what he was doing," I said to Abigail.

"Did you expect him to agree with you? Of course he's going to say he knew what he was doing. Suicide can be rational, but it seldom is," Abigail said.

"Can you imagine hating life so much?" I asked Abigail.

"That's not the question," Abigail said. "Haven't you ever thought that you can hate *your* life without hating life?"

I took a huge, greedy bite of Abigail's cherry pie and said to her, my mouth full of it, "I know it's possible to love it, without loving your own. I do it every day. Also, I know that sooner or later we will all become statistics."

"Yes," said Abigail.

———————

IN SEPTEMBER, when he died in an emergency room, one thought that came to me was that I no longer had to worry about Jasper and suicide. This wasn't my only thought, but it was one of them. There was a way in which Jasper's attempt, and knowing that he could do it again, that he could succeed, was worse, was harder to live with, than his death was. It wasn't that I loved him any less. But part of him, something of his character that had been forbearing and unassailable, had let him down. I had to find a way to love this different man.

Every morning now, when I come to life again, it amazes me to be in the world, that in the day ahead I will be able to witness some event, to hear on the telephone what friends are doing, where they dined the night before, to hear their menu and what they said to each other about someone else. It amazes me that today or tomorrow I can photograph a man or a woman and make them look better than they do; that I can read a book I've always wanted to; that I can go to a movie; that I can peel a sweet mango and cut it into pieces to eat while I read in the newspaper that astrophysicists are, at this minute, entertaining notions of establishing, in the next two or three hundred thousand years, photosynthesis on the planet Mars.

That, of course, is optimism. I don't think a lot about what life may be then, of what cities will have become, of what powers may be ruling. It scares me more than a little to imagine how the species may evolve, but all of this is for cheerful souls to contemplate. I may not extrude enthusiasm or effervesce with cheer, but buildings do go up, money changes hands, nations prosper and fall; possibly someone's friends grow cherries in their gardens, handsome men eat peaches; sounds come into being that are heard for the first time; new music is made with them; cuisines are reinvented, new machines come along, new techniques for old things; diseases are conquered, history happens, and movie stars still have babies.

I've not seen all the images. I haven't seen enough. Even without resources, without prospects, lacking health, lacking money, perhaps even unloved and unloving, there is still a world to grasp. If I cannot grasp it, it is there to be beheld.

I will do so. I will apprehend.

The body can feel, in illness, a distaste for all sensation, and this distaste can overwhelm the body, make it ache for cessation, for oblivion. I have known this, I have felt it. Jasper felt it, too, I'm sure. He felt it, I think, so keenly that he could not look ahead, could not see his way out of it. I didn't see all that much, either, really, but I did know that there were things left for me to see, and I kept on looking.

JASPER HAD told me he was leaving all his wine to me. There were unopened cases of splendid vintages. They would be ready for us to drink in ten or twenty years. When we bought our place in Paris together—our home away from homes—we agreed to leave, in our wills, our halves each to the other. Jasper had put it in his document, and kept after me until I did the same. We both made our wills in 1983 and did not, of course, ask to see copies.

Jasper had promised not to take his life without speaking to me, but when a man wants to kill himself what does he care about keeping his word?

In the deed of suicide, even in the thought of it, a man puts himself first. That's what suicide is.

On the seventh day after Jasper's return from Paris, I decided to call Oliver Ingraham. But instead of Oliver Ingraham, I called the hospital in Jasper's town. It was there I found him. He was in for pneumonia, he told me. When Jasper had it, in 1991, pneumocystis carinii was still the number-one killer among all HIV infections. I believe it still is among the poor and untreated. There is also something called breakthrough PCP, which becomes stronger than any prophylaxis that is used against it.

In Paris, Jasper had stopped bicycling. When I asked him why, he told me he didn't have the wind for it. That was the day I learned that Japser was not on any prophylaxis against pneumocystis. I asked him how this could be so. Ordinarily, when a patient tests positive for HIV antibodies, unless other symptoms are present prophylaxis against pneumocystis will be the first medication prescribed.

In all cases of HIV infection, the need is to combine different medications for different infections, which arise not from the virus itself, not directly, but from a lack of immune function. In medicine, these combinations are called cocktails. The doctor's aim, or the patient's, is to combine drugs that will not be antagonistic, that may even work together, in *synergy*. The combination of acyclovir with zidovudine, now standard, I believe, is an example of such a cocktail. It is believed that each of these drugs, when taken together, is made more effective. For a year, or longer, I had urged Jasper to ask his doctor about Bactrim, or pentamidine, or dapsone. Jasper said he would, then he told me that his doctor was looking into prophylaxis.

"Looking into?" I asked.

Months passed, a year. No patient should need to ask a doctor for standard treatment, especially when the doctor is in situ at a major hospital. Or in situ at a minor hospital, for that matter. The only reason for Jasper's doctor not prescribing one prophylaxis or another was ignorance—unless, perhaps, Jasper had expressed a wish to die.

To help a patient die is, as I read it anyway, to break the Hippocratic oath at the core.

I was relieved to have found Jasper but could not stop myself from thinking that in not letting me know where he was Jasper had sequestered his life from me. I felt left out, forgotten, secondary. This was a shabby reflex, but it was the reflex I had.

I asked Jasper, when I had him on the telephone, what time would be best for him to have me come see him. I was annoyed at having to ask, to plan my visit around Oliver Ingraham. This wasn't the first time I'd felt a little bitter about being a resident of the venue that worn-out Fannie Hurst had so sagaciously named "Back Street."

I always had been a little bitter. Sometimes I still am. And I don't mean bittersweet. There is not any sweetness to it; it's not cake mix.

Jasper told me not to visit. It was a long trip, he said, an effort. Of course it was, but I wanted to make the effort. I think what Jasper didn't want was for me to see him in a hospital. This vanity made sense to me, and I honored it.

I called every day. He told me Oliver Ingraham was coming every night. I said I hoped Oliver Ingraham was bringing Jasper lovely things to eat.

I told him how important it is to get up once or twice each day, to walk in the corridors. Otherwise, I warned him, his feet would stiffen, "drop," as therapists say; his muscles would atrophy, as mine had done.

Jasper was cantankerous, more so than usual. He rebuffed everything I said.

One night I called him in the hospital at nine o'clock. I wanted to tell him I'd walked eighty-nine blocks that day. I didn't tell him how long it had taken. I thought Jasper would welcome this news, but he was distant. He sounded chilly. When I asked him what was going on, he answered that it *was* rather late. Hospitals can sour anyone's spirits—no one is at his best in the hospital—but Jasper, I thought, was being crabby.

It was not becoming. I let it go and began to worry that Jasper was becoming a person with whom I'd let things go.

Later, I would read that exaggeration of a person's worst characteristics is common in the early stages of dementia.

———

JASPER STAYED in the hospital eighteen days. It takes at least twenty-one to treat PCP. When I saw him at the end of August, when he was out, it was the first time in almost two months. He didn't want to drive into the city, so we had agreed that I would call him from a bus stop in his town.

Jasper's house was a two-minute drive from the bus stop. He took fifteen. I leaned against a parked car reading an immunology textbook. It had been published eight years before, had nothing in it about HIV, but quite a bit about other immune disorders. It was an odd thing to care about, but I liked knowing that there have always been immune disorders, that they did not originate with AIDS.

I read about the thymus gland, which produces T-cells. The T is for thymus. I was reading that this function of the thymus was unknown until the nineteen sixties, and I was in the midst of wondering how exact a science immunology could have been without this understanding when Jasper pulled up in his car.

I saw his face through the window. Just from this I could see that he'd lost weight, a lot of it. Even in dark sweats, he looked wraithlike, cachectic. His face had lost pigment, and he looked older. He was still handsome to me but would not have been, I believe, to others. Even to me, he was not *as* handsome, but I didn't care. I had had the handsome Jasper. He would be fifty-nine in a week, and he looked it, and more.

In the car, when we said hello, I saw that he had chipped a tooth. It was his left front tooth; it was missing a corner.

"What happened?" I asked.

"I was carrying something down the stairs and lost my footing."

"Does it hurt?" I asked.

"I don't feel it," Jasper said.

"When was the fall?" I asked.

"Last week," he said.

"Last week, and you haven't had it fixed?" I asked.

"I'm waiting for an appointment," he said.

"Do you have an appointment?"

"I'm going to make one," Jasper said.

"When?"

"Later today, maybe tomorrow," he said.

We went to a place that served fried clams. Inside, the place had red vinyl booths, a counter with stools fixed to the floor, laminated menus, waitresses in hair nets.

I said, "Papa, you have got to gain some weight."

"I know it," Jasper said.

There was nothing I wanted to eat, but I wanted Jasper to have something. I saw platters borne by waitresses. Every one of them had one of those horrid little paper cups that hold wet coleslaw.

I ordered fried calamari.

I wondered how Jasper and I had come to this.

I ordered a lobster.

I knew how we had come to this.

Jasper ordered spaghetti and meatballs.

"Whatever for on *earth* did you order spaghetti and meatballs?" I asked. His choice alarmed me. There are just so many reasons not to order spaghetti and meatballs.

"It sounded good," said Jasper.

I offered a taste of calamari. He said he'd take it in a minute. He didn't.

Jasper seemed too tired to cut the meatballs. He moved his fork once or twice, but not to his mouth.

"This is not a comfortable place," he said.

"It isn't, really, is it?" I said.

"I'll wait for you in the car," he said.

"You're going to leave these ravishing meatballs?" I asked.

Jasper smiled, wearily. "I'll wait for you," he said.

"I'll come with you," I said, and started to get up.

"No, take all the time you want," he said.

It occurred to me that he wanted to be alone.

I watched him walk to the door. Then I watched him from the window. Then I watched him in the car. I saw him slump in the driver's seat.

The waitress filled my water glass. "Your friend left all his food," she said. She sounded like a mother. Possibly she had been one. Possibly she still was, I thought.

"I don't know why," I said. "It looks very good."

"We make the meatballs here," she said.

"How nice for you," I said inanely.

She took Jasper's plate away. She was almost despondent.

I didn't stay long, but I finished the calamari, and the lobster, too.

I was hungry.

———

IN PARIS, when Jasper took naps, I don't believe he slept, I think he just needed to lie down.

At least once each day I'd lie down with him.

Jasper lived on toast and honey. He left nectarines half eaten; boxes of raspberries went bad.

One night he said the first words I ever heard him say in his sleep. It was the only time I'd heard him do it.

He said three. The first was "please." Then he said "help," and then he said "me."

My instinct was to wake him. I wanted to get him out of the dream. But what could I have given him to waken to? Would I have held him in the dark until he'd sleep again? I thought he might say more and that in the morning I could tell him all. But nothing more came, and it was better, I decided, to let the dream play itself out, to let him waken free of it.

In the morning, and all the next day, I came close to telling him. I knew he'd resent it; I didn't want to be an interloper. Also, I was embarrassed. That's the truth of it. Embarrassed was the worst thing I could have been then, and the worst of it is, I still am.

———

WHEN I saw Jasper ten days later, the tooth had not been fixed, and under his chin was a large patch of beard he'd missed when shaving. I'd noticed it the week before, but it had been less noticeable. It was unlike Jasper to be carelessly groomed. It saddened me to see him in dark sweatpants again. For years he'd picked me up at 181st Street and we'd drive to his house. He'd always worn sweatpants. They were his at-home attire. It hadn't bothered me; he looked relaxed, comfortable, and he'd been fit, a fine specimen of traditional, old-fashioned, good-looking manhood—the basic stuff.

I usually put myself to a little trouble when Jasper came to me. I'd greet him with just-washed hair and would splash my skin with a little pear brandy. I got in the habit of changing the sheets every weekend. For a while, I did everything but disinfect the ashtrays. After a while I slackened off a bit, I suppose, but I always hid the *People* magazines. I also put away all the fag rags.

It felt better, making an effort for him.

I wondered how Jasper could have missed that inch of beard; the rest of his face was clean shaven. Jasper had told me that when you have HIV you have got to be more careful about your appearance. You mustn't let yourself go, he said. I agreed with him, but I wondered who it was he cared about looking good for.

The virus tends to speed metabolism. Many people cannot help losing weight, and there were other things Jasper could not avoid. He could not avoid blood transfusions, for example, because AZT made him anemic, as it did to about fifty percent of all people who took it, until it was discovered, after Jasper's death, that lower doses are safer and as effective.

It may even be safe to say that a dosage that doesn't kill is more effective than one that does.

Jasper knew I was taking medications that had not been approved by the FDA. In the hospital, he asked if I knew of any medication that would counteract AZT anemia. I didn't know of one, but I told him I'd ask around. I called the Gay Men's Health Crisis; I called the American Foundation for AIDS Research. I called the People with AIDS Coalition. Each one referred me to a different place, and after about twenty calls I found what Jasper needed. The drug is called erythropoietan, or EPO, and it's not a pill, it is an injection.

I told Jasper how to obtain it, gave him a telephone number his doctor could call. Jasper, though, would take no medication that had not been FDA approved. I tried a few times to talk him into taking EPO, or at least to get him to ask his doctor about it. All he did was tell me to get off his back. "Papa, you asked me to find something, and if you take this you can take AZT, and you will probably need fewer transfusions." I told him that taking this drug was the best thing he could do.

"I didn't ask you to find anything, Timothy," Jasper said.

"But you did. Don't you remember?" I asked.

"Thank you for your interest," Jasper said then. "But I don't want it."

Two months after Jasper died, erythropoietan, a natural body substance, which science had learned to synthesize, was approved by the FDA. The reason for the slow approval may have been that people make money by taking their time.

I didn't know what was stopping Jasper from getting his tooth capped, and didn't he always run a hand over his face after shaving?

That day we had another lunch. Jasper got halfway through a bowl of ghoulish-looking chowder. After lunch, which I again finished alone, we drove to a thrift shop. Jasper had filled the trunk of his car with clothes he wanted to donate. He heaped them in my arms. Among them were business suits I'd not seen him wear, but there were other things I recognized. There was a pair of wide-waled corduroy trousers, very like the ones he'd been wearing the night I found him waiting for me outside the West Side Y. I think they were the same trousers. I was sorry to see them go.

"Why are you giving all this away?" I asked.

"I won't be wearing any of it again," Jasper said.

"I guess not," I said. "Not if you give it away."

"Timothy, I have too much clothing. It's time to clear out some clutter," said Jasper.

Later, I realized what Jasper was doing that day. Of course, I knew even as he was doing it, but I could not let it be as clear to me as it was. Jasper was doing the proper thing, the tidy thing, which I will not do. I haven't the courage or the gentleness to do it for anyone.

I may not have enough love to do it.

I would not have done it for Jasper.

What Jasper was doing, and using my arms to do, was clearing things out for Oliver Ingraham.

Disorder is one thing I will leave.

seven

"WELL, HE always liked young boys," Oliver Ingraham said a year ago, when I told him Jasper had met me when I was nineteen. He made this reply with his eyes not on me. It was as if he didn't need to look at me to know that youth had been my hold on Jasper. That in the eighteen years Jasper had known me I had at any point ceased to be a young boy was a thought Oliver Ingraham was not apt to entertain.

We were less than five minutes into the dinner I'd been dreading for years. I had always feared it, but I'd always thought it would come much later. I thought it would stay far off for so long that by the time it came I'd be ready for it.

Naturally, I'd hoped it would not happen. Until Jasper became ill, and long before that, I'd had another hope, one I told to no one: that Oliver Ingraham would die before Jasper, would keel over one fine day, would be all-at-once dead, and that he would do this beautifully.

If Oliver Ingraham were out of the picture, I would have Jasper undivided for a piece of our life.

We wouldn't live in Jasper's house, or in mine, but in some other place, where neither of us had lived before, with anyone.

For a while I thought Paris would do. I changed my mind when everything started to end.

Two months before he died, when I had more or less given up all hope—Jasper had Oliver Ingraham come to Paris. It was arranged that I would leave, that Oliver Ingraham would come in July. He did, despite my protesting it to Jasper, and after that, after Oliver Ingraham had sat in chairs I had bought, after he had eaten what Jasper had cooked for him in my pans and served him on plates I had chosen, after Oliver Ingraham had seen photographs I had made, my work on our walls, and had slept next to Jasper in my place in our bed—where I had not brought Claude—I decided that Jasper and I would not live in Paris after all.

Too much had been taken from it.

I still believed Jasper would live. When we were in Paris, he didn't seem as ill as he must have been. He did have three transfusions in six weeks and lay down three or four times a day, but we'd been able to walk long distances together. In fact, Jasper would be slightly peeved when I could not keep pace with him. It was as if he'd forgotten that two months before I hadn't been able to walk at all. This can happen to anyone who stays several weeks or even months in a hospital and is not allowed to leave his room.

Later, a physical therapist had come to my house twice a week and taught me exercises to strengthen my foot and how to go up and down stairs, but he quit before my course of therapy was finished. In fairness to him, he'd had to check himself into a recovery center for an alcohol dependency and substance abuse. In other words, this therapist was an alcoholic and a drug addict. It must be believed by nearly everyone, and certainly by the jargon police, that if a thing is given a bland enough name it will become bland itself, lose its force. It wasn't the therapist's choice to quit on me: he'd lost control of his life, which is easy to understand. It can happen to everyone, and usually does.

Still, I felt he'd let me down.

It was a thirteen-hundred-dollar orthotic that finally enabled me to walk. Because I was without insurance and on Medicaid, the woman who made the orthotic offered to charge only the Medicaid rate. I have since been advised that thirteen hundred dollars is a far heftier piece of change than Medicaid will pay for an orthotic.

I wore it for ten days. I still have it in a drawer.

IN PARIS, without the orthotic, the hardest task was going down the steps into the Metro. One time Jasper and I were going to a dance concert, and I watched the lively spring in his step as he went down ahead of me. It looked youthful. I thought, "He'll live forever."

The dance was being performed in a magnificent glass-domed building, possibly built for the exposition, near Place de la Concorde. It hadn't been built as a theater, but an imposing stage had been set up in it. There was seating for hundreds of people, possibly thousands. To reach your seat you must ascend a tall bank of stairs, and, because Jasper had bought seats very near the stage, we then had to descend an equal number of steps, which were steep, and there was no railing, nor were there landings to break the descent.

It was not until all those difficult steps were behind me, when I reached my seat and looked up through that magnificent dome into the vast evening sky, that I realized what a superb space I was in, how perfect it was for watching a dance.

Jasper touched my leg for an instant. I felt just then as if everything horrid had been put behind me, almost as if I weren't ill and hadn't been, that I had not had carbuncles covering my face, had not ever been befuddled by toxoplasmosis, and had not known the fright of being unable to find, in what for seventeen years had been my neighborhood, the Thai place where I was to meet Gary and Abigail for dinner.

I knew I was in my neighborhood, knew that I was lost in it, and did not for one instant consider that anything was wrong with my brain. I thought that nothing was where it was supposed to be. Though it's not clinical dementia, toxoplasmosis has this in common with it: when you have it, you don't know it.

I might have guessed I had it if I'd known anything about it.

It is caused by a one-celled organism called toxoplasma gondii; it commonly lodges in the brain but can also affect the lungs, the liver, and the eyes. It is found in about forty percent of the pork and ten percent of the lamb sold in this country, and in much of the beef. It is common in France, among peope who eat steak tartare. Even a vegetarian can get it, if the vegetarian is also a cat lover.

While it is said to infect only one percent of the cats in America, when you have AIDS one percent is not something you should ignore. There was a time when less than one percent of the human population was said to have AIDS.

You can cook it out of meat, of course, if you want to eat dark-cooked lamb or a steak without any blood in it.

For a long time after my doctor told me I had it, I thought its name was toxicplasmosis. It seemed apt. Most people have been exposed to it, but if your immune system is intact the protozoa will seldom do harm. It can harm a newborn if the mother is infected, even when she is asymptomatic. When it is acquired this way, it can be extremely dangerous.

Although the antibody will show in a blood test, it

won't mean that you have active toxo. Unless your doctor will make a diagnosis on the basis of behavior, which no doctor should do, a CAT scan will be necessary. The only way a doctor can be absolutely sure is to take a biopsy of the brain, but no doctor will do this, certainly not to a patient with AIDS.

The first thing toxo does is annihilate short-term memory.

SULFADIAZINE AND pyrimethamine, the most common secondary prophylaxis against toxoplasmosis, are among the least expensive medications used to treat any HIV condition. A year or two ago the makers of sulfadiazine announced that the drug was unprofitable: they weren't losing money, but they weren't making much, either. It strikes me as odd that a medication that restores more or less—probably a little less—the acuity one had before the infection set in would be so unprofitable.

I don't know if the company raised the price. I am now poor enough to qualify for Medicaid, which, in New York State, pays for every AIDS medication approved by the FDA. In California, I've been told, there are medications for which Medicaid will not pay. In New York, my pharmacist bills Medicaid directly. I take about sixty thousand dollars' worth of medication each year. I paid it all myself for two years, when I had the money. I haven't that money now.

I would not have thought of New York State as having the best benefits in the country. I believe, perhaps falsely, that benefits are a kindess, a charity, and these are not virtues I had associated with New York State, and certainly not with the city of New York. But, in fact, New York State offers the best AIDS benefits in the country.

Being on benefits is another matter. They must be renewed at least once a year, you must have yourself reinstated again and again. Wayne, who does not have AIDS but works as an administrator at a clinic in East Harlem for people who do, has said more than once that retaining one's benefits and doing everything necessary to keep oneself well, or rather as well as one can be, is a full-time job. I was happy to hear him say this. I'd thought there was something wrong with me that made the maintaining of benefits such an ordeal.

I don't believe many people think as Wayne does. Wayne is smarter than most people. What is most often thought about people on benefits, I believe, is that they are taking advantage of the state, completely ripping off the city. When you pay with food coupons at a Korean fruit and vegetable market, you will be looked upon with hatred. Cash is transferable, food coupons aren't.

Even I have thought more than once that being on benefits not only puts me at the mercy of the government, which no doubt everyone is, but that it also makes me a parasite, a no-account, not quite a zero, but more of a negative integer.

This is not a complaint. I am lucky to have benefits. I am grateful to them; I could not live without them, but I would probably be grateful to a hole in the ground if it were the only place that would have me.

As things go today, if you are too weak or too confused to complete the renewal forms the organization may assume you are dead and will not maintain your file.

I hadn't noticed until just a second ago that the word "file" is the word "life" scrambled.

———————

THE FIRST time Jasper told me that Oliver Ingraham would be coming to Paris in July, my response was that I had heard nothing but raves about the Crillon.

Jasper was not amused.

I said it was our place, his and mine, that it had nothing to do with Oliver Ingraham. I told Jasper plainly and simply—I let there be no mistake—that I did not want Oliver Ingraham to say in our little house on the Quai d'Orléans. My actual words were, "I don't want him here."

I added that I would not be happy about it.

"You won't be here, Timothy," Jasper answered.

"Yes, I know. I'm being kicked out," I said.

"I wouldn't put it that way," said Jasper.

"How would you put it?" I asked.

"I'd say that you are giving Oliver an opportunity," Jasper answered.

"An opportunity that only an opportunist would take, and I am being forced to give it." That was my feeling on the subject. "What would you do if I forbade it?"

Jasper looked at me unhappily. "I suppose we could sell the place," he said.

"You would actually sell your half of this place for the sake of a man who makes his living selling second-rate antiques?"

I was appalled by his threat.

"You know, Timothy, sometimes you can be a pretty insensitive son of a bitch," said Jasper.

"What do you think you're being, papa?" I asked. "I'm just giving as I'm getting."

In fact, what I'd said turned out to be more prophetic than I could have known. I don't believe Jasper knew, either.

"Papa, I am asking you *not* to do this," I said.

"It's done," Jasper said. "Oliver already has his ticket."

"Not to this apartment, he doesn't," I said.

"I didn't object when you had Vivian stay a month," Japser said.

Vivian is my oldest friend. Oldest in the sense of age, also in the sense of long-standing. For a few years she has admitted to being ninety years old. I met her at a garden party in San Francisco the summer I got hepatitis. She is the woman with the lapis-lazuli ashtray in her all-white bathroom. Vivian has been married five times and has dedicated her life to public health, which is more than Oliver Ingraham has done. It's more than Jasper has done. Alas, it is also more than I have done.

Vivian once said to Jasper, who was buying her an awfully good dinner at a place called Chanterelle, "One thing you cannot take away is that I haven't worked just for money." This was not said without a trace of bitchiness, and I found it somewhat inappropriate; Vivian had drawn a handsome salary from the agencies she ran.

There was no comparison between giving an old friend a month in Paris and Jasper's kicking me out for Oliver Ingraham. Jasper had been in New York the month that Vivian came; I hadn't given him the boot. I would not have done that to him.

Suffice it to say that Oliver Ingraham came to Paris, and I thought briefly that Jasper and I might give up cities altogether. I even entertained, though for the briefest minute, the notion of giving up Jasper altogether. I detested Oliver Ingraham's taking over more of my life than he already had.

MY OTHER plan, before we became ill, was that Jasper and I would buy a vineyard, in Tuscany. We'd hire farmhands, who would do all the things we couldn't, the dull things mostly, and who would be happy for the work.

Better yet, we could start a vineyard, plant the vines ourselves, begin it from the ground. I'd met two men who had been smart enough to do this. They told me of a store near Pisa that sells nothing but grapevines. They had been able, in one afternoon, to fit one thousand vines into the back of their car. They hadn't needed a truck, they told me—all it took was their everyday sedan.

Within the year they had a harvest. These men also have olive groves and cold-press their own virgin oil. They sell their wine and their oil to the best trattoria in their town.

They are Americans, expatriates, though they do vote in presidential elections. They speak Italian the way I would like to speak French. They are also supreme food snobs. I wish I knew half, a third, of what they know about the art of eating. In New York, even if I could afford it, I wouldn't dare propose an Italian restaurant.

Theirs is undistinguished wine, they admit, but their oil is the best in Tuscany, and, since the best olive oil in Italy is known to be Tuscan, theirs, they claim, is the finest olive oil in Italy.

They brought me a bottle. It's the best I've tasted, better than any I've found in New York or tasted in Italy, even in Tuscany. I'd like to keep this bottle almost as long as Dominick has kept his maraschino, but oils, whether olive or hazelnut or pumpkinseed, do eventually go bad.

In other words, wine can be made, and, however it is done, Jasper and I would do it *that* way. We would learn together whatever is to be known about making wine.

There is, I was sure, much to be learned. It must be inexhaustible, all that one must know. Viniculture is more than watching vines grow, and behind viniculture there is oenology, a science and a passion. No doubt making wine is work, but not so difficult that thousands of people haven't been able to do it. I thought of the scores of vintners—not just in France or Italy, not just in California, but in Chile, in South Africa, in southeastern Australia—every one of them had been able to master the ground, to fructify their earth.

We would need an enterprise, but it wouldn't matter what. Jasper would stop importing; maybe he could *export*. I'd learn to drive, get over my abhorrence of driving machines. I'd drop my conviction that anyone without at least the intelligence of a Susan Sontag should not be allowed anywhere near a steering wheel.

Or we could, if we felt like it, become warm-weather nomads and practice an uprootable trade. We could live by the sea if we wanted, and I thought about that, about sleeping next to Jasper every night to the moaning of the tide, and of awakening with him every morning to the roaring of it, too.

We could have awakened this way every morning. Jasper would pull me from bed, and we would charge straight into the ocean.

Oh, perhaps we would not exactly *charge*.

That part I could live without.

Better, really, that we stroll into the surf like old men, which we would become, given time. I'd photograph objects, splendors, not people. I wouldn't have to look at any face but Jasper's, and I would not tire of it.

I considered all the possibilities and was rich with their plenty. With Oliver Ingraham out of the picture, things would be as they should have been.

These thoughts engaged me for the better part of a decade. I did not abandon them until Jasper said one night, in no context whatever, that he had thought about what it would be like for him to live with me. He'd thought about this only once, he told me, because he knew that to live with me would be, for him, an utter hell.

It was a life he would be unable to live, he told me in 1984.

_____

WE WERE having Father's Day dinner. Jasper didn't like it, but it gave me pleasure to observe Father's Day with a good dinner and a gift. They weren't ever big gifts, nothing like what I gave him on his birthday or on our anniversaries. On his birthdays I'd try to give Jasper something especially nice. I'd think of things I'd like to be given. For example, when Jasper turned fifty I gave him a pair of malachite cuff links. The problem was that since

Jasper had started having his shirts made he didn't have them made with French cuffs.

Observing Father's Day with Jasper made up for us not celebrating Christmas, and it made me feel that I belonged.

That Father's Day, when he told me he couldn't ever live with me, he said it as sadly as I'd ever heard him sound. We were at the table that Jasper had built for me, the one he had worked on for eleven months. This table—I still have it—is round and has spherical legs, which taper to thin wedges at their feet. The wood is black cherry. That night I had made an exceptionally fine *sauce rémoulade* for oysters that I had fried in beer batter with paprika, and, with a success that had startled us, I'd made a more-than-decent duplicate of something Jasper and I had tasted in New Orleans, at Galatoire's, just the week before, something they do at Galatoire's with crabmeat, with slivered mushrooms and sliced artichoke hearts, all sizzling together in buttery triumph.

With the oysters we drank Muscat Beaumes de Venise, and when Jasper made his observation we were drinking a 1976 Batard Montrachet, a haunting wine, though I have not ever found a wine to really complement an artichoke. I don't suppose there is one.

When Jasper said this to me at the table, I gave up hope that Oliver Ingraham would clear a way for me; even if he did, it would make no difference. I realized, and not for the first time, that I would not have more of Jasper than I had.

I no longer had the hope to distract me from fear.

But I didn't know how to abandon hope. So I pretended I still had some.

I hadn't ever been without the fear, really. It was with me before Jasper became ill, long before that—not a fear of losing him to someone else, though for a while I had that fear, too, but after I'd been with Jasper ten years or so that became less a fear, became almost no fear at all.

Why would Jasper want to start over with someone else, I asked myself, and reasoned that he wouldn't.

Of course, he could have started over with someone else *without* giving me up.

I don't know that he didn't. Until the last two years, unless one of us was out of town, Jasper was usually with me three nights each week; it wouldn't have been easy for him to have a fling of much consequence.

Of course, I am talking of another time, before minor flings became high risks, before people used protection. Even a tiny fling, even a protected one, can still have the gravest consequence. Two men have told me they've had condoms break. One of these men told me he could feel a difference, fortunately, that it felt much better unsheathed, he cared as much about his partner's safety as about his own pleasure, had another condom close to hand, and was not sorely inconvenienced. A woman, wanting to be safe, told me of the time a man withdrew from her upon completion of the act, which had been pleasing to both of them until they saw that the condom was hanging from the man in shreds.

One thing I know about condoms is that they should not be kept in a wallet, especially one that is carried in a back pocket: the heat of the body will melt the plastic, or the lambskin, or anything else the condom is made from, and that will make it that much likelier to break.

It was another fear that had been with me from the beginning, that is, from the beginning of my attachment to Jasper. The mind, I've read, cannot sustain a state of fear, so it sends much fear on its way. I read this in a novel. It was explained that the body has a mechanism that ignites only upon specific signals from the brain, specific signals of fear. This mechanism, the novelist wrote, filters brain waves, protects the body from the onslaught of fear. Fear, it was claimed, is a chain of chemicals linked together, and the filtering is the action of an enzyme. Without it, the body would be so weakened by the chemicals of fear, by their magnitude, that fear itself would break the body down.

After I'd read this in fiction, I began to see it everywhere. I didn't seek it out; it showed up uninvited. I saw it written about again as science. I decided that it must be with a fear like this, with a chemistry like this, that one will always prefer, if given a choice, to perish rather than to live without the one who is his love.

Of course, we are not given this choice.

I had always imagined I would find this true. With Jasper, I came to know it. I knew it quickly at first. Then it slowed to a kind of stasis, until I knew it with the certainty that will come sometimes with an illness, when it is grave, when the humors of the body begin to riot in your blood.

In my case, it was even simpler than this. It was arithmetic, the fact that Jasper had been alive more years— almost a lifetime more, in fact. Today, his miscarried child would be older than I, and I thought about that.

I thought about it all the time, that if Jasper had had a son, and his son had a son, then Jasper would, even today, have a grandson, and if then the grandson had a son, and if it went on in this way, there would always be a little Jasper in the world. This was a pleasing thought to me.

If there hadn't been the waves of dying; if there hadn't been this virus, which I had seen as a green-and-white image in a computerized electron microscope—a machine roughly the size of a child's bed—which revealed to me, beyond the power of an eye, a dark nucleus one hundred thousand times smaller, give or take, than a single human cell—the cell itself being much smaller than, as Anton van Leeuwenhoek was the first man in the world to see, a single grain of sand; a nucleus which the machine had magnified to three hundred and fifty thousand times its diameter, in order to make it appear smaller than a seed in a grape; if all the dying that has issued from this—and from that indirectly, and very probably in tandem with one or many other agents; if all the dying that has been going on for so long, that has not been stopped, that may not be stopped, ever—and which has probably just be-gun—if all that had never been, I would still have lost Jasper, if only to the law, the duration, of mortality.

Invariably, it comes to something as dull as this, as dull and arithmetical as the law of mortality, and it was this that gave my fear its ground.

———

"I WAS young once," Oliver Ingraham said. He gave out a thin laugh.

I didn't join him. It seemed likely to me that Oliver Ingraham wanted me to know there had been a better time for him. I expect a time comes to most of us when we will want this known.

I could have answered Oliver Ingraham that I had "al-ways" liked older men. I could have offered to him as an axiom that it is better luck to like older men than it is to like young boys, that, unlike a young boy, who will stop being young, an older man does not stop being older.

I did not say this to Oliver Ingraham, the reason being that it is clearly not so.

"I've been here before," Oliver Ingraham said.

This was what he had said when he'd come in.

I'd watched him cross the room and saw, as I hadn't when I'd met him the time before, that Oliver Ingraham was a tall man. When I stood up to greet him, I saw he was at least half a foot taller, which would put him at about six-five. Years before, when I was going to bath-houses, when I'd see a man as tall as Oliver Ingraham— unless he was lethally appealing in every other way—I usually would not look at him. Tall men are simply not, as Dominic would say, tasty to me. I like a man who can line up with me, eye to eye, foot to foot, balls to balls. Otherwise, frottage is awkward.

Oliver Ingraham was a heavyset man with silver hair. He had what appeared to be the vestiges of some erstwhile athleticism.

We'd agreed to meet at an Italian place where Jasper and I had been many times for dinner, but not for years. I chose it because it's a short walk from where I live, was likely to be uncrowded, and I remembered the pumpkin tortellini. I liked the pumpkin tortellini, and I wanted to be in a place where Jasper and I had been. There are dozens of such places, but this is the one that has the pumpkin tortellini.

In Italy it would have been pumpkin ravioli.

"You told me Bleecker Street," Oliver Ingraham said. "I looked on Bleecker Street."

"Did you?" I asked.

I knew one thing: I had not told Oliver Ingraham Bleecker Street. I had told him Sixth Avenue *near* Bleecker Street. I remembered going to some trouble to make that much clear.

Of course, Jasper would not have set out to meet me anywhere without first checking the address.

It's odd, isn't it?—no one thinks to use the telephone book. They don't think to dial 411. Or, rather, tap it, punch in four fucking eleven.

I said, "I'm sorry," to Oliver Ingraham.

"It's all right, Tim," said Oliver Ingraham. Oliver Ingraham sat down.

"Oh, but, Oliver, I *am* sorry," I said.

"I found you," said Oliver Ingraham.

OLIVER INGRAHAM and I spoken less than two weeks ago, the day before Jasper died. I'd called Jasper's house at eight in the morning, having tried to get him for more than a week. Oliver Ingraham answered Jasper's telephone. I asked to speak to Jasper Eisendorfer.

"He isn't here," Oliver Ingraham said.

I told Oliver Ingraham who I was and reminded him that we had met three years before.

"Yes," said Oliver Ingraham. He said it like a question.

"I'm a friend of Jasper's," I told Oliver Ingraham.

"Yes," said Oliver Ingraham.

"Where is he? I called the hospital, they told me he wasn't there."

"He's here, Tim, but he can't come to the telephone," Oliver Ingraham said.

"How is he?" I asked.

"When was the last time you saw him?"

"Nine days ago," I said.

"Well, then you know how he is."

"He was pretty sick then," I said. "Is he worse?"

Oliver Ingraham paused. Our conversation that day was full of pauses. Oliver Ingraham is a man who chooses to say as little as possible. Sometimes this is welcome.

"He's in terrible shape," said Oliver Ingraham.

"I've been trying to call him all week," I said. "There's never an answer. Is he in bed?"

"He's in the living room," Oliver Ingraham said.

"All day?"

"He stays on the couch," said Oliver Ingraham.

"Why doesn't he pick up the phone? I've let it ring fifty times," I told Oliver Ingraham

"Jasper can't walk well," Oliver Ingraham said.

He had walked awkwardly nine days before.

"But don't you have somebody there, a nurse or a health-care person?" I asked.

The last time I'd seen Jasper he had told me he would get someone. I hated that he had just been placating me.

"I suppose we should have something like that, but Jasper wouldn't want it," said Oliver Ingraham.

"Yes, and he probably doesn't *want* to be sick, either. But there has got to be someone in the house," I insisted.

"I'm here at night," said Oliver Ingraham.

"Where are you during the day?" I asked.

"I have a business to run. I have appointments in the city." Oliver Ingraham inflected the word "business" as though it were the most important thing in his world. He said it as though it were huge. He said it as though it were something.

Not every appointment I have is with a doctor. I'd started doing portrait work again. I had limited myself to two sessions a week, and unless it is commercial work, which I hadn't resumed, people have always come to me. I'll photograph them wherever they like, but they must first come to me. It's to their advantage to let me see them in the studio.

Oliver Ingraham deals in antiques. Jasper had told me he had a store on East Twelfth Street, as do many antique dealers. East Eleventh and Twelfth Streets are spotted with smallish antique stores. There is the man who sells horses from the Tang dynasty. There is the man who deals in Louis XIV, mostly chairs and love seats, garishly regilded. There is the man who deals in chinoiserie. There is the man who deals in the late Gothic period, and another who does only Queen Anne, and one whose store is full of Victorian furniture.

Years ago, I bought a sang de boeuf vase from the man who deals in old Japanese treasures. Over the years, I've bought one or two other things from him. When I first went to him he asked to see my card. I shook my head and told him that I was not a decorator and would not engage one.

This man, who for years has had in the back of his store a coromandel screen that eventually will sell for a little more than one would pay for a pleasant little house in the country, told me that interior decorators are called designers. I told the man I knew that. I said they can call themselves anything they like, and I would still not engage one.

Objects in a man's interior should, I said that day, thinking about it for the first time, be eclectic. That is, they should veer in that direction. They shouldn't look as though great time had been spent considering how well one piece would go with another.

Back then, I looked like someone with the wherewithal to buy things. In fact, I was. Overall, I'd say that I preferred looking like a young man with wherewithal. I miss being one.

The man with the sang de boeuf vase allowed me into his store. When an antique dealer has on his door, or emblazoned on his window, the words "To the Trade," it is only an easy way to discourage browsing.

These are harder times. I wouldn't even try to gain egress to such a place today. Lack of wherewithal usually shows. There is even sometimes a minor stench to it. The foulest incense cannot mask it.

It is probably more true of indigence than of the illness that a lowered self-esteem, verging on paranoia, usually tags along with it.

———

YEARS AGO, I asked Jasper about Oliver Ingraham. Before I asked, I asked if I could ask.

"May I ask you about Oliver?" I asked. We were sitting on my couch sharing a negroni.

"What do you want to know?" Jasper asked.

I hadn't thought that far ahead.

His response could have been taken as permission to ask anything at all, or could have been Jasper's way of asking how I dared ask.

"Is he terribly good-looking?" I asked.

"Terribly?" Jasper asked. "No."

"What does he look like?" I asked.

Jasper hesitated. "He's letting himself go," he said, a little pensively.

I wasn't sure what Jasper meant. Jasper lived by almost impossibly high standards. He even took his pleasures in a disciplined way. He took pleasure from discipline, it satisfied him or seemed to. Although he did not aspire to model male underwear, if he'd shaved his chest he probably could have. Recently I saw an advertisement featuring a bare-chested man in staggeringly good condition. I couldn't tell if he was good-looking; the photograph was cropped at the nape of his neck. The product advertised was men's shirts, but there was no shirt in the photograph, not on the body, not even wadded up in a corner. Unless I see at least a hint of contour, I assume a crotch has been padded. Jasper wouldn't have needed that or any kind of body doubling. He tended to expect, and he always preferred, men and boys who upheld similar standards.

It turned out that Oliver Ingraham is the man who deals in Victorian furniture. He has an associate. When you call the store, the associate, the partner, the factotum, answers and says, "Oliver Ingraham." Probably this man is not a partner. Possibly he is simply a man paid to answer the telephone and say, "Oliver Ingraham," in order to tell you that he is not Oliver Ingraham himself. "No," the man will say. "I am not Mr. Ingraham."

———

"JASPER CAN'T walk, and he's *alone* all day?" I'd asked Oliver Ingraham on the telephone about two weeks before. "Oliver, how can that be? I'll come, I'll take care of him, until you get someone."

Oliver Ingraham was quiet awhile. "I'll ask Jasper if

he'd like that. I know you are ill, too. Tell me, did you and Jasper have a physical relationship?" Oliver Ingraham asked.

Jasper must have finally told Oliver Ingraham something. I wondered why.

"Why don't you ask Jasper?" I said.

"I'm asking you," Oliver Ingraham said.

I was disinclined to disclose my life to Oliver Ingraham. His question struck me as being abysmally phrased.

"Yes," I said. "We do."

I would give not one detail of Jasper's life with me. That was ours, Jasper's and mine. Oliver Ingraham must have been eager, I expected, to dismiss me as nothing more than Back Street butt fuck. It couldn't be easy for him to accept that Jasper had had another life, one that hadn't included him.

I knew it wasn't easy. I'd accepted it for eighteen years.

I wondered if Oliver Ingraham had already asked Jasper. I wondered if Jasper had lied.

"You can understand that I have to ask you this," said Oliver Ingraham. "Did Jasper get this thing from you?"

It was my turn to pause.

"I can't know, Oliver," I said.

I knew Jasper hadn't gotten it from me.

All I said to Oliver Ingraham was that Jasper had been capable of getting this "thing" without me.

Oliver Ingraham did not respond.

His next question came quickly, almost as if the one before hadn't been the one he'd really wanted to ask.

"Have you and Jasper had any discussions about his assets?"

I could picture Oliver Ingraham. I could see the elements, the composition. I knew he was standing or sitting at Jasper's desk. Oliver Ingraham keeps a telephone in almost every room. In that house there is a basement, and in that basement there is a telephone.

Jasper has a workroom in that basement. His large

worktable abuts a short wall; his saws, some of which were his father's and some his grandfather's, and some of which are just collector's items, hang from copper prongs or hooks on a long wall. That wall has small windows near the ceiling. Otherwise, the basement is well underground, and Jasper had himself forced the hooks into the concrete wall. There are shelves on another wall for about three hundred paperback books.

When Oliver Ingraham watched television upstairs, Jasper sometimes went to read in his basement workroom. There is a battered old wing chair, with an ottoman that doesn't match it. There is a good lamp for reading. The worktable is the only piece of furniture in the house made by Jasper, unless, of course, you count the sawhorses. Jasper built those, too.

He built the table that he gave me down in that basement workroom, and all the bookcases that he made for me he made there, too. The bookshelves he has given himself are simpler affairs, but they show Jasper's respect for books, for the physical objects they are. They are lined up neatly.

It appalled Jasper to see me using paperbacks as coasters. Hardcover books with glossy jackets make, in fact, better coasters than paperbacks do. A damp paper towel will get rid of most rings. I've cleaned water rings that were years old. A bit of Windex works wonders.

I wouldn't buy coasters. They'd be just one more thing to lose.

Oliver Ingraham, that I know, hasn't much occasion to go down to that basement, yet he keeps a telephone in it. It is his line, it isn't Jasper's.

That morning I'd called Jasper's line, not Oliver Ingraham's. Jasper's telephone is in his study. He has only one. Except when I was in the hospital, and then when Jasper was, I don't remember speaking with Jasper for more than two minutes on the telephone.

What would we talk about on the telephone?

Why would we?

That is how I knew that Oliver Ingraham was standing or sitting in Jasper's study and was waiting for my answer.

The pause grew. It grew by itself. Then I let it grow. The silence deepened. When it had become as deep as I could stand, and deeper than that, I said to Oliver Ingraham, "Jasper isn't dead yet, Oliver."

I would not put myself through another second with Oliver Ingraham. I hung up. Whatever reponse he had, he could make it to himself.

I put the machine on, left the house quickly, and began a walk that kept me out until late in the evening. I walked around Gramercy Park, where nannies read romance novels as their infant charges snoozed in their canopied prams. If I'd had a key to that little park, that dear hush in the middle of the city, I would have gone from pram to pram, admired each darling creature. There must be, no doubt, many ugly babies in this city and the world, squadrons of them, platoons, but I had not yet seen one. Perhaps babies are unbeautiful only when they cry and scream. In Paris, parc de Monceau more or less belongs to nannies and their charges, though sometimes you will see a woman too well dressed to be a nanny, and these women may be the mothers, but at least as often you will see a grandmother, sitting or strolling with the carriage, or walking hand in hand with a child who is taking his first steps. In English, we call these children "toddlers," a cloying word, a belittling, disenabling label. Many grandmothers in parc de Monceau are impeccably groomed, elderly women of fashion who look absolutely smashing. A smart woman recognizes the time when she has ceased being succulent, but there is still elegance for her, that glamour closed on her, and she can become sage and gracious. The most a man can become is distinguished, but too few do.

A few times, but only a few, one of these women has smiled right back at me.

I walked up a few blocks of Third Avenue, where it is bleak, and then walked west to Madison. I passed Brooks Brothers amd Paul Stuart, some shoe stores, looked in Sherry Lehman's window, went into Books and Company and bought a paperback of Willa Cather's *My Mortal Enemy,* which I'd read in Paris and kept there. I walked through Central Park, stopping on dry grass to read a few pages—there is no one who writes like Willa Cather today. I ended up, without having planned it, on the corner of Broadway and 74th. I stood outside the Continental Baths and looked across the street at its lifeless facade for several minutes, possibly an hour.

I remembered Dominic's brittle observation, long before the epidemic, that I had been born at the baths, had been bred at the baths, and would die at the baths. I disliked giving credit to Dominic's prophecy, but in an imprecise way this can be said of too many of us.

I walked down Eighth Avenue, had dinner alone at a place called the Acropolis. It has been there as far back as I can remember. Jasper and I had been there once, in 1974. The food had been just all right, but I remembered that we'd had a good time together there. We'd laughed more than we ever had before. Our laughter that night at the Acropolis was copious and fun.

I looked up from Willa Cather and saw just then that I was the only customer in the place.

I had all the room in the world to think and it was at that instant it became clear that in Oliver Ingraham's mind Jasper's death was already a fact.

My mind jettisoned the thought. Good lord, I'd been bed-bound, just as Jasper was couch-bound, and I couldn't walk either, not for the longest time, but I hadn't been left alone all day. I had friends who came to see me, and others who called, and none of them had asked me what I was going to do with my "assets."

I was always hungry back then, six or seven times a day. That may have been another thing that saved me. Day after day, I'd lie abed, thinking of the magical dinner I would make for Jasper and me as soon as I'd be able. Of course, I did not forget myself, how could I, when for more than thirty years my life had been largely a matter of me-me-me? I let the glorious dinner evolve, picturing it in complete detail, until I could smell every taste. I knew that I could buy sea urchin from any of a dozen Japanese places, where they sell it on the half-shell at the sushi bars. For a few days I wondered if it could be used mysteriously in some odd and wonderful crepe batter. For a while I had a longing for that particular flavor and a longing, too, for saffron—remembering that in a long-ago century, Marco Polo's time perhaps, saffron had been more treasured than gold. It occurred to me, lying in bed with cookbooks and news magazines, which were all I read for a while, that *oursins,* which is a prettier name for sea urchins, when served uncooked are close to the color of saffron. I thought then of composing a dinner around that color, that a dinner could be wrapped in that color, could begin and end with it, and include at various intervals an item of green and of black and of white. Sautéed spinach leaves, chosen for size and symmetry, could be laid out singly on a large black dinner place, circled with slivered almonds, softened by a slow steep in butter; I thought of how thinly a fennel bulb could be sliced and of how white it might be, or how green. I thought of the black exterior of a grilled chateaubriand, and of the red its slices should be when it is cooked precisely *à point.*

Constantly, I told the care providers how to bake a potato or how to slice one almost translucently, or how to cut the potato, or rather the potatoes, into cubes after the skin had been scrubbed with a brush, and how much butter to use tossing them.

If I could do these things and get a little better, Jasper could do them, too. It hadn't come yet to me that he would not.

I objected to Oliver Ingraham's question almost as fully as I did the thought of Jasper dying. To give him an answer to it would have been as offensive as the question.

In fact, Jasper and I had talked about each other's assets. The day we closed on our place on Quai d'Orléans we celebrated by giving ourselves an excellent lunch in the just newly reopened garden of Le Pré Catelan. It was at that lunch that Jasper suggested, and strongly, that we each leave our halves of the property to each other. It was before the epidemic had become a problem, and it seemed odd to be talking will and testaments and such on that day. I would rather have waited.

Jasper said he would leave all his wine to me. I told him he would get my cases of framboise and also of poire, the rights to all my photographs, and whatever money I would have after taxes, which would not likely be much. I said I would count on him to give some of the money to Abigail and Gary.

He was adamant about the property. He said that he was sure I would not want to own it with Oliver Ingraham. I told him he was quite right about that.

"Why are we talking about this now?" I asked.

Jasper was not at all tightfisted about where we should have our celebration. He said we should have it in the Bois de Boulogne, in the garden of Le Pré Catelan, which had just begun to bloom. The first thing I noticed was a small boy child, a ganymede. He was ignoring his grilled John Dory and was, I thought, the most seraphic-looking French child I'd ever seen. The big white sun umbrella was turned to protect the mother and father from the sun's glare—it was bright, almost merciless that day—but the boy child was not under its circle of shade. He didn't seem to care, though, not at all, because he had turned his small, radiant self fully around in his chair and settled his eyes on Jasper.

They must have been the greenest eyes in Paris. It was as though his black pupils, by enlarging, had crowded all the green to the perimeter of the iris, so that green was laid over green, so that green had doubled and tripled. No leaf had ever been as green, or any jade of emerald, probably, and no eyelashes were as lavish, as dark and abundant.

This boy child was nine or ten. He was not only a treat to my eyes, he was a blessing to them. His beauty was almost a benediction—and his eyes were the best reason in the world to photograph in color, though I doubted that any film or any lighting could capture them.

"Papa, you have an admirer," I said.

"Timothy, please don't encourage him," Jasper said, almost pleading with me.

"He doesn't need encouragement," I said.

I was right about that. The child sprang a little awkwardly from his chair and began to parade around his table. He was wearing a little boy's summer suit, pale white linen. The trousers were short and they were cuffed. If I had seen short trousers cuffed before, I hadn't noticed them. Preening a bit, more than a bit actually, the child swung his arms about and looked over his shoulder, directly at Jasper.

"Ignore him, please, Timothy," Jasper suggested or, rather, ordered.

"How can I?" I asked. "He is helplessly in love with you. I know exactly what the poor little darling is suffering. He knows he has to break your heart, before you break his."

"You're such a twink sometimes," Jasper said. "No one will break anyone's heart today."

"I beg to differ. Behold, the angel cometh."

The little boy had left his table and was coming over to ours. He showed no hesitation whatsoever.

Every table in the garden was taken. Le Pré Catelan is not a place where ladies come for lunch. It's too long a

trip and too far from shopping. There was at least one
man at every table and some of them were good-enough
looking, in a respectable sort of way, but of all the men
at all the tables that day, this angelic boy had chosen Jasper. He was a precocious boy child, no doubt, but I
doubted he had shook hands yet with his libido; he probably hadn't even become vain yet, though you could see
this would only take some time. He was already sensible
enough to see that Jasper was the best choice that day in
the garden.

———————

OLIVER INGRAHAM had wanted to meet at 8:45 that
evening.

"Jesus," I expelled. "Time doesn't come in fifteen-
minute modules."

"What's that?" asked Oliver Ingraham.

"Modules are bitsy little units. I don't meet people at
eight forty-five, Oliver. I don't meet people at eight-fif-
teen. I will meet you at eight-thirty or at nine o'clock."

"What's wrong with quarter of?" Oliver Ingraham
asked.

"Nothing is wrong with a quarter of, I don't do it,
that's all," I said.

"Why not?" Oliver Ingraham asked me.

"Because I don't have to," I answered.

"How is eighty-thirty, then?" Oliver Ingraham asked.

"Not as good as nine o'clock," I answered.

———————

I CAME early. I sat at a table in the back, had a negroni,
and read—and read again—George Orwell's essay
"How the Poor Die."

The essay is Orwell's account of his stay at a public

hospital in Paris. It's hard to take. That's why I read it again.

Just about all my life, I've been late for just about everything—every appointment I've ever made, every date I've ever had, every class I've ever taken.

In airports, I am the frantic, foolish-looking fellow whom you always see running to the gate. People get annoyed. Abigail and Gary bitch all the time about this, and Dominic, who should know me better, has said that I come late so that I can make an entrance. Dominic says this because it is true of him, or it used to be. Dominic used to love making an entrance.

I was not late for Jasper, though. Not once. For Jasper, I was always on time. I managed this by being a little early whenever we met. Jasper was always on the dot. Six o'clock to Jasper was not six-fifteen or six-twenty. Tonight, to meet Oliver Ingraham, I came *very* early.

Dominic is wrong: I don't like making an entrance, and an entrance was the last thing I was going to make for Oliver Ingraham. I was not going to be the one who, seen by the other, must walk across a room.

I hate that. I've always hated to be seen walking across a room. I still do. Even more, I hate an open space, where the person I am walking toward will have nothing to look at but me. That is the most hateful thing. While it's happening I just want it to be over, I just want it to end. I hate the time it takes, every second of it.

It isn't the open space itself I mind, it is the obligation to cross it, to be seen crossing it, being looked at in that way, by anyone. *That* is what I hate.

It isn't agoraphobia.

It's worse than that.

It is a lack of poise.

One time I remember well. I was in school, in British Columbia, was nine and the only American boy in fifth-grade gymnastics. I was also the youngest. I was about to do a flip, a running flip over six boys who had formed a pyramid, when, from out of nowhere, the headmaster appeared in the doorway and called me to him.

I remember that I had to walk, with everyone looking at me, with every eye upon me, all the way to the other end of the gymnasium, which was vast. It was a frightening walk, all the way to the door of the gym, to the head, who, once I got to him, told me the president had been shot, and when he told me this I was slow to comprehend why the head had put me through such misery to tell me this.

One night I walked toward Jasper in Venice. He had come the day before. I'd had to photograph an actress in London. Jasper didn't want to be in London and suggested we meet in Venice. The flight from London was delayed, and it was about three in the morning when I finally got to Venice.

The city was asleep, more or less. At the hotel, the concierge told me they had not been able to give us our usual room, that Mr. Eisendorfer had preferred the Danieli, would I go by launch? It was a glorious night; I said I'd walk but told the concierge it would be good of him to send my bags along. He said they would be there before I was. I said that was splendid and started walking toward San Marco.

I had just started out, had found my way along narrowly cramped streets, and had just come onto San Marco, onto its sudden, thrilling immensity—it gave me a great delight to be again in Venice—and was thinking to myself that the chance of Jasper being awake for me was slim, and at that moment, at the far end of the square, looking small in the massive scale, was Jasper.

He must have been out looking for me. He had probably called the airline to ask about the flight. He was the only man in the square; I hadn't seen him for two weeks, and I started running toward him, and just as I was beginning, that was the instant, exactly the instant, that Jasper saw me.

He did not, of course, wave.

Nor did I. We were not people to wave at one another. Nor did I move. I stood where I was and waited for Jasper to come to me. I saw him look at me across the square and could see his puzzlement.

I wanted to be with him at once: I wanted all the time it would take for me to walk to him, or to run to him, and him to me—time in which we could only look at one another—I wanted it to end. Even more than this, though, worse, I found I could not bear for Jasper to watch me cross so vast a space.

It didn't surprise me that Jasper had ditched the Gritti—though I thought it terribly sweet of them, civilized, to speak of our "usual" room; we'd stayed there only twice before and were hardly regulars. They must keep meticulous records. The Danieli is under the same banner as the Gritti. Jasper and I had spoken two or three times about the Danieli, which is a little less costly and is, on top of that, not quite as out of the way as the Gritti. Some people like the Gritti *because* it is out of the way, and it may be true that the Danieli can be a little noisier than the Gritti—though it's still pretty quiet over there—and noise had bothered Jasper only toward the end, and it was his *not* hearing it that was the problem, not that it was loud.

Jasper had thought he was losing his hearing and asked me to speak up. I spoke quite loudly to him, and he was still annoyed with me for not speaking up *enough*. This went on for several months, until a doctor, an otolaryngologist, told him, in 1989, that he had wax in his ears.

I was glad Jasper could hear again. His partial loss had lessened his enjoyment of music, which was one of his greatest pleasures. He would rather listen to Mahler than look a long time at a Matisse.

Jasper never walked around with headphones, though. Isn't wax something one would feel? And couldn't I have thought of it? Shouldn't I have? I was reminded of

Norman Mailer's objecting to Arthur Miller's oblivious-
ness to cold sores in his wife's mouth, his wife having
been the legend named Marilyn Monroe. Norman Mailer
was not able to restrain his amazement at the fact of this
and asked his readers, rather temptingly, to speculate when
Arthur Miller had last kissed Marilyn Monroe.

This has, of course, nothing at all to do with my not
knowing Jasper had wax in an ear, but I often think about
it.

It occurred to me that there were possibly other things
about Jasper's decline, things more important than wax
and easier to discern, that I hadn't thought enough about
to observe them.

On earlier trips Jasper and I didn't mind the walk to
the Gritti, and the Danieli, while also on the canal, has
nothing even close to the Gritti's terrace, which is so
agreeable a place to have a grappa late at night, where it
is such a pleasure just to go right up to bed, while you
still have the taste in your mouth and the fire in your
belly—and because of this the choice was, actually, a little harder to make than it would seem to be, initially.

The Danieli does have a terrace on its roof. It has a
wider view of Venice than you will have from the Gritti's
terrace. I don't know if it actually floats, but the Gritti's
terrace more or less sways with the water—the tides, such
as they are, of the canal.

If you lay a pen on the tablecloth, wonderful, heavy
white linen, it is likely the pen will roll. It may even roll
off the table.

You can have coffee and raspberries in the morning at
either place, but the Danieli's roof isn't what I think of
when I think of a place to drink a grappa before going
to bed.

When Jasper and I stayed at the Gritti, I was horrified,
both times, by the same family. It must have been a family
from Washington State. The landmarks that speckled this
family's breakfast talk sounded to me like things in Wash-

ington State: Lake Washington, for instance, and the "floating" bridge; Mount Rainier and Frederick & Nelson.

I was horrified especially by the daughter, who appeared to be an only child. She was blonde and much too hefty, too fleshy, too thick of thigh and broad of beam for the tight, tight faded blue jeans that were her uniform for Venice. For three mornings I watched her gobble eggs. She always ordered extra bacon. She was about sixteen the first time, closer to twenty the next, and the years had not reduced her girth.

She was energetic and thumpingly North American. When I saw her the second time I was more than horrified. She was then a tall woman, which meant that there was nothing forthcoming for fat to grow into. Her mother called her Stephanie. Her father called her "Stephie." That is probably the story.

Why did she churn so agitatedly in my stomach? Quite possibly I was the only one who found her frightful. Jasper thought I made too much of her.

He used her name, though, once. When he told me I was buried in suet, he also said, "Timmykins, you don't want to get like Stephie-poo."

———————

AFTER JASPER had commented that Oliver Ingraham was letting himself go, I asked, "Have you said anything to Oliver about how he's letting himself go?"

"It wouldn't make any difference, he'd only be hurt," said Jasper.

"That didn't stop you from telling me I was getting rotund," I reminded him.

"I care how you look, Timothy. I worried that if you were pudgy at twenty-seven you'd look like hell at thirty-five. I also know that you care about being glamorous more than you care about anything else," Jasper said, not accusingly but with amusement.

"What on God's ravaged earth gives you that idea?" I asked.

"You do," Jasper answered. "Your quest, your desperation to be glamorous, drives everything you do. Your photography is all about glamour, and nothing but. So is everything you cook. So are the expensive flowers you buy and keep in stagnant water long after they're dead," Jasper said.

"What kind of living would I make, do you think, if I made people look no better than they do?" I asked. "Is it so awful that I'd rather cook something with a pretension or two than churn out mom's home cookin'? And papa-balls, my sweet, your cuisine isn't exactly farm style."

"I don't go as far out of my way as you do," Jasper said. "I don't scream 'fuck, shit, piss' when I burn garlic."

"Possibly because you never burn garlic," I suggested.

"And you do it all the time," Jasper said.

"That's why I scream about it," I said.

"When I told you you were getting a little thick in the waist, you starved yourself to the bone."

"Papa, you didn't say I was getting thick in the middle, what you said was that I had no cheekbones. You told me they were buried in suet."

"Is that what I said? That's not bad. It doesn't sound like me," said Jasper.

Actually, Jasper hadn't said "suet." The word he'd used was "fat." Suet, I believe, is cow fat. Or sheep fat. Goat fat?

"What makes losing weight an obsession with being glamorous?" I asked. "Why can't you think of it as a discipline?"

"Because it isn't a discipline, it's a mania," Jasper said.

"Sort of like spending your life lifting weights?" I asked.

"Not quite, dear Timothy," said Jasper.

———

TONIGHT, I wasn't about to give Oliver Ingraham that extra chance to judge.

I had to tell myself that the man across the table, with his reddened eyes, had lived with Jasper longer than I had known him. If Jasper were alive, he'd be with Oliver Ingraham. They would have grown old together. It had taken nothing less than death to part these men.

This was what I thought while waiting for Oliver Ingraham to speak. There must be something in this man, I thought, that Jasper had loved.

———————

THE NIGHT I asked Jasper to describe Oliver Ingraham, we were sitting on my couch having a drink. Jasper would come to my house, and we would always have a drink before we went into the bedroom to toss the ball. Usually, we had a negroni, sometimes we had sherry, or if I was making a dinner for us we might have Pinot des Charantes or a champagne framboise. In the summer, I made bellinis. I have found that a decent champagne is still quite drinkable, even lively, the day *after* it's been opened, so you can open a bottle and have a glass or two, you don't need to drink it all, and if it does go a little flat you can always poach a fish in it. It would be foolish to throw it away. A good cook is one who doesn't waste.

I make efforts against waste, but if something isn't delicious I *do* throw it away.

I'm not saying I've never had a failure.

For the first ten years or so, Jasper and I would always drink the same thing; if Jasper had sherry I'd have sherry. Around 1984, this began to change.

Jasper and I always played in the bedroom. Jasper and I did not, for example, play in kitchens. Jasper never bent me over the kitchen counter to have at me, nor did I ask

him to. Jasper and I weren't innovative. We didn't improvise much.

"Improvisation," by the way, was one of a handful of
words Jasper could not pronounce. There were one or two
others. When Jasper said "improvisation," it came out
"improvision." Something we saw off Broadway, for example pieces we saw in the seventies at the Performance
Garage, would strike Jasper as being "improvisional," or
something he'd cooked for us would be. One time he went
so far as to call something "improvositable." Even he made
a face when *that* came out of him.

Jasper was an articulate man; he just had a problem
with this word, and one or two others. I can't think of
the others now, I would have to hear him say them again.

The one I remember is "improvisation." I'd always
correct him, and he would laugh at himself, in a good-
natured way, which laughed at me, too, and he'd repeat
the word as I had said it—once—and then he would not
remember it when it came around again.

I didn't give up on him, though. I kept after him about
it, because it bothered me, just enough so that I could not
let it go. I cared that Jasper pronounce a word correctly,
cared more than it was worth, I realize now. It even came
to a point where I wasn't amused.

I think that leaving Germany must account for it. In
America, in Indiana, his father and his mother did not
allow German to be spoken in the house. This is said to
have been true of many immigrants from Europe, especially those from Germany, especially the Jews, and every
time Jasper said "improvision" I wondered if losing the
language of his childhood—having all the words he knew
ripped away—might have been, at that age, to Jasper, in
a way that it hadn't been for other children, shattering.

More than once it crossed my mind that Jasper was
not ever at home with the new words, that he might not
have really settled in them.

Of course, I make too much of this.

For the most part, Jasper spoke nearly perfect English. He corrected me sometimes. He used words handsomely, though he may have been too careful with them, a little too punctilious. Jasper was an exact man. Most of the time I liked listening to him, and he always listened to me. Jasper did not interrupt, me or anyone else, that I ever heard. The man simply did not interrupt. Ever.

But there were frequent little things he did in speech that irritated me. They were of no consequence, I knew they were of no consequence. Still, they irritated me. For example, Jasper used to say "infer" when he meant "imply." He did this for years. A lot of people do it. It irritates me. He finally got that one right, but he never did get "improvisation." He just couldn't get it. If you cannot pronounce a thing, how do you say it is missing from your life?

I wonder that.

So Jasper and I didn't improvise. We always played in bed. Except once. Once, we played on a beach.

Other people, two older men, were a hundred yards or so away. We didn't plan it, we just found ourselves at play. It was a bright afternoon, there was sun all around the world, no breeze at all. We let ourselves get out of hand. But that one time was exceptional. After that, Jasper wouldn't even let me squeeze him through his trousers in public—though I could never stop doing that altogether.

That one time was fun, playing with Jasper on the beach. I remember the fun of it. I remember everything about it, how slippery Jasper's skin was, how he smelled of coconut oil. I remember it all. I could live for the memory of that one time, for just that one heart-pounding, blood-thumping time with Jasper. It would be worth living for, too. With one memory worth living for, can't every last one of us be somehow ready to die?

———————

OLIVER INGRAHAM ordered a white-wine spritzer.

He didn't drink, he told me, didn't like the taste of wine. I thought of all the great bottles Jasper had in his cellar, the cases of superb Bordeaux and of the different cognacs, which, unless I asked for them, Oliver Ingraham would sell to strangers, who would probably drink them too soon.

Maybe he would just let them go bad.

That night, I wanted to drink a cold Tokay with the pumpkin tortellini and a robust Amarone with *ossobuco*. And I would have if Jasper and I were having this dinner. What would Oliver Ingraham think if I ordered these wines, even just one bottle, for myself?

I wondered this idiotically.

Why should I want to enjoy this dinner? Why should I try to? Shouldn't it be properly grim?

When I'd met Oliver Ingraham at Jasper's house, Jasper and I had been having dinner on the deck outside the greenhouse, where Jasper had tall jade trees growing taller in umbrellaed shade and was having a run of bad luck with orchids. From that deck, which goes around two sides of the house, and from the two-story greenhouse, which curves around a corner and is magnificently planted with varieties of hothouse flowers, is a view of the river.

Every morning Jasper or Oliver Ingraham would drive up to the mailbox for the *New York Times*. It was and will always be a house where no one who does not drive a car can live.

It is almost inaccessible, hard to find in the first place, and harder still, Oliver Ingraham told me that night, for an ambulance to reach.

The night Oliver Ingraham and I met by accident, in 1988, I was sitting alone on the deck smoking a cigarette. Jasper did not let me smoke in the house. The space for cars—the parking lot, so to speak—is visible from the deck, as was the deck visible to Oliver Ingraham. It was late evening, but there was lamplight on the deck. Oliver

Ingraham looked at me from where he stood. I saw him hesitate. I lighted one cigarette off another and tried to look composed, which I wasn't, of course—not at all.

Oliver Ingraham unraveled a water hose and began to wash his car. That year Oliver Ingraham had a Mercedes. Jasper was in the kitchen. After dinner Jasper would always clear things away immediately. I never do that; I wait until guests leave.

I went upstairs to tell Jasper that Oliver Ingraham had come home.

"Where is he?" Jasper asked.

I told Jasper that Oliver Ingraham appeared to be washing his car.

Jasper's mind worked quickly. In an instant he took everything into account. He went at once to Oliver Ingraham. I returned to the deck. Within the minute Jasper appeared, followed by Oliver Ingraham.

"You two should meet each other," Jasper said, and began introductions.

I stood up and extended my hand before Jasper could say my name. I gave Oliver Ingraham my name.

Oliver Ingraham almost draped his hand in mine. His handshake was like liquid.

Jasper said something about dessert and left me alone with Oliver Ingraham. I could have killed him for that.

I had tested positive a few months before. Jasper still thought he was negative.

Oliver Ingraham made me feel unwelcome. He also made it clear that he had never heard of me. Minutes later Jasper returned with clear glass bowls of grappa ice. I thought it was glorious and told him so. Oliver Ingraham took a taste of it. He didn't like it at all and said to Jasper, "You knew I wouldn't eat this."

"DID JASPER ever tell you about David Moss?" Oliver Ingraham asked me, ignoring his white-wine spritzer.

"The name sounds familiar," I said.

"He's an old friend of Jasper's. They met in Kansas City."

"Oh, yes," I said. "Isn't he the man who sends Jasper a birthday card every year?"

"That's him," said Oliver Ingraham.

"That's such a nice story, isn't it?" I said.

"He called this year on Jasper's birthday," Oliver Ingraham told me.

"That must have been nice for Jasper," I said.

"It wasn't," said Oliver Ingraham.

"Why not? What happened?" I asked.

"I told David Moss Jasper couldn't come to the phone," Oliver Ingraham told me. "I told him Jasper was sick. David Moss asked me what was wrong, so I told him Jasper had AIDS. He was silent. He said he couldn't talk, said he'd call back. That was almost a month ago. He hasn't called back."

I wondered if Oliver Ingraham would ever tell me anything I could be happy to hear.

"'Why didn't you ask David Moss to wait?" I asked. "You could have *gone* to Jasper, told him David Moss was calling, and helped him upstairs to the telephone. Clearly, Jasper meant something to this man, and didn't you think that Jasper might have wanted to speak to him himself? Maybe there was something Jasper wanted to say to David Moss. That didn't cross your mind, Oliver? Christ, it wasn't yours to tell."

"Tim, keep it down," Oliver Ingraham said.

I nearly told Oliver Ingraham to vanish in hell. I hadn't heard the worst.

Maybe I *had* been a little loud.

————

OLIVER INGRAHAM was talking about the night Jasper tried to kill himself. He'd come home late and found Jasper's note.

"I was frantic," Oliver Ingraham said. "I called the police, then the hospital. Jasper had been brought in by a couple who found him in the park. They'd found him lying under his car. He was lying there with the motor running."

A year ago, when I asked Jasper if Oliver Ingraham had found him, Jasper wouldn't talk about it. I hadn't known this part of the story. "Did he think he could asphyxiate himself in the open air?" I asked.

Oliver Ingraham made a face. "I don't know what he was thinking, Tim," Oliver Ingraham said. "The nurses at the hospital told me that when the couple brought Jasper in he screamed at everyone that they should have let him die. He shouted at everyone, 'I have AIDS, I'm going to die. I don't want to wait around for it.' "

I could not picture Jasper in the state Oliver Ingraham was describing. I had not ever seen him that way, out of control, nearly out of his mind, as Oliver Ingraham was making him sound.

"You know, Jasper wrote me a letter that night," I said. "He must have mailed it just before he went to the park. I never received it, though. It never came in the mail. Jasper must have thought he was writing the last words he'd say to me. He was saying good-bye in that letter. I wish so much now that I knew how he'd said it."

"Of course you didn't get the letter," Oliver Ingraham said. "The letter was destroyed."

'No, Jasper mailed it," I said. "In fact, he called and told me not to read it. That was sort of odd, I thought. But then, everything about that time was odd. Jasper was the last person I would have expected to try to kill himself."

"Tim," said Oliver Ingraham, "the letter was destroyed."

"Oliver, if he destroyed it, why did he call and tell me not to read it?" I asked.

Oliver Ingraham looked at me. I looked back at him. Then it came to me, and I thought that I had not before seen so transparent a face. If I kept looking at it, I would soon see through Oliver Ingraham's skull and into the workings of his mind.

I didn't ask Oliver Ingraham if he had destroyed the letter.

I wanted to be sitting on Jasper's granite counter, having a drink with him in his kitchen. I wanted to watch as he peeled asparagus for us, or chopped shallots. There were other things I missed, but this was what I missed just then.

I tried to change the topic. "Without Jasper to do it for you, are you learning to cook?" I asked Oliver Ingraham.

"No," Oliver Ingraham answered. "I have absolutely no interest in it. *None*."

He scorned the suggestion.

I thought of Jasper's costly kitchen being unused. "Don't you care what you eat?" I asked.

"Not really," said Oliver Ingraham.

"That's too bad. Jasper said people who don't know how to eat don't know how to live," I told Oliver Ingraham.

"It's not that I don't know how to eat, Tim. It simply isn't an issue for me. And I don't believe Jasper said that," said Oliver Ingraham.

"Maybe he didn't say it to you," I said quietly.

I knew there were some other things that Oliver Ingraham hadn't heard.

He would not have heard what Jasper had done for me when I came out of the hospital. That was in 1990 and was allowed by my doctor only with the condition that I have people looking after me round the clock.

The health-care agency I used—there are better ones now—had only four employees willing to work with an AIDS patient. One of them was a gigantically overweight, chain-smoking nurse. Her cough, or perhaps the vibration of it in the floor, awakened me two or three times a day. I made a pledge that if I ever smelled as much like an ashtray as this nurse did, I would do what I could to smoke less. The nurse was named Harriet and administered the acyclovir drip, which took six hours three times a week. Yet her shift was twelve hours, she slept in the living room. Harriet slept so soundly that even her stentorian snoring did not disrupt her slumber. I assumed she could sleep straight through a coughing fit. I slept in what had been the dining room, looking out into the garden, though there wasn't anything growing in it that October. On nice days I'd ask to be helped from bed into a garden chair. The garden was six steps down. That's when I needed the most help.

The other three care providers brought to my bedside the avalanche of medications I was taking every four hours. I'd get them down with fresh grapefruit juice and Pellegrino water. They made endless iced tea, endless lemonade, and Jasper marveled at how well they kept the house clean. Not wanting to seem ungrateful, I said nothing about it being easy to keep a house in good order when no one is using it.

Most of them were decent people with horrible jobs. One of them, Felicity, made wonderful fried chicken, but that was her only specialty. None of them could grill or bake or poach a fish, no one could trim an artichoke. Mostly I subsisted on Chinese and Indian food, taken out. I preferred that the health provider pick up the order, because that saved three or four dollars on tips.

Twice a week Jasper would come to see me. It was a long drive for him, too long just to come and say hello, so every time he came he would cook me something splendid for my dinner, a rare rack of baby lamb, not yet a month old, a wonderfully thick veal chop sautéed with chanterelles, a two-pound lobster, which he took out of the shell for me and served with fresh tarragon mayonnaise, tiny soft-shell crabs crisp with garlic and capers. I liked the tarragon mayonnaise and ate it, but I told him the raw egg in it might give me salmonella.

"Balderdash," Jasper said.

The next time he cooked lobster for me, he served it with butter and lemon. It was good, but not as good as fresh tarragon mayonnaise.

There was always a salad, usually green, but occasionally there would be freshly baked beets in it, Bibb lettuce or arugula, often with some chevre or a little crumbled Roquefort.

This food was cooked only for me, and Jasper waited to see that I ate all of it. He would not serve me in bed but made me have dinner at the table. He would not carry me to it, but he would help me walk. He didn't know, I'm sure, how sharply my foot hurt every time I put weight on it. Jasper ate none of this food himself. These dinners were usually under way by seven, too early for him to think about food. He usually left before nine, sometimes to meet Oliver Ingraham for dinner.

Jasper could not sit with me and have a long conversation, because every time he cooked for me he would clean up in the kitchen—any pan he'd used, any bowl, any counter space.

"Papa, come talk to me. You can leave the mess for the ha-ha help," I said one time.

The nights Jasper came, I would give the care provider money to go see a movie.

"Timothy, what do you pay these people?" Jasper asked.

"I don't pay them. I pay their agency. The agency gets thirty dollars an hour, and the workers probably get about eight of those dollars. The agency gets eighty dollars an hour for the IV nurse, who gets thirty-six dollars herself. Sometimes, to get them out of the house, I give them ten dollars to go see a movie or something, have dinner in a coffee shop. And, papa, they are paid for those two or three hours that they're not here. Felicity, the crabbiest of them, asked me, or rather told me, to give her twenty dollars so she could have a giant tub of popcorn, and a beer after the movie."

Jasper smiled. "And you did, didn't you?"

"Are you kidding? Or are you just out of your mind?" I asked. "Of course I didn't. I told dearest Felicity that she could go to the movie or have a couple of beers, that I wasn't made of cash. Which, by the way, I'm not. All this health-care poo-poo is wiping me out."

"If you really run out of money, Timothy, I will help you," said Jasper.

"Oh, papa, you don't know how much help I need," I said.

"You won't be able to live as you used to, but I won't let you starve," said Jasper.

"I'm hoping to get back to photographing people again, I said.

"How likely is that, really?" Jasper asked.

"Given time, there is some possibility," I answered. "Someday I'll get these monstrosities off my face, I'll get physical therapy sufficient to get me walking again, and I haven't completely lost my name. I will probably learn color, too. It's not as pure as black-and-white, and I don't like it as much, but it pays more handsomely."

These dinners were not at all like dinners with Jasper. After he'd been cooking them for a few weeks, I asked him why none of these dinners included a first course. I had not ever cooked Jasper a one-course dinner, and he had never done so, until now.

Jasper looked at me as though I had said something too foolish to believe. "It's a lot of work doing this much for you, Timothy."

"I know that, papa. Of course I know that. And I can't talk about how grateful I am to you," I told him. "I can't begin. I'm grateful that you're still in my life, that you didn't dump me when I got ill. I know people who have had that happen to them. One of them died quickly, soon after he was left. You can say AIDS killed him, but you can also say that he died from not being loved. But how much more difficult would it be just to make a little billi-bi. Once you clean the mussels, the soup almost makes itself. You strain the mussel liquor, heat some cream, whisk in an egg yolk, bring it all briefly to the boil, and that's it, you've made billi-bi. And if that's more than you feel like doing, why not just buy a little Scotch salmon?"

That was the night Jasper told me he'd rented a house for a month in Saint Barthélemy.

"Is Oliver coming?" I asked.

"No," Jasper answered.

"Can I come, then?"

"I can't take care of you," Jasper said. "You would have to be able to walk from here to Fifth Avenue."

It seemed likelier that Audrey Hepburn would come bang on my door insisting I take her picture than that I would be able to walk to Fifth Avenue in February, when Jasper would be going. It took me to the end of April. Jasper and I had loved Saint Bart when we had been there a few years before. The language is French, the currency is francs, there is a bay, and there is the ocean, too. Most of the cooking is French, and there are places to eat that would not be small potatoes in New York or even in Paris.

I didn't begrudge Jasper the trip. I didn't begrudge his saying that he couldn't take care of me. But in Saint Bart he stopped AZT because he did not want blood transfusions, and he took the sun, not his usual enormous dosage, but he would have been wiser not to take it at all. The sun is said to damage immunity, to kill T-cells. Jasper had so few T-cells he must have thought they weren't worth holding onto. I doubt the sun killed him any faster.

After Jasper died, Abigail told me what he said to her at a birthday party he gave me. Most of my close friends were there, and Jasper only told Abigail that he felt pretty terrible leaving me, but that he had to go to Saint Bart because he didn't know if he'd have another chance.

"That's right," I told Abigail. "That was Jasper, always ready to check himself out."

"That's a cruel thing to say," Abigail said. I think she was offended.

"I only say it because I love him," I told Abigail. "And I hate how he let himself die."

"Maybe he didn't think he had enough to live for," Abigail suggested.

"Why would he think that? Because he couldn't fuck anymore? There is always enough to live for. There is consciousness, Abigail, there are brain waves," I said.

"For many people, for most, I think, that isn't enough. Jasper thought you were going to die," Abigail told me then.

"Did he say that to you?" I asked.

"Yes," said Abigail.

"He didn't need me. He never lived for me," I said.

"I know that's what you think. Jasper probably dreaded what he feared would happen, and probably he dreaded his life without you," said Abigail.

"That's so corny," I snapped.

"Sometimes things are," Abigail said.

I granted Abigail that point because it was stingy not to.

I had dreaded my life without Jasper. In many ways I still do. I am healthier than I was then, maybe, but otherwise life without Jasper is pretty close to what I'd thought it would be.

Why shouldn't Jasper have had that feeling?

How much pleasure did it give me to fancy that I was the only one?

———————

OLIVER INGRAHAM had called me at six o'clock on the morning Jasper died. He said he had been awakened by Jasper's moans. There weren't any words in them, Oliver Ingraham said, they were only moans. He had called Jasper's doctor, and the doctor had dispatched an ambulance.

I was expecting Oliver Ingraham to tell me Jasper was dead. Instead, he talked about how long the ambulance had taken, an hour, or more. The driver had trouble finding the house, and, Oliver Ingraham did not say why, there was also a police escort. He described for me the howl of the siren.

I did not tell him that I know the siren sound. I hear sirens every night.

It hadn't been easy to get Jasper into the ambulance, Oliver Ingraham told me.

I asked Oliver Ingraham how much Jasper weighed.

Oliver Ingraham asked me what I was asking.

"I think he weighs about ninety-eight pounds," I said.

"Well, if that," said Oliver Ingraham.

"Why didn't you drag him up the stairs, put him in your car, and *take* him to the hospital?"

Oliver Ingraham said he had to wait for the ambulance.

"You don't just drive someone to a hospital, Tim. If I'd done that, he might not have been admitted quickly."

"Emergency rooms are for emergencies," I said. But I wondered then if Oliver Ingraham had a point; maybe an emergency is easier to recognize when someone arrives by ambulance. Maybe a police escort is a plus. Maybe all the theatrics are necessary.

Three years ago, a friend came to my house; we had a date for dinner. When he saw me, he told me I wasn't going to dinner, I was going to the hospital. I thought he was being extreme, and I resisted. He was firm, took my keys, locked my door, and drove me to the hospital. It *was* extreme, but that was what it took to save my life that night.

Oliver Ingraham said that the emergency nurses had told him he should be prepared: Jasper might not last the night. There was nothing he could do, they said, and told him he might as well go home and try to get some sleep. That is what Oliver Ingraham did.

When I got off the phone, I took a cab to the Port Authority and waited for an hour for the first morning bus. The bus did not stop at the hospital. It took another twenty minutes to get to it by foot.

It was too quiet for an emergency room, I thought.

The woman at the reception desk checked her log and told me Jasper wasn't registered.

She called someone inside and asked if anybody knew anything about a patient named Jasper Eisendorfer.

"Oh, did he?" I heard the woman say.

I told myself to assume nothing.

The woman told me someone would be with me soon. Another woman appeared directly.

"I'm here to see Jasper Eisendorfer," I said to the new woman.

She was calm, she was composed. This was her job. "Are you a relative?" she asked.

"Yes," I said. I knew that would cut through a lot of explanation.

The woman looked at me. This was her life. "Are you next of kin?"

I could only lie so much. "I am related by blood." This wasn't a lie, exactly. "Is he—seeable?" I asked.

The woman shook her head, just once. "No," she answered.

I looked at her.

I waited for her to explain.

"He passed away an hour ago," the woman said.

I tried to think how I could make her take the words back, tell me something else.

"You must have known how sick he was," the woman said.

This was her way of telling me it wasn't the hospital's fault.

A second passed. I've known him all my life," I said. I don't know why I told the woman this. It didn't change anything, but I wanted her to know. To this woman, Jasper was a man who had died on her shift. She knew less than that about me, but it had been given to her to break the worst news of my life. It was a part of her day.

"I can still see him," I said.

"No," the woman said. "You can't."

She wasn't being sharp. She was being nothing more than matter-of-fact.

"Why not?" I asked.

"I cannot let you see him," the woman said.

"Yes, you can," I said. I wasn't nasty, but I was determined.

"It's not allowed," the woman said. "Hospital policy."

"Oh, come on, you don't have a *policy* for this!" I said.

"Sir, we do." The woman stiffened. "We cannot open a body bag."

I must have heard the phrase before, or read it somewhere. I hadn't expected to hear it that day. I would have been able, I believe, to look at Jasper in death; I may have even needed to. But the idea of Jasper in a bag was unthinkable. I did not want my last sight of him to be accompanied by the snarl of a zipper.

The woman asked, would I be all right? Did I want to sit down? she asked. I did not want to sit down. I thanked her. I left.

From the street, I looked at the hospital. What a place, I thought, for Jasper to die.

On the way to the bus, I stopped and bought coffee and a cheese Danish. The Danish was in cellophane, which I couldn't unwrap. I couldn't see where the seam was. A waitress gave me a handful of paper napkins.

Why had I bought a Danish? I don't even like Danish. I left it on the counter. Someone would come along, find it wrapped, and eat it.

Outside, halfway to the bus stop, I sat on some damp grass. It had been sprinkling that morning. I lay down on it and covered my face with my hands.

It was too soon, as it would also be if it had taken a year, or two years, or three. How could I have stopped this? Without Jasper, what did I have?

I used the waitress's paper napkins, every one of them.

———

THERE WAS a message on my machine from Oliver Ingraham. He left his office number. I called it. Before Oliver Ingraham could speak, I told him I knew about Jasper.

Oliver Ingraham did not break the news to me. It would have been worse, somehow, to hear it from him. He asked how I knew, and he sounded surprised when I told him that I had taken a bus to the hospital.

"You were hoping to see Jasper alive?" Oliver Ingraham asked.

I did not answer.

"Tim, if I had known you wanted to go I would have made some arrangement," Oliver Ingraham said.

I thanked Oliver Ingraham. I didn't tell him that I hadn't wanted to wait for his arrangement. I wish I'd had the cash to take a cab that morning. If I had, I might have been there several minutes earlier, maybe even an hour.

On the bus, it had been in my mind that I could be there when he died, at the actual instant of death. It wasn't a question of whether I would have liked that. But I could have been the last thing Jasper would look at, and maybe he would have liked that a bit. Not knowing anything about what death will feel like, I think that Jasper would be, as my last sight of anything, the best I could have.

Oliver Ingraham told me then that there would be no service. That Jasper would be cremated, according to Jewish law, within twenty-four hours. That Jewish law is for burial. I don't believe there is a Jewish law for cremation. The Orthodox, of course, do not cremate.

I said nothing for a while. Then I said good-bye, and Oliver Ingraham said, "Wait a minute."

Oliver Ingraham said to me, "By the way, Tim, on the death certificate the cause of death is given as a heart attack."

"Did Jasper have a heart attack?" I asked.

"Well, his heart did stop," Oliver Ingraham said.

"But that's not quite the same as a heart attack, Oliver," I said.

What I thought then wasn't clear to me, not as clear as it has become. So I didn't say to Oliver Ingraham that Jasper's body, burned, would be of no use whatever to medical science; nothing would be learned from it. It also came to me that Oliver Ingraham was preventing Jasper from having an honest death. I remembered that when Jasper had sold Eisendorfer and Son he had told the people who had worked with him for more than twenty years that he had "a very rare blood disease." It's likely they all knew. Jasper sold the company to the people whom he had employed, some of them from the beginning. He took less than the company was worth. The new owners have not changed the name. It will always, one man told me, when I went to pick up a photograph Jasper had kept many years in his office, the company would always—at least while this man was alive—be known as Eisendorfer and Son. It was odd being in the Woolworth Building, in Jasper's office, that day. I had not ever been there for any reason but to meet Jasper.

It made me happy, what the man had told me. Most people, I'm sure, would slobber their name on the door and at the top of the letterhead. The man had told me in this indirect way that Jasper had been well liked by his colleagues. That made me proud of him. I was always pretty proud of Jasper, but this was a new way.

DUE TO Oliver Ingraham, Jasper will not be a statistic. He will not be counted among the thousands who have died, and are dying now, from this particular illness. I thought then of all the people—who knows how many there are?—whose death certificates slip around the truth. I dislike the cowardice of this, the falsehood. For the good of science, for the sake of research, and for those who have yet to live—for the future and even the sake of humankind—every AIDS death should be recorded as an AIDS death. What good does it do anyone to lie?

How important was it to Oliver Ingraham to be able to tell people that Jasper died of a heart attack? It's lies like this, as simple, as innocent as this, that make many truths unutterable.

An untold truth cannot be let go; there is no getting rid of it. It will always be waiting to close in around you. One way or another, the bitterest and most rancid truth will usually win.

EVERYTHING IN my house reminded me of Jasper. I could not sit at the black-cherry table, could not take a book down from a shelf. I couldn't look at any chair that Jasper had sat in, and he had sat in every one of them. I tried to lie on the bed. I couldn't. I looked at the photograph Jasper had given me, the one we had seen together in Soho seventeen years before; I looked at the man's face in the photograph, at his hand cupping his manhood, and I wondered if he, too, was dead.

A year or so later, all these things—the photograph, the tables and the bookcases Jasper built for me—have become remnants of his presence. But that afternoon, everywhere I looked I saw only his absence, and I felt nothing but the fact that Jasper would not look at me again, that his voice was also lost to me.

I went to a café across the street. From where I sat on Seventh Avenue, I watched as hundreds of people passed by. Most of them carried bundles, things they had bought from stores with names like New York Man, N.Y. Jock, All-American Boy. The names were printed on the bags. There were also names like Tower Records and World of Video. Every third or fourth person I saw was young and muscular and wearing as little as possible. All these men were going on with their lives, dressing for the weekend, buying new bathing suits for the beach, new jockstraps for the bars, listening to and possibly lip-synching Jessye Norman, or Diana Ross, or Barbra Streisand, or, God forbid, Madonna, watching the newest porn video, with or without a buddy. Life was quotidian. All anyone had to do was to go on doing it.

Oddly, I felt no envy.

I saw a woman walking a stroller. A baby was sitting up in it, taking in the late-summer afternoon with wide-eyed amazement. The baby's face was all bright eyes and pale skin and bright pink cheeks. It was, as all baby's faces are before they are stamped by the weight of living, nearly perfect. The stroller stopped at my table. I assumed that the woman had stopped deliberately, to indulge me with a longer look at her beautiful child. Mothers do that. It touches me. A baby was the perfect thing for me to see. It let me know that not all life had died that morning, and that right there, this minute, given me to look at, was a tiny life that was just beginning.

"Exquisite thing," the woman said. I looked at her, surprised, having recognized her voice, her tone, as that of Miss Fingerstop.

"How are you?" she asked, sounding as though she cared.

"Good Lord," I said. "I've been worse, I suppose. Don't tell me this darling child is yours?"

Miss Fingerstop was standing on the other side of a railing, which prevented the café and the sidewalk from spilling into each other.

"But it is, can you believe it?" Miss Fingerstop asked, tittering a little over the great unlikelihood.

"I take it that Mademoiselle Mercy has been laid to rest?"

As soon as this was out of my mouth, I was sorry I had asked. Why had I thrown back at her a time that she had done her best to put behind her?

Miss Fingerstop laughed, even made a little noise at it. "She's been vanquished. I killed off that little bitch a long, long time ago."

"Is this a little boy?" I asked.

"It's a little girl," Miss Fingerstop answered.

"Does this treasure have a name?" I asked.

"Of course she does. Her name is Timothea," Miss Fingerstop announced.

"You are, of course, kidding," I said.

"No, I'm not," said Miss Fingerstop. "We thought of naming her Justine, after Justin, but only for a minute. I didn't want to name my child after a novel. I'm hoping she'll live up to her name. The way she can do that is to become the perfect androgyne."

This had to be a joke. How many mothers raise their

daughters to be androgynes? It struck me as a somewhat outmoded aim. Then it came to me at once that perhaps few things had changed, that she was still perhaps the same Miss Fingerstop. She didn't seem as mendicant as she had before, but this was, after all, a first impression.

"He's the painter you were with at the party for Tom, isn't he?"

Miss Fingerstop nodded.

"Good for you," I said. "Good for you both."

"You're looking different in some way," Miss Fingerstop observed.

"I'm older," I said.

"And you're thinner, too," said Miss Fingerstop.

"Is there a Saint Timothea?" I asked.

"Are you still seeing that handsome man?" Miss Fingerstop asked.

"I nearly saw him today, but it didn't work out," I said.

Miss Fingerstop looked at me. There was a kind of appraisal in the way she did it. "So you are still seeing him?" she asked.

"I will always be seeing Jasper," I answered.

"Are you all right?" Miss Fingerstop asked.

Just about everyone I knew knows I nearly died. Some, I expect, are waiting for me to die altogether. There was no reason to have Miss Fingerstop be one of them.

Tonight I will have dinner with Gary and Abigail. I will tell them, probably in their garden, that Jasper died that morning. I hoped I could hold it to myself until then. There was no need to confide in Miss Fingerstop the inadequacy of my love to keep Jasper alive.

I answered her question by telling her that I had just got back from a long assignment, that the work had been grueling. I said I was pretty worn down by it all.

"Then you're just tired," Miss Fingerstop said.

"Yes, that's it," I said.

"Would you come for dinner when you're better?" Miss Fingerstop asked.

"I'd like that," I said.

"We're living just around the corner, on Grove Street. May I call you?"

"Please, of course," I said, pretty sure I would not hear from her. "It's good to see you again."

She returned a similar pleasantry, and then she was down the street. I watched her until she disappeared.

I picked up my glass and saw then that through our brief conversation Miss Fingerstop could easily have made out the name of the publication, *Treatment Issues*. The words had stared up at her the whole time.

The new Miss Fingerstop had let this pass without comment.

———

OLIVER INGRAHAM was telling me about the many trips he and Jasper had taken, to "really interesting, unusual places," Oliver Ingraham said. "Not just the usual clichés, but offbeat places."

He told me that he and Jasper had not been just typical tourists. This was his way of disregarding the trips Jasper and I had taken together, taken twice a year for almost eighteen years, to Paris, Provence, Antibes, Milan, Bologna, Rome, Venice, Florence, Certaldo, Pisa, Ravenna, Positano, Capri, or to Saint Bart, or to Cabo San Lucas, or to Cuernavaca, Uxmal, Chichén Itzá, San Miguel de Allende.

I knew he and Jasper had taken a Caribbean cruise, but that was before I knew Jasper. Otherwise, Jasper had not traveled with Oliver Ingraham in eighteen years.

"Why did you buy a place with such low ceilings?" Oliver Ingraham asked me. This seemed to me an abrupt change of topic. It's true, our ceilings in Paris aren't high.

Standing on the floor, you can stand on your toes, stretch, and touch the ceiling at its lowest point. They also slope a bit, our ceilings. Oliver Ingraham sounded angry that I had chosen a place with such a flaw. I wondered what business it was of his. He said he was certain that the low ceilings would hurt the resale value. "And don't you get claustrophobic?" he asked.

My answer was that I liked the low ceilings, that I found them cozy. I pointed out that rooms with low ceilings require less heat. I had no plans to sell the place, I told Oliver Ingraham. I did not add that claustrophobia had always struck me as being a state of mind.

I was trying not to get into that state with Oliver Ingraham. Oliver Ingraham looked at his watch. It may have been a Rolex. At that minute, just then, a tall figure in a dark suit appeared in the doorway. The figure made its way across the room to our table. He said good evening to Oliver Ingraham and said he had been looking for us on Bleecker Street. Then he looked at me.

"Tim, this is my lawyer," and Oliver Ingraham told me the lawyer's name. Then he introduced me to the lawyer as Tim Springer.

The lawyer said good evening and sat down with us at the table. He produced some papers. One was Jasper's will. I looked at it long enough to see the date. It had been signed two weeks after Jasper returned from Paris, when he was in the hospital with PCP. The lawyer must have paid a visit to the hospital, or at least dispatched a factotum. I doubt that this was done with any initiative but Oliver Ingraham's.

My name was nowhere to be seen; there was not any mention of property in Paris. Except for fifty thousand dollars to his sister and twenty-five thousand each to his nephews, everything had been left to Oliver Ingraham.

I slid the document across the table, back to the lawyer, without comment.

The lawyer told me that Oliver Ingraham was prepared to offer me a very fair price for my half of the apartment. He said something to the effect that half an ownership isn't really worth fifty percent.

This was the first time I realized that Jasper had left his half of our property not to me, as he had said he would, but to Oliver Ingraham.

I had a picture of Jasper and Oliver Ingraham in Paris. I imagined Oliver Ingraham pestering Jasper to change his will, pressuring a dying man to break his word—to another dying man.

Of course, I didn't see this, didn't even know if there had been any such scheme, but I imagined the pained expression Jasper would have had if he believed I would die soon, wondering what use I would have for a place in Paris. It would have made quite a bit of sense to Jasper: I was almost out of the picture, a creature of the past. Already dead in his mind, I didn't need his loyalty, not as much as Oliver Ingraham did.

Oliver Ingraham was the one who was going to be devastated.

Oliver Ingraham had hired someone to appraise the place in Paris and was offering me seventy thousand dollars less, give or take, than I would get on the open market. This wasn't what the lawyer said, but I did know what the place was worth.

A contract had been prepared, even though Oliver Ingraham claimed not to have seen the will, and Oliver Ingraham's lawyer offered me a pen.

We hadn't ordered dinner yet.

I did not look at the document. The lawyer explained that I was to give Oliver Ingraham something that sounded very like a thirty-year mortgage. I said nothing.

Oliver Ingraham watched as I gave the document back to his lawyer. I also gave back his pen.

Oliver Ingraham said, "You know, Tim, I do own other properties."

"I know you do, Oliver. Jasper told me."

The lawyer interjected. "You know, don't you, that Oliver can force you to sell?"

"Yes, I know that. I'm not sure, though, that he can force me to sell to *him*. First, he would have to prove to the French court that I had turned down an outside offer. I believe it needs to have been a reasonable offer. I doubt that any court in France would consider Mr. Ingraham's offer to be a reasonable one. As you must know," I said to Oliver Ingraham's lawyer, "these sales are made at auctions, in courts of law. It can take years just to get a court date, and selling a property at auction is a crackerjack way to lose money."

I just didn't want to be there. I stood up. I left. I made it to the door without saying that I could also force Oliver Ingraham to sell. I didn't say that I could oppose Jasper's will. To do so, I would probably need to assert that Jasper was demented when he wrote this new will. I would not say that of Jasper. For one of the first times, I did not waste time brooding over something I was not going to do.

I said only that I would not in this world or any world accept his cheesy offer.

Walking on Sixth Avenue, which was mobbed at nine-twenty, the thought came to me that I had adored a man for eighteen years; that what he had given me at the end—the outcome, his real legacy, apart from his kindness in letting me love him—was the newest of my opportunistic infections, possibly the most pernicious.

Lately, I've started talking to myself. I do it when there's no one around. Sadly, these are some of my liveliest conversations. Tonight I am surrounded by people; the world is hanging out, killing time. I look at many of them, the thousand wanderers on foot, and I hear myself saying aloud, though not to them, "Honey doll, sugar puss, you bunghole out of hell, straight from hell, I will not die for you today."

eight

"WHERE ARE you, honey?"
Dominic says. "It's pudd'n time."

Dominic will not let me forget that when we met I was in the habit of calling dessert "pudding." This was a hangover from Canada, in the same way that spelling "theater" with *re* at the end is a hangover. This was a hard habit to break; it had been drilled into me. Sometimes, if I'm tired enough, I still do it.

"I was just sort of elsewhere for a minute," I tell Dominic.

Tonight, in Los Angeles, Dominic orders strawberries. When they come, he asks the better-looking waiter for some dark brown sugar. The better-looking waiter replies that the house hasn't got any dark brown sugar.

Dominic's response is to me, not to the waiter, who is still much in evidence, probably waiting for Dominic to make some other impossible request. White sugar, maybe.

"You know, Timothy," Dominic says quietly, but not so quietly that the better-looking waiter won't hear, "if this were a top place, really top, someone would be sent out to *get* dark brown sugar."

I look up at the waiter and raise my eyebrows in apology. Actually, though, I think Dominic has a point. I've read of such things being done, of a waiter going out in search of an item requested but not in the larder. There is usually a mention of inclement weather. But I read of this pretty long ago, in travel books that were old even then. Such service is hard to find these days; I don't think there are places of that ilk anymore, and if you find one what you will end up with will be some pretty pricey dark brown sugar.

I'm not having dessert, but I ask the waiter what grappa he can offer. He names a few. The last one he mentions is one I like. It's expensive, though. Even in Italy, where Jasper and I discovered it ten years ago, in Santa Margherita, it was expensive. I ask the waiter how much it costs. A glass is thirty-eight dollars, he answers.

Someday I may be able to afford such an extravagance again, though I doubt it. Even in that case, I would think twice. Tonight I don't think twice. Since I cannot afford this grappa, I feel dislocated in the world, and I want the exorbitance of it right now. I don't want it sometime later, in a future I may not have.

I tell the waiter to bring it.

I've saved a long time for this dinner. I've lived on French toast.

The waiter brings the grappa to me in a homely, narrow glass with a tall stem, and with no character at all. I've always hated this kind of glass. It reminds me of a line attributed to Steve McQueen, who, according to a much-repeated anecdote, when he was served something in a wineglass—whiskey, as I recall—asked his waiter, "Can't you bring me a butch glass?"

Tonight, I ask the waiter to bring me, please, a brandy snifter.

Before the snifter has been brought, Dominic, without asking, pours half the grappa over his strawberries, roughly twenty dollars' worth.

"These berries need something," he says without compunction.

I restrain an urge to slap him; this urge is my keenest

desire. Dominic will always have money; his grandfather started a plumbing-supply business. It has thrived for almost a hundred years.

I am mute with anger.

I want, at this instant, to tell Dominic that Jasper is dead. He hasn't asked about Jasper in the thirty-six hours I've spent with him, not even in passing, nor has he commented on the remnants of herpes zoster lesions on my face, the scars the monstrosities left. They aren't glaring, they don't reach out with tentacles to grab you. They are, thank God, nothing like the horrors they were. Still, it does take a rather unobservant person not to notice them.

One needs, in fact, to be oblivious.

Since Dominic is not oblivious, that is, not completely, it occurs to me that in his silence he is being tactful. This would be so unlike him, I wonder if it's possible. I decide it couldn't be. I want to blame Dominic for Jasper's death, though I know he's not to blame. It wasn't Dominic's virus that killed Jasper, not necessarily. Nor can Jasper be blamed for Dominic's illness. Jasper and Dominic are each one of handfuls of people who could have given each other the virus. What I do think Dominic may have given Jasper, and what Jasper may have given Dominic, is *more* virus—reinfection, virus on top of virus.

It would be false to hold Dominic accountable. There is no blame, no villain.

Why do I want one?

I'm glad—or not glad—to have Claude to point to, not that I do, really. Glad isn't the word. The timing of everything with Claude makes it unlikely that my virus came from him—but not impossible, not completely. Some viruses *do* work at greater speed than others. Claude, the fact that I was with him in 1987, makes it impossible to be sure that I was infected by Jasper. This, of course, was the point of Claude.

There is, though, a way in which I would rather know I'd gotten the virus from Jasper. This thing, as Oliver Ingraham called it. At least then I'd be able to think that I got it from love.

Dominic and I had agreed to do this dinner dutch. I had thought, though, until he helped himself to my thirty-eight-dollar grappa, that I would treat him. Now and then everyone needs a treat: it has nothing to do with deserving one.

Now we'll go dutch, after all.

A bottle of maraschino will be enough of a treat. I will still give him that.

———

"DUMP HER, why don't you?" Dominic says to the prosperous-looking man on our way out. "You can do better."

Dominic says this so quickly that by the time the man absorbs it Dominic is gone.

"He had too much to drink," I say to the man.

The woman looks too stunned to be horrified.

The man looks at me. "Tell your pal it's lucky for him he's not a man. Tell him if he was, I'd give him a thrashing he wouldn't forget."

"I believe you would," I assure the prosperous-looking man.

I wish him a good night. And the woman, too. I wish it to the woman, especially.

"Whatever in the world did you do that for?" I ask Dominic, on the street.

"It just came over me," Dominic answers, as though that were an answer.

Dominic starts the car. We are on the freeway when I say, "Someday you're going to get in trouble, sweetheart."

Dominic laughs. "What more trouble could I be in, honey?"

I let it go.

We drive awhile. That is, Dominic does. We park on a street and walk a block or two on Santa Monica Boulevard. Robust, good-looking young men are everywhere I look. Many wear cutoffs. Many wear sandals. Most wear T-shirts that show off their worked-on bodies. The ones who really think they're something go shirtless. Waxing is the rage; there are no chest hairs out tonight. Dominic and I, in our summer blazers, with our loosened ties, get odd looks from more than a few of these toothsome-looking specimens, but mostly we walk unnoticed.

Tonight, everyone on earth is twenty-four years old. And everyone's good-looking but me.

So it seems.

"Isn't this a pigpen of pulchritude?" asks Dominic.

"Yes, indeed," I answer. "Pulchritudes, pulchritudes in the valley of perdition."

A man walks toward us. He's dressed in white, weightless-looking cotton. This one isn't good-looking. The cloth of his trousers is so thin you can see through it to the outline of his parts, which are immensely oversized. These massive deformities put me in mind of a kind of cyst, the giant ones called dermoid. These can grow inside the body. They can weigh as much as two hundred pounds. People don't understand why they're gaining so much weight. It puzzles them, they starve themselves, and still the cysts grow. Sometimes they grow hair, cartilage, teeth.

"He thinks he's a water buffalo," Dominic says.

We go to a piano bar. The piano, a Yamaha, has been painted high-gloss white. The clientele looks older than the studlings on the street. It is better dressed, or, rather, more dressed. In a tuxedo, an exceedingly thin man, probably in his seventies, slowly puts away a banana split.

I've had all the alcohol I need. I order tonic with lime, pretty sure I'll get lemon. Dominic orders a rusty nail. He wants to get drunk, he says. I know he won't. Dominic has never been arrested for drunk driving. He is proud of this. And why shouldn't he be?

Just behind us is a sign saying, "Telephones—rest-rooms." Behind an inside wall, a stairwell leads down to them.

There are not more than twenty men in the place. At the piano, a heavyset man in his forties, I'd guess, sings a ponderous rendition of "What Are You Doing the Rest of Your Life?" He brings nothing new to it; his inflections have been rehearsed, they are set, paralyzed in show-biz gel. When he's finished the audience of queens goes mad with applause.

Since Dominic and I came in, a man has been looking at me.

"Sing something," I say to Dominic.

"I don't do that anymore," he answers.

"Oh, please," I say. "Do it for me."

"I don't know if I still can," Dominic says. "I haven't sung anything in six years."

"That's much too long," I tell him. "I'm sure you can do it, sweetheart."

Actually, I'm not sure at all.

Dominic looks at me, almost pleading. This is one of the times—they aren't frequent—when doubting breaks through. This self-doubt is appealing in Dominic. It becomes him.

"Why not?" he says, with no confidence at all.

He walks to the piano, there is a lilt in his walk, and he takes an unlighted cigarette along for company.

The man has white hair. He is tanned. These are set off by his white shirt. He wears onyx cuff links and a voluptuous-looking pale yellow tie. He is broadly built but looks fit for his age. He's close to sixty, I'd say.

Dominic leans forward to consult briefly with the piano player. The lighting is dimmed a bit, but an overhead spot encircles Dominic, the piano player, and the white Yamaha in a bright pool. It makes Dominic's head glow a bit, and, because I am looking at him closely, I can see one blue vein rippling faintly under his scalp. Dominic looks good in this light, only a little gaunt. A decade ago, or longer, this was a sought-after look.

Dominic begins a rapid, capering version of "I've Got No Strings," from Disney's animated feature *Pinocchio*. In the movie this is sung by a little boy, a puppet, who has been given the ability to move without strings. He doesn't need a master to pull them. The puppet yearns, as does the old woodcarver, to be "a real boy." Pinocchio prays for this. One evening, his prayer is visited by an angel, who is, in this case, a beautiful blonde. She tells Pinocchio that if he can learn to tell the truth, to be honest and brave—"courage," I believe, was the angel's word—his wish will be granted.

This is the film that also has the song that promises, "When you wish upon a star your dreams come true."

I don't hear in Dominic's singing any of the damage that I know has been done, nor, I think, does anyone in this audience hear it. All Dominic's flaws are inaudible tonight; his singing gives them no egress. It is as if all the cocktails, all the sex and cigarettes, and even the symptoms of illness have been lifted from him, in order for this moment to occur.

No one speaks while Dominic sings. The audience, every faggot in the room, is silent when, without pausing, Dominic drops his voice almost to a baritone and begins a new song, his hand still at his side, the unlighted cigarette clamped between his fingers. This time he sings quite differently.

"Give me some men," he begins, "who are stout-hearted men . . . Who will fight for the right they adore."

Usually, this number is sung boisterously, with a snap, as upbeat as an army-recruitment jingle, though in fact it is from an old Broadway musical called *The New Moon*. It is sung quickly, much too quickly for anyone to think about it.

Tonight, Dominic sings this song in his different way. He sings slowly, and so solemnly the song is as plangent as a dirge. He gives everyone plenty of time to think about it.

"Start me with ten, who are stout-hearted men."

Each word stands alone. Dominic looks slowly around, without expression, at the men in the room. They are looking at him, too. They can take this song however they want it, Dominic seems to be telling each one of them, in every cadence he brings to the lyric.

> And I'll soon give you ten thousand more,
> Shoulder to shoulder, and bolder and bolder
> They grow as they go to the fore . . .
> When stout-hearted men can stick together
> Man to man.

For an instant the room is frozen. Silence lingers in it. Dominic lowers his head, unsure of what his effect has been.

Then every man applauds him as one.

———

SOMETHING IN what I have just heard makes me less certain that Dominic should go home. I can't *make* him call his mother, and though I could call her myself I don't think I will. The news should not come by telephone, from a stranger. I was wrong to scorn the postcard from the Viennese musician. Such news should be written. There are many reasons for this. A written message is less apt to evaporate. Without it, you might think that you'd dreamed it.

I could write to Dominic's mother, but it seems less urgent than before.

Four years ago, if I'd had a mother, I probably would have called her. That is, if I'd had *a* mother; I don't know that I would have called the mother I'd had. As I told Dominic at dinner tonight, I don't have that to think about.

If I *had* called, who can say it would have been the right thing, the best thing to do? Certainly, no one can say it was the only thing.

Dominic returns to the table, gulps his rusty nail. The white-haired, broadly built man who looks fit for his age is still looking at me. I don't know what to make of him.

"That man in the corner hasn't stopped looking at me since we came in," I say to Dominic, quietly.

Dominic turns to look at the man. He gives a quick appraisal. He turns back to me and says, "Doll face, suck on that and beat me to heaven."

I go downstairs to check my messages in New York. As I wait for the tape to unwind, the white-haired, broadly built man passes me and goes into the men's room. From the rear he doesn't look quite as fit, but he *is* holding up well.

I have five messages. Two are offers of work.

I go into the men's room, see the man's shoes under the stall. His trousers have not been lowered. I clean my glasses at the sink, washing my hands in the process. There is no sound coming from the stall, and the door is open.

I put my glasses in my jacket pocket and move to the open door.

I stand in it a moment, looking at the man. I don't know that I want to do what I am about to do. The man is sitting fully dressed on the seat. I take one small step forward, and the broadly built man reaches out to me. I take another step forward, toward his outstretched hand. Then the man is opening my trousers, he is pulling my prick out from the opening he has made. He wraps his hand around it. This is already more than I have done in five years, since Claude, and it amazes me that any man has found me desirable enough to look at me for twenty minutes while Dominic sang, and to make himself available—to *me*.

I almost need this, just the pleasure of being in another man's hand. He leans forward to blow me, but I put my hand over his mouth. I tell this man, who isn't at all bad-looking, to pull out what Jasper called my "apricots." Of course, I don't call them that to him.

He does. He flicks at them with his fingers. He jostles them lightly. He gives them a bit of a squeeze.

I tell him to lick them, and he looks up at me, and then, of all things, he does.

I tell him to use *all* of his tongue, and he does.

This has always been one of the great feelings in the world to me. Physically, I mean. It may be the one I liked most. Jasper always said it felt pleasant but that I didn't have to do it to him for such a long time. Not enough men do this for each other; they don't think of it, they have to be asked. Don't they have balls of their own? There are men who do it too quickly; they don't linger. This white-haired man must know the joy his tongue can give, or maybe he just likes doing it.

He seems to. I clutch his hand and hold it still. I begin to fuck it. I was never this way with Jasper. Pretty soon, I know that I can make it even better, so I move his hand from me and start in on myself.

I tell him to use that tongue he's got. I talk butch and dirty. I take all the time I want.

I love a joy prolonged.

The man encloses me in both hands, and he tugs at my scrotum.

He uses his tongue on the base of my prick. I keep my thumb over the tip of it. With the other, I slide slowly down, then even more slowly up. I am loving my own skin. Someone could touch my arm right now, and just that would be lovely.

The white-haired man licks the underside of my prick, almost to the tip. His tongue laps the edge of my hand.

I'd go back twelve years for an old-fashioned suck.

I want to see what this man has but decide only to trace it through his trousers. Then I decide not even to do that. I don't want to make a comparison. This man will not be Jasper. He won't be Claude. He won't be Carlton Gabrielson.

This man is foreign to me. Every man is. I will not trust them again. But his tongue isn't foreign. All I want is his tongue licking my balls. I push his head forward and press my balls into his mouth. He groans. What pleasure does this give him? Does he feel the way I felt when I did this with Jasper?

I could stand this way for hours, getting licked by this broadly built man. He's handsome, actually. I loosen his tie, open his shirt to tweeze his nipples. I find a mass of chest hair. It is as dark as Jasper's, and this man has more of it. It is thicker, more lustrous, than Jasper's.

His nipples are hard, like an ardent young man's.

I rub his chest in a way I think he will like, and he seems to. He sighs. I feel its outline, all the dense hair on it. I press him forward and rub my balls against his luxury.

I loved doing this with Jasper.

I slap my prick against his face. Everyone likes that. Even I liked it, years ago, when a fellow didn't overdo it. Jasper, when he did this, did it just enough, just right. The man undoes his onyx cuff links. He lays them on the floor, left of my left foot, in the margin as it were, outside the frame of our lust. They are not preciously small. They are not ostentatiously large. Each one is the size an onyx cuff link should be.

I help him remove his immaculate white shirt. I notice that it is from Sulka, which means it was handmade for him.

He has kept himself in good condition. That is relative though.

He will never be nineteen again, but he's as good as a man past his prime can be. I am standing, so it's easier for me to hang his shirt over the door. There should be a hook for it, but there isn't one.

What will we do if someone comes in? I wouldn't be able to stop. It probably wouldn't matter; anyone who comes in here would be, ipso facto, a fag.

Every part of me is becoming stronger, focused, intent. I spit in my hand and use it even more slowly, gripping the base and I stroke with pressure. I don't want it to be over. I want it to last, to go on, but my body begins to spasm, and I feel everything build, that marvelous tremor in my feet begins to take over, and the man groans with me as I aim for his chest. Then, at the moment, I cup my hand against him to catch the great white instant, the glorious burst of coming.

Except for my telling him what to do, the man and I have not spoken. Finished, we skip the banalities, too. We don't ask names, don't exchange numbers. We smile at each other, though, for a time.

I pick the onyx cuff links off the floor. "Don't forget these lovelies," I say, looking at the handsome white-haired man.

Taking them he looks at my eyes. He puts one of the cuff links into a trouser pocket. He hands the other one out to me.

"Why don't you keep this one?" he asks me. This gesture, extravagant and generous, appeals to me in a way I do not analyze. It feels better, in an unexpected way, than his tongue on my balls. I've had these old pecans licked a thousand times. This is the first time I've been offered a single cuff link, onyx or otherwise. "Whatever are you going to do with one onyx cuff link?" I asked this elegant, divine-looking man.

"Everytime I open my cuff link drawer and find only one," the handsome man answers, "I will remember you."

"But, I didn't do anything for you, technically," I say almost with apology.

"No you didn't. I could tell you weren't in the mood. But you gave yourself to me, and that, young man, is luscious.

"I don't need your cuff link to remember you."

"Keep it anyway. It's rude to turn a present down," the man tells me.

We took no risk. None. We did nothing dangerous, and I don't feel a need to have done anything more. Oh, maybe I would have liked to cling to him, or him to me, for us to embrace, even to kiss, but that would overreach. What we did, no matter what pleasure it gave me, was, after all, just a little friskiness in a men's room. It was my first of those, in fact. The man left before I did. When I went upstairs the white-haired man had gone.

I do know one thing: the white-haired man and I, if we are not each a little more alive for being together, we are not any deader for it, either. The pleasure this man gave me will last a long time. I will remember it.

I know something else.

I know that in the long, vicious, trivial scheme of things, this is not worth remembering. None of it matters a fig.

nine

HE NEVER thought to put honey in tea. "It was you," he said to me, "who taught me about honey in tea."

A little thing, a spoonful in a coffee mug. A plastic mug, because a china cup might drop from his grasp, because sometimes his hands would shake. He never knew when it would happen.

A year later, at dinner in Los Angeles, Dominic looked at one hand and slapped it with the other, to make it be still. The hand obeyed, stopped trembling; it lay quiet, flat on the table.

Dominic forbade his hand to shake; Jasper allowed it. Jasper looked at his hand once, then did not look at it again.

A mug of apricot tea with a spoonful of avocado honey, with three spoonfuls, because nothing tasted sweet enough to Jasper. Nothing had for the last six weeks. He even put sugar in Coca-Cola, a sugar granulated a little differently to dissolve in cold liquid, a sugar he had found for me a year before, when nothing tasted sweet to me.

Jasper never drank Coca-Cola before. One time, in Provincetown, we stopped for fried clams and deep-fried onion rings, amazingly crisp, at a place that served no liquor. It was a place for junk food, but Jasper and I agreed that it was as good as junk food gets. It was glorious junk food. We were, both of us, mad for it, and Jasper asked for a sip of my Coke.

I gave him one, and he made a face of revulsion, horrified that I would drink anything so sweet.

The last six weeks, he'd been pouring sugar in the stuff. He got a taste for grape soda and put sugar in that, too.

I brought him lunch the last day I saw him. I took it to his house. He'd told me on the telephone, "Keep it simple, please, and light." For years, Jasper had claimed that I served him too much food. I brought him a small loin of pork, cooked the night before with mustard, with brown sugar, a fair amount of bourbon, and a few pitted prunes. I pitted the prunes myself; prunes you buy already pitted will have sulfur in them. I brought Jasper some peeled yellow peppers in a light sheen of hazelnut oil, with just a dribble of balsamica. I brought him a simple tart of one perfect fig, sliced on a layer of *crème patisserie,* on very light pastry that I had made two days before with finely ground hazelnuts, no flour, which I had chilled for forty-eight hours and rolled out every four, before rolling it out the final time and baking it that morning.

This was not, of course, an easy lunch to make for just the two of us. But it *was* simple, it *was* light, and I hoped that Jasper would like it.

He took not even one bite.

He told me that he preferred to stay downstairs when I called him to the table, that I should bring his lunch down to him. Now that I think of it, I don't know, really, why he had me bother, not that it was a bother, but it was difficult. It was a little hard to carry a plate down, because I needed one hand for the rail.

I laid two thin slices from the center of the roast, and four strips of peeled yellow pepper, on the best plate I could find.

Jasper had been trying for a while to find some dinner plates like the big ones we have in Paris. We have them there—that is, I have them there—in red and in green. Actually, they are what people call service plates. Jasper liked the red ones. There is an amount of blue in the color, and he had looked for them in New York, in two or three places. They were a standard Limoges pattern; they should have been easy to find in New York. I don't know why Jasper couldn't. He decided finally to order them, but before he had done so we went to Mexico, where Jasper got ill—where I did, too—from oysters on the half shell that we ate—it seems foolish now—on the beach at Puerto Vallarta.

That is, it seemed likely that the oysters had triggered something latent in his body that had been waiting for them.

I had a minor reaction, but Jasper was ill all that night, and ill for the rest of the trip. He stayed in bed, with the curtains closed to the beach. We came back to New York three days early.

He got a little better in New York, but just a little; he was not himself again, not ever, not altogether.

So Jasper didn't have those handsome red plates.

More than once, I've wondered how much longer Jasper might have stayed well if we hadn't gone to Mexico, if we hadn't had the oysters, if Jasper had just not ever put one of those fucking oysters in his mouth. But this is like most of the wondering I do, there is no point in it, nothing comes of it, nothing at all, and I am reminded constantly of how Jasper would always tell me that he did not like to speculate, and how much he wished that I would do less of it.

It is in the back of my mind that I play with questions like this, only there that I waste time with them. I have wasted years with them. In the back of my mind, there they are, all the time, disquietingly.

They thrive.

I took the plate that I'd chosen down the stairs to Jasper in the living room. That room had a view of the river, down through a patch of trees. The river there is wide. It looks, and is, I think, much wider where Jasper lives than it is in the city, near where the old piers used to be.

Jasper was lying on the couch, not looking at the view. No music was playing in the room. Jasper always had music in his house, something was always playing—a Bach unaccompanied cello suite, a Shostakovich string quartet, one of Mahler's symphonies. Jasper especially liked Mahler's Second Symphony, the one called *Resurrection*. That is the one that I like most, too. We'd heard it at Carnegie Hall, on three different Easters. We'd heard it in Venice, at Teatro La Fenice, in the summer of 1986. There were times when Jasper would interrupt—stop talking, or stop me from talking—in order better to hear a passage, some part of a score that was just coming up, that would at any minute be heard. One time he always did this was at the first sudden pizzicato in the second section, I believe, of Bartók's Sixth Quartet.

There were times when I did not enjoy being shushed by Jasper, but they were not too many, really. Sometimes Jasper would stop reading in a book to hear some music better, though most of the time he could do both things at once. I've never been able to read with any music playing, not at all, but for Jasper I would pretend I could.

Anything was worth pretending for Jasper.

When I brought him his lunch, he did not sit up. He said something about how nice the plate looked, and it was then that he told me he hadn't eaten for six weeks.

"Not at all?" I asked.

"No food," he said.

I said, "But I've seen you eat, papa, at those hideous lunches we've been to out here."

Jasper said, "I faked it."

"Do you throw food up?" I asked.

He said he did not throw food up. He said, rather testily, that he hadn't said he'd thrown anything up, had he? He'd *said* that he'd gotten nothing down.

"Get it down?" I asked. "Do you mean you can't swallow?"

"No," he said. "That's not it."

"What do you mean, then?" I asked.

He said he had meant that he couldn't get anything down. He asked me not to make him repeat himself.

"But what do you mean, get it down?"

"I mean I can't get it down. I can't get anything down."

"What happens when you try?" I asked.

An inability to swallow solid food, I knew, was a complication, just as dizziness and fever are symptoms, as a seizure can be, of one thing or another, or another. There are a number of disorders, pathologies, of which being unable to swallow food can be a complication, one possibility being pneumocystis of the esophagus, or esophagitis, or gastritis.

This can be painful, according to what I've read of it. A person afflicted will stop eating altogether, yet be without hunger, because all hunger will leave him.

In fact, I have not seen this pain described. The men who write about the pain and the men who have the pain are not the same men, but the pain is mentioned in every article I have read about pneumocystis when it is acute, when it is in the esophagus, or in the stomach, or in the bowel.

They don't call it agony. They don't want to, I suppose. Agony is not a word I have seen in science.

But Jasper hadn't said he couldn't swallow. He hadn't mentioned pain.

I asked him, did he have pain when he tried to get food down?

I thought that if Jasper could mention pain to me, at least it would then be mentioned.

Jasper said he didn't know, he hadn't tried for so long.

He was not a man to talk about pain.

I thought about this when Jasper asked me to make him tea. I went up the stairs again to his new seventy-thousand-dollar kitchen, and I thought about it while I boiled water.

I was thinking about it when I brought the mug of tea down the stairs to him, on a tray with the jar of avocado honey. He was sitting up on the couch, under the fur blanket I'd given him eight years ago, the year he turned fifty. This was before we knew or thought much at all about the pain that the fur animals suffer in the traps. Back then, I didn't know any better than to give Jasper fur, and it was, anyway, not new fur, not a new blanket. It was old when I bought it.

It was from an estate auction, I'm afraid.

Jasper said when he opened it that he thought a sable blanket was a bit much, but it wasn't his reluctance that had kept him warm for eight winters, when the nights were cold.

It was good old fur.

The tea steamed in the mug. I watched Jasper bring it to his face. He breathed in the steam, as though it were, to him, an exquisite mist. He sipped from the mug. I heard him sip.

"This is good," he said.

He swallowed.

"This is so good," he said. I heard every swallow.

I could smell the three spoonfuls of honey that I had stirred into the tea.

Jasper held the mug close to his face, as if the room were cold.

It was September. The room was too warm for me.

Jasper's hand trembled, holding the tea. He seemed satisfied by it, by the tea, by the honey in it, immensely. He said that it was just sweet enough, the amount I'd put in was just right.

He repeated that the tea was good, and he swallowed some more of it, painlessly, or so it appeared.

I watched Jasper drink the tea, and I was already remembering the way he looked drinking it.

That was when he told me that he had never thought to put honey in tea.

"You taught me that," he said to me. "I learned that from you."

Jasper was holding the mug of tea at that minute, he was drinking it at that minute, it was happening just then, and it was already becoming a picture remembered.

It had already fixed.

I knew then how Jasper would look when I looked back at him.

As it turns out, a year later, I have many other ways to see him.

Tea with honey. He had not thought about that. He learned that from me.

Through my life, I have never had to take care of anyone. On that day, I thought that if I could take some care of Jasper my life would be repaid.

I would believe in a Lord, if a Lord would give me that. I would believe in any Lord, in any deity at all, in anything at all; in God even, I would believe. If He would let me keep Jasper alive, I would believe that the God was in the heaven.

I wanted to believe that such a God will be repaid, and gladly. It was, of course, desperation to call upon God at the end of things, to turn to Him just then, but where else would a Lord be found, if not in that Godless end?

I wanted to repay.

Tea with honey was the last thing I gave to the man who was my life.

I did not believe then, as I have come to, that God had already been, that Jasper in my life was what I would have of God.

It had been more than it might have been.

Jasper had been in my life against odds, had stayed a long while, and we had known flight.

I am still owing.

FOR THE BEST IN PAPERBACKS, LOOK FOR THE

In every corner of the world, on every subject under the sun, Penguin represents quality and variety—the very best in publishing today.

For complete information about books available from Penguin—including Pelicans, Puffins, Peregrines, and Penguin Classics—and how to order them, write to us at the appropriate address below. Please note that for copyright reasons the selection of books varies from country to country.

In the United Kingdom: For a complete list of books available from Penguin in the U.K., please write to *Dept E.P., Penguin Books Ltd, Harmondsworth, Middlesex, UB7 0DA.*

In the United States: For a complete list of books available from Penguin in the U.S., please write to *Consumer Sales, Penguin USA, P.O. Box 999— Dept. 17109, Bergenfield, New Jersey 07621-0120.* VISA and MasterCard holders call 1-800-253-6476 to order all Penguin titles.

In Canada: For a complete list of books available from Penguin in Canada, please write to *Penguin Books Canada Ltd, 10 Alcorn Avenue, Suite 300, Toronto, Ontario, Canada M4V 3B2.*

In Australia: For a complete list of books available from Penguin in Australia, please write to the *Marketing Department, Penguin Books Ltd, P.O. Box 257, Ringwood, Victoria 3134.*

In New Zealand: For a complete list of books available from Penguin in New Zealand, please write to the *Marketing Department, Penguin Books (NZ) Ltd, Private Bag, Takapuna, Auckland 9.*

In India: For a complete list of books available from Penguin, please write to *Penguin Overseas Ltd, 706 Eros Apartments, 56 Nehru Place, New Delhi, 110019.*

In Holland: For a complete list of books available from Penguin in Holland, please write to *Penguin Books Nederland B.V., Postbus 195, NL-1380AD Weesp, Netherlands.*

In Germany: For a complete list of books available from Penguin, please write to *Penguin Books Ltd, Friedrichstrasse 10-12, D-6000 Frankfurt Main I, Federal Republic of Germany.*

In Spain: For a complete list of books available from Penguin in Spain, please write to *Longman, Penguin España, Calle San Nicolas 15, E-28013 Madrid, Spain.*

In Japan: For a complete list of books available from Penguin in Japan, please write to *Longman Penguin Japan Co Ltd, Yamaguchi Building, 2-12-9 Kanda Jimbocho, Chiyoda-Ku, Tokyo 101, Japan.*